CATHERINE HART
two-time winner of the *Romantic Times* Reviewers' Choice Award, is back with a tantalizing tale of love in the wild West . . .

SWEET FURY

Taught to survive the rigors of the Old West by her outlaw family, Samantha Downing could hold her own with the roughest cowhand. Texas Marshal Travis Kincaid had never known a prisoner as hard to control as Sam . . . or one as easy to love. Soon the tables were turned on Travis, and he found himself a willing captive of Sam's earthy charms.

Catherine Hart writes "Thrilling adventure . . . beautiful and memorable romance!"—*Romantic Times*

THE STORM RAGED AROUND THEM . . .

As Travis lay over her, Sam's body trapped beneath his, his breath suddenly caught in his throat. They were both soaked, their clothes clinging like second skins, and with every frantic wriggle, Travis became more aware of her. Sam's face was streaked with mud. Her dark eyes were snapping with anger, brilliant with fury. Ridiculous as it was, right here, right now, she was more beautiful than any woman he had ever known, and at this moment he wanted her more than he'd wanted anything in his life. He felt as if he might die if he could not claim her.

She was shouting curses up at him, trying to wrench her wrists from his hands, when he lowered his face to hers. "Shut up, Sam!" he growled. "Shut up and kiss me."

SWEET FURY

CATHERINE HART

LEISURE BOOKS NEW YORK CITY

*To my many devoted fans, who have
taken the time to write and tell me
how much they appreciate my books
—this one is for you! Read and enjoy!*

A LEISURE BOOK ®

May 1990

Published by

Dorchester Publishing Co., Inc.
276 Fifth Avenue
New York, NY 10001

CHAPTER 1

The night was dark and wild, as wild as the surrounding Texas countryside. Wind-driven rain pelted the earth, filling the brim of Sam Downing's stetson until it overflowed down the back of the dark slicker and inside Sam's collar. Sam shivered and squinted dark eyes through the driving rain. It was a hellish night with lightning flashing through the sky and thunder rumbling like a bear with a bellyache. Nothing could be heard above the sound of the storm, and this made Sam more anxious than ever.

Truth be told, Sam was never at ease on any of these forays, day or night, when Pa was in the middle of a dangerous scheme. Somewhere out there, beyond the small rise that would have blocked the view even in good weather, Sam's pa and three older brothers were robbing the south-

1

bound train, while Sam waited in the cover of the trees. Pa claimed that seventeen-year-old Sam was too young to do more than stand lookout on these capers. As a result, Sam was torn between relief and jealousy most of the time.

There was no disputing the fact that Tom, Billy, and Hank were bigger and tougher, at ages twenty-five, twenty-three, and twenty-one respectively. They had more weight, height, and muscle than Sam could ever hope to have. Pa called Sam the runt of the litter, but it was not meant maliciously. They were a close-knit family, Old Bill Downing and his offspring, looking after one another in good times and bad, sticking together through thick and thin. When Sally Downing had died of consumption five years back, the older members of the family had taken little Sam under their protective wings. Now Sam rode with them, but never in the center of danger, never in the thick of the action. They always included Sam in the planning, but when it came to executing the plan, Sam had the safer, lesser role.

Sam sighed and shifted restlessly in the saddle. What in tarnation was taking so long? The train had groaned and screeched to a halt at least ten minutes ago, and according to Pa's timetable, they should be on their way by now with the money from the mailcar stashed in their saddlebags. There was supposed to be a big payroll on the train this trip which meant extra guards, but Pa hadn't been all that concerned. He and the boys could handle it easily, according to Old Bill.

A shot rang out in the darkness, and Sam

jumped in the act of brushing a hank of straggling red-gold hair from a dripping forehead. Straining to hear, Sam caught the sounds of far-off shouts, then the dull sounds of mud-muffled hoofbeats coming nearer. Seconds later, Billy raced by on his mare. "Gitta move on, Sam! Pa's been shot, and we gotta git hid right quick!"

On his heels came Hank. "Where's Pa?" Sam called to him.

"Right behind me. Come on, Sam! Ride!"

Sam did as ordered, listening for sounds of Tom and Pa coming up behind. Fear made Sam's dark eyes huge in a pale, young, freckled face. Breathing was suddenly difficult, as if a fist had lodged in the youngster's windpipe. A bit of relief came when Pa and Tom caught up, but Sam could tell that Pa was hurting. His face was white against his dark beard, a grimace of pain twisting his mouth.

"Hang on, Pa," Tom said in a voice made husky by the same fear Sam felt. "We'll head west a ways, then double back south toward Oakville and git us a room for the night at the hotel."

They made Oakville by midnight, and an hour later Pa was lying white-faced on the bed in the hotel room. "I can't do it, Pa," Sam told him.

"Shore ya kin. Ya got to, Sam. I can't rightly go to the doc with a bullet hole in my shoulder, now kin I? You got the smallest hands of us all. You kin dig out that bullet as easy as rollin' off a log. I trust ya, young'un."

"Ya got to, Sam," Tom affirmed. "The bullet has to come out soon. We'll help ya any way we can."

"Pa's right, Sam," Billy added. "We'd take him

3

to a doctor if we could, but if we do we'll be hangin' ourselves sure as sunrise."

"Awright," Sam agreed reluctantly, "but I cain't do it alone. Ya got to stay and tell me what to do. I ain't never dug a bullet out o' anyone before, and I don't reckon I'll want to again, especially kinfolk."

"It ain't like Pa went and got shot a'purpose," Hank put in. "That fella with the gun surprised us as we was ridin' off. Probably more luck than sense that he managed to wing Pa."

"Depends on whose luck you're talkin' about. Pa came away with a bullet in him and only Sam to doctor him. I wouldn't want to be in his boots." Tom shook his head in mock dismay, serving to lighten the tension a bit.

"Yeah, but we got the payroll," Billy pointed out. "That should make Pa feel a mite better. There must be a thousand dollars here." Billy hefted the bulging saddlebags.

"Count your gains later, Billy," Sam advised grimly. "Git your tail downstairs to the kitchen and bring me some clean rags and a pot o' boilin' water, and I could use a pair o' scissors if they have some handy, a small pair. No sense makin' this hole any bigger than it already is, huh, Pa?"

Old Bill nodded agreement. "And bring me a bottle of their best whiskey, son," he grated through clenched teeth. "I need something to dull the pain, and Sam kin use it to clean the wound once the bullet is out."

"And don't dally, brother," Tom told him. "Pa's lost a lot of blood already, and if Sam don't get things straightened out soon, we may have to take Pa to the doc whether we want to or not."

Half an hour later, Sam bent over the groaning patient. Old Bill's teeth were sunk deep into a leather belt as Sam worked over him, alternately using nimble fingers and the small scissors to dig the bullet out of the hole in his shoulder. "Wipe the blood away, Tom," Sam instructed. "I can't see a blamed thing. I'm doin' this mostly by feel, anyway, but it would help if I could see part of what I'm doin'."

Tom obliged. Then, with a clean rag, he wiped the sweat and damp hair from Sam's forehead and eyes. "Better?" he asked. When Sam nodded, he added teasingly, "I keep tellin' ya that ya need a haircut, Sam. When ya gonna listen to what your big brother tells ya?"

"When mules fly," came Sam's distracted answer.

"Yeah, Tom," Hank laughed. "Ya keep teasin' about Sam needin' a shave, too, but there ain't nothin' but peachfuzz and freckles on that homely puss."

"Hush, you two, and pay attention here," Sam admonished. "Hank, bring that bottle over here again and get ready to pour. Tom, git your big fingers out of my way for a minute." Face screwed up in intense concentration, Sam slowly pulled the chunk of lead from the wound. Sam didn't take the time to wipe the sweat from stinging eyes. Holding bits of shredded flesh from the wound, Sam ordered. "Pour the whiskey now, Hank."

As the potent brew seared his torn flesh, Old Bill groaned in agony. "Sorry, Pa," Sam muttered through quaking lips, wanting nothing more than to crawl away and have a good cry, but there was still the wound to bandage. Then someone had to stay nearby and watch that Pa didn't start running a fever.

"It's awright, Sammie. Ya done good," Old Bill moaned. "Ya done real good."

Three days later they rode out of Oakville. Old Bill's wound had not festered and was beginning to show signs of healing. It was really too soon for him to travel, but they all knew they dared not linger too long. To make matters worse, what had seemed to be a lot of money in the saddlebags had turned out to be a few greenbacks masking bundles of useless cut-up newspaper. The total take from that disastrous night's work was a measly hundred and fifty dollars. The real payroll, if it had been on that train, was undoubtedly now safe in the hands of the people it had been intended for.

The few dollars the Downings had stolen would not last them for long. As soon as Old Bill was sufficiently recovered, they would have to plan another heist. The trouble was, the Downing gang was fast making a name for itself in northern Texas, and that made each robbery all the more dangerous. Wanted posters were already popping up in various towns and along stage routes, and undoubtedly in every sheriff's office within a hundred-mile radius. Their only remaining advantage was that there were no pictures to go with the posters as yet, only vague descriptions of the brothers and father. They would have to lay low for as long as the money held out, and then they would have to be extremely crafty and careful.

As they rode along, Sam's mind began to drift back to better times, before Mama had died. Not that Sam disliked life with Pa and Hank and Tom and Billy, but it had been different when Ma was alive. They had lived in one place for the first few years of Sam's life. Then they'd moved about a bit after losing their farmland in Kansas, selling it for a portion of its worth. But it was nothing like now. Now they were on the move almost constantly, mostly on the run and one step ahead of the law.

Sam recalled tales Pa told of earlier years, when the boys were young. Sam had been born only months before the Civil War broke out, and remembered little of that time. Pa and the older boys remembered the rough times then, times when Kansas was torn between North and South, wanting to straddle the line of neutrality and catching the devil from both sides. They had lost their newly-built house, when Quantrill's raiders had come through, hell bent on destruction, burning the house and killing all the livestock. The Downings had just enough warning to run to the woods and hide, or they would all have died that fateful night. Sam could not remember hiding in the bramble-choked gully, clutched tightly to Sally's breast while their house and barn burned, lighting the night sky for miles, but the older boys remembered, and Pa had never forgotten nor forgiven.

Bill had been fighting for the North, leaving Sally and their children to face the terror of that night alone. It was months later before he learned of the tragedy that had befallen his family. Unable to get home, he had experienced a helplessness and guilt that rode him like a dark demon for years afterward. Perhaps that guilt was the reason Old Bill had taken the twelve-year-old Sam with him and the boys on their lawless flight, rather than turn the child over to a friend to raise for a while longer. Bill had a fiercely protective streak toward his family. Never again would his children face calamity without him. If they faced disaster, they would do it together.

The night of the raid had been the turning point for the Downing family. All of Sally Downing's prize possessions had gone up in flames, all the cherished momentos of early marriage, each item of her girlhood reduced to ashes, even those few furnishings that had been her mother's and her grandmother's. They had nothing to their names but the clothes on their backs, and those were nightclothes.

They had no money in the bank in town, all their hard-earned cash had gone up in blazes with the house. They had only the land they stood upon, and that not worth much, since Quantrill and his men had even set fire to the fields, destroying the few crops Sally and her sons had managed to plant, crops so near to harvest, and along with them an entire year's labor and profits.

In desperation, Sally had gone against everything she believed in, gone against what Bill would have wanted, and written to her family for money to get by on. They had sent what they could spare, not being prosperous themselves, and, somehow, Sally and her children had made it through the long winter months ahead. With the help of neighbors, they built a small, one-room sod cabin, like the one she and Bill had started out in when first coming to Kansas. Since their money went for cooking utensils, tools, and food, they had swallowed their pride and accepted used clothing from charitable friends and neighbors who had been more fortunate the night of Quantrill's raid.

Come spring, Sally had borrowed against their land to buy seed and replant their farm fields. With only the small boys to help her, the yield was small, but she managed to keep a roof over their heads and food in their mouths through sheer determination. Bill managed a furlough at Christmas that year, arriving home thankful to find his family alive and well, but dismayed at the circumstances to which they had been reduced in his absence. Only Sally's insistence made him return to his unit rather than remain with his wife and children.

When the war was over the following spring, Bill returned and tried to make a go of his farm. Again, he had to borrow from the bank in order to plant his fields. Drought and locusts destroyed most of his crops that season, pushing him further in debt. The next year it was too much rain, flooding the fields and killing the new seedlings.

That was when Bill lost the will to hold on to the land. He sold the farm, and after paying off what he owed at the bank, he barely had enough left to buy provisions, load up a wagon, and move his family westward. They moved around a lot after that, Sam recalled. Bill tried his hand at several things. He hired himself out as a farmhand for keep and small wages for a while. Then he hired on at a ranch in Colorado for a spell, while Sally cooked for the ranch hands. They got by fairly well, since Tom was soon old enough to work alongside his father, and finally Billy, too.

The year Sam turned ten, and Hank fourteen, Sally caught a bad cold that turned into pneumonia. She was sick for many weeks, and her lungs were terribly weakened. Never really regaining her strength after that, the next winter, she got sick again, and this time the cough lingered. It sapped her strength so much that even the slightest exertion exhausted her. When she began taking to her bed more often and spitting blood, Bill knew the worst was happening. His beloved wife was dying, and there wasn't a thing in the world he could do to prevent it.

When Sally died, Bill lost more than a wife; he lost his soulmate, his guiding force in life. Without her, he was like a ship without a rudder. He buried his grief in a bottle, losing himself in a drunken spree that rarely found him sober. Before long, he lost his job. Though Tom and Billy, and even Hank, who was now sixteen, could have stayed on at the ranch, they refused to work there if their father was not welcome. The five of them drifted from place to place for a time, but there were few spreads large enough to hire four men at once, unless it was for the brief time of roundup and branding, especially when it meant taking on a next-to-useless twelve-year-old in the bargain.

It was during a trail drive from Waco to Abilene that their lives took another turn. The drive was a murderous trek, with disaster courting them every step of the way. There were storms, flooded streams, stampedes, even an Indian raid to contend with, as well as a trail boss who was the devil in disguise. When the cook, who was supposed to be keeping an eye on Sam, nearly let the youngster get kidnapped during the Indian raid, Bill decided there must be an easier way to turn a profit than eating tons of dust mile after mile and risking his family's lives as well. If they were going to risk life and limb, it would be for better profit than this! Besides, it was rare that they could all find decent-paying employment at the same time and find suitable lodging that allowed Sam to be with them. Between jobs they often found their stomachs as empty as their pockets.

It was then that Bill chose a way of life he would never have considered while Sally was living, but he did it so that he and their children could stay together. He would not even consider abandoning Sam in order to make things easier for the rest of them. The next thing the Downing clan knew, they were following Bill blindly into a life of crime. The first few attempts were rather inept, and it was a wonder they didn't all land in jail. Then they hit a streak of luck, where things went smoothly. They robbed a stagecoach near Dallas, netting a quick hundred dollars from the passengers, but little else. Then they hit a bank in Denison, near the Texas-Oklahoma border, and made off with several hundred dollars, which saw them comfortably through the winter in a little cabin near Santa Fe. Whenever the funds got low, they would waylay unwary travelers and relieve them of their money and jewels.

Quick escapes became a way of life for all of them. Danger rode on their tails constantly, but they accepted this as inevitable and part of the life they had chosen. They stole everything from horses to cattle, to bankrolls. They robbed trains and stages, banks, hotels, even a prosperous saloon or two, but they never intentionally robbed children, widows, or anyone who could not afford to lose a few dollars. They had known too well what it was to be poor, and they would not inflict that need on a fellow unfortunate soul.

There were even times in the course of their travels that they shared their ill-gotten gains with those less fortunate than themselves. Their unstinting generosity kept them from accumulating much of a fortune for themselves. That, and their growing notoriety, kept them from buying more land and settling someplace into a decent life once more, but by now the die was cast. They were well and truly outlaws, running from the law at every turn. While some recalled their generosity, even comparing them to Jesse James's gang, Sam Bass, or Robin Hood, the law took a dim view of the Downing gang's activities.

If Bill Downing had his personal regrets, he rarely voiced them. If he ever longed for a more peaceful existence, he never said, and neither did his offspring. They were all together, and that was the most important thing to Bill, worth the hazards that confronted them. If he wished that Sam or Hank, the youngest of his brood, had more schooling, or the more refined manners that Sally would have taught them had she lived, he kept such thoughts to himself. They would manage without learning their letters. Sure, they were ruffians, but they had learned how to fend for themselves, how to think on their feet, how to sleep in the saddle, how to shoot straight and true, how to live off the land if need be. Even Sam could outride, outshoot, outthink, and outdrink most full-grown men. And the kid had uncanny luck in a poker game, without ever having to cheat! Who needed booklearning when a person had those talents?

If any one of them had complained in earnest, Old Bill might have considered reforming. They could always go down into Mexico and buy land, or maybe head out to California and start over. But none of them did complain, and Bill didn't really want to start again from scratch without Sally. She had been the backbone of his energies and ambitions, and without her, he just naturally took the easiest course, whether right or wrong, in providing for his little family. In spite of everything, Bill was a good and devoted father, if not a very shining example to follow.

None of the younger Downings were blind to their father's shortcomings, including Sam. Now, riding behind him, on their way to a new hideout, Sam was tired of running from place to place. More and more often, Sam longed for some permanence, some stability in their nomadic existence. Sam was not as strong as the rest of them, never would be, and knew it. Yet Sam carried on. Sometimes, while half-dreaming, Sam longed for unknown things, perhaps better clothes, a better education, a home. The strange longings were never clearly defined, only a vague restlessness of the soul.

As fiercely loyal as the others, Sam shoved personal feelings aside. As long as they could all be together, everything else would work itself out in time. Sam just wished they could stop looking over their shoulders in fear of the law on their trail. It would be such a relief to live in peace for a short time, not worrying what lay ahead or behind, not wondering when one of them might be shot or killed, whether they would all end up in jail someday soon or hung for their various crimes.

With a bone-weary sigh, Sam pulled the stetson lower to shade the sun from aching eyes. The mare's hooves seemed to telegraph an echoing chant to the youth's tired brain. *Maybe someday. Maybe someday. Maybe someday. Maybe someday, what?* Sam thought, but there was no ready answer.

CHAPTER 2

In the northern town of Tumbleweed, Texas, which lay just a day's ride south of Dallas, and which the local citizens preferred to call Tumble, Marshal Travis Kincaid sat behind the old scarred desk in his office. Born too late to fight in the War Between the States, he was nonetheless well suited for the job he now held. At twenty-six years old, he had already served a short time in the U.S. Cavalry, served for three years as one of the illustrious Texas Rangers, and for two years as a U.S. Marshal here in Tumble. He was a tall, well-built man, with shoulders broad enough to carry the heavy responsibilities of his office. Though not famed for being the fastest draw in those parts, he had a reputation of being unerringly accurate when forced to use his gun, and this skill had saved his life on numerous occasions. He was handsome, much sighed over by the ladies, with thick blond hair, a rather rakish mustache, and piercing eyes the most unusual shade of turquoise. It was fact as well as rumor that many a man had taken one long look into those sharp, relentless eyes and allowed himself to be arrested, handing over his gun rather than face the bold marshal in a showdown.

This particular hot May afternoon, Marshal Kincaid was studying the newest wanted posters and telegraph messages that had just come in. He frowned when he came to the notice of the Downing gang. Those fellows were fast becoming a thorn in the side of every marshal and sheriff in northern Texas. So far no one had been able to give a decent description of the members of the gang. In fact, some folks claimed there were four men in the gang, while others swore there were five. There was an older man, supposedly the father of the others, a young man still thought to be in his early teens, and three of varying ages in between. Since they wore bandanas over their lower faces, and hats pulled low over their foreheads, it was difficult to tell what they looked like. That made Travis's job that much harder. They seemed to be hitting small towns at random so no one knew where they might turn up next, and with no accurate description to go by, they could be in and out of Tumble before anyone was the wiser, except, of course, those they managed to hold up before they left!

Just a few days before, they had held up the train north of there. The thousands of dollars they had attempted to steal had been destined for the banks in several nearby towns, including Tumble. Fortunately, the Downings had made off with very little of it, thanks to the idea of hauling the money in the regular baggage car and disguising bundles of cut-up newspaper to replace it in the mailcar. It had been a smart maneuver, but not one they would readily fall for again soon. Someone had to apprehend them soon. So far no one had been hurt in one of the Downings' hold-ups, but that didn't mean someone wouldn't be in the future. The possibility of violence erupting in one of these situations was all too real, no matter what the pattern had been in the past.

Travis sighed and handed the notice to his deputy. "Same old thing, Chas. At least Sam Bass has decided to give us a breather. Heard tell he took a herd of cattle up to Dodge. Don't know how much truth there is to it, but it's been quiet for a while now, and it's for sure he's not in Denison any longer."

"Count your blessin's, my ma always says," Chas answered. "The James gang has been keeping to Missouri, and that's one thing to be thankful for. And that young fella, Billy the Kid, has kept to New Mexico and Arizona so far." Chas waved the notice in the air. "Ya think the Downings might be headin' our way?"

Rubbing the back of his neck to try to work the kinks out of his aching muscles, Travis said, "No way to tell, Chas. In one way, I hope not, but in another, I wish we could nab those culprits once and for all. If I could just lay hold of one of them, I know I could get an accurate description of the rest of the gang. Then maybe we could catch them all in short order. For now, all we can do is keep a sharp eye out for strangers, four or five of them together."

17

Chas watched his boss work his shoulders in an arc. "Sore back?"

"Yeah. I swear, I hate these days behind this desk. I'd rather ride a hundred miles in one stretch than do all this paperwork. It's the one part of this job that I really despise."

Chas grinned. He'd worked with Travis for two years now, and they were friends as well as deputy and boss. "Molly would be more than willin' to help you relieve all that tension, ya know."

"Maybe too willing," Travis replied with a wry grin. "Among all those words of wisdom your ma is always teaching you, didn't she ever tell you that something that comes too easy may not be worth having?"

"Now, Travis, Molly isn't a bad girl, even if she does work in the Silver Nugget."

Travis's eyebrows rose fractionally. "Sounds like you might be sort of sweet on Molly."

"What if I am, not that I'm sayin' I am for sure, ya know?" Chas asked in a slightly belligerent tone.

"I think you'd make a right nice pair."

"Ya wouldn't mind?"

"I don't have any claims on Molly. If you want her, go after her. Actually, Miss Nola is more what catches my eye," Travis admitted in a rare moment of confidence.

"Rafe Sandoval's daughter?" Chas's features took on a musing look. "Oh, well," he shrugged, "might as well set your sights high, I guess. Might as well aim for the daughter of one of the richest ranchers in the territory, if she'll have ya."

It was Travis's turn to shrug. "She seems interested enough. Of course, it hasn't really gotten to the courting stage yet, so don't go runnin' off at the mouth inviting everyone in town to the wedding, Chas. I've gone to Sunday dinner exactly twice, and I plan on asking her to the church social in a couple of weeks. I'm sure not ready to make a trip down the church aisle with anyone just yet. I want to get to know the woman fairly well first, see if she and I can get along together, you know?"

"Sounds like a smart plan, if it works," Chas said skeptically.

"Why the look? What's wrong with the idea?"

"Well, Trav, ya know I'm not all that smart about women myself, but I listen real good when the other fellas I know are talkin'. Seems there's a goodly number of them got the surprise of their lives when the sweet little thing they were courtin', who wouldn't say boo to a goose or raise her voice over a whisper, suddenly turned into a screechin' shrew a few weeks after the weddin'. Not all of them married in haste, either. They really thought they knew the girl. Seems more than a few of the little darlings were hidin' their true natures until after the 'I dos,' so be real careful, my friend."

"I intend to, Chas," Travis assured him. "I surely do intend to. After all, there's no real rush. I'm plenty young yet, and I have Mrs. Willow to clean and cook for me."

"Hell's fire, I don't see why ya have to have Mrs. Willow cook for ya at all," Chas exclaimed in disgust, "with all the Sunday-dinner invites ya get and all the pies and such the eligible ladies of this town push your way all the time! If ya don't watch it, ya'll wind up with a potbelly the size of Texas before you're thirty!"

"Just as long as I don't lose my mustache, Chas," Travis added with a low laugh, his long fingers smoothing the well-trimmed growth over his upper lip. "I have to admit, it's my one true vanity."

The Downing gang rode up to Denison less than a week later. Upon finding Sam Bass gone, as Marshall Kincaid had told his deputy, they wandered south from the Oklahoma-Texas border. They waylaid a stage not far from Denison, grabbing a quick couple hundred dollars. In Sherman they held up the bank, tying up the bank employees and making a clean getaway without alerting any of the citizens or the town sheriff. Then they decided to bypass Dallas. They set their sights on smaller quarry instead, deciding to head for the quiet little town of Tumble and another unsuspecting little bank.

CHAPTER 3

Sam's horse shifted restlessly in the hot sun. Sam was beginning to feel as restless as the horse, if not downright anxious. Pa and the boys had been in the bank for what seemed a lifetime. Had something gone wrong? There hadn't been any shots or shouts, but they should have been out by now. Left outside once again to guard the horses, Sam felt as conspicuous as a fox in a henhouse. In an effort not to stand out, Sam had dismounted and was leaning nonchalantly against the hitching rail. Beneath the brim of the stetson, Sam's eyes swept the street for signs of trouble, all the while keeping one eye on the door of the bank two buildings down, but everything seemed normal. If only they would hurry!

Across the street from where Sam stood waiting, Marshal Kincaid watched unseen from the window of the hotel lobby while behind the hotel desk, Harry Jacobs, the owner, nervously awaited Travis's signal. Chas Brown had already been alerted by Harry's wife, when Travis had become suspicious. Chas was now on alert in the barbershop, as was the barber, Lou Sprit, a veritable mountain of a man and the best damned dentist ever to hit the West.

"You really think it's them?" Harry asked in a gruff whisper.

"Could be. There's five of them, one of them old and one not old enough to have whiskers." Travis's intense gaze never left the bank door, even as he answered the newly-deputized Harry. Travis had been having a leisurely breakfast in the hotel dining room when he chanced to glance out the window and spot the five strangers hitching their horses. There was nothing really that suspicious about the small group of men, but Travis's senses were suddenly alert.

Two of the men had sauntered into the bank, while two more had wandered into the general store. The fifth one, the youngest, had stayed by his horse. A few minutes later, the two in the general store had come out again, and calmly joined the other two already in the bank. That was when Travis had gone into action. Better to be prepared than caught completely off guard. Travis just wished he could be sure this really was the Downing gang, wished that he might have had some forewarning before they had gotten this far, before they had gone into the bank.

There was no telling what was going on in there at this minute, but the longer they were in there, the more Travis began to sweat. Old Mrs. McPherson, who was ninety if she was a day, had gone into the bank a few minutes before the men. The feisty old gal might take it into her head to lay her cane across someone's head before letting them take her life's savings. Travis's only comfort was in knowing that so far the Downings had never seriously wounded anyone. Surely they wouldn't hurt the old woman—if it was the Downings, and if they were, indeed, robbing the bank.

Travis's gaze shifted slightly to the kid with the horses. The boy seemed a bit nervous. Every few seconds the lad would glance toward the bank, and though he leaned almost lazily against the hitching rail, the toe of one well-worn boot repeatedly scuffed the dusty earth. The marshal's keen eyes noted this as he quickly scanned the street.

Travis frowned. At this hour of the morning, there were several people already out and about; ladies doing their morning shopping before the heat of the day, men going into the feed and supply stores soon after they opened, children chasing about eager to spend a penny on sour candy or licorice whips. There had been no time to warn everyone off the streets. To do so now would alert the men in the bank and possibly endanger the lives of those innocent people inside. If the bank were actually being robbed, Travis could only wait until the men came out. Then he and his deputies would have to let them mount their horses and start out of town before giving chase. Travis could not chance a stray bullet hitting some unsuspecting bystander. It was a tricky situation, one that made Travis extremely uncomfortable.

Suddenly the door of the bank flew open, and

four men came hurrying out, carrying six canvas bank bags. As they ran to their horses, which the waiting lad had now untied, Mrs. McPherson toddled out the bank door and shrieked, "Stop! Thieves! Stop 'em! They robbed the bank!"

So much for Kincaid's plan not to alarm the thieves or the citizens of Tumble!

The robbers mounted their horses and amid shouts and cries of anger and alarm, raced their horses down the street toward the south end of town. At the same time, Kincaid, Brown, Jacobs, and Sprit grabbed the reins of the nearest horses, disregarding whose animals they might be, and prepared to follow. Catching sight of Isaac Hand, a local merchant, Travis shouted, "Go check on the people in the bank. If anyone is wounded, get Doc." With that they were gone, racing after the cloud of dust kicked up by the robbers' horses.

The Downings were hightailing it out of Tumble as fast as their horses could carry them. Damn! They'd have been long gone without anyone knowing if it hadn't been for that noisy old woman! They had tied and gagged the bank employees, but Old Bill had balked when it came to doing the same to the frail old lady. Now it looked as though that might have been a fatal mistake, and they would be extremely fortunate if they weren't all in jail before noon and swingin' from a noose shortly thereafter.

Sam was riding hell bent for leather, cursing father, brothers, and the old woman all in the same breath. Tom and Billy had each thrown a sack at Sam as they'd run for their horses, and now Sam was trying to ride, to stuff the sacks of money into the two saddlebags behind the saddle, and to handle a gun at the same time. It was a juggling act fit for a circus!

Hank raced by, having succeeded in securing his loot already. "Spur that nag, Sam!" he yelled, casting a worried look behind them.

Sam did the same, and nearly came unseated at the sight of four horsemen fast gaining on them. It did nothing for Sam's morale to note that Pa and all three older brothers were out ahead, leaving Sam to bring up the rear. "Damn and blast!" Sam spurred the mare, but she was running full-out as it was. "If I ever get out of this, I'll trade you in on a mule! I swear it!" Of course, it really was not the little mare's fault, and Sam knew it. The horse had caught a stone in her hoof the week before, and it was still a bit tender, from the way she was beginning to favor it now. Just when speed was of the essence, Bess was not going to be able to deliver!

The distance between Sam and the others was increasing. Likewise, the distance between Sam and their pursuers was lessening. Sam ducked instinctively as a bullet whistled past, too close for comfort. Sam spared a glare for Hank, who had fired the shot. "Who ya tryin' to kill, Hank? Me or the posse?" *Hank always has been a piss-poor shot*! Sam thought, dodging the return fire and drawing a bead on one of their pursuers. Sam's aim was true, hitting the man in the thigh and causing him to fall from his horse. Pa had rules about that, too. He'd taught all his young'uns to aim to wound, unless it was absolutely necessary to do otherwise.

Chancing another look behind, Sam saw the gun fly from another of the men's hands, and he clutched at his upper arm with a cry of pain. Two down, two to go! At least one brother was improving his aim, and without looking, Sam's first guess was Billy. He could hit a gnat at a thousand paces! Sam grinned as the distinctive sound of Old Bill's rifle split the air and another man fell, his horse shot out from under him. That left only one.

As Sam was getting ready to crack off another shot, Bess stumbled. For a split second, the horse tried to recover, then went down onto her knees, sending Sam flying over her head. By some strange quirk, Sam's hat stayed put, as if nailed on. With a startled cry, Sam went spinning in a glorious cartwheel, then landed heavily belly-first. There wasn't even time to brace for the fall. Sam's breath gushed out in a painful rush; the gun went flying, landing several feet away.

For the briefest instant, Sam lay stunned, trying vainly to draw breath into aching lungs. Danger spurred Sam to action, but it was already too late. As Sam lunged desperately for the Colt, a shot rang out. Almost simultaneously, the gun leapt further out of reach. Sam gave a second shout, and heard it matched by Billy's. Even as the lone rider approached, Sam saw Billy wheel his horse around and start to ride back to help. "Sam!" he called, fear and desperation in his voice.

"No, Billy! No!" Sam waved Billy back, fearing for his safety if he dared come closer. "Go on! Leave me!"

Billy hesitated for just a second. "We'll be back for ya, Sam!" he hollered, then turned and raced after the others.

"Get up, kid. And don't even think about trying for that gun again." The voice seemed to come from a long way up, and Sam looked up to see a mounted rider glaring down. The man had the most intimidating stare Sam had ever encountered, with piercing, turquoise eyes framed by thick, brown lashes. But those eyes weren't the only thing pointed at Sam. A gun was leveled at Sam's chest from less than four feet away, and beyond the gun was a glistening tin star pinned to the man's vest.

Sam started to rise, looking helplessly after the others as they disappeared over a slight rise. Suddenly Sam gave a weak cry of pain and sank to the ground again.

"Kid, if you're trying to pull one over on me, I'll shoot you here and now," the marshal warned with a growl.

"I'm not!" Sam panted. "It's my ribs. I fell on a rock when I landed, I guess." Sam clutched the offending ribs tightly and grimaced. "And my ankle. I think it's broke."

Travis dismounted. After he had picked up Sam's gun and stuck it in his own gunbelt, he bent to help the boy up. His big hand went about the lad's thin upper arm, and Travis thought to himself, *The kid is skin and bone!*

Sam groaned in agony, trying unsuccessfully to bite back the pitiful cry. Travis looked down into a dirty, scraped face dominated by huge, pain-filled, black eyes. Beneath the grime, the kid's face was pale, and for a brief moment Travis felt a twinge of pity. Then he shrugged it off. This boy, young as he was, had shot Chas, and with his deputy out of commission, there was no way Travis could chase after the remaining bank robbers. Of the four pursuers, he was the only one not wounded, and now it was up to him to get this kid back to town and in jail and see that the doctor patched up the others. With a look of disgust, Travis sighed. Chas had a bullet in his leg, Harry Jacobs had one in his arm, and big Lou Sprit had broken his leg tumbling off his horse. And Ike Harrison would be screaming bloody murder because his bank's money had not been recovered. What a disaster!

"Come on, kid. You either walk or ride back to town." Even though his tone was gruff, Travis pulled the boy to his feet as gently as possible, careful of the boy's ribs.

"I'll ride." Then Sam thought about Bess for the first time. "My horse?"

Luckily, Bess had fared better than Sam. The little mare stood quietly awaiting her rider. "She's favorin' her right foreleg," Sam muttered.

Travis helped Sam mount, taking the precaution of removing the rifle from its scabbard on the saddle. His brow rose slightly when he recognized it as a Winchester '73. The kid's handgun was a Colt Peacemaker. The Downings obviously did not stint when it came to their weapons. These were the finest a man could own. He bent to examine the horse's foreleg. "The leg's fine. No sprain or break. She doesn't want to put her weight on the hoof."

Sam nodded sulkily. "Bruised it last week on a stone. Ya sure the leg is awright?"

Travis's eyes narrowed. "Better than Lou's, which is broken, or Chas's, which has a bullet in it that came from your gun."

With an uncaring shrug, Sam answered. "I didn't notice none o' you holdin' your fire. Guess y'all just ain't as good a shots as we are."

It was all Travis could do not to jerk the little

braggart down out of the saddle and give his rear end a good tanning. "You are an insolent brat. How old are you anyway—uh, Sam, isn't it?"

Sam squinted down at him. "Tain't none o' your business, Marshal."

"Since you are going to be a guest in my jail, I'd say it's plenty business of mine." As he spoke, Travis was tying the boy's hands to the pommel of the saddle. He gave the rope an extra strong tug, watching the boy wince. "I heard the one you called Billy call you Sam. That is your name, isn't it?"

"Yeah," came the hissing reply.

"And your age, son?"

"Seventeen, an' I'm not your son." Sam glared down at the lawman.

"No, you're Bill Downing's son."

Sam gave a terse laugh. "Think what you want, lawman."

"I think for someone who has yet to grow his first chin whisker, you've got a real sassy mouth on you, kid." Travis looped the reins over the horse's head so he could lead it behind his own. "Welcome to Tumbleweed, Texas, Sam," he said with grim humor.

With Chas and Harry riding double, and Lou groaning like a wagon wheel in need of grease, they made it to town an hour later. As they rode down the main street, they created quite a stir. Word spread like wildfire that the marshal and his posse were back, all shot to hell, and with only one prisoner. Travis was hard put not to scream at them to all go home and tend to their own business, but the money that was stolen that morning was theirs, so he clamped a lid on his temper and rode on grim-lipped and silent. When they reached the jail, he sent the Miller boy running for Doc Purdy and set several men to helping the injured men dismount. Amid much clamoring and confusion, he ushered his limping prisoner into the jail.

"When do I git to see the doc?" Sam demanded after having the cell's door clanged shut.

"Just as soon as he's seen to the others. You aren't going to die from those ribs of yours." Travis hung Sam's gunbelt on a rack behind his desk, along with the belt from the boy's britches, which Sam had been reluctant to give up. No wonder. The youngster's pants had nearly fallen down without the support of the belt. Travis had rarely seen such a skinny frame on a boy his age.

Sam glared out from between the bars at him. "Don't see why I can't have my belt."

"Could be I don't trust you not to hang yourself with it," Travis answered bluntly. "The good people of this town want to reserve that pleasure for themselves." Travis could have sworn he saw the boy blanch beneath the dirt on his face, yet he recovered quickly.

"My pa an' brothers will break me out o' here long before that happens. They're gonna come for me, ya know, an' they'll more 'n likely kill ya when they do."

"I expect they'll try," Travis conceded.

"Least ya could do is give me the makin's of a cigarette while I'm waitin' for the doc," Sam continued to complain. "If'n ya ain't generous enough to share yours, ya could at least git me mine from my saddlebags."

Travis would have ignored the request, but he

was curious to see what else Sam's bulging saddle-bags would reveal. As yet he had not had the time to search them. He was somewhat relieved to find a sack of money crammed into the top of each bag. "Two out of six is better than nothing at all," he said to himself. It improved his mood enough to throw Sam the bag of tobacco and papers he found in the bottom of the saddlebag.

Sam grunted what Travis took to be a word of thanks, and as Travis watched, quickly and expertly rolled a cigarette. "Ya gonna make me sit here an' suck this thing dry, or are ya gonna give me a light?"

Travis tossed him a match. When it fell short of the mark, Sam bent to retrieve it. It was too much to ask from the battered ribs, and Sam groaned aloud in pain. Tears glistened momentarily in the pitch-black eyes, but were quickly blinked back. Sam took several shallow breaths to dispel the wave of darkness that threatened, and fell back on the small cot, gingerly hoisting the injured leg onto the lumpy mattress. It was some time before Sam finally lit the cigarette. "I ain't gonna let the doc cut on my boots, neither," Sam grumbled, blowing a smoke ring toward the ceiling.

Travis shook his head and grinned. "You've got a lot to learn about being in jail, boy. Not only will you let the doctor work on your injuries any way he sees fit, you'll be taking a bath as soon as he's done with you. I don't want you stinking up my jail while you're here." Travis was amazed to see the quick look of panic that crossed the boy's face. "Hey, kid! Being clean isn't all that bad, you know. You just might come to like it after you get used to it."

* * *

Doc Purdy arrived a couple of hours later. "Heard your prisoner needs tending, Travis," he said in a gravelly voice. He was a pleasant man in his mid-thirties, with receding brown hair, twinkling blue eyes, and a good start on a potbelly. "You sure have kept me hoppin' today. Business hasn't been this good since the stairs at Mattie's brothel collapsed last New Year's Eve. I must have set twelve legs and twenty arms that night." Doc chuckled in remembrance. "And I stitched more than one head the next day, too! Amazing what a rolling pin can do in the hands of an angry wife!"

Travis joined the doctor in his laughter. "I'll remember that, Doc. Now, why don't you see what you can do for Sam, here." Travis unlocked the door to the cell. "Maybe he'll stop his complaining then and give my ears a rest. He says his ribs hurt and he thinks he may have broken that right ankle."

Doc Purdy set his black bag on the floor and looked at Sam. "Kind of young to be getting yourself in this sort of fix, aren't you, boy?"

"I ain't shot," Sam retorted grumpily. "If my horse hadn't stumbled, I wouldn't be here now."

"I'm not talking just about your injuries. I meant you're a mite young for robbing banks and shootin' deputies." While they were talking, Doc Purdy swiftly cut the boot from Sam's foot and started examining the swollen ankle. "Don't think you broke it, Sam. Just sprained it good."

Sam glared down at the ruined boot. "Ya owe me a pair o' boots, Doc."

"And you owe me my fee," the jovial doctor retorted. "I'd say we'll come out about even."

When the doctor asked Sam to remove his shirt,

Sam balked. "Can't I jest hitch it up a mite?" he suggested, casting a glance in Travis's direction. "Ain't I got a right to no privacy at all? It's bad enough he took my belt an' my pants are about to fall down."

Travis's eyebrows rose over amused eyes. "Why so shy, Sam? You haven't got anything I haven't seen before, you know."

"I don't doubt that," Sam grumbled low, "but you ain't seein' mine!"

"All right. All right. Don't get all riled up," Doc put in quickly. "Just roll your shirttail up so I can get a look at those ribs."

Sam did so hesitantly and very gingerly, every movement painful in the extreme. Sam couldn't help but flinch as the doctor probed and prodded at each discolored rib. As Doc Purdy's fingers felt along Sam's upper rib cage, Sam's breath was sucked in tightly in dismay. Doctor and patient stared at one another in mutual shock for several long silent moments. "Travis, I think you have a problem here," Purdy said finally in a hushed, solemn voice, his eyes still locked with Sam's.

"He broke the ribs?" Travis asked.

"No, the ribs are just badly bruised." Purdy hesitated a moment, then said softly. "Unless I'm sadly mistaken, and the worst doctor God ever put breath into, your Sam here is actually a Samantha. Travis, you've arrested a young woman."

CHAPTER 4

"I've what!" Travis's jaw nearly dropped to his knees, his face taking on a color Sam had only seen once when Hank had eaten a raw egg on a dare from his brothers. She could swear the marshal's mustache even quivered as he stood rooted to the floor and stared in disbelief. "No, I can't have. I didn't. He isn't . . ." Travis's voice trailed off as he looked almost pleadingly at Doc Purdy.

Doc almost felt sorry for him. "She," he corrected, "and she most certainly is. I didn't get to be a doctor without learning the difference between a man and a woman. Sorry, Travis, but your prisoner is without doubt a female."

Travis shook his tawny head, still stunned. "But he, er, she—she has no—er . . ." Travis's hands came up to simulate female breasts, his face

35

changing from its former ghastly hue to a dull red as he stumbled over his words.

Sam sat up, pulled her shirt down, and watched warily as the doctor and the marshal exchanged comments over her head as if they had almost forgotten she was there. In truth, she wished she could disappear, because Marshal Kincaid didn't seem at all pleased with the sudden change in her gender. The devil take that nosy, old doctor for searching out her secret!

"Yes, she does. Take my word for it, Travis," Purdy assured the marshal. "Bent over as she was to ease the pain in those ribs, and with the boy's clothes and that shirt seven sizes too big, I can understand why you missed them, but the young lady does have breasts."

"I ain't no lady," Sam piped up in the husky voice that had also served to disguise her gender.

Travis's intense gaze swung to her. "That's probably the first truth out of your mouth today," he agreed through clenched teeth, advancing on her with measured steps, his eyes searching her frame from head to toe. "Look at her, Doc. Does that look like any woman you've ever seen, let alone a lady?" He went on without waiting for an answer. "He, er, she's grubby from the top of that battered hat to the tips of those run-down boots! She walks and talks and looks like a boy. Sweet hell, she even sat here and smoked a cigarette while we waited for you!"

Hemmed in on one side by the doctor and on the other by the cell wall, Sam could not react fast enough to stop him when Travis suddenly reached out and whipped the hat from her head. Long tangled strands of red-brown hair tumbled down about her shoulders and face. "Oh, God!" Travis groaned, as if in more pain than Sam. "It's true! I was hoping, by some miracle, you were wrong, Doc."

While Travis was bemoaning the facts, Sam grabbed her hat back from his limp fingers and plunked in back on her head. "Touch one more thing of mine, Marshal, an' I'll rip off that shaggy mustache of yours an' feed it to ya!" she threatened heatedly, her black eyes shooting sparks.

Purdy, who was fast recovering from the surprise of discovering that Sam was a girl, laughed. Travis didn't. Involuntarily his fingers went up to smooth his mustache, his eyes narrowing into bright slits as he returned Sam's glare. "Someone needs to teach you manners, girl, among other things."

"Who? You?" Sam challenged, her chin rising defiantly.

"Oh, no! I wouldn't take on that task for all the tea in China! They couldn't pay me enough to put up with the likes of you!"

"Uh, Travis, I wouldn't be too hasty," Doc Purdy advised. "You just might wind up eating those words. The fact remains, now that you know that Sam is a girl, you can't keep her locked up in this jail. You are going to have to make other arrangements."

Travis groaned again and ran long fingers through his hair. "You're right, Doc. I just hadn't thought that far ahead yet." He paused thoughtfully, then frowned as no ready solution came to mind. "What in blue blazes *am* I going to do with her?"

Sam smirked, enjoying the sight of two grown

men in a situation they obviously wanted to avoid like the plague. "You could always let me go. Could end up saving ya your purty hide if my pa doesn't have to come git me."

"Over my dead body," Travis growled.

Sam nodded almost pleasantly. "That's what I was gittin' at."

Travis leaned over her until they were face to face, only inches separating them. "Let's get this straight, little girl. I'm not afraid of your father, or your brothers, or your cousins, uncles, in-laws, or outlaws. I am well aware that they will probably come after you and I'll be ready and waiting. You are in my custody now and you'll stay in my keep until I say differently. Anyone wants you, they'll have to get by me first. Do you understand that?"

Sam grimaced. "I hear ya, Marshal. I ain't deaf and I ain't dumb."

"You haven't had much schooling, either, from the way you talk."

"I ain't needed none." Neither of them was willing to give an inch.

"As long as you are in my care, we'll see if we can't correct that. Maybe if you have something to occupy your mind and your time, you won't have time to get into too much more trouble."

"I ain't goin' to school, Marshal." Sam was adamant.

"You'll go if I say you will." Travis was just as headstrong.

Sam gave him a hateful smile. "Ya know the old sayin', Marshal. You kin lead a horse to water, but ya can't make him drink."

Travis grinned back nastily. "You'll drink or you'll drown."

"Meanin'?"

"You'll learn if it kills you."

Doc Purdy cleared his throat loudly, thus gaining their attention. "I guess this means you'll be taking Sam home with you?"

Travis shook his head. "To tell you the truth, I don't know what to do with her." As Sam started to open her mouth again, Travis glared at her. "Not one word out of you, or I'm going to lose what little hold I have on my temper and tan the daylights out of you, girl or not," he warned. Turning back to the question at hand, he asked Purdy. "Got any suggestions, Doc?"

Doc Purdy shrugged. "Do you think Parson Aldrich and his wife would take her in?"

Travis nearly snorted at that. "Those two kindly old folks? Lord, Purdy, Sam would rob them blind and be long gone within an hour."

Sam bridled at this, and could not hold her tongue. "I wouldn't rob no preacher!" she declared angrily.

"Why not? You certainly don't strike me as the religious type, Sam," Travis taunted.

Sam refused to back down. "We Downings never steal from the church or from folks we know can't afford to lose a few dollars. We may do a lot of things, but we've never killed no one yet, an' we don't steal from orphans an' widows."

"Aha!" Travis's brilliant eyes lit with triumph. "So you are Bill Downing's kid. Until now, I wasn't absolutely sure it was the Downings who held up the bank this morning."

Sam could have bitten off her tongue to hear Travis admit this. Damnation! Her big mouth would be the death of them all yet!

"And what about poor old Mrs. McPherson?" Travis went on. "She's the old woman who was in the bank this morning. Your family robbed her, and she's a widow. Not rich, either."

"Uh, Travis," Doc interrupted. "There's something you ought to know about the bank robbery this morning, besides the fact that no one was hurt. It seems the Downings went out of their way not to take from anyone who could not afford it, just as Sam says. They told Ike Harrison to fill the bags with money from the larger accounts only, and not to touch those of folks who were having a hard time of it. Ike had never heard of such a thing! And Mrs. McPherson was there to make sure he did just that! That old biddy wasn't about to lose one thin dime of her meager savings, if she had to shoot Ike herself."

"Then why did she scream bloody murder afterward?" Travis frowned.

Purdy shrugged. "Just doing her citizen's duty, I reckon."

"Well, regardless of whether she would rob them blind or not, Sam can't stay with the Aldriches."

"What about Nan Tucker?" Doc suggested, naming the town's schoolteacher.

"No. She'd be a good one to teach Sam during the day now that school is out, but she couldn't take Sam to live in with her. Not without a husband to keep Sam in line. Besides," Travis said with a sigh, "she's baked me too many pies for comfort already. I'll gladly pay her to teach Sam, but anything else would be too great a favor. Nan might get the wrong idea, and it would be like letting a bee loose in a field full of clover. Before I knew it, I'd be up to my eyeballs in wedding plans."

Purdy laughed in agreement. "Why don't you just take Sam home with you? You're going to have to keep an eagle eye on her anyway, if you think her folks really will come after her. You can't put that danger and responsibility off on someone else's plate. Besides, you have plenty of room in that big old house, and Elsie comes in to cook and to clean. She could help you keep an eye on your little prisoner when you are working." Purdy chuckled again and winked at Travis. "You have to admit, Trav, Elsie certainly keeps you in line. Surely she could handle a mere girl. You could even ask her to live in for a while, to keep the gossip down."

Travis considered this a minute. "Do you think she would?"

"I don't see why not. All her own children are grown now, and she's all alone in that little house of hers. She might like the idea of having a young girl around to teach women's skills to again."

"It wouldn't hurt to ask her, I suppose," Travis said hesitantly.

"The worst she could do is say no," Doc agreed.

So it was settled, all without Sam's agreement, or even her knowledge. When Travis turned to see her reaction to his decision, he found her curled up on the cot, sound asleep. One arm was flung out over the edge of the cot, the other clutched tightly about her sore ribs. "Tuckered out, I guess," he said softly.

Doc nodded. "Let her sleep. I'll come by later and bind those ribs and that ankle for her. She'll be stiff and sore for a few days yet."

"At least I have that in my favor. For the first few

days I may not have to worry about chasing her all over the countryside. You know, Doc, even when I thought she was a boy, I felt rather sorry for her. Can you imagine what her life must have been like up till now, being dragged all over by that outlaw family of hers, no decent home or clothes or education, constantly on the run?"

Doc Purdy shook his head. "Must have been rough on her." He picked up his bag and headed for the door. "One word of advice, Travis," he added with a slight smile. "I'd watch that soft streak if I were you, or that little gal is going to get the best of you yet."

Their first major confrontation came later that day. Travis took Sam home and introduced her to Elsie Willow, his housekeeper. Sam wasn't sure exactly what to think of the crusty older woman, but when she heard Elsie issuing orders to Travis like an army drill sergeant, she decided not to take offense at Elsie's gruff attitude. It seemed to be the woman's normal manner.

When Travis instructed Sam to take a bath, Sam grumbled a bit just for the sake of appearances. Secretly, she was thrilled at the thought of being clean again, and a long hot bath would go a long way toward relieving some of the stiffness and soreness from her body. Even when Travis warned that if she didn't emerge from the tub sparkling from head to toe, he would scrub her clean himself, Sam didn't really mind too much. She intended to squeak by the time she was done.

But when Elsie came into the small room off the kitchen where Sam was bathing and, as ordered by

Travis, removed all of Sam's clothes, Sam's temper flared. "Why?"

"Dearie, they're as filthy as you were. Surely you don't intend to put grimy clothing on a clean body?" Elsie explained.

Sam calmed down a bit at the woman's logical reply. "I've got a clean change of clothes in my saddlebags, wherever Marshal Kincaid has put 'em," she offered. "Could ya ask him for 'em, please, ma'am?"

"I'll check on it for you," Elsie promised.

Some time later, as Sam finished her bath and was wrapping herself in a fluffy towel, Elsie returned. Instead of the requested items of clothing, she carried with her a dress and underwear. Losing control and pointing at the dress, Sam said, "What's that?"

"Now, don't try to tell me you've never seen a dress before, 'cause I don't believe it," Elsie told her.

"If that's for me, take it back an' git me my own clothes. I ain't wore a dress since I was ten, an' I ain't about to start now." Sam's eyes threw dark flames that reinforced her stubborn stance.

"Oh, yes, you are," Elsie stated firmly. She could be as stubborn as this little gal. "Young ladies do not run about dressed in tattered men's pants that show all their curves and old flannel shirts that look like a miner wore them to work every day for a solid year."

"I done told your marshal, I ain't no lady. An' I ain't wearin' no dress!"

"In this house you will, and you'll learn to like it. It's high time someone took you in hand,

Samantha. You've run amok too long. Between us, Travis and I are going to make a lady of you whether you are willing or not." Elsie lay the dress and petticoat over the back of a chair and put the chemise and underdrawers on the seat. Then she stood by and folded her arms over her ample bosom. "You start with the drawers and the chemise," she instructed. "I noticed when I burned your other things that you didn't seem to own a set of either. Rule number one: Ladies always wear underwear beneath their dresses."

Sam stood seething, looking from the clothes to Elsie and back again. Elsie didn't seem inclined to back down on this issue. Elsie had taken her other clothes so what could she do? As she was about to give in, Sam heard Travis call, "Elsie, Sam isn't giving you any problem, is she?"

That lit the fuse to her explosive temper all over again. Dressed only in the short towel, with her hair streaming down her back in wet tangles, Sam bolted from the room. Out through the kitchen she hobbled as fast as she could, then along a short hall toward the front parlor, Elsie in hot pursuit. She didn't stop until she was face to face with Travis, who was sitting in an old easy chair reading his paper. Before he could recover from the shock of seeing Sam before him in nothing but a towel, she marched up to him, ripped the paper from his hands, and demanded, "Who died an' made you God, I'd like to know?"

Travis was too dumbfounded to reply at first, as he stared at the young woman before him. Was this the dirty little urchin he had caught this morning? He could scarcely believe his eyes! Gone was the dirt and dust that had effectively concealed her gender and her fair features. He could now see a sprinkling of freckles across the bridge of the small uptilted nose, the proud shape of high cheekbones set below snapping black eyes, the stubborn yet dainty chin. Her hair, which had appeared to be a bland red-brown before, was now a glorious red-gold that resembled a newly-minted penny, streaming over her bare shoulders in a thick, glistening mane.

And saints help him, how had he ever missed those long, thick eyelashes, the lush shape of those pouting, alluring lips? Lord, but he must have been half-blind not to have noticed those pert breasts, now thrusting themselves half out of the towel with her every angry breath! And such long, shapely legs on such a small girl! Noting the curve of hips barely concealed by the brief towel, Travis wondered how he had ever thought of her as a short, skinny boy. Even once he had known she was a girl, having been told she was seventeen, he had thought of her as a child. Certainly he had never envisioned her as the lovely young woman who stood before him now, ready to tear his throat out with her bare hands.

"Did ya hear me?" she was demanding, and Travis blinked back to his senses. He almost lost them again as Sam placed a fist on each shapely hip, nearly unloosening her precariously-wrapped towel.

"What the devil do you think you are doing, parading through the house in that towel?" he growled in a voice made gruffer than he'd intended by sudden desire.

Sam didn't even blink at his irate tone. "If some thievin', low-down snake hadn't made off with my clothes, I'd be wearin' 'em now, instead o' this towel!" she threw back.

"If you don't keep a better hold on that damn thing, you're gonna be wearing nothing at all!" he roared in extreme agitation, sweat popping out on his brow as her towel slipped another precious inch. Travis glanced helplessly to where Elsie stood in the doorway, bemused by Travis's reactions. Rarely had she seen him in less control of himself.

Elsie spread her hands out before her in a gesture of apology. "Sorry, Marshal. She slipped past me slick as a whistle. I'd never have guessed she would dare run out undressed."

"I want my clothes back." Sam shifted the attention back to her immediate needs. "Now!"

Travis didn't move from his chair. He merely pinned her to the spot where she stood, like a butterfly pinned to a board, with that particularly searing stare of his, and Sam could feel her resolve wavering. "Your clothes have been burned, Samantha," he said firmly but more calmly. "You will wear the dress you've been given."

Sam swallowed hard, but would not give up completely yet. "I don't take nobody's charity." Her chin went up proudly.

"It's not charity. I destroyed your clothes, and I replaced them with those I felt more appropriate. Fair trade."

"Not to me, it ain't." Tears of anger and frustration welled up in her eyes, and she fought to blink them back. She didn't want his charity, and she certainly didn't want his pity!

His steady gaze never wavered. "You will wear the dress, Samantha, if I have to button you into it

myself. And the underthings as well," he added
sternly.

She glared at him mutinously for a long moment, deciding that this man probably would carry
out his threats. At last she handed him his hard-
won victory. "Awright, but only if ya stop callin'
me Samantha. Both of ya," she said, her glance
including the housekeeper. "I go by Sam, or
Sammie."

Supper might have been a silent affair had it
been left to Sam. She was still seething at having
been forced into the dress. Elsie had fixed chicken
and dumplings, one of Sam's favorite meals, and
one she rarely had the opportunity to enjoy. For
dessert, there was a mouth-watering apple pie.
Now here was a meal Sam could appreciate, sore
ribs, throbbing ankle and all! At least she thought
so, until Elsie and Travis started berating her for
her lack of table manners.

"Good God, Sam!" Travis exclaimed. "Slow
down before you choke on something! Nobody's
going to steal the food from you. You are tucking
into it like a half-starved lumberjack!"

"Sam, use your fork for those peas, dear. How in
creation do you manage to balance them on that
knife blade, anyway?" Elsie was almost as amazed
as she was appalled.

"Turn your fork right side up when you put it
into your mouth, Sam."

"Please refrain from wiping your mouth with
the back of your hand. That is what the napkin is
for."

"Please chew with your mouth closed."

"So help me Hannah, if you dare belch aloud

like that again, I'm going to whack you in the mouth with a knife handle!" That from Travis, though Elsie had been about to suggest something almost as drastic.

On and on it went, until Sam began to wonder if the joy of consuming the delicious meal was worth having her two tablemates screeching at her. It seemed like a century before the meal was done.

Because of her injuries, Sam was excused from helping in the kitchen; however, Travis assured her that she would be expected to do her share of the chores in the near future. "Your being here will add to Elsie's work a great deal, and I expect you to help out where Elsie feels is best. Look at it as helping to pay your keep," he told her with a sly smile. "I know how you detest charity of any kind."

Doc Purdy came by shortly after supper, surprise very evident on his face as he viewed the miraculous change in Sam's appearance. He stuttered and stammered, and even through her own embarrassment and discomfort, Sam felt his hands shake as he bandaged her ribs and her ankle.

Not long afterward, Elsie ushered her upstairs to a spare bedroom, giving Sam a long, cotton night-gown. She was so tired that she barely took note of the room or its furnishings. She sighed gratefully as she sank into the thick mattress, wondering briefly how her pa and brothers were faring. She didn't even notice when Elsie locked the door behind her. She was already drifting to sleep.

An hour later, Travis looked in on her on his way to his own bed. He nearly swallowed his tongue when he peeked in to find her sprawled naked across the bed, all the covers kicked off and the nightgown thrown heedlessly into a heap on the floor. "Lord, give me strength," he muttered in fervent prayer, rolling his eyes heavenward and quickly closing the door on his way out. It certainly looked as if he would need it, with Sam around. And it was either ask for strength, or pray to be struck blind!

CHAPTER 5

Yanking on the knob of the locked door, Sam screeched, "Let me out of here! Do y'all hear me?" She pounded on the thick wood with her fists and threatened loudly, "If y'all don't come soon, I'm gonna answer nature's call right here on the floor!"

In the kitchen below, Travis nearly choked on his coffee, aiming a blistering look toward the ceiling, where Samantha Downing was yelling loud enough to raise the dead. Elsie met his look and chuckled as Travis grumbled, "Wouldn't put it past the rotten little brat to do just that!"

"Then you'd better get a move on, Marshal," Elsie advised dryly. She turned back to the hotcake batter she was stirring and grinned to herself while making private bets on how long it would be before shining gray hairs joined the gold in Travis

Kincaid's head, put there by his troublesome young prisoner.

Tumble's normally calm marshal shoved back his chair, stomped toward the stairs, and yelled, "I'm comin', you loud-mouthed little baggage! Pipe down before I put a boot in your mouth!" As he twisted the key in the lock, he paused long enough to hope that Sam was decently dressed, in the nightshift at least.

She was, but barely. The nightgown, one of Elsie's, was entirely too large for Sam's smaller frame. It hung off of one shoulder, baring it to Travis's gaze. Sam hadn't bothered lacing the front ties, and the bodice gaped open, giving him ample view of the soft inner curves of her sweet young breasts, while sufficiently hiding the rosy peaks thrusting impudently against the soft fabric.

Biting back a groan, Travis raised his turquoise gaze to her flushed, angry face, framed by a wild halo of unruly red-gold waves. Her dark eyes were blazing back at him. "'Bout time you got here, Marshal!" she ranted, her lips pouting at him. "A body could drown in his own—"

"Don't you dare say it!" Travis growled, cutting short her words. "Rule number one around here: No cursing from you! It isn't seemly for a woman to talk that way, and I won't have it from you!"

Sam smirked at him. "You an' your housekeeper better get yourselves straight," she told him with a shake of her head. "Accordin' to her, rule number one is always to wear underdrawers!" In defiance, her eyes cut swiftly to the linen undergarments folded neatly on a nearby chair, and, unbidden, Travis's eyes also strayed in that direction.

Fighting the color rising on his neck, he said, "Then I'd suggest you do that, Sam. And while you're about it, get yourself into your other clothes. I'll not be taking you to the outhouse dressed in your nightshift."

With a laugh, Sam said mockingly, "What's the matter, Marshal? Afraid of what your neighbors might think of ya?"

"Not particularly," he answered, his tone softer now, but rife with warning as he glared at her. "But you might have a concern about what they think of you. You're not their favorite person, Sam. You and your family made off with quite a bit of money yesterday, and the townsfolk are itching to lynch somebody. Just because you're a girl, won't make them want revenge any less."

Though her face paled slightly, her chin rose stubbornly. "Ya gonna turn me over to them?" she challenged.

"No. I had in mind trying to get them to help you," he told her.

A frown drew her brows together. "Help me? How? Help me escape?"

This drew a sharp laugh from him. "Hardly, my witless little urchin! I thought they might feel sorry enough for you and the way you've been raised to want to help turn you into a decent, young lady. It might take their minds off their anger long enough to save your scrawny neck from a noose!"

"Sorry for me? Sorry for me!" Sam shrieked. "Why you almighty ass! I don't need nobody's pity, least of all yours! Take yourself an' your righteous town an' suck rotten eggs! Hell'll be sproutin' icicles b'fore I ask for your help or your dad-blasted pity!"

He had to admire her spunk, if not her language. The girl couldn't be stupid enough not to realize the precarious spot she was in. Still, if either of them were to survive this time together, some ground rules had to be laid and abided by. He couldn't let this pint-sized bandit get the upper hand. "I thought you were in such an all-fired hurry to use the necessary," he reminded her.

Her face screwed up, and with it her upturned nose. "The what?" she questioned.

"The outhouse. Ladies call it the 'necessary.'"

"Oh." Sam considered this a moment. With a shrug, she said, "Yeah, I guess that fits."

Travis hid a grin. "Get yourself dressed, and I'll be back in a couple of minutes to help you down the stairs."

Once more she drew herself up to her full, if minuscule, height. "I kin git myself downstairs, Marshal. I ain't some helpless ninny."

It was his turn to shrug. "Suit yourself, Sam. Just don't try to sneak out the front door on your way. It squeaks something awful, and I'm sure to hear it. And don't take all day. Elsie has breakfast started."

Luckily, the dress Kincaid had provided buttoned down the front. Getting her arms through the sleeves, with her ribs bound and sore, was a bit tricky, but Sam managed to squirm into it at last. Grimacing at her reflection in the mirror over the bureau, she ran her fingers through her tangled hair as best she could. Without comb or brush, it frizzed out in a riot of curls. "Should've taken

Tom's advice and whacked it all off long ago!" she groused to herself.

Elsie had taken her hat along with her other clothes, and Sam didn't know where her saddle-bags were. They certainly weren't in her room. Even before she'd begun rapping on the door and demanding to be let loose, she had scoured the room thoroughly, looking for a way to free herself or anything she might use as a weapon. Though this room was on the second floor, she considered tearing the bedsheets into strips and making a rope with which to climb down, regardless of how tender her ribs might be. But Marshal Kincaid must have thought of that also. He had thwarted this plan by securely nailing the windows shut. Drat! And search though she may, Sam could find nothing even remotely resembling a weapon.

As she glanced about the room once again, Sam had to admit that it was a rather nice room—much better than that jail cell! On the two long windows on either side of the bed, crisp blue curtains were tied prettily back with matching ties. Lying folded across the end of the bed was a colorful patchwork quilt, and on the floor beside the bed was a little braided rag rug. The bed itself was nothing fancy, just a wood frame and headboard, but it supported a wonderfully soft feather mattress. Sleeping on it last night had been like sleeping on a cloud! It wasn't often these days that any of the Downings could claim such a luxury; usually they bedded down in their bedrolls on the hard ground.

Against one wall stood a small, sturdy wardrobe. Upon checking it, Sam had found it empty except for a stack of bed linens. Likewise, the drawers of the bureau were empty. Except for a hand-embroidered dresser scarf, and the mirror hanging over it, only a single candle resided atop the dresser. A ladder-back chair stood near a small, round table, the only other piece of furniture in the room. On the table was a small bookrack holding half a dozen books, and a kerosene lamp. Evidently, the marshal didn't trust her not to set the house afire, for he had not left any matches in the room.

By holding tightly to the bannister for support, Sam managed to hobble barefoot down the stairs without mishap. For a moment, she stood staring wistfully at the front door, wondering if she might chance it. Even as she contemplated this, from the end of the hallway near the kitchen, someone cleared his throat noisily. Whirling about, Sam met Travis Kincaid's unsettling gaze. He was leaning against the wall, his arms crossed over his broad chest, watching her.

Shaking his head at her, Travis smiled nastily. "Don't even think about it, Sam. You wouldn't get three feet, and it would be all the excuse I'd need to blister your behind for you."

Sam glowered at him. "Nobody ain't never whomped me, an' you ain't gonna be doin' it now! My own pa never laid a hand to me!"

"It might have done some good if someone had taken a belt to your backside a long time ago," Travis told her. "Maybe you wouldn't be the god-awful ruffian you are today if they had."

"I manage jest fine, thank ya." Sam's chin rose in defense of herself and her family. "Me an' mine don't need no fancy duds an' manners, or a lot of nonsense clutterin' up our lives, an' I don't need you tellin' me what to do about it."

A look too close to pity to suit her came over his face. "Sure, Sam. You do so well that you landed in jail, so well that you're all of seventeen years old and barely aware that you're not a man." His gaze raked over her from head to toe. "Good grief, girl! Haven't you ever wanted to live a normal life?"

"Depends on what normal means to a person, I'd say," she retorted stiffly. "My pa an' brothers are all the family I have in this world, an' they're all I need."

"What about a husband, Sam, and children of your own? Don't you want a real home?"

Her laugh was rough, the husky tone of her voice rasping pleasantly over him as she answered, "Now what would I want with a husband an' a passel o' kids taggin' on my coattails? Marshal, I got troubles enough without that! When I want a man, I'll take me one, without all the glorified promises an' problems."

His eyes narrowed as he studied her. "Have you had one yet?" he asked softly, surprising both of them with his question.

"A man?" she asked.

He nodded, almost holding his breath as he awaited her answer. Why the thought bothered him, he didn't know, but it did. Clean and dressed properly, Samantha was a pretty little thing. No, that wasn't true. She was beautiful, in a wild, untamed sort of way. Living the way she had, Travis would not have been surprised to learn that she had already taken a lover or two. The thought entered his mind that it was even possible that her own brothers or father might have molested her; after all, what did he really know about them, other than the fact that they were criminals?

That pert little nose of hers rose into the air as she faced him haughtily. "I don't rightly think that's any business of yours, Marshal."

"I'm making it my business, Sam. Since I'm giving you shelter in my own home, and making myself responsible for your well-being, I have a right to know if I'm giving aid to a woman who is with child, or not."

"I ain't exactly asked for your help, Kincaid," she reminded him sourly. "As I recall, you sort of insisted."

He walked slowly toward her, his intimidating eyes locked with hers. "Answer the question, Samantha," he grated softly.

It was amazing how piercing those eyes of his were, how they made her insides quiver. Considering retreat the better part of valor at this point, she said snippily, "No. Ain't yet came across a man who took my fancy enough to want to bed down with him."

Travis hid a sigh of relief. Of course, she could be lying to him, but he didn't think so. As a U.S. Marshal, and a Texas Ranger before that, Travis had questioned numerous people on both sides of the law, and most of the time he could tell when they were telling the truth. His instincts told him that though she was belligerent, Sam was telling the truth now.

"Could be you just haven't met the man who could tame you, Sam," he said before thinking, again surprising both of them with his hasty words.

Her black eyes threw sparks at him. "That man ain't been born, Marshal," she boasted arrogantly, unwittingly challenging the male in him.

"Hasn't he?" he murmured, holding her bold stare.

Breakfast was strained. Samantha was still smarting over the humiliation of having Kincaid escort her to the outhouse, and wait just outside the privy door until she had finished. Bars or no bars, she was still his prisoner, and the thought grated.

For his part, Travis was wondering what on earth had possessed him to say such things to her, to challenge her by suggesting that he was the man who could awaken her to womanhood! Sam was a child, and a nasty, ill-bred one to boot! What had come over him? He was nine years older than she, quite old enough to know better and to be able to control his tongue and his temper.

Chastising himself for his own behavior, he knew the best thing would be to hand the girl over to someone else's care, to have as little to do with her as possible. However, as Doc Purdy had pointed out, there really was no one else. He, Travis, was responsible for her, like it or not.

It was with both a sense of guilt and of relief that he left her in Elsie's care and went about his business as town marshal, after making certain that all of his guns were securely locked away in his room. With her injuries, and without her horse, Sam wouldn't get far if she tried, and Elsie was not one to put up with any nonsense. The gruff house-keeper had raised six children of her own, and she could certainly handle one half-grown, hateful girl. If Sam thought otherwise, she was in for a grand surprise.

Sam soon learned this for herself. For all her years, Elsie had experience on her side. "As soon as you finish eating, you can clean off the table and start washing the breakfast dishes," Elsie told her. "There's a pot of water heatin' on the stove."

Immediately, Sam bristled. "Ya got me into this dratted dress, woman, an' that's enough. I sure ain't doin' no dishes."

Elsie merely smiled and nodded. "Suit yourself, gal, but I'll be making a big pot of vegetable soup for lunch, and if you'll excuse my braggin', you haven't tasted anything like it this side of heaven. Now, if you want some of it when it's time, you'll get off your fanny and do those dishes like I said. Think about it, Sam."

Her lower lip protruding, Sam said, "As a prisoner, I got a right to be fed, but I don't have to work."

"Is that so?" Elsie commented casually. "Where did you hear that? As far as I know, Travis doesn't have to feed you if he doesn't feel like it, and I sure as tarnation don't. You're not my prisoner to keep, dearie."

"Then ya won't mind if I just sort of mosey on out o' here," Sam smirked. With effort, she pulled herself out of her chair and started toward the kitchen door.

Behind her, she heard Elsie say sternly, "Take one more step, young lady, and you'll be nursing lumps on that bright little head of yours for a month of Sundays!"

The authority in the housekeeper's voice rang clear, and Sam turned to find Elsie brandishing a long wooden spoon like a war club. Despite the fact that Elsie resembled a plump pigeon, Sam had the feeling the woman could outrun her if need be, at least until her ribs and ankle had time to heal some.

"Oh, awright!" she grumbled, with an exaggerated pout. "I'll wash the dad-blamed dishes!"

"Good!" Elsie gave a brisk nod and lowered the spoon. "I knew you'd see things my way, if I explained them so you could understand."

While Sam rattled the breakfast dishes around in the tin pan, Elsie diced up vegetables and beef for the soup, explaining as she did so. "Now listen to what I'm tellin' you, Sam. I don't go around giving away my recipes to just anyone, you know."

In spite of herself, Sam was intrigued. She'd never been much for cooking. Truth be told, rabbit stew was the limit of her cooking talents, and that barely edible. Her biscuits came out more like soot-covered rocks. Even Billy cooked better than she did, much to her chagrin. Her brothers were constantly teasing her about it. If Elsie could teach her a trick or two while she was here, Pa would surely be grateful. Of course, if Sam had her way, the cooking lessons would be short-lived, since she planned to escape the first chance she got.

Once the soup was simmering merrily on the stove, Elsie demonstrated the proper way to prepare fluffy, delicious biscuits in the bricked-in oven. "Of course, you can do the same thing over an open fire in a dutch oven. The trick is knowing how much baking powder to use, and how long to let them bake without burning. It's a matter of taking pride in your skills, Sam. I've always believed that if you're going to do something, then learn to do it well."

Put that way, Sam agreed with what Elsie was saying. Hadn't Pa said much the same when he'd first taught her to trap and to shoot? Why Sam had never applied that same philosophy to cooking, she didn't know, but it made sense now. Wouldn't Pa and her brothers be surprised if she really learned to cook? If there were time, maybe she could even get Elsie to teach her how to make an apple pie as good as the one she had eaten the night before. Now wouldn't that be the cat's whiskers!

A short while later, Elsie handed Sam a dust rag and instructed her to dust the furniture in the parlor. "Just go nice and easy, and it shouldn't task your ribs too much." Then, to Sam's amusement, the woman asked, "Do you sing, Samantha?"

Sam's ribs gave a sharp twinge as she burst out laughing. "I've heard mules brayin' better than I sing!"

"Well, give it your best try, dearie," Elsie said with a sly smile. "I want you to sing nice and loud, so I can hear you from upstairs, while I make the beds. Mind now, if I hear you drifting away, I'll be down here in a blink and take that spoon after you! And that's mild compared to what Travis will probably do if he hears you tried to run off!"

That said, the plump housekeeper waddled up the stairs. "Sing, Sam!" she commanded imperiously. "Sing!"

CHAPTER 6

Before Travis reached the picket fence that marked the edge of the small lot on which his house stood, he heard the racket coming from inside. Common sense told him someone, probably Samantha, was trying to sing, and doing a terrible job of it. He winced as a particularly sour note assaulted his ears. If he didn't know better, he'd swear someone had locked a pack of baying hounds in his house!

As he lifted the latch to the front gate, he smiled apologetically at the woman at his side. Nan Tucker was Tumble's schoolteacher, and Travis had just spent the last half hour talking her into tutoring Sam. He'd also done his level best to try to explain the girl to Nan, but Travis feared Nan would have to experience Sam for herself to truly understand the situation. How could anyone properly explain the little red-haired hellion he'd caught yesterday?

Until now, Nan had obviously thought Travis was exaggerating, but now she turned a startled face his way. "What is that awful noise?" she asked tremulously.

"Nothing to worry about," he assured her. "Just a trapped cat." Beneath his breath, he added, "An angry she-cat, most likely." If not for a few of the words drifting along with the caterwauling, he would never have recognized the tune as "Oh! Susanna." Sam sounded more like a mad moose at mating season. He grimaced again at the sound. It would have to be mid-May and warm enough for the windows to be open! Travis was willing to bet his neighbors were simply delighted with him about now.

The two of them had just mounted the three wooden steps and stepped onto the front porch, when the front door creaked open slowly. As it did, the volume of noise increased considerably. As they stood watching, a female rump, covered in blue-flowered cloth, backed slowly out the doorway. Beneath the hem of the skirt, two bare feet edged backward.

Leaving the door wide open, and singing as loudly as her tender ribs would allow, Sam crept outside. As she was prepared to swing about and make a hobbling dash for freedom, her bad ankle collapsed beneath her, causing her to stumble backward. With a shriek, her arms spinning like twin windmills, she felt herself begin to fall.

Two strong arms wrapped themselves about her before she could take a tumble down the stairs. A familiar voice asked mockingly, "Going some-where, Sam?"

Her heart leaped to her throat, then plummeted to her feet. "Jumpin' Jehoshaphat!" she screeched. "Do ya have to go around sneakin' up on a body like that, Kincaid? Ya damn near scared the be-Jesus out o' me!" Craning her head around, she shot him a look that could have boiled water.

Travis's scowl more than matched hers. "I thought I told you I wouldn't have you cursing in my home," he said with a frown.

"I ain't in it," she pointed out.

"You're *not* in it," Nan Tucker corrected reflex-ively.

Sam's head swiveled around, and she frowned at the newcomer she hadn't even noticed until now. Dressed in a drab skirt and jacket that almost matched her mouse-brown hair, the woman re-sembled a plain little wren. "That's what I just said," Sam responded, wondering who this person was and why she was here. "This your woman, Kincaid?"

As she watched, fascinated by the response her bold question brought, Travis and the woman both turned several shades of red. Finally, the marshal found his tongue. "No, she is not my woman. This is Nan Tucker, the schoolteacher I've hired for you."

Sam's nose wrinkled, even as she squirmed out of Travis's arms. "I done told ya I ain't got no use for book learnin', Marshal, and no use for a schoolmarm, neither."

Nan Tucker cringed visibly at the way Sam was mutilating the English language. "I'd say we have our work cut out for us," she murmured in dismay.

Nodding his head, Travis agreed. "Might as well get started," he suggested.

To Sam he said amiably, "Look at it this way. At least you'll be able to read the wanted posters with your name on them." Taking her firmly by the arm, he propelled her toward the door.

"There you are!" Elsie called from the foot of the stairs. "I knew the minute you'd stopped singing that you were up to no good, young woman!" To Travis, she apologized. "Sorry, Marshal. I was tryin' to get some work done upstairs."

"It's all right, Elsie. No harm done, except maybe a few of the townsfolk wishing they had gone deaf listening to Sam trying to sing."

That delectable lower lip popped out again as Sam complained loudly, "'Tain't my fault! I tried to tell her I can't sing worth a hoot, but she wouldn't listen to me!"

"It *isn't* your fault," Nan corrected again, earning an odd look from Sam.

"'Course it ain't. I jest said that! Why are you so dad-blamed set on repeatin' everything I say? Ya deaf or somethin'?"

Elsie choked back a laugh as Travis explained. "Miss Tucker is trying to correct the way you speak, Sam."

With a toss of her head, Sam's red-gold hair flew across her shoulder. "Ain't nothin' wrong with the way I talk," she said, taking immediate offense. "Most folks understand me right enough."

"Most folks are probably just too polite to correct you," Travis amended.

Due to his superior height, Sam had to tilt her head back to look down her nose at him, but she managed all the same. "That lets you out of the polite folks then, I reckon," she said, putting him in his place for once.

With some reluctance, for she hated to miss anything that might be said, Elsie went to the kitchen to prepare a pitcher of lemonade. With similar reluctance, and a sour disposition, Sam allowed herself to be led into the parlor. "Sit!" Travis ordered, pointing to a seat on the divan.

"I ain't no dog!" Sam grumbled, shooting him yet another dark look.

"You're no lady, either, but we're going to do what we can to correct that, and like it or not, you are going to cooperate." The sparks flying from his brilliant eyes warned her he would take no nonsense from her now.

Sullenly, Sam threw herself onto the divan. It was painfully obvious from the way she sat with her legs sprawled apart that Sam was more used to wearing trousers than a skirt. "Samantha!" Travis growled, his face growing red again. "Sit up straight, if you please, and kindly hold your legs together! And pull that dress down!"

Nan looked as if she might faint, so mortified was she at witnessing such a scene. She practically wilted into the cushion next to Sam.

"Well, hell's bells, if you'd jest give me back my pants an' be done with it!" Sam yelled back, yanking at the offending skirt.

Next to her, Miss Tucker almost strangled on a choke of dismay. Trying to be helpful, Sam leaned over and gave the woman a sharp whack on the back, and the poor lady almost flew onto the floor.

Travis bellowed. "Sam!"

"What!"

He shook his head and sighed. At least she had

quit thumping Nan on the back. "Nothing. Just sit there and behave, and listen to what Miss Tucker has to say to you."

By this time, Nan was quite flustered, but she managed to stammer, "Miss, uh, Miss . . ."

"Downing," Travis supplied, when Sam just sat there sulking.

"Miss Downing, I thought we might begin with the basic alphabet, and the sounds of the letters. Have you had any schooling at all?"

When Sam maintained her silence, Travis snarled at her, "Answer her, Sam!"

"Never needed none," Sam grumbled, ignoring Travis's grunt of disbelief.

"Haven't you ever wanted to be able to read a book, Miss Downing?" Nan gaped at her as if Sam had committed the ultimate sin.

Sam's chin came up defensively. "I know some of my numbers, leastwise enough to git by."

"That figures," Travis put in with a sneer. "You probably had to learn to count so you could tally up your stolen money from all those robberies."

"Travis, please!" Nan objected, her pale-lashed, hazel eyes practically eating the man alive, and her voice so sweetly modulated that Sam almost gagged. Travis might deny wanting this woman, but it was clear to Sam that Nan Tucker would gladly have him! Of course, the poor, homely thing probably looked the same way at any man under eighty. It was plain to see that Nan Tucker was well on her way to being a spinster, if something didn't happen soon.

Turning once again to Sam, Nan asked softly, "How is it you learned your numbers, dear?"

"Ya got to know 'em to play poker," Sam retorted proudly, "an' I play the best da-darn game o' cards ya ever did see, if I do say so myself!" Hating herself and Travis for having to watch her tongue so carefully, she shot Travis a spiteful look and caught him gloating. "Well, I do!" she claimed heatedly.

"I should have guessed," he commented dryly, stroking long fingers over his mustache.

"Oh, dear!" Nan exclaimed breathlessly. "Oh, my dear!"

"My name's Sam!" she grated in exasperation. "I'd be obliged if ya used it."

What followed turned out to be the longest, most discouraging afternoon Sam could ever recall, if she discounted the disastrous result of yesterday's capture by one obnoxious, self-important marshal. Using a slate Miss Tucker had thoughtfully brought with her, Sam learned to print her name. Then, she laboriously copied the numerous, confusing letters of the alphabet the schoolmarm tried to teach her. Even when Miss Tucker had left, Sam was forced to continue her lessons, with Travis or Elsie looking on to make sure she did.

By supper time, the letters were swimming before her eyes, and she was sure she would see them in her sleep that night. What useless drudgery! What drivel! She needed to read like a frog needed hair! And if the good Lord had intended for her to write, He would have filled her fingers with ink and replaced her fingernails with quills! Such a bother over nothing!

"As soon as the swelling in your ankle goes down, we'll take you to get some decent shoes," Travis told her.

"And stockings," Elsie added, for good measure. She had been concerned that Sam might injure herself more, running about barefoot as she had for the past two days. Only this morning, the poor girl had stubbed her toe on the table leg and howled in agony.

Sam wrinkled her nose in distaste. "If by shoes you mean a pair of those god-awful ugly things Miss Tucker wears, you kin jest forget it, Kincaid. I wouldn't be caught dead in those! I want a pair of boots."

"What you want and what you'll get are two different things," he responded with another of those smug smiles that turned the edges of his mouth and mustache upward. He could be so blasted irritating!

Sam gave him a nasty smile of her own. "Like I said, you kin buy 'em, but that don't mean I'll wear 'em, but it's your money to spend any way you want. Like my mama always said, 'A fool an' his money are soon parted.'"

"Actually, I think Ben Franklin was first to say that," he told her, earning an indifferent shrug for his efforts.

"What was your mama like?" Elsie asked, giving Sam a sympathetic look. "I take it she must have died when you were very young."

A soft, dreamy look came over Sam's face, intriguing Travis as he awaited her answer. It was the first time he had seen her look so vulnerable, so sweetly feminine.

"My mama was an angel!" she said, sighing. "She died more 'n five years back. Sometimes now, it's hard to recollect her face, it's been so long, an' that jest makes me want to bust out bawlin'. I do recall she had the most beautiful hair I've ever seen. It was long, an' sort of reddish like mine, an' she wore it twisted up on her head. But when she let it down, it was like a cloud of fire a-fallin' all the way past her waist." Suddenly self-conscious, Sam's hand went to her own tangled tresses, and with a rueful laugh, she admitted, "I guess that's why I never took Tom's advice an' cut my hair off, even if it is a bother at times."

A lump formed in Travis's throat as he thought of Sam cutting off all that glorious red-gold hair. He was glad, despite himself, that she had resisted the temptation. If she even dared suggest doing such a thing while she was in his care, he'd threaten her with the worst thing he could devise. Just yesterday, Sam had finally put her pride aside and asked him if she might have her comb and brush from her saddlebags. Now, freshly washed and brushed out, her hair streamed down her back and over her shoulders like a flowing flame.

Clamping down on his wayward thoughts, and the path they were heading, Travis asked, "What about your father and brothers? I've been meaning to ask you about them. What are they like, Sam?"

It was as if a cloud had passed over the sun, so swiftly did her attitude change from sweet to sour. "Nice try, Marshal," she said tartly, "but I ain't fool enough to tell you nothin' about 'em that's gonna help you hang 'em."

Sighing heavily, he tried once more to reason with the stubborn little wench. "Sam, if you'd only stop to consider your own situation for a minute. Can't you see that the more cooperative you are, the easier things will go for you? You're in some mighty deep trouble, girl, and I'm just trying to help you. Being a young woman won't keep a noose from about your pretty little neck, you know. You're still guilty of robbery, and God knows what else, and a judge won't take kindly to that."

"I'll learn my letters. I'll wear this dad-burned dress. I might even try on a pair of those ugly-lookin' shoes," Sam conceded stiffly, "but I ain't snitchin' on my own kinfolk. You kin sit there and sweet-talk me till ya turn blue in the face, but you ain't makin' me do no harm to my family, judge or no judge, rope or not."

Tears glittered in her black eyes, and she blinked them back angrily. It had only been three days since her capture, and already she missed them all so much that she thought her heart would burst with grief. She knew, without doubt, that they would come for her, that they would try to rescue her if they could, but they probably thought it safer to lie low, for a while anyway. Sam understood it would be foolhardy for them to rush in right away without some sort of plan, but the waiting and wondering were so hard! If only she could find a way to escape on her own, she knew she could find them somehow.

"Your loyalty is admirable, Sam, and I understand how much you must care for them, but you're the one in hot water right now. You've got to look after yourself."

She glared at him. Finally, Elsie said softly, "I know you think they'll come for you, Sam, and you're probably right, but when they do, Travis will be waiting for them. It's just a matter of time before your father and brothers are caught. Surely you're smart enough to see that."

"No!" Sam shook her head in denial, her hair flying across her shoulders. "No. They're not stupid. They won't get caught."

"You did," Travis was quick to remind her, "and if they want you back, they are going to have to come after you sooner or later. Like Elsie said, I'll be waiting, and I'm not going to let them waltz in here, grab you out from under my nose, and waltz back out again free and easy." His voice took on a cutting edge, as he continued with deliberate cruelty, "The law has been trying to catch the Downing gang for a long time now, and the fact is, right now they're four, fat trout, and I've got the right bait on my hook—you! I'm going fishing, Sam, and I'll be darned if I don't mean to catch the whole mess of them."

He was deadly serious, and Sam knew it. Seeing the determined glint in his eyes, she knew he would do his level best to capture her family. It galled her that she had gotten herself into such a situation where he could use her this way, to lure her father and brothers into his net.

If she thought for one moment that they would be caught, Sam would rather they not even try to rescue her. If it came to a choice of them being hung or leaving her behind, she would choose their safety, even if it meant never seeing any of them again. She'd rather lose them that way, knowing they were safe and well, than have their deaths on her conscience and mourn over their graves.

That evening, as if she didn't already have enough problems, Sam noticed the first painful twinges that heralded her monthly flow. *Oh, drat!* she thought to herself. *Why'd I have to be born a girl?* Her brothers never had to put up with all this! They just went their merry way through life, as content as fleas on a dog! They never had this mess and fuss. Boys had all the luck! Why, they didn't even have to pull down their drawers half the time to answer nature's call! She, on the other hand, had no choice but to find a bush and bare her bottom whenever she had to go! God must have been mad at the world the day he fashioned the female body!

Knowing this was going to get worse before it got better, Sam decided to do herself a favor and help herself to Kincaid's liquor supply. She'd seen half a dozen bottles lined up on a shelf in his study, the marshal's private supply. This in mind, as soon as the supper dishes were done and Elsie ushered her out of the kitchen, Sam made a beeline for the study.

As quiet as a mouse, she turned the knob and let herself into the room, only to find Travis sitting behind his desk, scribbling on a piece of paper. Dagnabit! Why couldn't that man ever be where he was supposed to be, when he was supposed to be? He was continually fouling up all her best plans! Right this minute, he was supposed to be in his easy chair in the parlor, reading the paper and drinking a cup of coffee, as he'd done every other night!

Resigning herself to failure, Sam started to back out of the room, but Travis had already noticed her. Though he did not look up from his work, he said, "Come on in, Sam. I'll be finished with this in a minute."

Trapped, she walked into the room. Feeling his attention on her, though he had yet to raise his head, she pretended an interest in the books that lined one wall. Several minutes went by, and she was starting to fidget, when he finally laid the pen aside and asked, "Did you want something, Sam?" Those turquoise eyes pierced her with their brilliance as he sat watching her.

"Nothin' much," she replied with a lame shrug. "Jest lookin'." On an inspiration, she asked, "Ya got any books with pictures in 'em? There ain't much entertainment around here, an' I kinda thought it'd give me somethin' to do."

Though she couldn't understand for the life of her why, her conscience twinged as a pleased look crossed his face and he smiled at her. "Sure, Sam. Let me see what I can find for you."

Her luck took a tiny turn for the better as he rose and went to the bookcase across from her. His back was to her and the six beckoning bottles of liquor. Carefully, Sam edged her way toward the liquor. Quick as a wink, she grabbed the smallest bottle and hid it in the folds of her skirt as Travis turned toward her, a book in his hands.

"This might interest you. It's a collection of prints from paintings by famous artists from all over the world." He held the book toward her.

With her free hand, she took it from him. For just a second, their fingers brushed, and Sam felt a jolt of heat streak through her hand and up her arm. Such an intense shock from such a fleeting touch! Before she could even think to hide her reaction, her dark eyes went wide with surprise. Her gaze flew to meet his, and she saw a flicker of wonder on his features, as if he, too, had felt the same thing and was as startled by it as she was.

For a long moment they stared at one another.

Then, still shaken, she stammered, "Kin I take this to my room an' look at it?" Her heart was racing, and something was wrong with her breathing, and if she didn't get out of this room and away from his disturbing presence, she didn't know what fool thing might happen next!

"Sure," he said softly, his voice slightly husky for some odd reason she could not begin to guess at. His eyes seemed to be locked with hers, and it was all she could do to break contact with them and turn toward the door. In her haste, she almost stumbled, almost forgot to keep the bottle hidden as she reached for the knob of the door.

"Sam?"

Her back to him, she stopped. "Yeah?"

"I hope you like the book."

CHAPTER 7

"Travis! You've got to do something with that girl!" Elsie's voice fairly quivered with indignation. "This is the last straw!"

Looking up from the papers on his desk, Travis frowned. "What's she done now, Elsie?" It hadn't been more than three hours since Sam had left his study, intent on going to her room to look at the book she'd borrowed. He could not imagine what kind of trouble she'd managed to invent in such a short time and with so little available to her in that bare little room.

"Look at this!" Elsie held up several long strips of cloth for his inspection. At his befuddled look, she explained hotly. "This used to be a perfectly good bedsheet, in case you don't recognize it now! She's torn it to shreds, and when I asked her what she thought she was doing, sitting there on the floor in nothing but the skin God gave her, tearing up the linen, she just hiccuped and started to giggle! I don't now how or where she got it, but I could swear that rotten little urchin is as drunk as a mule skinner!"

Travis's eyes widened, then narrowed suspiciously. His gaze swung to the shelf where he kept his liquor, taking inventory of his limited stock. Where six bottles used to sit, there were now only five. "Why, that conniving little witch!" he muttered between clenched teeth! "Wanted a book, did she?"

Rising from his chair, Travis's long strides carried him swiftly toward the door. "I'll take care of this, Elsie! I'm going to teach that sneaky, red-haired wench a lesson she won't soon forget! So help me Hannah, she's going to regret trying to pull the wool over my eyes this time!"

Elsie hurried after him as fast as her short legs would allow. "Travis!" she called breathlessly. "You can't go in there! The girl doesn't have a stitch on!"

Too late! He was already shoving the door to Samantha's room open. "All right, Sam! Where's the bottle?" he demanded loudly, his eyes shooting flames at her.

Sam sat on the floor amid a puddle of sheets, merrily ripping them into strips. With her long hair streaming over her shoulders, and her legs tucked under her, she reminded him of a mermaid, a very tipsy mermaid in a Roman toga. She gave him a slightly befuddled look, then grinned up at him. "Howdy, Marshal!"

"The bottle, Sam!" he repeated sharply.

Behind him, Elsie stopped in the doorway, suddenly unsure of what to do. As long as she had known him, she had never seen Travis Kincaid react so swiftly and irrationally toward anyone as he did with this girl. He was usually so calm and easy-going, so unflappable. But this snip of a female certainly knew how to light the fuse to his temper! Not that Elsie thought he would hurt her, but where Sam was concerned, Travis seemed to lose his reason.

Elsie almost cringed when Sam rose on her haunches, nearly losing her covering as the sheet slipped low over Sam's breasts and rose even higher on the girl's bare thighs. Sam crawled the few feet to where an empty liquor bottle lay half-buried in the sheets. "This whacha want?" she asked, waving it gaily in the air.

Travis gaped at her. In all his born days, he'd never met a woman as bold as this elfin bandit! Why, here she sat, all but naked, as unconcerned with her near-nudity as if she were fully clothed! She didn't even have the common decency to blush! Or the wits! Of course, downing an entire bottle of whiskey would ease anyone's inhibitions, he supposed, but her actions still shocked him, a feat not easily done.

"You drank that whole bottle?" he asked incredulously, deliberately battling down his desire. He was supremely conscious of Elsie standing in the open doorway, taking in the whole, incredible scene with open-mouthed curiosity.

"Wasn't half bad, neither," Sam admitted, squinting up at him. "You got good taste in liquor, Marshal."

"Apparently, so do you," he stated grumpily. "Out of several to choose from, you stole my best Kentucky bourbon."

A smile as innocent as a babe's crept over her lips, replaced a second later by a loud hiccup. "You're stinkin' drunk!" he accused, his mustache pulling up at one side as he stared down at her in disgust.

"Take more than that itsy bottle to git me drunk!" she shot back. "Why, I could still shoot the wings off a gnat at a hundred yards!"

He watched her weave slightly as she tried to focus on him. Torn between anger, and a sudden impulse toward laughter, Travis said, "You couldn't see a gnat if it landed smack on the end of your nose right now!"

Sam frowned, her lower lip pouting in that particularly fetching way of hers. "Gimme my Colt, an' I'll show ya what I kin see!"

At this, he did laugh. "Not on a bet, you pint-sized, gun-toting hooligan! I'd have to be the dumbest thing in boots to give you a gun!"

"At least you have boots!" she whined pathetically, turning wounded brown eyes his way.

Those large, liquid eyes reminded him of a deer's, and for just a moment he wondered if they would look that soft, that velvety, in the aftermath of passion. Bringing his wandering thoughts under control, he commented wryly. "Yeah, and I have a few less sheets, from the look of things." His own eyes hardened as he shot her an accusing glare. "What were you doing, Sam? Trying to make a rope to climb out through the window?"

"A lot of good that'd do me! Ya nailed the

blamed windows shut, ya weaselly varmint!" she reminded him. Completely uninhibited, she flipped the hair over her shoulder, the sudden movement baring one breast to his startled gaze.

Behind him, Travis heard Elsie gasp in shock again. A fiery tide of raw lust shot through him, almost choking him. Tearing his gaze from the tantalizing sight of her, he glanced hastily about the room in search of the illusive nightdress Sam shunned so regularly. He spotted it lying half under the bed. Snatching hold of it, he quickly knelt and dragged it over Sam's head, trying not to notice her enticing curves any more than he already had.

She protested loudly at this rough treatment, and tried to wriggle away from him as he proceeded to stuff first one arm then the other through the sleeves of the gown. "Blast you, Kincaid! It's hot as hell in this room! There ain't enough air in here to keep a fly alive! I don't want this blamed nightshirt on!"

"You'll wear it if I have to harness it to you!" he grated gruffly. "I don't care how hot or uncomfortable it is, you're going to abide by decent behavior in this house!"

A sound suspiciously like a snicker came from the doorway, drawing Travis's attention to Elsie. Upon glancing her way, he found her stifling a laugh, her hand clamped over her mouth and her plump body jiggling mirthfully. "And what, pray tell, has you bound up in stitches?" he growled irritably.

"You—you put it on backwards!" Elsie managed between giggles, pointing toward Samantha.

"Well, at least it's covering her!" he grunted.

He grabbed the empty whiskey bottle from the floor and eyed Sam disgustedly. "Now, about those sheets, Samantha," he said. "If you weren't making a rope, what were you doing?"

Sam shook her head, then wobbled back and forth like a fishing cork as the movement made her dizzy. "Can't tell ya," she said, her words beginning to slur as the potent liquor began to affect her speech.

It had been a long day, and promised to be an even more wearisome night if he could not get the images of Sam's naked body out of his mind. Travis had put up with all he was going to from her. "You'll tell me, or I'll beat it out of you!" he threatened softly. "I'll wring your scrawny neck if I have to!"

"I won't!" she wailed, tears rising suddenly to swim in her eyes. "I can't!" She cast a pleading look toward Elsie. "Please!" she whimpered, seeking an ally in the other woman.

Sam's tears and her suddenly vulnerable attitude took all of them by surprise, Sam included. She couldn't remember the last time she had begged for anyone's help. Shaking her head, she thought the whiskey must have been stronger than she'd thought to make her behave so strangely.

"Sam?" Elsie asked tentatively, coming forward and bending awkwardly before the girl. "What is it? You can tell us."

"Not him," Sam said with a jerk of her head toward Travis. "I ain't tellin' him."

"Will you tell me?" Elsie persisted.

After a moment's thought, Sam nodded reluctantly. Leaning closer to Elsie, she whispered into the woman's ear, "My monthly's gonna start, and I needed rags. I didn't want to ask nobody, so I jest tore up one o' the sheets."

Knowing that Samantha, as tipsy as she was, was whispering loudly enough for Travis to hear, Elsie shared the girl's embarrassment. As she felt her own face heat, she hoped Travis would be gentleman enough not to mention this fact to Sam.

She needn't have worried. His own embarrassment had Travis so tongue-tied, that he couldn't have spoken at that moment to save his soul. He stood there for a moment, turning a dull red from the neck up, then turned and stomped from the room, leaving Elsie to handle things.

"And the whiskey?" Elsie asked once he was gone.

"For the cramps," Sam admitted around a huge yawn. Suddenly the amount she had consumed was beginning to tell on her. Her eyelids felt as if they had lead weights on them.

Elsie sighed and shook her head in dismay. "If you'd said something to me, I would have given you some laudanum to ease the pain. You didn't have to resort to strong drink, Samantha."

"Always worked b'fore," the girl muttered, barely able to force the words past her lips. She was so sleepy, so blessedly relaxed!

"Come on, dearie." With some effort, Elsie levered herself upright and tugged gently at Samantha's arm, urging her to stand. "Let's get you to bed before you pass out on the floor."

Sam resisted, too content at the moment to care where she slept, until Elsie said, "If you don't get yourself up, Travis will be back in here to do it for you, and I don't think either one of you want that to happen."

Sam barely made it crosswise over the mattress before her eyes closed in blissful sleep. On her next breath, a delicate snore issued from her parted lips, making Elsie chuckle despite herself. "Part angel, with a good part devil mixed in," she murmured as she drew a sheet over Sam's body. "And like as not, the devil will win out most of the time. We're going to have to work on that, my girl. Yes, we certainly are going to have to work mighty hard to let the angel triumph once in a while."

"We can't jest ride into town, big as you please, an' git our Sammie back," Old Bill told his three sons. "That marshal will be layin' for us for shore. We got to have us a plan, boys. A good one."

They were hiding out in the woods several miles outside of Tumble. It had been three days now, and the Downings were all anxious about Sam. They had to do something soon, before any harm could come to her.

"What if they go an' hang her?" Billy asked, voicing the dread they all felt.

Old Bill shook his head. "If he's got half the brains God gave him, that marshal won't do anythin' that stupid, Billy. With Sam alive, he's holdin' all the aces in his hand an' most likely knows it. He probably figures we'll be back for her sometime soon."

"Do you reckon he's found out she's a girl yet?" Hank ventured.

Old Bill's lips thinned into a grim line. "More 'n likely," he admitted, "but if he's laid so much as a hand on her, I'll kill him. I'll slit his throat from ear to ear!" Fire leaped from his dark eyes in a promise of vengeance.

"If he's just waitin' on us, how we gonna git her back?" Tom asked.

"Well, I been thinkin' on it, an' the best I kin come up with is for one of us to ride into town an' nose around a bit, find out whatever we kin," Old Bill said. "Now, I can't do it, not with my shoulder wound opened up again. Besides, I'd be the first one they'd recognize." During that mad dash out of Tumble, Bill's gunshot wound had opened, and he'd lost a good deal of blood once more before they had finally stopped to rest. For the past three days, he had been recovering, nursing the shoulder and hoping it wouldn't fester.

"I'll do it, Pa," Tom volunteered.

As the oldest, Tom would have been the logical choice, but Old Bill shook his head. "No, Tom. Ya look too much like me, an' we can't take the chance. An' Billy's colorin' is too much like Sam's not to notice." The older man's gaze leveled itself on his youngest son. "Hank, looks like this'll be up to you. Think you can handle it without bringin' the law down on top o' all o' us?"

Hank nodded solemnly. "You jest tell me how to go about it, Pa, an' I'll do it."

Hearing a strange man's voice in the kitchen when she came downstairs the next morning, Sam was reluctant to enter the room. However, other than leaving the house by the front door, which squeaked every bit as loudly as Travis had warned, she had to go through the kitchen to get to the back door and out to the privy at the rear of the house.

Squaring her shoulders, and taking a deep breath for courage, Sam walked quietly into the kitchen.

No sooner had she crossed the threshold, than Travis's head came up, those sharp, blue-green eyes measuring her, taking in the unusual pallor of her face. "Good morning, Sam," he said quietly, announcing her arrival to the other two people in the kitchen.

Immediately, the other man swiveled in his chair, sending Sam a dark, curious frown. Elsie turned from the stove, offering Sam a welcoming smile. "How are you feeling this morning, Sam?" she asked. "Eggs are about ready."

"I feel like I been pulled through a knothole backwards," Sam grumbled in greeting, the thought of food making her stomach turn. "I don't think I want any breakfast, thanks. I'll make do with some o' that coffee."

"What's the matter, Sam? Hung over?" Travis did not even try to hide his grin.

"Jest sick o' lookin' at your ugly puss all day, every day," she snapped back.

He laughed, the sound going straight through her throbbing head. "I want you to meet Chas Brown, my deputy. Chas, this is the little sharp-shooter who put the lead in your leg during the chase."

Chas was staring at her as if she had grown three heads! Of course, by now it was all over town that the bandit they had captured that day had been a girl, but he still couldn't believe his eyes. Why, she was no bigger than a minute, and without those boy's clothes and all that dirt, he would never have recognized her. She was downright pretty!

Sam stood her ground, not sure what to expect,

as Chas continued to gape at her. This man had every right in the world to hate her, to want revenge. Were she in his place, she would be mad as a wet hen, faced with the person who had shot her. As he continued to sit there, Sam shifted uncomfortably. "Uh, I reckon I should apologize for shootin' ya," she ventured. "I want ya to know, I wasn't tryin' to kill ya, jest aimin' to stop ya from chasin' us. I hope your leg heals real soon."

If anything, Sam's words left Chas even more befuddled. His stupefied gaze sought Travis's. "Is she joshin' me, Trav? Is this some sort of joke?"

"Knowing Sam," Travis said, his mustache twitching with humor, "I think she is perfectly serious, and trying to make amends. In fact, I think we're witnessing a minor miracle here. If I'm not mistaken, this is the first actual apology we've heard from her."

"No need to belabor it, Marshal," Sam grumbled irritably, "an' you kin wipe that silly grin off your face before that moth-eaten mustache you're so blamed proud of falls off in a fit!"

"Now, that's not what you told me last night, little darlin'," he retorted, winking broadly at her.

Sam's face flamed as she blinked back at him. Her mouth dropped open, then closed again with a snap. Frantically, she tried to remember anything that might have passed between them the night before, but her memory was as fuzzy as her head felt this morning. Oh, why did she have to drink so blasted much last night? Her startled gaze flew toward Elsie, seeking help, but the older woman seemed to be choking on something at the moment. Elsie's eyes were watering, her hand clutching her chest as she struggled for breath.

Forgetting her own discomfort, Sam became alarmed for her. "Well, jest don't sit there!" she shrieked at Travis. "Do somethin' to help her!"

As Travis started from his chair, Elsie waved a staying hand at him. "It's all right!" she wheezed, brushing at her tears.

Chas's curious gaze made the rounds from Elsie to Sam to Travis. What was going on here? Since Sam's arrival, Travis had been as touchy as a sore-tailed bear and about as predictable. Chas had never thought he'd see the day when anyone but Elsie could sass Travis and get away with it, but this little gal had just done it without blinking an eye, and Travis had laughed it off! And if one were to take the marshal's words seriously, there was something going on between him and his female prisoner, and that most definitely was not Travis's way! Had everyone in this house gone crazy, including him?

"Well, Chas, are you going to accept Sam's apology, or not?" Travis asked, casting laughing eyes at his friend and deputy. "I can guarantee it will be the only one you'll hear from her. From the looks of her, it pained her just to voice the words once."

Sam glared at him. "Go to hell, Marshal Kincaid."

He grinned back. "If I do, can I take you along to introduce me? You *are* the devil's granddaughter, aren't you?"

"Now, Travis, let the poor girl be. You know she's not feeling well this morning," Elsie advised.

Chas chose this moment to intervene. "Miss, uh, Miss Downing, I'd be pleased to accept your apology. I can't say I'm too happy about being laid up this way, and little use to the marshal. And having the doc dig the bullet out wasn't my idea of fun, but I guess I'll live. And if I had to be shot by someone, I reckon I'd rather it was you. All the same, I'd feel a lot better if ya'd promise not to do it again real soon."

Despite her aching head, Sam smiled and chuckled. "Ya got my word on it," she told him. She liked the young deputy. There was something really nice about him. He seemed kind of shy and unsure of himself, sort of like a puppy you couldn't resist just because he was the runt of the litter. You couldn't help but like him.

"Now there's a promise you can bank on, all right," Travis mocked. "The word of an outlaw."

Suddenly, without warning, Travis found himself the object of three sets of blazing eyes, all intent on making him feel their wrath. Without a word, Chas got up, nodded to both Elsie and Sam, and left. Elsie slammed the coffee pot down on the stove top and announced huffily, "Cook your own dinner, Marshal Kincaid. I'm taking the day off, and I won't be home until late." She untied her apron and tossed it into Travis's lap as he stared at her in mute disbelief.

To Sam, she said, "And don't let this insufferable man try to tell you anything of any importance happened between the two of you last night, because it just isn't so. I was there the whole time, and I know."

After Elsie marched from the room, Sam headed for the back door, her back straight and her head held at a proud angle. Travis, who had been silent until now, suddenly found his tongue. "Where do you think you're going?" he demanded.

"To the outhouse, Marshal, and you're not invited."

"I told you before, Sam. Ladies call it the 'necessary.'"

Over her shoulder, she shot him a smile that would have given a lesser man frostbite. "You kin call horse droppin's roses if you want, but they still smell like manure."

Somehow, Travis was certain her cutting analogy had nothing to do with their discussion of the proper term for the privy and everything to do with him as a man and a person. He also knew he deserved her anger. His comments had been uncalled for, and beneath him as a gentleman and a U.S. Marshal. It was seeing her smiling at Chas that way, so free and easy, that had made him see red! She never smiled at him that way, like she really meant it!

Rising, Travis went to the window, and watched her as she walked across the yard, limping slightly. What was it about her that got to him so badly? She was a seventeen-year-old brat, with the manners and mouth of a mule skinner, and the body of a temptress. She had no education, no morals, and more pure stubbornness than a jackass. Yet, she had more pride in herself, just as she was, than anyone he had known. In her own way, she was the most honest person he had ever met. She intrigued him, she puzzled him, she tempted him without meaning to, and even as he resented it, he had to admit to himself that he wanted her as he had never wanted any other woman.

"Why her, God?" he moaned aloud, allowing himself a moment to wallow in self-pity. "Why not Nola, or Nan—anyone but Sam?"

CHAPTER 8

Travis had rounds to make. He had two prisoners in jail who required his attention. Of course, one was the town drunk, who only needed a few hours to sober up before going home, and the other was a rowdy, young cowboy who needed time to consider how to behave himself in Mattie's brothel. Still, Travis had duties to attend to, and now Elsie had deserted him, leaving Sam in his care for the day. What was he supposed to do with her?

For about ten seconds, Travis considered locking Sam in her room, but he wouldn't put it past the little varmint to find a way out of it while he was gone. There was the hall closet beneath the stairs. It had no windows and sturdy hinges, but Travis couldn't bring himself to lock Sam into that tiny, dark space and leave her there like some animal.

The girl was wild, yes, but she was still a human being and deserving of better treatment. Besides, he wouldn't be setting a very good example of how civilized persons acted if he did such a thing, now would he? And the whole idea was to civilize Sam, wasn't it?

Casting a disgruntled look at her, he said, "Go do something with your hair, Sam. Braid it or something, so it looks decent. You're coming along with me today."

"Why?" Her dark eyes were belligerent and wary.

"Because I said so," he told her shortly. "Get moving. I haven't got all day to sit here and wait for you. I have work to do."

She considered telling him that her ribs and ankle hurt more than they really did, asking him how she was supposed to accompany him in such a condition, but she resisted the temptation to aggravate him. Truth be told, Sam was heartily sick of being confined to the house. She would have walked barefoot over hot coals for the chance to get out for a while, and she certainly wasn't going to let a few minor twinges of pain stop her now. Nor would bare feet, though she did wish she had her boots back.

They hadn't gone three steps across the front porch, however, when Travis became aware of her limitations. "Blast! I forgot about your injuries!" he grumbled, glaring at her as if it were all her fault. With a sigh, he adjusted his long strides to match hers. "We'll just have to take it slow, I guess. Remind me to take you by the general store, and we'll try to get you a pair of shoes."

"Boots!" she muttered beneath her breath. Still,

he must have heard, because he grinned down at her in that superior way of his that made her ache to rip his mustache off!

Travis offered his arm to her, but Sam shuffled along on her own. "Hey! I'm trying to be a gentleman, Sam!" he proclaimed, miffed at her rejection of his gesture. "I know you're mad at me, but that's no reason not to accept a little help when you need it."

Sam stopped short and stared at him in confusion. "What the heck's got your feathers ruffled now, Kincaid? I ain't done nothin' wrong."

"I offered you my arm, Sam. You didn't take it."

The frown on her face deepened. "Your arm?" she questioned. "What am I supposed to do with one o' your arms, when I got two good arms o' my own? Now, ya want to be helpful, offer me a good leg to stand on!"

Travis burst out laughing. He couldn't help himself. "Oh, Sam! You're a treasure!" When he stopped chuckling, he explained. "When a gentleman puts out his arm like this," he said, extending his elbow toward her, "a lady is supposed to slip her hand into the crook of his arm."

"What for?"

"So he can help her walk beside him."

Sam let loose a disbelieving guffaw. "Never heard of such nonsense!"

"Now, Sam, surely you've seen men and women walking together before," he said, daring her to lie to him.

"'Course, I have," she retorted smartly, "an' I seen plenty o' women walkin' jest fine all on their own, too!"

"Well, when they walk together, it's considered

the polite thing for a man to offer his arm, and for the lady to accept," Travis insisted firmly, once more extending his elbow toward her.

Grudgingly, feeling extremely silly and self-conscious, Sam poked her hand into the crook of his arm. "I still say, if a woman'd wear decent boots instead o' them infernal shoes, she could walk by herself anytime an' anywhere she wanted, without needin' no help, or havin' to worry about fallin' over on her face!"

"Shoes or not, you need my help right now, so simmer down and accept it without all the fuss, Sam. Lord, you'd think I suggested you take hold of a snake!" Travis's good humor was fast dissolving in the face of Sam's stubborn attitude.

"Amounts to the same thing, if ya ask me," she grumbled beside him.

"I didn't ask you," he snapped irritably, "so just shut your mouth, or I'll take you right back inside the house and we'll forget the whole thing!"

"What set the burr under your tail?" she asked. When he stopped walking and glared down at her, she conceded. "Awright! I won't say another dad-blasted word! Jehoshaphat!"

In the general store, Mrs. Bertha Melbourn put her long, thin nose in the air and acted as if she would rather be serving Benedict Arnold than to help fit Sam with a pair of shoes. Sam wasn't so very pleased with the idea herself. The old prune-faced proprietress had cold, bony fingers, and she wasn't any too gentle in handling Sam's sprained ankle.

Mrs. Melbourn shoved one ugly high-topped shoe onto Sam's newly-stockinged foot and reached for the other. "Next time you bring her in for something like this, Marshal, please make sure she washes first. Her feet are filthy!" she sniffed disdainfully.

"Bertha, how was she supposed to arrive with clean feet when she walked over here?" Travis asked reasonably.

Rather than answer, Bertha gave Sam's ankle a vicious twist as she fitted the other shoe onto her foot. Despite herself, Sam yelped. "Dammit, you old witch!" she yelled. "You did that a'purpose!"

Travis groaned. He should have known this was not going to be easy, but Sam was only making matters worse! "Sam, apologize to Mrs. Melbourn at once!"

Sam turned stormy eyes in his direction. "When hell freezes solid!" she snarled. "She twisted my sore ankle, an' these clod-hoppers she's sellin' us are about three sizes too small! She's a mean-minded woman, an' she should be apologizin' to me, not the other way around!"

"Well! I never!" Mrs. Melbourn huffed.

"Maybe you oughta! It might improve your mood some!" Sam shot back, before Travis could intervene.

"That does it! If this is all the thanks I get for trying to be helpful, you can just forget it!" Mrs. Melbourn rose and stomped toward the front of the store. "Fit those shoes on her yourself, Marshal! I'll not cater to a common criminal and be made to take abuse as well!"

The dark look he gave her made Sam want to shrivel up and disappear, but she'd be eternally damned if she let him know it! She thrust out her chin and glared back at him. "All right, Sam! Since we have to do this ourselves, let's get it done with,'' he announced grimly, kneeling at her feet. He picked up one foot, propped it against his leg, and began lacing it.

Sam yanked her foot back. ''Kincaid, I'm tellin' ya, the blamed thing is too small! My toes are curled up six ways from Sunday in there, an' the blood has already stopped flowin' past my ankles!''

''Quit exaggerating, Sam!'' he grumbled.

''I ain't kiddin', Travis. I'll be lame b'fore I ever take the first step in these things!''

Sam's eyes locked with his, and Travis thought he saw something akin to pleading in hers. With a resigned sigh, he pressed his thumb down on the toe of the shoe. His brows rose slightly when he felt her toes cramped against the end of the shoe, with no room to spare. Indeed, it did feel as if her toes were bent inside the shoe to accommodate the small fit. ''Why, that spiteful hag!'' he muttered.

''Told ya so!'' Sam announced churlishly.

It took him several minutes to pry the too-tight shoes from Sam's feet and locate another pair in the proper size. To her dismay, Sam finally limped out of the store in a brand-new pair of the most awful shoes she had ever worn. ''If they end up hangin' me, Kincaid, I want to be buried in my boots!'' she told him sulkily. ''If you dare let them put me to rest in these things, I'll find a way to come back an' haunt ya forever!''

''Then we'd better find a way to save your neck, hadn't we?'' he returned grouchily. ''It might help if you could keep from making enemies of all the townspeople, Sam. Screaming and cursing at them is not the way to make friends.''

''If she's the best this town has to offer for

friends, I'm better off havin' enemies," Sam groused. "Nasty old biddy!"

Travis made his rounds, with Sam trailing behind him. When he stopped at the bank to speak with Ike Harrison about a shipment of gold due to arrive soon, Ike glared at Sam with malevolent eyes. "We'd better speak in private about this, Marshal," Ike said, pointing at Sam. "That one is likely to tell every bandit in five counties all she hears."

"Now, Ike. Sam isn't going anywhere to tell anything to anyone," Travis said calmly.

"You may be sure of that, but you can't convince me. What if she manages to escape? I still say, girl or not, she should be locked safely behind bars in that jail of yours."

In order to satisfy the bank manager and to insure that Sam stayed put, Travis resorted to handcuffing her to a sturdy railing while he and Harrison went into the man's office to discuss their business. Sam had stared holes through his back with those black eyes of hers. He knew she was mortified, though she refused to show it by word or action. She merely stood there, erect and stiff as a board, and silently condemned him with her eyes.

Of course, as he was releasing her, Parson Aldrich and his wife came into the bank. If Travis had felt low before, he was even more shamed when Alma Aldrich sent him a sad, accusing look and turned her sympathetic gaze upon Sam. "Oh, Travis!" she said, shaking her fuzzy gray head at him. She made a couple of tsking sounds that almost had him bowing his head before her. "Is that really necessary?"

"It was the only way to make sure she wouldn't escape, Mrs. Aldrich. Please try to understand."

Sam pulled her hand free of the loosened restraint and rubbed at her wrist, rolling her eyes in disgust at Travis's placating tone. "I think I need those boots after all," she muttered. "It's gettin' kinda deep in here."

"Sam! Behave yourself for once!" Travis hissed, then turned a blinding smile toward the parson's wife. "Believe me, Mrs. Aldrich, I have gone to great lengths to avoid hurting this young woman. Elsie and I are trying our best to make her comfortable and to teach her all those things she has missed learning while living the life she has." Behind him, Travis heard Sam making gagging noises, as if she were about to be sick. When he got her alone, he swore to himself that he was going to beat the tar out of her!

"Oh, you poor dear!" Alma cooed. "What a life you must have led!" she exclaimed softly to Sam. "I never gave a thought to that before, but you must have missed out on so much!"

The parson spoke up for the first time in defense of Travis. "Now, Alma dear, I'm sure Marshal Kincaid is doing the very best he can for her."

"Yes, Mr. Aldrich, I'm sure he is," his wife responded. After thirty years of marriage, she still called him Mr. Aldrich. "But a man can only do so much! There are things only another woman can teach a girl."

"Oh, Elsie has been living in for just that purpose," Travis assured her quickly. "And Miss Tucker is coming in several days a week to instruct her."

"That's all well and good, but a young lady needs more than household skills and an education. Her spirit must be fed, too. Don't you agree, Mr. Aldrich?"

"Most assuredly, my dear," the parson concurred. Peering pointedly at Travis through the speckled lenses of his wire-rimmed eyeglasses, the reverend suggested, "We will see you in church this Sunday, won't we, Marshal? With your young charge in hand?"

"I'd planned on it, sir," Travis responded politely, if somewhat insincerely.

Sam groaned audibly, something Travis also felt like doing but was denied at the moment. If there was one place he wanted to avoid taking Sam until she learned better manners, it was to church! On the other hand, he couldn't think of a place she more needed to go! The little bandit probably hadn't seen the inside of a church in her life! Still, to set her loose among that many of the townspeople was like lighting a match in a fireworks factory! There was no predicting what horrible catastrophe might occur!

To add insult to injury, this Sunday was the church social. Before Sam had landed in his lap, Travis had intended to invite Nola Sandoval to go with him. With everything that had happened lately, he had completely forgotten, but Nola was sure to be there anyway. How was he supposed to explain Sam to Nola? Oh, word of his female prisoner had undoubtedly reached Nola's ears by now, but hearing about Sam and meeting her were two entirely different matters, a fact to which Nan Tucker could readily testify.

After leaving the bank, and the parson and his wife, Travis was sure the rest of his day was bound to improve. He was wrong. They were passing the barber shop, when big Lou Sprit hobbled out to waylay them. "Hold up there a minute, Travis! I want to get a look at the gal who crippled me!"

The day of the hold-up, Sam had been in too much agony to pay much attention to the other members of Travis's posse. Now she stood gaping in awe at the mountain of flesh blocking her way. Great Gertie! She'd never seen a man as big as this one! She hadn't even realized it was possible for a man to grow so huge! Why, her nose only came to the middle of his chest, and she had to tilt her head to stare up at his ruddy face.

What she saw did nothing for her shaky composure. The barber was scowling down at her with fire in his eyes! As if that and his immense size weren't enough to scare a body out of its wits, he was brandishing a gleaming razor in his hand!

Sam's mouth went as dry as the desert. Her mouth flew open in wordless terror. Her knees threatened to give way beneath her as she began to tremble, and to her humiliation, she had to grasp tightly to Travis's arm to keep from falling. "K–K–Kincaid! Do somethin'!" she whispered. "Tell him I didn't have nothin' to do with his leg gettin' broke!"

Travis was amazed beyond belief and secretly delighted. So, the little rapscallion was frightened of something after all! Travis had begun to think she would spit at the devil himself! "Now, Sam, how can I tell Lou something like that?" he mocked. "If it hadn't been for you and that outlaw family of yours robbing the bank, Lou would never have been deputized that day, and if we hadn't been chasing you, he wouldn't have been hurt."

From behind Sam's back, Travis shot Lou a look

that warned him not to try to hurt the girl. Throwing a little fright into her was one thing, but Travis would allow no real harm to come to his young prisoner.

"Damn you, Kincaid!" Sam wailed. "This ain't funny! Tell him I wasn't the one who got him hurt!"

Relenting somewhat, Travis said, "Well, you didn't fire the shot that brought his horse down."

"Hear that, mister?" Sam asked, turning wide brown eyes up at the barber. "I didn't shoot you or your horse!"

Sprit growled at her, the sound rumbling through his broad chest like a gigantic gong. Scared spitless, Sam almost climbed into Travis's arms like a monkey heading up a tree for safety!

It was almost more than Travis could do not to laugh. "Why, Sam, I didn't know you cared!" he crooned gloatingly, a wide grin splitting his face.

"You better not let him hurt me!" Sam cried out, trying to regain her bravado. "It's your sworn duty to protect me!" For all her brave words, Sam still clung to him as tightly as possible, trying to hide herself against his chest.

Though his arms came about her to hold her to him, Travis commented lazily, "How is it I don't recall anything like that in the oath I took?"

"In that case, I think I've got some revenge comin' to me," Lou responded with a sly grin. "I think I have just the thing, too. Travis, bring the girl into my shop."

"What do you have in mind, Lou?" Travis asked, half-carrying a squirming, squealing Sam into the barber's establishment.

Two other men, one half-shaved, and the other

waiting his turn for a haircut, sat staring at them as they entered. Lou ignored them, except to order the man from the chair and direct Travis to deposit Sam into it and hold her there. "Been quite a while since I've had anyone to practice my dental skills on," he replied tauntingly, giving an evil laugh at the stark terror that crossed Sam's face.

"No! You can't do this! Travis! You can't let him! Please!" Sam was beside herself, willing to swallow all pride to escape this fate worse than death! She strained against the arms holding her in the chair. "Oh, God, Kincaid! Please! I'll do anything ya say!"

Travis's eyebrows rose at this. "Well, now! This is quite a turn-around, Sam. Did I hear you would do anything, if I keep Lou from pulling a few of your precious white teeth?"

"A few, hell! I'm gonna pull every damned one of them!" Lou vowed vehemently.

"Yes! Yes!" she squealed. "Jest keep him away from me!" Her eyes went even bigger as Lou pulled open a drawer and came toward her with a menacing instrument that resembled a thick pair of pliers. His hand came out to clamp her jaw roughly, prying her mouth open.

"Hold on there a minute, Lou. Maybe we ought to see how cooperative my little prisoner intends to be. Seems she's mighty willing to make amends right now."

Travis eyed Sam intently. "You ready to talk to me now, Sam?"

Even with Lou's huge paw grasping her jaw, she managed a small nod.

"Let her loose," Travis told the barber, brushing Lou's hand back. For a long, silent minute, Travis stared at her. Her nerves were screaming by the time he finally said, "Tell me about the Downings, Sam. How many of you are there altogether?"

When she hesitated, Lou brandished the tongs again. "F–f–five," she admitted shakily.

"Including you?"

She nodded affirmatively, her tongue sneaking out to moisten her dry lips, her gaze swiveling rapidly from Lou's hand to Travis's face, and back again.

"What are their names?"

The pain showed on her face as she listed them haltingly, her heart breaking with every word she was forced to utter. "Bill. Billy. Hank, and Tom."

"And Bill is your father?"

Again she nodded.

"Which of your brothers is the oldest? Billy?"

With a shake of her head, she corrected him. "T–Tom is the oldest."

"And after him?" Travis prodded.

"Billy, then Hank."

"Then you're the youngest," Travis deduced. "How long have you been with them, Sam?"

As frightened as he knew she was, she dared to glare at him. "Always. Since the start."

"And when was that?" he insisted.

"Awhile after Mama died."

Travis sighed in exasperation. "Holy hell! It'd be easier letting Lou pull your teeth than it is to drag information out of you! How long has that been, Sam?"

"About five years, if ya gotta know!" she snarled, her temper beginning to outweigh her fright. "Lord, I ain't never met a man as nosy as you!"

Wagging a warning finger at her, Travis cautioned, "Now, now, Sam! Don't let your sassy mouth get the better of your good sense. Lou's just itching to get his fingers on those pearly-white teeth of yours."

Immediately, Sam clamped her mouth shut, waiting in dread for the next question.

"Any of you ever kill anyone during your hold-ups?"

"I told ya b'fore, that ain't our way! Pa don't take kindly to killin'!"

"But he does take kindly to robbing people," Travis sneered. "That doesn't exactly make him a saint, you know. Why did you and your family start stealing when you did?"

Sam shook her head at him. "I don't remember," she said.

"Don't lie to me, Sam. I want to know why."

"I said I don't recollect, Marshal!" She practically screamed the denial at him. "I was only twelve at the time!"

His face registered his shock, as he swiftly calculated the timing in his head and realized that what she was telling him was the truth. Good God! Sam had been but a child when her father and brothers had first introduced her to a life of crime! When she had admitted it had been five years now, he hadn't stopped to think how young that would have made her. Now he was appalled and more than a little ashamed of himself for carrying this charade so far. Whatever Sam and her family had done, Sam was hardly responsible for starting it or for being involved in it.

From the startled look on Lou's face, he was realizing this, too. So were the other two men, who had been avidly listening to every word. "Sam, I'm sorry," Travis said earnestly. "I didn't know."

When she failed to respond, merely staring woodenly at him, he turned to Lou. "I think this has gone far enough," he stated quietly. "I'm taking Sam home now."

As Travis lifted her from the chair, Lou stood looking on, sheep-faced. "I'm sorry for scarin' you so bad, Sam," he told her in his gravelly voice. "I'm really not such a bad fella, once you get to know me."

Sam craned her neck to level a sour look at him. "Can't prove it by me," she retorted, her spirit beginning to revive once more. If there was anyone in this town she meant to avoid in the future, it was Lou Sprit. Just to cover her bets, she added less spitefully, "I still say I had nothin' to do with your leg gettin' broke."

Lou grinned down at her and extended a beefy hand. "I'm willin' to call it even if you are, little girl."

She thought about it a minute, then let her hand disappear into his. "Even," she agreed reluctantly. They might never be friends, but this barber was one man she didn't want for an enemy. He was much too big—and he pulled teeth!

CHAPTER 9

"**T**ravis! I can't believe you would do something that awful!" Elsie had come storming into the house as Travis was attempting to fix supper for himself and Sam. Sam had bluntly told him to fend for himself. She sure as the devil wasn't about to cook for him, even if she did know how, which she didn't.

Setting her reticule on the table, Elsie placed both hands on her ample hips and continued to rail at him. "It is all over town that you and Lou Sprit were terrorizing the daylights out of Sam, threatening to pull all her teeth! How could you? I'm absolutely ashamed of you!"

"So am I," Travis admitted humbly, completely taking the wind out of Elsie's sails. "Sam has hardly spoken a word to me since we've been home—not that I blame her." He slanted a thoughtful look at Elsie. "Did you know that Sam was only twelve when her father and brothers began taking her along on their robberies? Is it any wonder she's turned out the way she has? I think I understand her a little better now, though I'm not proud of the way I gained that bit of information today."

"That poor baby!" Elsie was aghast. "Where is she now?" If nothing else, perhaps Elsie could offer a bit of comfort to her, a little late mothering to a girl who'd had so little of it in her life.

"She's upstairs in her room. Says she doesn't want any supper. She just wants to be left alone."

"I think I'll go try to talk with her," Elsie said.

"Tell her I'm sorry, will you?" Travis asked. At Elsie's questioning look, he added, "I tried to tell her before, but she just wouldn't listen to an apology from me. Maybe she'll accept one from you, on my behalf."

Elsie nodded. "I'll try, Travis," she promised.

Upstairs in her room, Sam paced restlessly. Contrary to what Travis might think, she had more on her mind than the fright he and that giant barber had given her this afternoon. Hank was in town!

Sam had seen her brother as she and Travis were walking back to the house. He'd been standing across the street in front of the general store, casually watching people pass along the town's main street, when Sam had first noticed him. He'd spotted her and the marshal almost immediately, then confused Sam by looking straight past her as if he'd never seen her before. A second later, his gaze had returned for a closer look, and Sam could almost see the surprise in Hank's eyes, though not a muscle in his face betrayed him. The only thing Sam could figure was that Hank had not recognized her at first, never having seen her in a dress!

Hank had followed them along the street, discreetly, of course. Already angry at Travis, Sam used this as an excuse not to speak to him, lest he somehow notice her growing excitement, and as soon as they had reached Kincaid's house, she had come straight to her room to hide and plan. Hank would come for her, probably sometime tonight after everyone else was asleep. She would be ready and waiting for him, ready to do whatever it took to escape with him. Somehow, she would find a way to signal him, so he would know which room she was in.

With that in mind, Sam went to the window, silently bemoaning the fact that her room did not have a rear window, one located over the back porch and looking out over the back yard, where escape would not be so noticeable or difficult. Neither did it have a front window. There were just these two long windows on either side of her bed, both facing the side yard.

Outside the one window, a huge tree blocked most of the view, so if she were to signal Hank, it would have to be from the other window. However, the tree did offer a possible escape route. Sam would leave it up to Hank to devise a way to rescue her, for there was no way she could manage to climb down that tree unaided, with her battered ribs and ankle. If only she still had her boots and trousers, it would make things so much simpler. Also, she was going to hate having to leave Bess behind, but if it came to a choice of leaving the horse or hanging, the mare was a small loss.

When Elsie tapped lightly on her door and entered the room, Sam jumped guiltily away from the window, her heart thumping in her chest. She breathed a little easier when the housekeeper smiled and said, "I guess you're still a mite nervous over what happened today at Sprit's place. I heard about it, and I've just finished dragging Travis over the coals for his part in it. Of course," she added with a shrug, "he seems pretty ashamed of himself already. That was a low, despicable thing to do to you."

"The man's a skunk!" Sam agreed with a scowl. "If they want to hang someone, he's my pick."

Elsie laughed. "Come on, Sam! He's not that bad!"

"Well, I ain't either! I ain't never killed nobody, never even wounded anyone real bad!"

"Of course, you're not bad, honey," Elsie concurred. "Just a bit misguided." She put a comforting arm about Sam's shoulders and gave her a hug. "Why don't you come down and let Travis apologize to you? I'd give a whole week's wages to hear that!"

With a shake of her head, Sam refused. "No. I want to be by myself right now, if ya don't mind. I got me some stewin' to do, an' it's best I do it alone. B'sides, it won't do the marshal no harm to think a bit more on how bad he's treated me. It might make him think twice b'fore he does somethin' that low-down again."

"Aren't you even going to come down to supper?" Elsie asked slyly.

"Not if Kincaid's cookin', I ain't," Sam avowed vehemently.

"What if I fix you a little something?"

Sam shrugged. "I really don't want to tangle with the marshal no more today, Elsie. I guess I'll skip supper tonight." Sam hoped she wouldn't regret not eating, but she couldn't chance sitting beneath those probing blue eyes of Travis's. He might guess something was in the wind. Too, she needed to try to signal Hank.

"All right," Elsie relented with a sigh. "I guess it wouldn't hurt to fix you a tray and bring it up here to you. Just for this one time, now, mind you, and only to make Travis all the more miserable. And I'm not fixing a morsel for him, either! He can eat humble pie, for all I care. It might do him some good, for a change."

Squinting through the darkness outside her bedroom window, Sam tried in vain to catch a glimpse or even a tell-tale sound that might herald Hank's arrival. It was late, long past midnight, and darker than the inside of a goat outdoors. Sam had been waiting for hours, quiet as a mouse, and her nerves were beginning to fray terribly. Where was that brother of hers?

Patience never had been her strong suit, and matters had been made even worse when Travis had made an unexpected visit to her room to check on her. Her heart had leapt into her throat and threatened to choke her when she had heard his footsteps creep to a halt outside her door. Then a key had grated in the lock.

Fully dressed and suspiciously alert, Sam had

dashed from the window, diving headlong into the bed and hastily pulling the covers up tight beneath her chin. She'd almost died when he had tiptoed quietly to the side of the bed and stood looking down at her for what had seemed to be three lifetimes. Only God knew how he had missed hearing her thumping heart, or how she had kept from jumping out of her skin when he had lifted a strand of her hair and smoothed it back from her forehead.

By the time he had left her room, locking the door behind him, dots of perspiration were dampening her brow, and she was trembling so badly she could scarcely stand on her own again. Several minutes went by before she wondered how often he had made these middle-of-the-night forays into her room, unannounced and unnoticed, while she slept comfortably nude and blissfully unaware of his presence. Lord, that man had more nerve than a toe with an ingrown nail! If she didn't plan on never seeing him again, she would have considered strangling him!

"I hope he got a good eyeful, 'cause it's the last he'll ever see of me!" she grumbled to herself. She could only be thankful he hadn't pulled back the covers and discovered her fully clothed, because he would really have been suspicious then!

A rustle of leaves in the still night caught Sam's attention. With her nose pressed flat against the pane, she peered through the branches. There! That hulking black spot about halfway up the tree must be Hank! The dark blob moved upward, miscalculated and slipped downward about three feet, and stopped. What curses she couldn't hear,

Sam could well imagine, as Hank rubbed briskly at his skinned shinbone.

Finally he was level with her window, and inching his way along the nearest branch. Sam held her breath as her brother balanced himself precariously, then launched himself onto the outer windowsill with a dexterity that surprised them both. Swaying on the small ledge, his feet wedged sideways and his fingernails digging into the splintering wood frame, Hank whispered loudly, "Open the window, you ninny!"

"I can't!" she hissed back. "It's nailed shut. Both windows are, an' the door is locked!"

"Damn!" After a moment, he suggested, "We're gonna have to break the glass, then."

Immediately, Sam sat down on the floor and began to remove one of her shoes, muttering to herself as she did so, "At least these ugly, blasted things have some useful purpose!"

"Whacha doin'?" Hank asked in a frantic falsetto tone that threatened to set Sam giggling, despite the peril of discovery.

"I'm fixin' to bust the window with my shoe. It's all I've got that'll work," she told him.

"No, ya idiot! You'll shower glass all over me, an' I'm liable to lose my footin', which ain't the greatest as it is!" he warned. "I'll break the glass from this side." After a few contortions that Sam had to admire, Hank finally managed to draw his pistol from his holster. "Stand back!" he instructed, aiming the butt of the gun at the pane.

"Wait!" she breathed, wincing as his aborted thrust almost sent Hank tumbling from the narrow windowsill before he finally regained his balance.

He glared through the glass at her, and she sent him an apologetic half-smile. "Let me get a blanket off the bed first to smother the sound, or they're sure to hear the window breakin'."

Once she had braced the blanket and herself against the inner pane, Hank tapped lightly on the glass. As it cracked, splinters tinkled like miniature bells onto the floorboards at Sam's feet. The tiny, silvery sounds seemed overly loud to her ears, though her good sense told her otherwise. Laying the blanket on the floor, she and Hank worked quickly to clear the windowpane of most of the jagged edges still remaining.

"Okay, I'll go first, and you follow behind me," he told her quietly. "That way I kin catch ya if ya start to fall. Jump as far as ya kin and latch onto any branch ya touch first."

"I can't!" Sam groaned. "Hank, I got me a bad ankle, and near-busted ribs, and a skirt about to trip me up jest walkin'! There ain't no way I kin make it down on my own!"

"You got to, Sammie," he said, grimacing at their predicament. "Now, hitch your skirts between your legs, and loop the ends through the waistband. That'll be almost as good as pants."

"What about these shoes?" she moaned, glancing toward her feet. "The soles are as slippery as a swamp bottom."

"Where are your boots?"

"Gone."

"Then take the shoes off an' go barefoot. Jest watch out for the glass."

A minute later, Sam was leaning out the window, her face next to Hank's knee, judging the distance she would have to jump. If there had been

114

more light, her brother would have been startled to see the fright on her face. With knots in her stomach, she watched Hank brace himself on the small ledge, gather his muscles, and leap forward. Amid a loud rustling of leaves and a smothered grunt, he landed on one branch, latching onto another with both hands.

Hesitantly, Sam eased herself into a sitting position on the ledge. More than anything, she wished she'd learned how to pray, because she could sure use some extra help about now. As she leaned forward, preparing to let go, Hank hissed from below her. "Stand up! You can't make it like that, ya simpleton!"

"I gotta!" she answered low, shutting both eyes and trying to swallow the lump in her throat. She knew her knocking knees and bad ankle would never support her enough to stand. "Catch me, Hank!" she begged on a whimper. "If ya let me break my neck, Pa'll never forgive ya!"

Before she lost what little courage she had mustered, she pushed off with her good foot and both arms. Mere seconds and an eternity later, she crashed into Hank, knocking him askew on his perch. Beneath their combined weight, the limb gave a loud crack, and before either of them could alter their positions, it gave way beneath them. Down they tumbled, arms and legs flying in every direction in a frantic effort to stem their fall, as branches snapped and crunched in their wake.

Startled and unable to stop herself, Sam screamed. Hank's yelp echoing hers didn't make her feel any better about all the noise they were making. Stealth was not of as much importance now as saving their necks anyway. Hank landed with a dull thud, but Sam was not as fortunate. Suddenly she found herself dangling in midair, upside down, her skirts settling over her head. Another sharp shriek was torn from her as her mad flight downward was halted abruptly.

By now, dogs were barking and they heard sounds of someone stumbling about in the house. Hank was barely on his feet and reaching for her as a light shone through the broken window in her room.

"Hank! Help me! My skirt's snagged on a branch, an' I can't reach it!" Sam cried, twisting about in a fruitless effort to free herself. She dangled out of her brother's reach.

Above her, Travis roared, "Sam!" Though she couldn't see him past the skirts billowing about her head, Sam knew the exact moment Travis thrust his head through the window. Hank's head jerked up as if by a puppet's string, his hand going for the gun at his hip.

"No, Hank! He's a U.S. Marshal!" she warned. They both knew how much trouble they would be in if Hank shot the lawman. Hank sent her a helpless look, torn between wanting to help her and not wanting to get caught. "Go on, Hank!" she urged, holding back the tears that stung her eyes. "No sense both of us gettin' nabbed. Run!"

He nodded quickly. "I'll be back, Sammie. Don't you worry none. We ain't gonna let ya hang. We'll save ya somehow!" A bullet kicked up the dust near his feet, cutting short their parting.

Dodging through the shadows, Hank scurried away. As she dangled from the limb, hot, angry tears dripping into her hair, Sam heard the muffled sounds of horse's hooves as Hank made good his escape. "Dang, darn, and damnation!" she sniffled, feeling extremely sorry for herself.

She didn't have long to wallow in her misery. One minute she was cursing softly to herself, and the next she was staring down into sizzling aqua eyes. "I ought to let you hang there all night!" Travis snarled up at her. "If for nothing else than to prove that there is more than one way to skin a cat, and more than one way to hang an outlaw! Maybe your own blood pounding in your ears will knock some sense into that thick skull of yours! You have got to be the orneriest, most stubborn damn female I have ever had the misfortune to meet!"

"You gonna yap all night, or are ya gonna cut me loose!" she snapped back, completely disregarding her own helplessness. It was bad enough to miss escaping and finding herself once more in his keep, let alone listening to him lecturing her as she hung from a branch like a blasted possum!

His eyes blazed a warning. "Shut up, Sam! Just wise up and shut your mouth! You're in no position to be giving orders, not with your skirts around your ears and your bloomers showing up brighter than a full moon!"

A short while later, Travis shoved her unceremoniously up the stairs, past a wide-eyed Elsie, and into his own bedroom. The door slamming behind them sounded like a death knoll. Whirling about, Sam faced him, her own eyes huge in her flushed face. "Jest whacha think you're doin', Kincaid?" she blustered.

He sneered back at her. "I'm making darn good and sure you won't be going out any more windows tonight. From now on, you'll be in my sight day and night, and if any more of your brothers show up to rescue you, they'll come face to face with me first."

Unbidden, her gaze slid to the bed. "I ain't sleepin' in the same bed with you."

"Suit yourself," he answered bluntly, sliding his gun beneath the far edge of the mattress and reaching for his handcuffs. "You can sleep on the floor if you want, but you'll still be right beside me, within arm's reach." Snapping one manacle about her wrist and the other low on the bedpost, he shackled her securely. As she sat and stared at him in shocked silence, he nonchalantly tossed a blanket and pillow onto the floor. Then, as brazen as you please, he shucked his pants and crawled into bed before dousing the lamp. "Sweet dreams, little bandit," he mocked. "Try not to snore too loudly, will you? You've already disturbed my sleep enough for one night."

Yanking her wayward mind away from thoughts of his magnificent male nakedness, she managed to mutter, "Don't I even git my nightshift? It ain't gonna be too comfortable tryin' to sleep in this dress, ya know."

"Then take it off," came the unconcerned answer. "We both know you never use the nightgown anyway."

That silenced her for a long minute. He could almost feel the heat of her blush in the dark room. "And how am I supposed to do that, tied up to the bedpost, Marshal?"

"That's your problem, darlin'," he yawned. "You figure it out. It'll give you something constructive to do with that busy little brain of yours."

CHAPTER 10

Parson Aldrich droned on, the monotonous tone of his voice nearly lulling Sam to sleep as she sat on the hard church pew between Elsie and Travis. She wished she dared yawn, but the last time she'd done so, she'd earned herself a sharp jab in the side from Travis's elbow. Now he was glaring at her for sliding down in her seat. She was sitting on her spine, and if she slid any lower, she knew she'd probably end up on the floor. Still, she felt like a freak in a side-show, on display for all to see. From the time they had entered the churchyard, all eyes had turned her way, and she could feel them boring into her back this very minute.

Thanks to Elsie, she'd at least had a decent dress to wear this morning. Her only other dress now had a huge rip in the skirt, where it had caught on the branch last night. Then again, if Elsie hadn't purchased this new dress for her, Sam wouldn't be in church right now, enduring this torment.

It was time to stand again and sing, much to Sam's dismay. Of course, they would have to be seated in one of the first pews! Travis's hand clamped about her arm urged her to her feet as he thrust his hymnal toward her. She glared back at him. Then she shrugged inwardly. Well, if that was the way he wanted it, so be it!

It took a moment for Sam, unfamiliar with the hymn, to pick up the melody by ear. Mrs. Aldrich, bless her heart, was pumping it out, loud and clear, on the old organ. Hymnal in hand and an angelic expression on her face, Sam suddenly joined in the singing, bellowing the words for all she was worth, off-key and a full beat behind everyone else, since she could not read the words, needing to hear them first.

Next to her, Travis stiffened and stopped singing. Above the starched collar of his shirt, his neck glowed red, the color rising into his face. The veins in his neck stood out as he clenched his jaw tightly, and another vein ticked rhythmically at his temple. His fingers clenched tightly to the hymnal he shared with Sam, his knuckles showing white as he attempted to jerk the book away from her. But Sam, a sweetly mischievous smile etching her lips, refused to release the hymnal.

On Sam's other side, Elsie, too, stopped singing. Now the housekeeper's shoulders were shaking in silent laughter, and little choking sounds erupted past her pursed lips. Behind them, several snickers were heard among the parishioners. Parson Aldrich had the strangest expression on his face, as if he'd swallowed a fishbone and gotten it lodged in his throat. His wife, however, seemed extremely pleased and kept smiling and nodding at Sam as if encouraging her in her efforts.

Meanwhile, Sam's husky alto rose in volume with each verse, her southwestern drawl distorting words and notes alike. The congregation of Tumbleweed Trinity Church had never heard a rendition of "Shall We Gather at the River" delivered in quite this fashion before. Many of them were trying so hard to hold back their amusement that they sounded every bit as bad as Sam before the song was done. The end result resembled a pack of coyotes howling at the moon.

Travis wanted nothing more than to dig a hole, crawl into it, and pull it in after himself! He could not recall ever being so publicly humiliated and he had no one to blame but himself! For the rest of the church service, he sat hunched in his seat, a frown pulling at his mustached mouth, and prayed that this one morning, Parson Aldrich would dismiss the congregation without a closing hymn.

Walking down the center aisle of the church following the close of the service was something akin to running a gauntlet. As Travis held tightly to Sam's arm, he could feel her trembling, though she did not betray her nervousness by word or any overt action. She held herself erect and proud, her face a carefully set mask of unconcern.

Still, Travis's own embarrassment melted in the face of hers, for he knew she must feel tremendously awkward before all these curious eyes. "It's all right, Sam," he whispered. "Nothing bad is going to happen." Though she did not answer, he saw her swallow hard.

Sam didn't put much faith in Travis's reassurances. From what she could tell, very little separated this crowd from that of a lynch mob. Several ladies drew their skirts aside as she passed by; others hid smiles and giggles behind raised hands. Many a churchgoing person now forgot the prayerful attitude of moments ago to glare openly at her. Others stared with curious eyes. Mrs. Melbourn, from the general store, was whispering loudly to a woman at her elbow, and shooting sour glances in Sam's direction. The bank manager was frowning at her in a menacing manner. All in all, it was not a welcoming atmosphere, and Sam wondered if this was how prisoners aboard a pirate ship had felt when made to walk the plank.

The only ones who seemed genuinely glad to see her this morning were the pastor and his wife, and Lou Sprit. The three of them were standing by the door, beaming at her as if their faces were about to split. It was silly, since Sam scarcely knew any of them, but their smiles bolstered her flagging courage. As she and Travis drew near to them, Sam managed a wobbly smile in return.

"Oh, my dear!" Alma Aldrich cooed, holding her arms out to envelope Sam in a quick embrace. "How delighted I am to see you here this morning! And don't you look nice! Doesn't she look nice, Mr. Aldrich?"

The parson's head bobbed in agreement. "Indeed, she does." Then he asked the inevitable. "How did you like the service this morning, Miss Downing?"

Put on the spot, Sam could not immediately recall one word of the man's sermon, and she hated to lie to a man of God. In desperation, she stammered, "I liked the singin' best, I reckon."

An odd silence followed her statement, with everyone looking extremely uncomfortable, until Alma said, "Have you ever considered taking singing lessons, Miss Downing? You have such a strong, rich voice. All it really needs is some training. I'd be happy to take you on as a pupil."

Travis couldn't be sure, but he thought he saw Parson Aldrich hide a grimace. Sam seemed stunned, unable to formulate a reply. "That's kind of you, Mrs. Aldrich," Travis said, taking charge, "but not at all necessary."

"Oh, but I want to contribute to Miss Downing's reformation!" Alma exclaimed. "In my own small way, I, too, would be teaching her something, don't you see?"

"Well," he hedged, as Sam blushed to the roots of her hair, wishing she could disappear in a puff of smoke.

"Oh, go on!" Elsie put in suddenly, giving Travis a nudge from behind. "What harm can it do?" Beneath her breath, she muttered loud enough him to hear, "Lord knows, it might even do some good, and save all our ears in Sundays to come!"

The church social that afternoon was another trial for Sam, but again Travis insisted they go. "It's an excellent way to get to know people, and to let them know you. Just, please, behave yourself. If you want to save your neck, you are going to have to make some friends in town, Sam."

With everyone else dressed up in their Sunday best, Sam stuck out once again like a sore thumb.

Oh, the dress Elsie had bought was nice enough for everyday wear, and Sam would never have known the difference had it not been for all the other young ladies she saw that day. While the older women wore darker colors, the ones Sam's age wore brighter hues, trimmed in embroidery and ribbons. Lace frills and ruffles adorned the gowns, creating a delightful rainbow of color as the girls clustered together in groups to giggle and gossip.

The main topic of their hushed conversations this day was Samantha Downing, Marshal Kincaid's outlaw prisoner. As Travis led her about, introducing her to Tumble's citizenry, whispers rose in their wake. Mostly out of respect for the marshal, people were polite to her in his presence, but when the introductions were concluded, Sam did not receive any invitations to join their exclusive groups. She stood to one side with Travis, Elsie, and Alma Aldrich, trying her best to hide her anger and hurt.

As if all this were not bad enough, Sam looked up to see a beautiful, young woman headed in their direction. The lady simply oozed self-confidence and charm, as she sent Travis a dazzling smile. Ignoring Sam entirely, she put out a daintily gloved hand and purred, "Travis! Shame on you for ignoring me so these last few days! Why, I almost didn't come today, because of you, you know."

Her rosy lips formed a come-hither pout that defied her words and made Sam suddenly want to double up her fist and plant five hard knuckles right in the woman's mouth. Where this idea came from, Sam was not sure. Nor was she sure of how to deal with her instinctive dislike of this lady, or the fiery feelings of jealousy that suddenly erupted within her. Never, in all of her seventeen years, had Sam ever felt such burning jealousy toward anyone!

"Now, Nola, you know I haven't been ignoring you on purpose," Travis was saying smoothly, in a soothing tone that made Sam's eyes widen with surprise. "I've just been too busy to get out to the ranch since the hold-up."

"So I've heard," Nola admitted dulcetly, her sharp gaze cutting to Sam in an accusing manner. "This, I take it, is the little outlaw who's been taking up all your time." Nola's eyes raked Sam from head to toe as she sniffed, "I hear she's living with you."

Mrs. Aldrich gasped aloud at the insults Nola was voicing. Almost immediately, Elsie rushed to Sam's defense. "Sam's staying with Travis, but so am I, I'll have you know."

"Oh, there's no need to explain," Nola said hastily, sending Travis another blinding smile. "I'm sure Travis has his reasons, after all."

"I couldn't very well keep Sam in a jail cell, Nola," Travis put in mildly.

"No, no, of course not," Nola concurred sweetly. Her gaze hardened once more as she assessed the young girl before her. "Sam, did you say?" she trilled. "My, how quaint!"

"It's short for Samantha," Travis said, his brows drawing together slightly as he contemplated Nola's attitude toward Sam. He'd never seen Nola act this way before, and it had him baffled.

"Oh, but Sam seems to fit her so much better, don't you agree?" Nola asked. Her lips still held a smile that didn't quite reach her eyes.

Skirting an actual answer to her comment, Travis said, "That brings up something I've been meaning to ask you, Nola. Would you be willing to come by the house a couple of times a week and tutor Sam in the ways and manners of a lady?"

To her credit, Nola's smile stiffened only slightly. For a mere instant, she looked as if she'd swallowed a cannonball, but she recovered her poise quickly. "Why, Travis! I'm honored that you would ask! I'd be delighted, of course!" she gushed.

"Nan Tucker is tutoring Sam in some of the schooling she has missed, and Elsie is teaching her things a woman needs to know about the house," Travis went on to explain. "Even Mrs. Aldrich has kindly volunteered to give her singing lessons. However, when it comes to the finer matters of ladylike deportment, I can't think of anyone more suitable than you."

Sam could not believe her ears! Why the nerve of the overgrown galoot! Here he stood, talking about her as if she were invisible, and practically slobbering over himself to please this woman! In all her days, Sam had never witnessed anything this revolting or wanted so desperately to knock two heads together! Even Elsie looked absolutely dismayed and disgusted. Why, he hadn't even had the common decency to introduce her properly! Even she knew enough to do that!

Fortunately, before her temper could explode, Elsie dragged her away, not even bothering to make their excuses. "Let's go get us some lemonade to wash down the bile," the housekeeper said, wrinkling her nose. "Right now I could give Travis Kincaid a swift kick in the pants, which is where he is wearing his brains these days, I'd guess! Men!'' she snorted. ''I swear they're all as blind as bats! What he sees in that woman is beyond me, and then to have the stupidity to ask her to teach you how to act like a lady! When the good Lord gave out brains, Travis must have thought He said trains, and asked for a slow one!''

For the first time in days, Sam really laughed. ''Oh, Elsie! I like you!'' she declared. ''That Nola might be considered a lady, but you're a woman to admire.''

Beaming, Elsie made a mock curtsy. ''Why thank you, dear. I do respect your judgement—in this case, at least.''

During the course of the afternoon, Sam did gain a few new friends, not all of whom met with Travis's approval. First there was Lou Sprit. The barber, a confirmed bachelor, suddenly took it upon himself to be Sam's guardian angel. He never left her for more than a few minutes at a time. When it came time to eat, he even filled a plate for her and brought it to her, seating himself next to her at the table. He scowled at the young men who defied their parents and dredged up enough nerve to approach Sam. He even scowled at Travis from time to time.

Poor Sam didn't know what to do or think about all this. She'd never had a beau before, never had time for one, but she knew instinctively that this was what Lou was behaving like. Though it did wonders for her battered female ego, it still did not sit well with her. Unless she missed her guess, Lou was old enough to be her father, or near enough to count. Besides, after the scare he'd given her the day before, Lou was not one of her favorite people right now. The only thing that made her hold her tongue was the fact that she did not want to make this big bear of a man angry with her again. Neither, however, did she appreciate having him get so downright friendly!

It did cross Sam's mind that Travis, wanting to spend more time with the beautiful Miss Nola, might have asked Lou to keep an eye on her, to make certain that she did not try to escape again, but that still did not account entirely for the way Lou was behaving. No, if she had to place a bet, Sam would put money on Lou wanting to spend the afternoon with her for his own purposes, and she wasn't sure quite how to deal with this.

It was all quite depressing to sit here, trying to force food down, when she really felt like creeping off somewhere and having a good cry. Sam wasn't used to feeling this way. It was all so new to her, these feelings roiling about inside her. A few days before, she wouldn't have cared a hoot whether some other girl had a prettier dress. Now it hurt in ways Sam could not define. It pained her to be snubbed by the others, to know that they were talking about her behind their hands.

More than anything else, it hurt to see Travis paying court to Nola, to see him smile tenderly down at her upturned face, to know that he was being so blasted charming to her, while he'd been so hateful toward Sam all this time. Butter wouldn't have melted in his mouth, she was sure, and it galled her to sit and wonder what sweet, honeyed words Travis was spouting that were bringing such a delightful glow to Nola's face.

And Nola—sweet, sarcastic Nola. Why did the

woman have to be so blamed beautiful! With her shining dark hair piled into an intricate coil upon her head, and her intriguing dark eyes, and her faultless olive complexion with those perfect features, she resembled a Spanish figurine. Every movement was so disgustingly graceful! Her teeth were even straight, for heaven's sake! Couldn't she have at least one fault, other than her catty nature to which Travis was undoubtedly oblivious, to make her seem more human?

Next to Nola, Sam felt absolutely shabby, something she'd never had to consider in the past. Her own lack of manners was glaringly evident, compared with Nola's. In fact, with the other woman as an example, Sam measured up as woefully inadequate in the female category, and it wasn't making her feel very kindly toward anyone, most particularly Travis and Nola.

The most disturbing thing, though, was the very fact that she was having these feelings at all! Why should she care who Travis Kincaid smiled at, who he devoted his attentions to? He was her enemy, her jailer! Good grief, she didn't even like him most of the time! Since the moment they'd met, he'd gone out of his way to be hateful to her, or so it seemed. That she had instigated at least half their arguments did not come into consideration at this point.

So why was she acting like a jealous idiot over him now? Why did each smile he sent toward Nola cut through her like a sharp knife? Why did her gaze keep returning to him time after time, as if eager for the very sight of him? Why did he suddenly seem so outrageously handsome, so undeniably desirable, mustache and all? Why were her palms sweating, and her heart beating so painfully in her breast?

If she could have read Travis's mind, Sam would have felt a great deal better, for he didn't care any more for the way Lou was fawning over Sam, than Sam liked the way he was behaving toward Nola. Every time he turned around, he found Lou hovering over Sam like a protective husband, and that silly grin plastered on Lou's face was enough to make a body ill! Travis wanted to tell the man what a fool he was making of himself. He wanted to march over to them and demand that Lou stop smiling at Sam that way, that he quit hovering over her so solicitously.

Travis found himself so preoccupied with keeping an eye on Sam and Lou that he barely heard a word Nola was saying to him. He nodded and made what he hoped were the appropriate responses. Hell, he could have been agreeing to almost anything and not known it!

Giving himself a mental shake, Travis tried to jerk himself back to the conversation, before it became obvious to everyone where his mind was dallying. And dallying it was! While Sam might not be decked out in a dress as fine or fancy as the other women's, or her hair done up in the latest fashion, she was a beguiling sight just as she was. The dress Elsie had bought for the girl was the slightest bit too snug across the bodice, and Sam's breasts strained enticingly against the fabric. No doubt Lou and half the male population of Tumble were also aware of this! The very thought set Travis's temper simmering!

The simple waistband only served to accentuate Sam's miniscule waist and the flare of her hips. Her long, red-gold tresses were a shining tangle down her back, making his fingers itch to comb themselves through the blazing mass. And those big, round dark eyes of hers, so like those of a fawn! A man could lose himself in those eyes and never care if he saw the light of day again! When it came to lips, Travis had never seen lips as full, as luscious, as downright tempting as Sam's. A woman shouldn't be allowed to have lips that alluring, or if she did, it should be against the law to display them in public! She should be made to go around in a veil, like they did in the Eastern countries!

Once more Travis yanked his wayward thoughts back from dangerous paths, wondering what on earth was wrong with him that he couldn't keep from thinking of Sam in this way, couldn't seem to stop desiring her. Today certainly wasn't the first time by any means, and probably not the last, but it still bothered him. Sweet hell, she bothered him more than he cared to admit. Just the thought of her sweet, naked body brought beads of sweat to his brow and made his trousers uncomfortably tight.

He had to keep reminding himself of the difference in their ages, of the fact that Sam was an outlaw, his prisoner. Besides, she despised him and made no bones about it! Still, with every fiber of his being, Travis wanted her, and he didn't want anyone else looking at her the way Lou Sprit was. He didn't want any other man smiling at her, or bringing a smile to her lips. Especially, he did not want anyone else to touch her.

Sam was fast becoming an obsession with him, like it or not, want it or not. Travis was afraid he was about to make a complete fool of himself over her before too long, and he didn't know what to do to prevent it, or even if he wanted to prevent it—and that scared him the most.

When the young deputy, Chas Brown, arrived at the gathering with a pretty young blonde on his arm, Sam suddenly discovered she was not as alone when it came to being snubbed as she'd thought. For some reason totally unknown to Sam, none of the church women wanted anything to do with Miss Winfrow. Even Elsie, who Sam thought extremely fair-minded, shunned her. A few of the men nodded hesitantly, then hastily resumed their conversations, but most behaved as though they had no idea who Molly Winfrow was.

It was all very awkward, and Sam felt sorry for both of them. Poor Chas turned red and glared at everyone, as if daring anyone to say a word, while Molly tugged at his arm and whispered frantically in his ear. Whatever she said to him, Chas's response was a vehement shake of his head. Without a word, he led his lady to the refreshment table and helped her fill her plate. Then, with a glance about, they headed toward the very table at which Sam and Lou were sitting.

"These seats taken?" Chas asked almost belligerently, with a hard look at Lou.

Lou shrugged indifferently. "Nope."

After seating them both, Chas turned to Sam. "Hello, Sam. How are things goin'?"

Sam rolled her eyes at him in disbelief. "Chas, ya

gonna tell me Kincaid didn't tell ya I tried to escape last night? Hell, I reckon this entire town heard about it within an hour."

"That's a fact," Lou admitted sheepishly. "We just didn't want to make a big fuss over it."

"Chas," Sam said, leaning forward a bit, "ain't ya gonna introduce us to your lady friend here?" This comment earned her a nudge and a frown from Lou, though she couldn't fathom why, and an odd look from Chas.

Chas seemed as if he were trying to decide if she were serious or kidding him. Deciding she was serious, he said, "Sam, I want ya to meet Molly Winfrow. Molly, this is Sam, er, Samantha Downing."

"Glad to meet ya, Molly," Sam told the woman with a sincere smile.

Molly, on the other hand, was a bit more reserved in her greeting, as if she still weren't sure of how to react. For a moment, Sam was under the impression the woman did not care to be associated with a criminal and meant to snub her, as some of the others had. Then, slowly, Molly shook her head and said with a regretful sigh, "Miss Downing, it's plain to see you don't have any idea who I am, or why the others don't want nothin' to do with me. Honey, I work at the Silver Nugget. I'm a whore."

Sam didn't bat an eyelash at this blunt announcement, though Chas flinched openly and Lou groaned out loud. To Molly's amazement, Sam's smile grew wider. "Is that all?" she asked with a husky laugh. "I'm an outlaw. Now, which of us do ya reckon will make it to hell first?"

This brought a genuine grin to Molly's face, making her even prettier than she'd seemed at first. A sharp burst of laughter erupted from Lou, and he slapped his thigh in delight. Chas relaxed and sent Sam a grateful smile. His relief was short-lived, however, for at that moment Travis joined their group.

"Chas, I'd like a word with you, if you don't mind," Travis said sternly, his sharp aqua gaze melting the smiles on all their faces. "Privately."

Not put off at all by his warning look, having been on the receiving end of them too long to be intimidated by them now, Sam blurted, "Travis, have you met Miss Winfrow?"

Lou shook his head at Sam and groaned again, waiting for the fireworks to start. Travis took him by surprise by replying almost pleasantly, "I'm well acquainted with Miss Winfrow, Sam." Turning to Molly, he said, "Afternoon, Molly. Nice to see you."

"Afternoon, Marshal," Molly muttered, ducking her head in embarrassment.

Travis's next remark was directed at Sam, along with a particularly pointed look. "Sam, I believe Elsie is looking for you."

Knowing what he was up to and not about to let him get away with it, Sam was deliberately obtuse. "Why would she be lookin' for me? I been sittin' in the same spot half the day, an' she's been by here four times, at last count."

She could almost hear Travis's teeth grating against each other as he ground out, "She wants to speak with you, Sam. Now!"

"Awright! Awright! Don't git your dander up!"

Sam barked back, scooting her chair back before Lou could assist her. "Molly, it's a pleasure meetin' ya."

Elsie was, indeed, waiting to speak with her. Drawing Sam aside, she hissed, "You're not to speak with that woman! She's a harlot!"

Shaking her head sadly, Sam looked the housekeeper in the eye and asked, "Does that make her any worse than most of us, Elsie? Most of all, me? I know I wasn't payin' much attention in church this mornin', but wasn't the parson preachin' about forgiveness an' such? Didn't he say the Lord Himself said, 'Let him who is without sin cast the first stone'? An' not a one o' them people throwed one rock, 'cause none o' them was lily-white, neither."

Elsie wasn't the only one to hear Sam's words, nor the only to one to bow her head in shame. In the hush surrounding her words, Sam realized this and blushed hotly, not knowing what else to say, but not ready to back down, either.

Once more, Alma Aldrich came to her aid. "You are quite right, Samantha, dear. I am often dismayed at how quick we are to condemn others, while we, ourselves, are not blameless." With that, the parson's wife determinedly headed for Molly's table, her shoulders as stiff and straight as those of any army general.

"Yes, but neither are we supposed to lie down with swine," Bertha Melbourn intoned loudly. "As my papa used to say, 'If you lie down with dogs, don't complain if you get up with fleas'!"

"Ahh," Parson Aldrich, responded quickly into the consenting murmur following Mrs. Melbourn's statement, "but our Lord Christ, according to the gospel of Saint Matthew, chapter nine, verse thirteen, says also, 'For I am not come to call the righteous, but sinners to repentance.' Now I ask you all, should we, as Christians, not follow our Lord's example? Should we not try to guide our fallen brothers and sisters along the path to righteousness, rather than always turning deaf ears to them?''

There weren't many who could squarely meet their neighbor's eye following that profound query. Placing his arm about Sam's shoulders, thus making her once again the unwilling object of attention, Parson Aldrich added, "This young woman is newly arrived among us. She, who is woefully ignorant of the Scriptures through no fault of her own, is the wisest among us today. She is like a babe, new to the world and the Word, yet even she can see that we are often too self-righteous to be good Christian missionaries."

From someone in the crowd came a murmured, "Out of the mouths of babes!" Another declared quietly, "Amen!"

Standing to one side, where he had urged Chas for a lecture on decorum, Travis stood in open-mouthed amazement. He'd been about to haul Chas over the coals for introducing Molly to Sam, thus ruining all his hopes of having Sam accepted by the community. Now, in the face of Sam's words and Pastor and Mrs. Aldrich's, what was he to say?

Somehow, in her own rather blackened innocence, Sam had made them all look like self-righteous prigs—and damn if she wasn't right! Even as he shook his head in bewilderment, Travis admitted a grudging admiration. Then he shivered as he wondered what other surprises Sam might have in store for them, particularly for him, in the future. She was turning out to be so blasted unpredictable that it made him shudder just thinking about it!

CHAPTER 11

"Oh, no, ya don't!" Sam told him, shaking her head and backing away from the handcuffs Travis held. "I ain't sleepin' on the floor by your bed like some trained dog no more!"

"Well, I'm certainly not stupid enough to offer you your old room back, at least not until I have a chance to get that broken window boarded up," Travis told her bluntly.

"What about Elsie?"

Travis cocked a golden brow her way. "What about her?"

"I could share. her room, if she didn't mind awful much."

At this, Travis smiled, not a gentle smile, but one of those devilish smiles that always set Sam's stomach tumbling. "No, Sam. I happen to know

Elsie sleeps very soundly. She wouldn't make a very good watchdog for the likes of you." Again he rattled the handcuffs at her. "That leaves me and my room. Sorry, Sam, but you brought this on yourself when you tried to escape."

Sam's chin came up defiantly, and she glared up at him. "Then grab a pillow an' sleep on the floor yourself, if ya have a mind to, Kincaid, but I'm sleepin' in that nice, soft bed tonight. Once I'm back with Pa an' the boys, Lord knows when I'll have the chance to enjoy a real bed again, so I might as well make good use of it while I kin."

Half-stunned, Travis stared at her. Finally he said, "Sam, I'm not giving up my bed."

"Fine," she retorted simply. At his questioning look, she added, "Nobody asked ya to. We kin share the bed, Kincaid. Makes me no never mind, either way."

Now Travis really was perplexed. If he'd suggested their sharing the bed, he was sure she would have thrown a screaming fit. But here she was, calmly suggesting just that, as if it were an everyday occurrence and not in the least odd or sinful. In fact, she was already starting to unbutton her dress, not at all concerned that he was standing there watching!

"Uh, Sam," Travis said slowly. Even to his own ears, his voice sounded extraordinarily husky, and he hastily cleared his throat. Reluctantly he dragged his gaze from the gaping bodice of her dress, concentrating in vain on her face. "In case you've forgotten, I sleep in the altogether."

There was a glint of mischief in her dark eyes, and a hint of a smile lurking at the corners of her mouth as she answered, "So do most of the folks I know. So do I, when I kin."

Her dress dropped to the floor. In her petticoat, Sam plopped nonchalantly onto the edge of the bed and began to unlace her shoes. As she bent forward, the top of the petticoat sagged, giving Travis an uninhibited view of a good portion of ripe, young breasts.

Travis sucked in his breath and cursed to himself. Blast it all, what was she trying to do to him? Surely she wasn't so naive as not to know what she was doing to him? How in blazes had he gotten himself into this mess? Better yet, how was he supposed to spend the night in the same bed with her and not avail himself of her? It had been bad enough sharing the same room with her last night, and he'd barely gotten a wink of sleep just knowing she was within arm's reach. This would be ten times worse! This was like offering heaven to a hell-bound man!

Suddenly an idea occurred to him. "Sam, how long did you talk with Molly Winfrow this afternoon, and what did she tell you?" Surely that had something to do with Sam's actions tonight!

Casting a glance in his direction, Sam tugged at the second shoe. "Not long. Why?"

"What did she say to you?"

The second shoe off, Sam reached for the top of one long black stocking, baring most of one leg to his fascinated gaze. Lord, but the girl had the longest, shapeliest legs! Travis had to use all his inner strength to concentrate on her words as Sam answered calmly, "She told me she worked at the Silver Nugget as a whore, an' that was why the other women didn't want to be around her."

Now she was absently rolling the other stocking down, and Travis could feel the heat searing through him. "What else did she say?"

Curiosity and exasperation mixed in the look she threw him. "Why are you so goldurned nosy all of a sudden? She didn't say nothin' else, 'cause ya walked up about then an' made me leave. Now, does that satisfy you?"

His eyes narrowed to blue-green slits as he studied her face. She met his look squarely, not giving an inch. Then she stood and stretched like a cat, arching up on tiptoes and reaching both arms toward the ceiling. Her breasts strained at the muslin. Her earthy moan of pleasure covered his groan of agony, as his body responded to hers.

"I been wantin' to do this all day, but I'd of split the seams right out o' that dress," she commented lazily, as she let her body relax once more. "And those shoes are jest as uncomfortable as they look. See here, where they rubbed right through the socks!"

As she bent to indicate a spot on her ankle, Travis almost lost his composure. Was Sam being deliberately provocative or just her natural, artless self? Either way, it was playing havoc with his senses. Travis felt as randy as a goat, the front of his trousers about to burst open on their own!

"Sam! For heaven's sake, show a little modesty, will you? I can practically see—uh—er . . ." Travis's voice trailed off as Sam reached for the hem of the petticoat and unconcernedly peeled it upward and off. As she tossed it to the floor, Travis grabbed her nightshift and threw it at her. "Here!" he ground out gruffly, his voice sounding like a bullfrog's. "Get into this and into bed by the time I come back."

He stomped from the room, slamming the door in his wake. He was halfway down the stairs when he swore he heard soft laughter coming from his room.

Though Sam had been sound asleep by the time Travis finally crept quietly into bed, they awoke the next morning with arms and legs entwined like strands of old knitting yarn. Sam was lying half over him, her nose tucked into his neck, puffs of warm breath tickling his skin with each exhaled breath. One of her arms was draped over his chest, while his was wrapped about her waist, his hand clutching a wad of nightgown covering her bottom. A section of the bedsheet was trapped between them, having first wrapped itself about them until they resembled two mummies in one tangled wrapping.

One of Travis's feet was securely locked into the twisted sheet at the end of the bed, and he was afraid to guess where his other foot might be. He was, however, excruciatingly aware of where Sam's knee was lodged. It was nudging his manhood, and he could only pray she would not awaken with a jerk, or he would be walking stooped over for several days to come.

Travis was still contemplating the best manner of extricating himself when Sam yawned and began to stretch awake. The threatening knee nuzzled closer, brushing up over him in an exquisite caress, then down again. A deep groan tore from his throat, and he squeezed his eyes shut, praying for strength. Slowly releasing a ragged breath, he opened his eyes to find Sam staring sleepily down at him. Her eyes were soft and slumberous, her hair streaming wild and loose over her shoulders, the strands teasing his bare chest.

If he had expected her to pull away and blush with maidenly embarrassment, Travis was doomed to disappointment. Of course, Sam hardly ever did the expected. She blinked sleepily at him, took note of the situation and their position, and grinned impishly at him. "Guess I should have warned ya I'm a bed hog," she murmured, her voice slightly raspy yet. "By the time I was three, Billy refused to share the same bunk with me. Said I stole all the covers every night."

Travis stared up at her, for once at a loss for words. Finally, he muttered, "I think I know how he must have felt." He was about to suggest that they try to untangle themselves as carefully as possible, when there came a sharp rap at the bedroom door.

"Travis!" Elsie called from the other side. "Travis? You awake? Jim Hastings just rode into town with a bullet hole in him, and Doc says—" Elsie's words gave way to a sharp gasp of dismay as she opened the door to assure herself that Travis was inside and listening, since he hadn't yet answered her summons. The housekeeper's mouth hung open, working ineffectually for several seconds before it snapped shut again. Her eyes widened as they traveled over the two in the bed, taking note of their intimate position. Color suffused her stiffening features.

With effort, she gathered her ruffled dignity, and huffed. "Well, I see I'll have to be a mite more careful about opening doors in the future around here! Still, it is an emergency! Doc wants you over at his place right away—if you can drag yourself away from your morning amusements, Marshal!"

She backed out of the doorway, pulling the door shut as she went. "Wait! Elsie! It's not the way it looks! Elsie!" Travis was shouting to himself, because Elsie was not staying to listen.

Mortified, it did Travis no good to discover Sam still lying over him, trying to stifle her giggles against his chest. "Damn it all! It's not funny!" he growled, trying to untangle himself.

In his hurry, he hopped from the bed and promptly fell to the floor, one leg dragging covers and Sam with him. She landed square on his chest, and the air whooshed from his lungs as her knee connected solidly with his stomach. "Ugh!"

It took a moment for the stars to stop circling in his head, but when they did, he pushed Sam from atop him and eyed her with disgust. "Will you stop laughing like some crazy hyena?" he demanded, watching as she brushed tears of mirth from her cheeks. "Hang it, girl! Don't you know the trouble you've caused?"

This served to douse her humor instantly. "I've caused?" she shrieked. "I've caused? Look, you dandified idiot! I ain't the one who insisted we share this room to start with, so don't go blamin' me for the way things are now. B'sides, what's all the hollerin' about, anyway?"

He stared at her in astonishment, as if she'd gone daft. "What's all the hollering about?" he repeated stupidly. "Can't you guess?" By now, Travis had untangled himself from the covers, located his trousers, and was poking his legs into them, while

Sam lay watching as if this were an everyday event for them.

"Well, I reckon it's Elsie findin' us tied up in bed together."

"Very good, Sam!" he grumbled sarcastically, hopping up and down as he tugged on his boots. "In case it's never been pointed out to you, nice young ladies do not bed down with men who are not their husbands! Decent folk frown on that sort of thing around here!"

"It's not as if we did anythin'!" she retorted, hiking herself up from the floor and straightening the skirt of her nightgown.

"That's beside the point! Besides, who would ever believe it if we claimed our innocence?"

"And how are they gonna find out, Kincaid? Who's to know, unless you go shootin' your mouth off all over town? As soon as we explain things to Elsie, she'll calm down, an' I really don't think she's the sort to go blabbin' everything she knows, anyway, even if she doesn't believe us."

Travis finished buckling his gunbelt around his waist. "You still don't understand, do you?" he sighed in exasperation, tossing her a dark look. "It's simply beyond you to distinguish between right and wrong, what's moral and what's not, isn't it? Sam, it doesn't matter that nothing happened between us, it's still not right for a woman to sleep with a man she isn't married to."

"I don't see why it makes a difference for a woman, when men do it all the time an' nobody seems to think that's so awful wrong," she answered poutingly.

"Well, I don't have time to explain it to you

now," he said stiffly. "Just take my word for it. That's the way it is, the way it always has been, and the way it always will be." He headed for the door, adding, "If word of this gets out, your reputation will be in shreds, and mine won't look any too good, either!"

"I'd say my reputation is pretty well shot to hell, anyway," she called after him as he walked from the room, "but yours is a horse of another color." She scurried after him, catching him just as he was about to leave the house. Leaning over the banister, she deliberately eyed the front of his trousers and said with a smirk, "It might help appearances some, though, if ya button up your pants b'fore you go, Marshal, and quit wavin' that thing around like a flag at a parade!"

Altogether, it was a terrible day! Elsie was angry, and it took quite a bit of explaining on Sam's part, since Travis was not there to help, before the woman finally calmed down enough to listen. At last Elsie relented, deciding to believe Sam's avowal that nothing had happened between the girl and the marshal.

"I tell you, Sam, I was mightily shocked when I opened that door to find the two of you together like that, and I couldn't decide which of you had disappointed me the worst."

Sam hid her hurt deep inside, but could not help but ask, "Would it've been so awful if we had done somethin', Elsie? After all, the marshal ain't exactly the ugliest duck I've seen."

Eyeing her thoughtfully, Elsie said slowly, "No, he isn't, and you are a very lovely young woman, but that is beside the point. Decent people do not fall into bed without being married to one another. It just isn't proper."

"Oh, horse feathers! Nothin' I do is proper, anyway, an' most likely never will be!" Sam exclaimed in exasperation. "It ain't proper to wear pants! It ain't proper to swear! It ain't proper to smoke or drink or play cards! It ain't proper to belch out loud, or to wipe your mouth on your sleeve! Hell's fire, nothin' that's useful or fun is proper in this here town! Why, it's a wonder y'all think it's proper to use the outhouse!"

Things went quickly from bad to worse, especially when Travis returned before noon to grab a quick bite to eat and pack a few things in his saddle bags. "I've got to ride out and scout the area where Jim Hastings was shot," he told them grimly. "I don't know how long I'll be, so Chas will be by in a few minutes to look after Sam." Left unspoken were the words, "So she won't escape." She was well enough to do so now, and they were all aware of how easy it would be for her to elude Elsie if she got the chance.

"How is Jim?" Elsie asked hesitantly.

"He'll live. He took a bullet in the side, and lost a lot of blood, but Doc says he's going to be fine." A dark look came over Travis's face as he added, "Jim thinks it was the Downings who attacked him. Luckily, he managed to stay on his horse and make it to town."

"No!" Sam blurted, shock and disbelief written across her features. "No! Pa would never do such a thing, an' he wouldn't let the boys, neither! He don't believe in shootin' down innocent folk!"

"Sam, for God's sake, grow up, will you?" Travis shouted, whirling on her. "Your family aren't saints! They're nothing but a bunch of bandits!" His eyes flashed at her like brilliant turquoise lightning.

He might as well have slapped her. His words cut through her like a sharp sword, the pain surprising her in its intensity. Unwanted tears swam in her eyes, but she blinked them back and lashed out at him with harsh words of her own, her back as stiff as a ramrod and her face a mask of pride and anger. "You think, jest 'cause you're the marshal of this one-horse town, that you're so high and mighty! Well, let me tell you a thing or two, mister! We Downings might be outlaws, but we got our own code o' honor, an' we abide by it! We don't go gunnin' down jest anybody for no reason! We don't steal from poor folk, we don't betray kin, and we don't backstab our friends!"

Neither of them said another word to each other after that, though Travis did warn Elsie to keep a sharp eye on Sam. All of Tumble, it seemed, was up in arms again over this latest episode, ready and eager to hang any Downing they could lay their hands on. Tempers were high, and common sense low, and the best thing for Sam to do was stay out of sight and mind until things cooled down a bit.

Within minutes Travis was gone. Chas came soon thereafter, followed almost immediately by Nola Sandoval. "This just makes my day!" Sam groused irritably. "Tell her I don't need her help, nor want it, neither," she pleaded with Elsie. "Make her go away. If there's one person I don't need to see today, it's her!"

Personally, Elsie agreed, though she didn't say

so. Travis had asked Nola here, and it wasn't her place to tell the woman to leave. "Now, Sam, you're upset, and rightly so, but we can't be impolite to Travis's guest. Truth be told, there's probably a lot Miss Sandoval can teach you, if you just listen to her and take note. She might appear a bit uppity at times but she is a proper lady."

"There's that word again!" Sam grumped. "And Miss Sandoval ain't all lady, neither. I'd lay odds on that!"

Chas, who was listening avidly to this exchange, asked with raised brows, "What is she then, Sam?"

"Mostly witch, I'd say." Then she flashed a smile at him and Elsie, "And I hope ya know I'm watchin' my cursin' when I say that!"

Elsie stifled a giggle. "Miss Tucker would be proud of you, Sam."

Nola, none too pleased to find Travis gone, took her spite out on Sam. "Good heavens!" she exclaimed snootily. "How can Travis stand to have you around? I have never met anyone less feminine or with fewer manners than you!" Looking down her aristocratic nose at the younger girl, she sniffed in disgust. "Why, it will take a miracle to transform you! It will be like trying to make a silk purse out of a sow's ear, and everyone knows that is impossible to do. To begin with, you simply lack breeding!"

In remarkable parody of her reluctant tutor, Sam wrinkled her own nose. "Breedin's for horses and cattle and married folk, so I've been told. I got no need for breedin' lessons, Miss Sandoval, and I don't think that's what the marshal had in mind for you to teach me, neither."

From his chair in the corner of the room, Chas smothered a chuckle, earning himself a chastising look from Nola. Elsie quickly hid a grin as she placed a tray with tea and cookies on the low table in front of the divan, and hurriedly left the room.

"Well," Nola sighed, "I suppose we might begin with the proper way to serve tea, since Mrs. Willow has seen fit to provide it."

"Mrs. Willow?" Sam asked. Then her brow cleared. "Oh, you mean Elsie."

"One does not address one's servants by their given names, Miss Downing. Neither does one allow a servant to address oneself in so familiar a manner."

"Travis does," Sam pointed out.

"Which is undoubtedly why he has employed me to teach you proper decorum," came the haughty reply.

Privately, Sam wondered just how Travis intended to pay sweet Nola for her efforts. The thought rankled more than it should have.

Several minutes later, Sam sat feeling extremely ridiculous, her pinky extended in the manner Nola had demonstrated. "This is downright silly!" she jeered. "Why, it's a wonder a body don't poke his own eye out, tryin' to drink this way!"

"Silly or not, it is the proper way, so just do it!" Nola snapped, her patience severely strained. "And sip your tea, dear girl. Do not gulp it or make those disgusting slurping noises, if you please! You sound like a hog at a trough!"

"You should know," Sam muttered low.

Nola's eyes narrowed. "What was that?"

"Nothin' important," Sam assured her. "Jest clearin' my throat."

"Then do so more quietly, please, as a lady would."

Looking the woman directly in the eye, Sam smiled with false sweetness. "Tell me, Miss Sandoval, do you ever break wind, or don't ladies never do that, neither?"

To Sam's immense satisfaction, Nola turned bright red and, in her haste to swallow a mouthful of tea, began to choke. Tea spewed from her mouth, splattering the front of her dress, as she sputtered helplessly. In his corner, Chas doubled up with laughter, howls of mirth shaking his entire body. He was incapable of coming to Nola's aid, even had he been so inclined. From the hallway outside the parlor door, Sam heard Elsie snorting with unbecoming glee. It was the brightest moment of Sam's entire disheartening afternoon.

CHAPTER 12

Travis was definitely not in the best of moods that evening. After getting back into town, he'd gone to the hardware store and bought a pane of glass with which to repair Sam's broken bedroom window—the last piece of glass large enough to fit. As luck would have it, the thing broke as they were loading it into the bed of the wagon, and it would take at least two weeks to order another and for it to arrive.

So, he'd come home with a load of lumber instead, muttering darkly to himself and glaring at everyone. With much banging and grumbling, he then proceeded to board up both of Sam's bedroom windows. As fast as Sam was recovering, Travis did not want to chance another middle-of-the-night escape attempt. However, within two hours, the small airless room was as hot as an oven, impossible even to breathe in, let alone sleep there.

In defeat, with obvious ill humor, Travis dragged the mattress from Sam's bed into his own room and flung it onto the floor next to his bed. "Put some fresh bedding on that!" he ordered Sam with a growl. It was the only alternative he could think of, short of sharing his own bed with her and most probably awaking to find her draped all over him again. That kind of temptation he could do without!

With a sharp shake of her head that sent her loose, copper hair flying across her shoulders, Sam said slyly, "Not if you're thinkin' I'm gonna sleep there, chained to your bedpost like some dadburned slave. Now, if you intend to use that mattress yourself, I'll be right happy to make up your new bed for ya."

His temper was hanging by a thin thread. Through gritted teeth, Travis told her, "Sam, I'm not going through another scene like we had this morning. Not only was it improper, but it will most likely take a good week to soothe Elsie's ruffled feathers again. We can't sleep together, at least not in the same bed, and that is all there is to that!"

"Suits me fine, Mr. Fancy-pants Marshal!" Sam retorted smartly, her eyes narrowed into dark slits. "I ain't too fond of sharin' my sheets with you, neither! But I ain't sleepin' on the floor!"

"All right!" he roared, glaring daggers at her. "I'll take the blasted floor, then. Will that satisfy you, you hateful little baggage?"

He looked so put out that Sam almost laughed. Only good sense made her bite back her giggles.

"And no handcuffs! I can't sleep with those things clankin' all night, an' my arm twisted up like that."

His eyes flamed blue-green, his long fingers flexing as if itching to clamp about her slim neck. "You just don't know when to stop, do you, Sam?" he asked in that soft, menacing way of his. Then, though it pained him, he conceded the final victory to her. "Luckily, I sleep lightly, and those bedsprings squeak loudly enough, that we can do without the handcuffs. Now—will you put the blasted sheets on the blasted mattress so I can try to get some sleep sometime tonight?"

She grinned openly at him then, daring his temper yet again. "Ya know, Marshal, ya really should learn to curse right, if ya aim to do it at all. It jest might help ya get rid of some of that orneriness buildin' up inside o' ya."

He made a strangled sound in his throat, his hands forming tight fists as he glared at her. Swinging about on his heel, he tromped from the room, slamming the bedroom door so hard that a picture flew off the wall onto the floor. A few seconds later, from somewhere downstairs, she heard his muffled, "Damn!"

Nola tattled, Travis ranted, Elsie sighed long and loud, and Sam sulked. This was the pattern of their lives for the next week and more. Each day, either Nan Tucker or Nola Sandoval appeared on the doorstep, sometimes overlapping one another's visits. Nola was scheming enough, however, to time most of her visits at a time when Travis was sure to be home.

The woman was the most devious, two-faced female Sam had ever met or ever hoped to encounter. When Travis was around to see and hear, Nola was charm itself, though even then her condescending attitude was hard to take. When he was gone, however, she was as hateful as a riled snake, venom in every word and action.

Still, Sam suffered valiantly through her lessons —why she couldn't say. Surely, she told herself, it was not to impress Travis Kincaid, who was being almost as nasty as Nola these days, when he even spoke to her at all. As far as Sam was concerned, Elsie was the only decent human being around the house, with the possible exception of Nan Tucker, for despite herself Sam was coming to like the mousy little schoolmarm. In rare moments, Sam even found herself enjoying some of Miss Tucker's laborious lessons.

This was not the case with Nola's lessons, however. Sam was made to walk the length of the parlor repeatedly, a book balanced upon her head, while Nola sat supreme in a chair, sipping tea and criticizing Sam's every step. "Keep your back straight, I said!" she would harp. "No, do not look at the floor. Keep your eyes straight ahead of you! You don't need to see what your feet are doing!"

"Books was meant to be read not carted about on a person's head!" Sam complained loudly.

"Sit with your knees together, if you please. How many times do I have to tell you the same things! Good Lord, but you are dense!"

Many were the times Sam was forced to bite her tongue to keep from uttering a scathing reply and telling Nola what she thought of her. Just when she thought she could bear it no longer, a sharp look from Travis would silence her. Never was there a word of encouragement from him, or a compliment on her progress from Nola, not that Sam really expected any. Only Elsie and Miss Tucker were kind enough to tell her how nicely she was doing.

"Now that I have taught your little charge how to walk properly, you really ought to do something about getting her some clothes that fit, Travis," Nola complained one day. "It is positively indecent the way her bodices gape open! Doesn't the girl own a corset?"

Hearing this, Elsie had to chuckle. She was sure Nola could have cared less if Sam wore a flour sack, as long as so much attention was not called to the girl's enticing figure. To anyone with eyes, it was plain to see that Nola was green with jealousy. If not for the fact that it threw Nola into almost constant contact with Travis, the woman would have long since refused to tutor Sam in any way.

Indeed, Travis had noticed the impudent way Sam's breasts thrust forward, especially with Nola insisting that she walk with her shoulders back and her head up. Her ripe, young figure was a pleasure to behold, and at the same time causing him untold moments of discomfort and lust. "I'll see to it, Nola," he consented, bowing to Nola's demands.

"Now wait a dad-burned minute!" Sam howled. "Ya—uh—you ain't—uh—aren't trussin' me up in no—er—any corset!" In spite of all Sam's resistance, Nan Tucker's lessons were taking hold in Sam's mind, reflecting more and more in her speech.

Travis glared at her, not saying a word. Beside him, but not within his direct sight, Nola smirked. "While we're about this impossible task, someone really should do something about that unruly mane of hair, too," Nola suggested, pressing her advantage. "She resembles some wild forest creature, with it flying about her face like that. If she can't learn to tame it back into a decent braid, or a demure bun, it should be cut to a more manageable length."

"No!" The word tore from Travis's throat before he even thought about it. "No," he repeated more evenly, but firmly. "You can try different styles, if you like, to see what suits her best, but not one strand is to be cut." His piercing eyes leveled themselves at Nola. "Not one inch," he stressed. "I hope I make myself clear, because if I find otherwise, you will both regret the day."

Sam already regretted her days or most of them. She learned to sit, to stand, to walk like a lady, to temper her usual long, boyish stride. She was taught how to eat, how to drink, how to chew her food, how to take small sips and bites. Along with this, how to handle her eating utensils properly, how to place her napkin across her lap, and to fold it neatly when she was done. There came the inevitable lessons on how to dress, and how to wear her hair, though her unruly locks tended to escape the most rigid hairstyle. Charming little wisps invariably sprang loose to cling about her face and nape in caressing curls, softening Sam's face despite all of Nola's efforts to the contrary.

When it came to sewing, Elsie and Nola, the most unlikely of allies, joined forces. While Elsie taught her the basics of cutting and measuring cloth, of making dress patterns and judging size, Nola attempted to teach her more intricate crochet stitches and delicate embroidery.

At this, Sam was hopeless! One would have

thought she had twice the normal number of fingers and thumbs! The yarn assumed a life of its own and always tangled beyond redemption; the embroidery thread became a rainbow-colored series of knots. Even Elsie finally had to admit that Sam was lethal with a set of knitting needles in her hands. "I hate to say it honey, but you'd better stick to the crochet hook before you mortally injure yourself or someone else."

Sam's first dress had an uneven hem and one sleeve three inches longer than the other. The collar was sewn inside out, and the buttonholes were randomly spaced and looked as if a mouse had gnawed on them. Still, it was the first garment she had ever sewn, and she was inordinately proud of it once it was done, though she thoroughly detested the actual effort of sewing the thing. Taking pity on her, Elsie helped Sam remedy her mistakes, at least to the point where Sam could wear it in public without garnering strange looks.

With renewed confidence, Sam then decided to crochet Travis a pair of socks with much the same result. This time, however, it was Travis who was forced to wear the mismatched pair, one much too long and the other so short the top barely covered his ankle. But wear them he did—not merely out of pride for Sam's efforts, if not the results—but because Elsie threatened to let Sam make him a new pair of trousers if he didn't! The thought of the probable maiming of his precious manhood was enough to make him cower!

If sewing was Sam's downfall, at least her cooking was improving. Under Elsie's patient guidance, this was one lesson Sam truly enjoyed. Unlike the sewing, this was an accomplishment she could carry with her once she rejoined her family, and Sam threw herself into it enthusiastically. Oh, she made a good many mistakes at first, but Travis valiantly ate her burnt offerings, the lumpy potatoes, and the half-cooked carrots. Little did she know that he'd begun praying devoutly each morning, asking God in all His mercy, not to let him die of indigestion or poisoning.

However, there at last came the day when Sam cooked an entire supper all on her own. In fact, she was so confident that she shooed Elsie out of the kitchen and refused even to tell the housekeeper what she was preparing. "It's a surprise," was all she would say.

By the time Travis came home that evening, tantalizing smells were wafting from the kitchen. Sniffing appreciatively, Travis smelled apple-cinnamon pie, and fresh-baked bread, but try as he might he could not identify the aroma of the particular meat Sam was preparing. Whatever it was was spiced with chili peppers and lots of onion.

"What is Sam cooking?" he asked Elsie.

Elsie shook her head. "It's a surprise, for both of us. Sam won't even let me peek into the kitchen."

"Then how did you manage to make sure she didn't escape?"

"Only Sam could make that much noise in a kitchen," Elsie told him with a shake of her head. "And she's been rattling pots and pans since noon."

Travis's stomach was rumbling with hunger long before Sam called them to the table. Once seated, he still was not entirely certain what she had fixed, but he hated to hurt her feelings by asking. It looked like pork, with some sort of chili sauce over it and little potatoes. It both looked and smelled delicious, and he told her so.

"Well, dig in!" Sam said with a pleased smile. "I think you're really gonna like this."

The meal was every bit as good as it appeared, but though the meat looked like pork, it did not taste like pork. It was hard to tell what it was, with the spicy sauce covering it, but halfway through his dinner, Travis suddenly had an awful thought. Carefully setting his fork aside, Travis asked quietly, "Sam, what is this meat we are eating?"

"I wondered when you'd ask that," she said with a grin. "It's somethin' I learned to cook when we were down by the border for a spell, the one thing I was sure not to ruin. It's armadillo."

Travis gagged, and Elsie's face took on a ghastly green cast. "What's the matter?" Sam questioned in confusion. "Lots of folks eat armadillo, and you were both enjoyin' it b'fore I told you what it was."

"And where, may I ask, did you manage to lay hands on this particular animal?" Travis croaked.

"Oh, I've had him staked out for over a week now, just layin' for the little varmint," Sam announced proudly. "Every mornin', comin' back from the outhouse, I've seen him scurry under the back porch. I finally caught him this mornin'."

Travis swung pitiful eyes in Elsie's direction, seeking comfort and commiseration. "Army!" he moaned pathetically. "She's cooked Army!"

"And we ate him!" Elsie nodded sickly.

Suddenly Travis bolted from his chair and dashed for the back door, Elsie close behind. Completely befuddled, Sam followed, but stopped when she heard the two of them retching. "Well, if that don't beat all!" she sighed, shaking her head. "Guess I shouldn't have told 'em what it was. They sure liked it well enough before they knew. Some folks are just downright squeamish!"

Before long, the two of them shuffled into the kitchen, pale and shaken. Sinking weakly into a chair, Travis pointed an accusing finger at Sam. "You!" he growled, glaring balefully. "You did that on purpose, just for spite! I know you did!"

"Well, how was I to know the two of you had such weak stomachs?" Sam grumbled, still not understanding. Disappointment and hurt mingled on her face. "All I did was try to fix a decent meal for you! I thought you'd be proud of me, finally cookin' somethin' without burnin' it!"

"All you did," he shrieked like someone demented, "was kill my prize-winning armadillo! Army was the fastest little racer in three counties, and you cooked him!"

"Now, Travis, be fair!" Elsie put in weakly, alarmed at the purple hue of his face, and the way his fingers clenched as he stared at Sam. "The girl had no idea the animal was a pet."

"I was training him for the big Fourth of July race coming up, and he was sure to win again this year," Travis lamented, laying his head down upon crossed arms. "Elsie, he's won two years straight!"

"I know, dear. I know."

Sam was dumbfounded, and suddenly feeling very guilty. "Travis, I'm so sorry! I honestly didn't know!"

She reached out to touch his arm, but he threw her off. "Oh, you knew all right!" he accused. "It was your way of getting back at me! God, you have got to be the meanest-hearted woman this side of the Mississippi!"

"Hell's fire!" she exploded. "How was I to know you kept such a danged fool critter for a pet? You never told me, and it's not like he was a cat or a dog, so's I could tell right off!"

Travis was so upset that he went for a long walk while Elsie and Sam cleared the table of poor, departed Army's remains. When he returned, he found Elsie in the kitchen, finishing up the last of the dishes. Sam was on the back porch, sitting on the top step and whittling on a piece of wood. Settling down beside her, Travis said quietly, "I'm sorry I yelled at you. It was an honest mistake on your part. I know that. It just came as such a shock. I apologize, Sam. Forgive me."

She pointed toward a small, flowering bush in the yard. "That's where I buried him." Then she handed him the piece of wood. It was fashioned in a cross, with the word "ARMY" carved into it. "Here. I'll leave you to do the final honors."

Her gesture touched him deeply, almost bringing tears to his eyes. "Sam," he murmured, tracing the wooden cross with his fingertips. But when he looked up, he was alone on the step, with only the creaking of the back door to tell him she had gone.

The wind whipped at the bedsheet with such force that it was almost torn from the clothesline. One wet corner snapped angrily at Sam's thigh. "Ouch! Dad-burned thing!" she yelled, backing off and rubbing at her smarting leg. She and Elsie had done the laundry together, another of Sam's recent domestic lessons, and now Sam was left alone in the back yard to hang it while Elsie prepared lunch.

Since that awful evening when Sam had served Army up on a platter, she had refused to prepare another meal. It had been three days, with Elsie constantly trying to convince her otherwise, but Sam was adamant. She had enough problems trying to deal with Travis right now without adding more.

As she struggled with the wet clothes, Sam's mind drifted. If her days of constant tutelage were torment, the nights had become pure hell. Sam was still sharing Travis's room, and it was becoming a unique kind of torture for both of them.

Every night, as she lay near Travis in the quiet, dark room, sleep eluded her. Beneath closed lids, she could visualize the long, clean lines of his naked body, so near and yet so far, and her own skin would begin to burn as if with a raging fever. Her heart would race, and her breathing would become erratic. It was all she could do to keep from squirming, as her every sensitive nerve came to life and yearned toward his. She wanted him with a desire that threatened to set the bedsheets aflame, and she wondered that he hadn't noticed her restlessness and commented nastily upon it yet.

The early-summer nights were hot, and within seconds, it seemed, the sheets were clammy, her nightshirt sticking to her like a damp rag. At any other time, she would have torn the thing off and flung it to the floor, but now, with Travis lying on the floor next to her, wrapped only in a thin sheet from the waist down, it would have been like throwing fat on a fire. He was so unpredictable these days, so touchy! There was no telling what he might do. Sam, who rarely feared anything, suddenly found herself reluctant to face his anger.

Each night they lay there, saying nothing, while the tension built between them until she could almost reach out and touch it. That he, too, found sleep elusive was small comfort.

Sam didn't even try to joke with him anymore or to cajole him out of his bad humor in the mornings. In silence, Sam would wait until Travis had dressed and gone downstairs before getting out of bed. The one morning she had leapt from the covers and begun dressing when he did, he had almost shouted the rafters off of the house, yelling at her about being indecent and decadent beyond belief.

Since then, she had stayed in bed, her nightshift tucked demurely about her, while she unabashedly and deliberately watched him dress. She didn't even try to hide her interest in his splendidly muscled body. Neither did she peek out from beneath lowered lashes, or stare in wide-eyed shock, or blush in maidenly modesty. She simply watched with frank appreciation.

Travis found her bold appraisal unsettling, even while it was complimentary. "Do you enjoy being a voyeur, Sam?" he asked one morning.

"A voy—a what?"

"A blasted peeping tom!" he explained, turning his back to her as he buttoned his pants.

Her husky laugh sent delightful shivers down his spine. When he turned to face her, Sam's eyes were alight with mirth. "More like a she-cat, in my case, I reckon, an' it'd be a little hard not to notice what's right in front of my nose, Kincaid."

"A lady would turn her back and close her eyes," he countered with a frown.

"A gentleman wouldn't strut around naked in front of her to start with," Sam shot back impudently.

Silence followed her remark. Finally, he said, "I don't strut."

"Oh, you surely do, Marshal," she giggled. "You strut like a full-feathered cock pheasant lookin' to impress the hens."

He'd speared her with those intense turquoise eyes, and asked in a low, seductive tone that sent tingles through her, "And are you impressed, Sam?" His penetrating gaze slid down to where the tips of her breasts were thrusting against her nightshift, evidence of her own arousal.

When his gaze at last returned to hers, she met it boldly. "I'm no saint, Travis, and I'm no angel. For all your tryin', you still have a ways to go just to make a lady of me. But, I am a woman, an' I know what I like. Yes," she said, her voice sliding over him like warm honey, "I surely do know what I like."

Now, as Sam stood in the hot yard hanging clothes, she fought her own confusion. This morning, she had opened her eyes to find Travis standing next to the bed, staring down at her. Try as she might, she could not decipher his odd mood or his serious look. Before she could guess what he was about to do, he leaned down and drew her up against him, enclosing her and supporting her in his strong arms.

Without a word, he lowered his head and kissed her. His warm lips plied over hers, caressing and demanding, and stealing her breath away! Hers melted beneath his, welcoming him intuitively, without thought or delay. When his tongue sought entry, her lips parted in natural compliance. Lightning danced in her veins as his tongue slid into her mouth, insistently invading, to begin a fiery dance with hers.

Somehow, of their own, her arms had come up and twined about his neck, locking him to her even more firmly. Her fingers delved into his crisp blond hair, as his entwined in hers. Through the thin cotton of her nightshift, her breasts tingled with pleasure, her aching nipples seeking contact with the thick, springy hair on his chest. With a moan of intense longing, her body arched artlessly into the curve of his.

A deep groan tore from him, and Travis drew back, releasing her lips momentarily. Sam drew in a ragged breath, her head spinning dizzily. Then his teeth were nibbling delicately at her lower lip, his hands brushing along her back and sides, edging ever nearer her breasts. "Sam!" he murmured throatily. "Sam!"

Then she giggled. She couldn't help it! Of all things, she'd never considered how ticklish her lips were, especially to the brush of a mustache against them. Now she knew, and combined with all the other delicious sensations racing through her, it was too much! She dissolved into helpless laughter, at the same time trying to suck her lips tightly together to allay the erotic tingling.

The mood was broken. As she lay tucked beneath him, Travis glared down at her, his eyes glittering with indignation. "Why not share the joke, Sam?" he demanded stiffly.

With shaking fingers, she scrubbed vigorously at her lips in an effort to bring normal feeling to them again. Travis, thinking she was attempting to rub the touch of his lips from hers, flung himself from the bed and began to pull on his clothes, his every movement seething with anger and wounded male pride.

"Travis!" Sam pleaded. "I'm sorry. I didn't mean to laugh, but your mustache was ticklin' me somethin' fierce."

He shot her a menacing glare. "I've never had any complaints before," he retorted heatedly.

"Well, I've never kissed a man with a mustache before, either," she explained. "I guess it came as sort of a surprise."

"Don't worry your head over it," he snapped. "It won't happen again. It shouldn't have happened in the first place." In a matter of minutes, Travis was back to being the staid, stern marshal, putting duty first.

"Why not?" she asked quietly.

"Why not, what?"

"Why shouldn't it have happened?"

"Because you're my prisoner, Sam, and I should have more sense than to lose my head like that. It was all my fault, and I'm sorry."

Nothing could have been more deflating to Sam than to have him apologize for having kissed her. "Are you sayin' you're sorry you kissed me, or sorry you liked it?" she demanded to know.

"Both, I guess," he answered with a wry smile and a shake of his head.

Shaking out another towel, Sam pinned it to the line with barely-suppressed fury. She'd dressed and come down to find Travis had wolfed down his breakfast and was heading out the door for his office. Halfway down the stairs, she'd heard him call back to Elsie. "By the way, I forgot to tell you. You don't have to fuss over tomorrow's dinner. You and Sam have whatever you like. I've been invited to Sunday supper at the Sandovals', and I'll probably be late getting back."

As he reached for the door handle, he'd stopped, shooting a cold look over his shoulder at Sam. He'd meant for her to hear him, had known she was standing there all the while. Travis had consciously and deliberately hurt her.

Now Sam was mad at herself as well as Travis, for she suddenly realized how much she had let this arrogant lawman get under her skin. Somehow, someplace along the line, she had come to like him, come to admire him, come to look forward to his company and even the many arguments they shared. During the last few weeks, he'd become important to her in so many ways, to the point where a sharp word or look could cut her to the bone and leave her aching. That kiss this morning had shaken her whole world. Desire had exploded through her, blinding her to everything but her need for him.

But now the blinders were off, and Sam could see clearly and what she saw scared her. She was perilously close to losing her heart to this man, to falling headlong and desperately in love with her enemy. This just wouldn't do! No, she couldn't let this happen, for Travis obviously did not feel the same way toward her as she was coming to feel toward him. Oh, there were times when she was sure he wanted her, caught him staring at her with lust gleaming in those devastating blue-green eyes of his. However, Sam was not so naive as to mistake lust for love. If the man cared even the tiniest bit for her, he would not be planning to go to Nola's for supper tomorrow night.

All that aside, Sam and Travis were totally mismatched. What had she even been thinking? Tarnation! The man was a U.S. Marshal—and she was an outlaw! There was no denying it. For most of her life she had lived outside the law, running just ahead of it, always looking back over her shoulder. Travis was the law, through and through. It was in his blood, it was his life. The two of them went together like oil and water, in opposition to one another in all ways—always.

I have to get away! Sam thought in sudden panic. *I don't belong here! I belong out there with my family, with Pa and the boys! I ain't some Cinderella, like in that story Miss Tucker's been teachin' me! Damnation! As much as I hate her, Nola is right about one thing. You can't make a silk purse out of a sow's ear and you can't make a lady out of someone like me. It's time everyone stopped foolin' themselves, and that includes me! It's long past time!*

Sam glanced hastily toward the house, then to the half-filled laundry basket at her feet. Merely by scooting the basket a short distance to the left and following it, she stood hidden behind a long row of billowing sheets. With the laundry lines filled, Elsie could not possibly see her from the kitchen window.

A grim smile twisted Sam's mouth. "Sorry, Elsie. You shouldn't have relaxed your guard today, of all days!" she muttered.

Seconds later, Sam, her injuries healed, was furtively dashing through back lots, dodging behind outbuildings, bushes, trees, anything she could find, making her way steadily and stealthily toward the rear of the livery where Travis had stabled her mare.

CHAPTER 13

"Travis! Travis!" Elsie dashed down the street toward the jailhouse, her rotund little body bobbing along at an amazing speed. As she reached the step to the boardwalk in front of the jail, the heel of her shoe caught, flinging her forward. Though her screams brought several people running, it was too late to prevent injury. Elsie lay whimpering on the walk, agonizing pain shooting through her right hip.

Travis was two doors down, buying tobacco, when he heard Elsie's cries. By the time he pushed his way through the crowd gathered in front of his office, Chas and another man were trying to lift Elsie to her feet. Tears were streaming down the housekeeper's paper-white face, and she was moaning in anguish. "Elsie! My God, what happened?" Travis exclaimed.

"She tripped and fell, Marshal," a bystander supplied.

"Travis!" Elsie hissed through clenched teeth, reaching out to try to clutch his arm. "Sam's gone! One minute . . ." Elsie paused on a wave of pain, then continued breathlessly, "One minute she was in the back yard hanging clothes, and before I knew it, she was gone. I looked all around the house . . ."

"It's okay, Elsie. I'll find her," Travis told her. "First, let's get you to Doc's place." Ever so gently, as if he were handling a newborn babe, Travis lifted Elsie into his arms. "Hang on, darlin'," he crooned, cradling her close. "I'll take care of everything, and what I can't fix, Doc Purdy will. I promise."

By the time he got Elsie settled with Doc Purdy, began a search of the town, and discovered that Sam had stolen her mare from the livery stable, Travis figured she had a good hour's head start on him. Ed Howard, the owner of the livery, had been working in the tack room and never noticed the girl at all. The only thing Ed could tell Travis was that Sam must be riding bareback, because her saddle was still in his tack room, along with the bridle. Nothing but her mare was missing.

Travis wasted no time in saddling his own horse. Stopping by the house long enough to discover that Sam had taken none of her belongings with her, he set out to track her and bring her back. He'd find that slippery little sneak if he had to turn over every rock in the territory! Then, if she was damned lucky, he wouldn't break her neck! He'd just beat her to within an inch of her life!

* * *

Clutching Bess's mane and clinging to the mare's heaving sides with her bare thighs, Sam cursed a blue streak. She had no food, no water, no saddle, and now the insides of her thighs were being rubbed raw because she'd had to hike her skirts up in order to ride straddle. Over-all, this escape could have been planned a lot better, if she'd had time to think about it. Lord sake, she didn't even have a weapon with her, and that was one of the first laws of the wilderness!

To top everything, Sam had no idea where to begin looking for her family. Hank, bless his sweet, stupid soul, hadn't thought to tell her where they were camped, giving no thought to the possibility that his attempt to rescue her might not succeed! Now she would have to search the surrounding countryside all around Tumble, trying at the same time not to run into Marshal Travis Kincaid! She didn't even try to convince herself that he would not follow her. The man took himself and his position too seriously to let her escape so easily. Sam's only hope lay in locating her pa and brothers, or they her, before Travis caught up with her.

As if she didn't have enough trouble, the sky was darkening rapidly. Ugly black clouds had blocked the sun, and thunder rumbled ominously in the distance. Sam didn't know whether to laugh or cry! In all the time she had been a prisoner, it had only rained once and then lightly. Now it looked as if they were about to get a real gully-washer!

To avoid getting caught in a flash flood, since she was not really all that familiar with the lay of the land around Tumble, Sam would have to stay to higher ground. In turn, while the rain might wash out her trail, it would also limit the amount of ground she could cover, thus making it twice as easy for Travis to find her. It would also lessen the chances of running into her family. Mother Nature sure had picked a fine day to turn fickle!

Lightning forked downward, lighting up both sky and land in blinding brilliance. As her mare shied, Sam clutched tightly to her mane. "This is no time to get skittish on me, Bess!" Sam muttered. With her knees, she urged the horse forward. She had to find a place to hole up, a place to hide from Travis until the storm passed.

Several miserable hours later, Sam sat shivering in the dark. It was too risky to chance building a fire, even if she could have found some dry wood, which was doubtful. The rain had been pouring down in torrents for hours, and Sam was soaked to the skin. Her hair was plastered to her skull, sending streams of water down her back and face.

The only cover she could find was beneath a tangle of bushes amid a pile of rocks on a small knoll. With the lightning still flashing, she'd had to forego hiding under the trees. So here she sat, huddled into a dripping ball, with only a nervous horse for company.

Below her, where the valley began to dip, Sam could see swift streams starting to form where none had been before. All about her, the ground had become a sea of mud. For thirsty though the soil might be, the sun-baked earth could not absorb all this rain at once. When the rain finally stopped, within hours the hot Texas sun would again bake all the mud to the hardness of brick.

"You know, Bess," Sam grumbled irritably, brushing her hair out of her face with muddy fingers, "Parson Aldrich was preachin' about a battle where the blood will be up to the bridles of the horses. If he thinks that's somethin', he should see this. I'll bet there are places around here where the mud would reach the arse-end of a ten-foot Indian!"

Some time later, Sam was jolted out of her misery by the bright flare of a match being struck on a rock just four feet from her hiding place. Between the rain and thunder, she hadn't heard the intruder's approach. Her startled gaze followed the match as it rose toward the man's face. Even before the flame lit the lean features sheltered by the man's hat, Sam knew who was standing there. Her heart drummed a cadence of doom as she saw Travis leaning against a large rock, calmly lighting a cigarette.

He exhaled, and the smoke drifted toward her, as if to show him where she hid. Deep down inside, Sam knew that Travis already knew she was here. He was toying with her, waiting to see if she would reveal herself. Long minutes dragged by, neither of them speaking, both waiting out the other. At one point he turned his head and stared directly at her, and Sam shivered anew at the anger blazing from his eyes. Then he turned away, resuming his unconcerned expression, while Sam stubbornly held her tongue.

Finally Travis sighed, tossing the cigarette butt to the ground at his feet. "This is ridiculous. I know you're there, Sam. I've been standing here watching your mare's tail switch back and forth until I'm getting dizzy. Come on out and face the music." Again he turned to face her.

"Go dance with somebody else, Kincaid," she snapped back. "I ain't in the mood."

"Sam!" he yelled. "Now!"

"Oh, hell! Guess I might as well. You're stubborn enough to stand there until you take root!" Slowly Sam crawled out from the center of her bush, emerging with leaves and twigs tangled in her hair and mud everywhere else. "How'd you find me?" she demanded.

"I didn't," he answered with a nasty grin that did not bode well for her. "Rusty did." With a jerk of his head, he gestured toward his horse, ground-tied a short distance away.

"That's some smart horse you got there, Marshal." Her voice dripped sarcasm.

"Not really, but he's persistent. Seems Bess is coming into season, and Rusty's interest has peaked."

Sam grimaced. "That ain't all, either, I reckon. You should have named him Randy instead. It'd suit him a darn sight better."

His short laugh held little humor as his eyes traveled over her in an insolent manner. "You're a mess!"

"Yeah, well, it ain't like I been pickin' daisies in the sunshine, ya know!" she answered flippantly, lapsing into her former incorrect speech pattern, tossing her straggling hair over her shoulder. Her dark eyes blazed up at him, but could not hold his condemning stare for long.

"You cause more trouble than one woman is

worth!" he shouted. "When I left town, Elsie was in Doc Purdy's office because of you."

"What?" On hearing this, Sam's head shot up. "How? What happened?"

"She fell and hurt her hip trying to find me to tell me you were gone."

"Is . . . is she hurt bad?" Guilt flooded her. The elderly housekeeper had become a good friend.

"For your sake, you'd better hope not."

Swallowing sharp words and wounded pride, Sam said, "I'm sorry. Honest. I wouldn't cause Elsie no harm a'purpose." Hanging her head, Sam was the picture of remorse.

A gust of wind sent a violent quiver through her as she stood before him, rain beating down on her bare head. "Damnation, girl! You're so cold you're turning blue!" he exclaimed suddenly. "You're going to catch your death of pneumonia!" Swiftly, he started to whip the waterproof poncho over his head, intent on offering it to her.

It was the only chance she was likely to get, and Sam took it. Before he could rid himself of the awkward garment, she was off and running, slipping and sliding down the muddy hillside. With a loud yell, Travis was after her like an enraged bull.

She was halfway down when he lunged for her, knocking her flat. Not about to accept defeat so easily, Sam squirmed and fought like a wildcat, screaming curses at him as she clawed for a handhold in the oozing mud. Though he was twice her size, Sam was as slippery as an eel, and Travis had a time of it trying to hold on to her, let alone subdue her. Flipping her over to face him, Travis put his full weight atop her, reaching for her flailing arms. "Damn it, Sam! Give it up!"

In answer, she flung a fistful of mud into his face. Travis shook the mud from his lashes, blinking and glaring at her as she tried to wriggle free. Retaliation was swift as Travis grabbed a glob of ooze and smeared her face with it. "How do you like it, brat?" he bellowed, at last managing to snare both of her wrists as she sputtered and spit.

They glared at each other in fury, both breathing hard and straining against one another. Mud covered them like a brown blanket, from head to toe, as they lay panting in the downpour. Dirty droplets dripped from his hair onto her face, streaking it even worse.

As Travis lay over her, Sam's body trapped beneath his, his breath suddenly caught in his throat. They were both soaked, their clothes clinging like second skins, and with every frantic wriggle, Travis became more aware of her. Sam was filthy, her face streaked with mud, and her hair caked with it. By all rights, her dark eyes should have been all but hidden in her dirty face, but they were snapping with anger, brilliant with fury. Ridiculous as it was, right here, right now, she was more beautiful than any woman he had ever known, and at this moment he wanted her more than he'd ever wanted anything in his life. He felt as if he might die if he could not claim her!

She was shouting curses up at him, trying to wrench her wrists from his hands, when he lowered his face to hers. "Shut up, Sam!" he growled. "Shut up and kiss me."

His blunt order shocked her into silence. For an instant, she caught the strange gleam in his eyes. Then his lips were sliding over hers, his tongue invading her mouth. She tasted mud and Travis, and sweet heat. The finest brandy could not compare or compete with this soul-searing kiss! It went straight to her head, blocking out all thought, save for him.

His tongue danced with hers, sending streams of pure flame through her. Her body on fire, burning alive with sudden desire, Sam forgot to fight him, forgot that he was her enemy. When he released her wrists to frame her face with his hands, her arms wound about his neck to pull him closer. As his lips left hers to plant tiny kisses across her brow, her nose, her eyes, whispering to her how much he needed her, Sam was lost. "Yes, yes," she moaned, her head turning, trying to recapture his firm, warm lips.

His mouth blazed a fiery trail along her throat, his fingers delving into her hair. With all the confidence of a born courtesan, Sam directed his mouth toward her yearning breasts. It was all the urging Travis needed, for he could not wait to taste the rosy buds. Careless of buttons and ties, he tore open the front of her once-white blouse and unlaced the front of her sodden petticoat and chemise, feasting his eyes on her pale, thrusting breasts and the strawberry tips pouting up at him so temptingly.

His tongue was lightning, his mouth almost burning her flesh as he lapped and suckled first one breast, then the other. "You are so beautiful!" he murmured. "As smooth and sweet as wild honey!"

Sanity had deserted her, but Sam didn't care. She was too consumed with desire, too caught up in this heavenly torment Travis was creating with his mouth and his hands. Her own hands were brushing frantically up and down his back, feeling the play of muscles beneath his wet, clinging shirt. His back was so warm beneath her fingertips, but his shirt was hindering her. She wanted to feel his hot flesh against hers, with nothing between them but their passion!

With that in mind, Sam's hands went to his chest, her fingers fighting with the stubborn buttons, until she had his shirt undone and tugged halfway down his arms. With his help, her blouse and his shirt were both flung aside, the bodice of her petticoat pushed down about her waist, her chemise discarded without regard.

As his burning flesh, softly covered with golden hair, brushed against her bare breasts, Sam gasped aloud. Never had she felt anything so glorious! Rain drenched them, and thunder still shook the heavens, but a thousand stars swam behind Sam's closed eyelids.

He kissed her again, stealing the breath from her lungs, robbing her of her very soul! His talented tongue slid smoothly into her mouth time and again, sending an ache to the center of her being. Her entire body was throbbing with a desire so immense that she didn't know when or how he had managed to remove the rest of their clothing. She only knew that he had, that they were both gloriously naked and clinging to one another in a mad fever. His hands were charting her body, doing marvelous things that had her curling her toes into the mud beneath her. His hot, throbbing manhood was prodding against her bare thigh.

It occurred to Travis, in a fleeting moment of rational thought, that they were both crazy. Here they were, naked and half-buried in mud, in the middle of a thunderstorm, making love! Then Sam's tongue snaked into his mouth, her hands smoothly caressing his flesh, and Travis gave up trying to think. He only wanted to feel, to take Sam beneath him and make her his once and for all.

When his hands parted her thighs, his fingers delving into that bright patch of curls that guarded her feminine secrets, a sudden flash of uncertainty assailed her. But when she would have tried to draw back from him, to close her thighs to his wandering hands, he soothed her with soft words and caresses. "Don't, love. No. Don't deny us both now. We've come too far to stop short of heaven now."

She opened to him then, entrusting her body and her heart into his care. Travis was right. She had come too far and she wanted him too badly. If they stopped now, she might never know where all this smoldering passion was leading and she wanted desperately to know, to have him teach her what it meant to be a woman in the most important way of all.

She cried out in surprise and delight as he gently fondled her, expertly finding that hidden nub of desire that sent liquid fire skipping through her veins, only to pool in raging passion deep within her. It was as if her insides were aflame and melting, her bones turning to jelly, and the wettest, warmest place of all was where Travis was touching her now.

As his mouth played upon her breast, his fingers stroked her, long, smooth caresses that had Sam wriggling beneath him and fighting for breath. Her heart was racing, so many emotions assaulting her at once, that she was sure she would die from sheer bliss. Yet even now she wanted more, knew instinctively that the best was yet to come, waiting just beyond her grasp. Little animal moans were tearing from her throat as she wordlessly begged him for the heaven he had promised her.

Then his manhood was prodding at the entrance to that secret chamber no man had ever before invaded. Slowly, carefully, he nudged into her, and her body, primed to eagerness, at last welcomed him. There was a final moment of resistance as he breached her maidenhead, a sharp twinge of pain that brought a gasp from her lips, but it was soon past. With honeyed words, he soothed her, waiting once more for her body to accommodate him.

Then he was moving within her, smoothly stroking to the very heart of her, calling her to join him on the rapturous journey. "Oh, sweetheart, come with me! Come with me!"

She had thought her desire could flame no higher, but as he plunged deep within her, her passions rose to new heights. Her hips rose naturally to meet his thrusts, as if her body had been waiting a lifetime for this moment and knew exactly what to do, all on its own. Bedazzled, Sam opened her eyes to find Travis gazing down into her face, his rapt expression echoing her own, his brilliant eyes shimmering with desire.

Then passion engulfed her, wave after wave of pure ecstasy washing through her, and she closed her eyes tightly against the intense pleasure. Her hands clutched at his shoulders as spasms of splendor shook them both, and her blissful cries blended with his as the earth tilted beneath them and the heavens shattered into a million glittering bits about their heads.

CHAPTER 14

Their loving had been a whirlwind ride, an emotional journey more exciting and beautiful than anything either of them could have imagined, but now it was over. Slowly, their breathing calmed, and their hearts resumed their normal beating. With a soft sigh of lazy satisfaction, Sam at last opened her eyes to gaze up at her lover. Travis was somehow smiling and frowning at the same time.

"If I didn't know better, I could swear the earth is still moving," he muttered with a shake of his head, as if to further clear his mind.

"I know," she concurred. "I feel it, too."

The sensation came again, and her eyes widened with fright as Travis exclaimed, "Sweet hell! It really is moving! Hold on, Sam!"

No sooner were the words out of his mouth, than

the section of muddy ground on which they lay slid downhill. Sam screamed, holding onto Travis for dear life, as their earthen sled gained momentum, sending them tumbling downward at an alarming speed. She clung to him like a bear cub to a tree limb, her eyes closed and her face buried in his chest, as Travis scrambled frantically, trying to gain a solid foothold in the mud, grabbing at rocks and brush on their way.

Finally he managed to snag hold of a small tree, its roots holding fast as it took their combined weight. Mud continued to pelt them, and for a few minutes Sam feared it might bury them. At last it stopped, and she dared to open her eyes. "Is it over?" she gasped. "Are we all right now?"

Grunting and spitting mud, Travis finally sighed. "Yeah, if you call being stuck halfway down a muddy hill in your bare skin safe." He rested a moment, gathering his strength, then instructed her, "Climb onto my back, Sam. Easy now. I'm not too sure how long this little tree will hold us."

When she had squirmed around, wrapping her arms about his neck and her long, bare legs about his waist, Travis began to climb, clawing his way up the steep, slippery hillside inch by precarious inch. To Sam, it seemed for every foot up they climbed, they slipped down two more, but Travis forged determinedly on, dragging Sam with him. At last they reached a point eight or nine feet from the crest of the hill and could go no further. It was too steep here, too slippery, with no handholds. Not one to admit defeat, Travis told her, "Okay, Sam, work your way up to my shoulders, until you can stand on them. Once you're over the top, you can throw a rope down to me."

On her first attempt to climb onto his shoulder, Sam lost her grip and her balance, sliding down atop him to a point where her head rested between his knees. With a shriek, she clasped her arms about his thighs, and dug her fingers into his flesh.

"Ouch! Damn, Sam! Watch it, will you?"

Recovering from her momentary fright, Sam couldn't help but grin. "Talk about givin' a gal somethin' to look at!" she taunted. "You got a real cute behind, Marshal."

"Sam!" he growled back. "Quit ogling me and do as I said. I can't hold on like this forever."

"Oh, stop your bellyachin'!" Sam slithered her way back up his slick body, finally succeeding in getting her knees propped onto his shoulders. "Sort of like tryin' to hold onto a greased pig!" she told him, digging her hands into his hair and hoisting herself further until she was standing wobbily.

Stretching up on tiptoes, she reached for the crest, her fingers clawing for a hold. "I still can't reach!" she informed him as he grunted and growled below her. "I'm gonna have to stand on your head."

As she planted one foot on his muddy head, he groaned and stiffened his neck. "Here goes," she announced heartily. Using his head as a springboard, Sam launched herself up and over the top, in the process, mashing Travis's face into the mud. He came up sputtering to hear her triumphant cry. "I made it!"

"Good!" he huffed. "Now go get the rope from my pommel and find something sturdy to tie it to, and throw the free end down to me."

For one glorious minute, Sam entertained visions of leaving Travis where he was, of taking her mare and riding off. Then she recalled those wondrous moments of lovemaking, and her heart softened toward him again. No, she couldn't leave him like this. Besides, if she did run off, he'd be mad as a wet hen when he finally did manage to get up by himself, and he'd be after her like the devil himself.

Deciding she'd had about all the excitement she wanted for one night, Sam dutifully got the rope and helped pull Travis up. They made a crude shelter by draping Travis's poncho over the bushes, but before they could crawl inside, they had to find their missing clothes and sluice the worst of the mud from themselves.

Travis came out the winner when it came to locating his clothes. He found his gunbelt, pants, and his boots, though he had to pour the mud out of them. His socks and shirt were not to be found. Neither were Sam's underthings. Also gone were her shoes, and she wished the horrid things a hearty good riddance. Only Sam's dress and her stockings were found, the rest of her clothes, and Travis's, undoubtedly buried in the mud along the hillside.

It seemed ridiculous after all that had happened for them to dress in their remaining wet clothing. As it was, they would be fortunate if neither of them came down with pneumonia, or at least a good chill. Since building a fire in this downpour was next to impossible, Travis reluctantly decided that the next best thing would be to huddle together beneath the shelter, the two of them sharing the one dry blanket Travis always carried as a bedroll for those times when he could not make it back to town.

"I'm hungry," Sam complained as her stomach gave a loud, protesting growl. By the flash of the lightning, she saw the hateful look Travis sent her way.

"Tough!" he snarled, his bad mood back now that he was forced to sit skin-to-skin with her and try to ignore the desire that was already rearing its head again. "You should have thought of that earlier, before you decided to run off."

"Well, look who's talkin'!" she said, making a rude face at him. "You came out here with no food and one lousy blanket! Not even a lick of whiskey on you, neither!"

Travis glared. "I hadn't planned on starting a hotel, Sam. Quit complaining and for God's sake, stop wiggling!"

"I'm cold!"

"You're hungry; you're cold! Is there anything else, since you're bent on griping all night?"

"Yeah, now that you mention it. I sure could use a cigarette about now, if you could spare the fixin's."

He frowned down at her. "I would have thought we'd broke you of that habit by now."

"Shows what you know, Kincaid," she shot back sassily. "I been sneakin' a smoke at least three times a day since I been stayin' with you. Now, how about bein' decent about it and sharin' one with me?"

Considering it the lesser of two evils, since he really would rather have made love with her again, he deftly rolled a cigarette and lit it. Taking a deep draw on it, he passed it to Sam.

"Thanks."

They sat quietly, passing the cigarette back and forth between them. "Do you realize how ridiculous you look, sitting there dripping mud, smoking that thing?" he muttered at last.

"No more silly than you do, I reckon," she sneered. Though they'd tried to wash most of the mud off in the rain, they still looked like a pair of chocolate candies. Travis most resembled an irritable raccoon, with two bright eyes shining out from twin mud rings. Even his mustache was stiff with the stuff.

Silence reigned for a time, until Sam spoke once more. "Travis?"

"What now?"

"Would you kiss me again?"

He gaped at her, wondering if she had somehow read his thoughts. "No," he said shortly, hoping she could not see the flush creeping up his neck.

"Why not? You seemed to like it well enough before."

Flicking the stub of the cigarette out into the rain, he bought a few seconds as he watched it flare brightly before it went out. "The problem is, I liked it too well, Sam," he answered finally. "That's why I lost my head the way I did. What I did was wrong, and I'm sorry."

"Sorry?" she echoed with an agitated frown. "Would you care to explain that remark, Kincaid?"

"I'm sorry I took advantage of your innocence, for robbing you of your virtue. I had no right to do that."

"If I'm not complainin', why should you? Dang it all, Kincaid, you can be the most aggravatin' human bein' I've ever come across!" Crossing her arms over her chest, she tried to turn her back to him, but his tight hold on the blanket prevented this.

He glared at her, his hot aqua eyes burning into her. "I'll be hanged if I ever understand you, Samantha Downing! Any other woman would be in tears by now, ranting and raving and throwing dire threats at me! Don't you have any shame at all? Don't you regret giving yourself to me?"

"I do now!" she shouted.

Trying to bring his temper under control, as well as his baser feelings, Travis told himself to ignore the impudent thrust of her breasts, now pushed into prominence over Sam's crossed arms. The rosy nipples seemed to be taunting him. "I don't mean to insult you, Sam. It's just that I'm surprised you're not upset about this. Didn't you want to save yourself for the man you would marry, for someone you loved?"

Sam swallowed the words that rose to her lips, words that would have declared her love for him. Surprised by the depths of her own feelings for this man, she retorted sharply. "I'd of been old and wrinkled if I decided to wait for that to happen."

Travis's lips twisted in a self-mocking smile. "So you decided I'd do for lack of anyone else available?"

"Don't twist my words, Marshal. What's eatin' you is that we made love, and I'm honest enough to admit I enjoyed it, even if you're not."

"What do you want from me, Sam?" he groaned. "Blood?"

She faced him now, her breasts grazing him as

she turned into him. "No. I want you to kiss me again. I want to go all warm and tingly inside when you hold me. I want you to make me feel like a woman."

Her arms came up around his neck, pulling his lips toward hers. Her black eyes seduced him, her parted lips enticed him, her breasts burned like pokers against his chest until Travis could scarcely breathe. "Sam, you don't know what you're doing," he murmured, weakening rapidly.

"I might not have known the first time, Travis, but I'm a fast learner," she said in that whiskey-warm voice of hers. "I most certainly know what I'm doin' now."

With a deep groan, Travis surrendered, letting her pull his lips to hers. Her kiss was hot and sweet, and every bit as demanding as his had been before. Her breasts branded themselves into his chest; her tongue delved between his lips to search out the moist heat of his mouth. Her tongue tangled with his; then, in a move that shook him to his toes, Sam deftly sucked his tongue into her mouth with a slow, sure pressure.

Travis was lost; he could not have denied her if he'd wanted to. His arms came about her, gathering her close to him. As they clung tightly to one another, the chill left their flesh, replaced by a shimmering heat pulsing between them.

"I want you. I want you," Sam whispered, her breath warming and tickling his ear.

He shivered. "I want you, too, darlin'."

Sam's response was immediate and startling, as she climbed into his lap, her legs straddling his. Burying her face into the hair on his chest, she nuzzled closer, until Travis thought he would explode then and there. In an effort to slow things down and give himself time to prevent such an untimely occurrence, Travis bent her back over his arms. With a hunger he'd never known, he suckled her breasts, lavishing them with wet, warm kisses, teasing her until she trembled in his embrace. His tactic had one drawback. In this position, the soft curls between her thighs were pressed intimately against him, and as she thrashed and moaned, she was arousing him even more.

Breathless with desire, on fire for her, Travis was more than willing to let her have her way. Lifting her and bringing her down on him, he groaned with ecstasy as her silken heat closed tightly about him. Sam gasped as he filled her yearning body. Then, with his hands cradling her bottom, guiding and aiding her, she rode him with all the fervor of youth, with all the searing passion in her body and the budding love in her heart. Together, they soared with the power of eagles, straight into the blinding light of the sun.

They were halfway back to town when Travis, his face set in serious and determined lines, told her, "As soon as I can arrange it, we'll have Parson Aldrich marry us."

Sam almost fell from her horse, thrills of shock echoing through her. "What?" she shrieked, when she finally found her tongue. "Have you gone plumb loco, Kincaid? Why in blue blazes would you even suggest such a stupid thing?"

Travis blinked at her in surprise and shook his head, sure he was hearing her wrong. He'd figured she might object at first, but not this strongly. "Sam, it's the right thing to do—the only thing. Surely, even you can see that, after what happened between us last night."

"I don't see why," she said stubbornly, her chin rising. "My brothers have all bedded their fair share of women, but they didn't marry any of them. I don't see what makes this any different."

The woman had a born talent for making him angry. "Your brothers can't get pregnant, Sam," he informed her stiffly, the muscle in his jaw beginning to jump. "I'd say that makes one hell of a difference, sweetheart."

"Don't you 'sweetheart' me in that uppity way of yours!" she screeched. "I don't care what you say, I'm not gonna marry the likes of you!"

"If it turns out you're carrying my child, I don't see that you'll have much choice in the matter," he pointed out.

"Well, maybe I won't be! Maybe we just ought to wait and see, before you shackle us into a marriage neither one of us wants!"

"You are the most obstinate, mule-headed woman! I swear, you're enough to drive a preacher to drink!" Travis leaned toward her, his eyes glittering with fury, his mud-coated mustache twitching. "We're going to get married, and that's the end of it!" he roared.

"I wouldn't have you on a bet! Get this through your head, Kincaid. I'm not marryin' you, and you can't make me!"

"We'll just see about that, you little hellion! We'll just see!" The wicked light in his eyes made her want to flee as fast and far as she could, but Travis held tightly to the rope on her horse, daring her to try it.

They were quite a sight, riding into town in their muddied clothes. Sam's hair was sticking out stiffly in all directions, and despite the hot sun beating down on him, Travis had been forced to wear the poncho, since he never found his shirt. The last thing he wanted at this point was any gossip about him and Sam. It was enough that Sam was returning minus her shoes.

Pulling their horses in front of his office, he dismounted. But before he could assist Sam, she slid neatly off her horse. "I've got to check in with Chas, and find out how Elsie's doing. Then we'll go home and get you a bath," he told her.

Sam sent him a blistering look but said nothing. She hadn't spoken one word since he'd made that asinine suggestion of marriage. Inside, Sam was seething. While she thought she loved him, she sure as the devil wasn't going to marry this exasperating man if he didn't feel the same. If he was considering marriage to salve his conscience, or because she might bear his child, he was whistling in the wind. He could argue until he was blue in the face, for all she cared, but unless he loved her, Sam wasn't about to marry him. An outlaw she might be, but even she had her pride.

No sooner had they entered the marshal's office, than Chas was beside himself and talking a mile a minute. "Travis! Thank God yer back!" Chas's eyes shifted to Sam. "And thank goodness ya have Sam with ya! We've got trouble, Travis! Big trouble! The Downings have kidnapped Nan Tucker and Nola

Sandoval and they're holding them for ransom. They want to trade them for Sam!''

Sam's heart stopped, and Travis fought to breathe. Their eyes locked in mutual dismay, all their tumultuous feelings jumbled into one long, heart-rending gaze. This was it. This was the end of their short, volatile relationship. They both knew that Travis would have no other choice but to trade her back to her family. This was good-bye.

CHAPTER 15

"**H**ow did the Downings manage to kidnap the ladies, and what makes you so sure it was the Downings?" Travis asked, recovering somewhat from the first shock of Chas's announcement.

"They left a note, Trav. A ransom note, saying they would trade the ladies for Sam," Chas hastened to explain. "As best we could figure, neither Nan nor Nola had heard about Sam's escape. They both showed up at your place for Sam's lessons, about the same time the Downings took it into their heads to arrive in force to rescue Sam. When they failed to find either you or Sam, they took the other two women instead."

"When and where are we supposed to make this exchange? Did they say?"

"The note said this evening, at sunset, half an

hour's ride west of town near that old Indian gravesite."

"That figures," Travis said with a grimace, and admiration for Bill Downing's cunning. "We'll be riding right into the sun when we meet them, and soon after the exchange is made, darkness will cover their escape." He turned to frown at Sam.

"Don't look at me," she said. "It ain't—uh—isn't my fault Pa's not stupid!"

"Well, I'm sure glad ya got back here with Sam in good time." Chas heaved a sigh of relief. "Let me tell ya, Rafe Sandoval is fit to be tied over his little girl bein' taken by a band of outlaws. He's out for blood."

"Hmph!" Sam snorted. "I feel a darn sight sorrier for Pa and the boys havin' to put up with that snooty witch, than I do for Miss Fancy-pants! Five minutes of her mouth, and they were probably regrettin' takin' her!"

Both men glared at her. "What about Nan Tucker?" Travis reminded her. "Don't you have any compassion for all the pain and fright she'll be going through? And what about the shame both of them will bear after this?"

Sam stared, aghast. Her chin came up and her shoulders went back as she faced him defiantly. "My brothers and Pa wouldn't stoop that low, Kincaid, unlike some folks I might mention! They won't touch those women!"

"You'd better hope like hell they don't!" someone growled from behind her. Swiveling on her heel, Sam turned to face a tall, angry man with thinning dark hair and snapping black eyes. His lips were drawn back over his teeth in an ugly snarl as he reached out and grabbed the front of Sam's dress. Her teeth rattled as he shook her hard. "You'd better pray they don't hurt a hair on my daughter's head, or so help me God, I'll kill you with my bare hands!"

"Rafe! Rafe! Turn her loose!" Travis had to shout to be heard over Rafe Sandoval's ravings. "Now!" he commanded, yanking on Rafe's arm.

The man released her and stood staring at Travis as if wondering who he was and why he was defending Sam. The strange moment passed, and Sandoval resumed his tirade. "Damn you, Kincaid! Where were you when you were needed? We pay you to protect the decent citizens of this town, not to go gallivanting about the countryside chasing snot-nosed brats! What do you intend to do about all this?"

"Simmer down, Rafe. We'll get your daughter back, and if I hadn't gone after Sam, we wouldn't have her to trade for Nan and Nola."

"And if you'd been here to begin with, those outlaws wouldn't have either of them!" Rafe countered furiously. "If Nola is hurt in any way, I'll personally see that you hang right along with the rest of them! You have my word on that!"

With a short nod, Travis said, "Fine. Now I think we'd better sit down and make some plans. Chas, go get Lou Sprit and stop by the hotel and see if Harry will be willing to ride with us. Check the saloons, and if Mike Morris is sober, we could sure use him. And see if Bucky can get someone to cover for him at the Silver Nugget. He's a fair shot with a rifle."

As Chas left, Travis turned his attention to Sandoval. "I suppose you want to go with us to get Nola."

"You suppose right, Kincaid. Wild horses couldn't keep me away. I want to catch those bastards and watch them hang! Better yet, I say we shoot each and every one of them on sight!"

"I know you're upset, Rafe," Travis told the distraught man.

"Upset? That doesn't begin to cover the way I feel! Murderous is more like it!"

"If you're coming with us, you'd better settle down," Travis advised firmly. "We can't go off half-cocked here, or someone is going to get hurt."

"Damn right someone's going to get hurt!" Sandoval roared. "Dead hurt!"

"I meant the women," Travis corrected bluntly. "We can't just go in shooting at anything that moves, or it could mean one of the women's lives. No one wants to chance that, Rafe, least of all you."

Sandoval blanched. "No," he croaked. "I wouldn't want that. But, damn it all, Travis, I want those outlaws to pay!"

"All in good time," Travis agreed. "The first order of business will be to make the exchange— safely. That's all we need to concentrate on tonight. Once the women are safe, we can go after the Downings."

Sam felt sick. Since Rafe Sandoval had let go of her, Travis hadn't given her a thought. His concentration was solely on the upcoming exchange and catching her family so they could all hang. Thinking she could stand there until she rotted for all he cared, Sam helped herself to a chair. Tilting it back against the wall, and giving the outward appearance of not having a care in the world, Sam sat fuming.

Hell fire! Nothing was going right lately! First she'd gotten captured, then Hank's attempt to rescue her had gone awry, and when she'd finally managed to escape, Travis had caught her again. She'd been stupid enough to give her body and heart to this mule-headed marshal who had a heart of stone, and now her father and brothers had really stirred up a hornet's nest by kidnapping Nola and Miss Tucker!

If she hadn't been so depressed, it would have been almost laughable! Here she had escaped, only to have her family choose that exact day to try to rescue her! If she'd been here, she'd probably be with her family and halfway to Mexico by now! No wonder she hadn't been able to find them! They'd been in Tumble trying to rescue her! If they didn't quit getting their signals crossed, they were all going to end up with nooses about their necks!

To make things worse, the man she loved was now planning how best to rescue the voluptuous Nola. It seemed to Sam that Travis was altogether too ready and willing to trade her back to her family, with no regrets! Where was all the talk about weddings now? Or had Travis already forgotten the way they'd spent the previous night, locked in one another's arms? Travis was also giving no thought to the fact that this was her family he was discussing so calmly, determinedly planning their downfall. It didn't seem to matter a whit to him that he was talking about hanging the four people Sam loved best in this world!

Sandoval's voice pulled her back from her musings. "I'll have a dozen of my best men waiting at the west end of town," he was saying. "We'll get those bloody bastards tonight!"

Travis shook his head. "No. Half a dozen men of my choosing will do nicely. We don't need to go out there looking like an army, or we might sour the whole deal. If that happened, God only knows when you'd see Nola again or in what condition."

Sandoval's face darkened. "With my men, we could lay a trap for them," he insisted. "We could have them all before they even knew what hit them, I tell you!"

"And I said, no. It's too chancy. I know what I'm doing, Rafe, now let me do things my way and don't give me any trouble about it. Hell, we've got enough problems without you trying to muddle up the plans. Just trust me and let me do my job."

Though he nodded in agreement, the other man still looked dissatisfied. "All right, Kincaid, but screw this up and it's your neck! Remember that! I'll meet you here when it's time." He shot Sam a hateful glare and stomped out without another word.

The sun was a bright orange ball hovering above the western horizon. Any second now, Sam expected to catch sight of her family. She rode beside Travis, at the front of their party of eight riders. The others, Sandoval included, fanned out behind and to each side of them.

Sam was jittery, and she couldn't convince herself that it was the thought of seeing her family again or the sadness of leaving Travis. Several times, she had glanced around to find Sandoval scanning the landscape with something akin to smug determination on his face. For a man who was about to enter a very ticklish situation, he seemed altogether too sure of himself, and Sam had the uneasy feeling that Sandoval knew something the rest of them were unaware of. Shaking her head, Sam tried to tell herself she was being silly, but the feeling persisted.

It felt strange to be riding in her boy's trousers again. For some reason, Elsie had not burned them. Instead, the housekeeper had laundered them and sewn up the various rips and tears in Sam's old garments. After her bath, Travis had returned the clothes to her. He'd also brought her a new pair of boots. "Thought you might need these, Sam," he'd told her, his bright gaze sweeping over her freshly-washed face and shining hair.

Past the knot in her throat, Sam had thanked him. He'd stood there a moment longer, as if waiting for her to speak again, or perhaps wanting to say something else to her. Instead, he'd given a shake of his blond head and left her to get ready.

Now she turned to him. "Don't reckon you'd be willin' to give me my guns back, would you, Travis? I'm kinda partial to that Winchester, you know. I've had it since I was twelve."

Travis sent her a lopsided grin. "I wondered when you'd get around to asking for them." Reaching behind him, he handed her the rifle, watching as she slipped it into the scabbard resting alongside her saddle. Then he handed her the Colt, butt first. "They're not loaded, by the way," he added, his aqua eyes twinkling.

"Didn't imagine they were," she answered with a shrug.

"What did Elsie have to say to you when you said good-bye?" he wanted to know, his voice suspiciously husky. He'd taken her by Elsie's daughter's house, where the housekeeper was recuperating from her injuries.

"Nothin' much. Just told me to behave myself, if I knew how." A wavering smile touched Sam's lips. "I packed some sewin' stuff, and a book Elsie gave me, and that blue dress I made. Elsie said it'd be all right, so it's not like stealin'. I just wanted you to know."

"It's okay, Sam," he assured her softly. "I'm glad you packed the dress. You look real pretty in it."

Sam nodded, afraid to trust her voice any further. Tears were already stinging behind her eyes. If getting caught by Travis the first time was terrible, parting from him was downright painful.

Facing forward, Sam's heart gave a leap. Just ahead, she could see her pa and three brothers waiting atop a slight knoll. Nola was seated before Billy on his horse, while Nan was held in front of Tom. Forcing a smile to her lips, Sam waved to let them know she was okay.

Seconds later, the riders faced one another, a distance of only twenty feet separating the two parties. "Sam and I will dismount together," Travis called back over his shoulder. "The rest of you stay on your horses, and don't any of you make any stupid moves. I don't need any dead heroes on my hands." This last was directed particularly toward Sandoval.

At his signal, Sam dismounted, taking the reins of her horse in one hand, ready to lead Bess slowly forward. Travis's hand on her arm stopped her. "I'm going to miss you, Sam," he said, his eyes holding and searching hers. "I can't remember what I did for excitement before you turned up, and with Elsie laid up, there won't be anyone around to sass me the way you do."

"You'll get by," she choked out, blinking back the tears that threatened to blind her. If this was the last time she saw him, she wanted to remember everything about him, down to the last tiny detail. She wanted to recall the way that lock of blond hair fell down over his forehead, the stubborn tilt of his head, the glint in those magnificent turquoise eyes. Her fingers ached to reach up and stroke the soft bristles of his mustache, her lips to feel the warmth of his just one last time before they parted. "I reckon I might miss you a tad, too, Kincaid. It ain't, er, hasn't all been bad. At least I learned to write my name and to read a bit and to speak proper. Maybe someday I'll write you a letter."

"You do that, Samantha Downing," he said softly, his hand coming up to brush her cheek. "I'll look forward to it."

For a breathless moment, Sam thought he might kiss her, but his gaze swung swiftly away and leveled itself at Bill Downing. "Send us one of the women first, then Sam and the other woman will walk out at the same time."

Ignoring the marshal, Old Bill called to his daughter. "Ya awright, Sammie? That lawman didn't hurt you none, did he?" All the while he spoke, his rifle was pointed toward Nan Tucker.

"I'm fine, Pa." It was a lie. Sam's heart was thudding so hard against her ribs that she thought she might die at any moment. Giving herself a mental kick, Sam told herself not to be such a ninny. *I'll get over him*, she promised herself silently. *A little heartache never killed anybody.*

Giving a nod, Old Bill signaled for Billy to release Nola. The girl slid shakily to the ground. As they watched, she turned and said something to Billy, though they could not make out her words. Then she walked toward her waiting father.

Suddenly, as Tom began to help Nan dismount and Sam started forward, gunfire erupted. With a terrorized scream, Nola stopped in her tracks, not sure which way to head for safety as bullets seared the air. Startled, Tom's horse reared, almost tearing Nan's arms from their sockets as Tom yanked her back into the saddle before him. Old Bill had his repeater to his shoulder, returning fire, Hank following suit. Billy kneed his horse into a run, heading straight toward the frozen Nola, on a collision course with Rafe Sandoval, who had his gun leveled at Billy.

It all happened in the blink of an eye, yet all so clearly to Sam's disbelieving eyes. In seconds, it seemed everyone was shooting wildly at everyone else. Lunging for her horse, intent on reaching her family, Sam was tackled from behind. Next she knew, she was lying face-first on the ground, Travis's big body over hers, sheltering her from the barrage of gunfire and successfully thwarting her attempts to wriggle free.

Still, she saw the flash from the muzzle of Sandoval's gun, watched as Billy tumbled from his horse to lie still on the ground. She heard Hank's cry of dismay, Nan's hysterical pleas, and Bill Downing's harsh command to his other two sons. With tears running down her cheeks, she saw Pa and Hank and Tom wheel their mounts and flee, taking Nan with them, saw them glance back once before they disappeared over the rise of the hill.

The moment Sam felt the weight above her give slightly, she was out from under Travis and running toward her fallen brother. "Billy! Billy!" Throwing herself onto the ground next to him, she stared at the crimson blood swiftly staining the front of his shirt. His face was as white as death, and she could not tell if he was breathing.

On instinct alone, Sam reached for Billy's gun, whipping it from its holster before anyone could guess what she was up to. In the next instant, she had the barrel leveled at Rafe Sandoval, not at all concerned that his weapon was pointed toward her. "You murderin' bastard!" she hissed, fire flashing from her dark eyes. "You killed my brother!"

Her finger was tightening on the trigger when she heard Travis growl close behind, "Don't do it, Sam!"

Slanting a look in Travis's direction, Sam's heart stopped. His Colt was aimed at her head, his face grim, his eyes deadly. There was no doubt in her mind that this man, her jailor, her lover, would shoot her if he had to. Something in her chest ripped open, the pain almost paralyzing her.

"Give me the gun, Sam. Hand it to me now." His voice was harsh, yet at the same time hypnotic. His eyes held hers without pity.

Neither of them would ever know what might have happened next, had Billy not groaned in agony. Sam's eyes flew to her brother's face, half-afraid she had imagined the sound. Billy's eye-lashes fluttered slightly, and Sam drew in a long, shaky breath.

Slowly, as if in a dream, she watched Travis's hand come forward, watched her own fingers release their death grip on the pistol. Trembling from head to toe, Sam, who almost never cried, bent her head and wept with relief that Billy still lived; in fear that he'd been spared only to hang; in grief that she and her family were still parted; and in anguish over the cruel shattering of the last of her new-found, naive ideals of love.

CHAPTER 16

Tumbleweed, Texas was abuzz with excitement! Their marshal had captured a second member of the Downing gang, but Travis was a mean man to cross these days. He was furious that Rafe Sandoval had gone against his orders and secretly brought his own men along for the exchange of the women.

While Sandoval was loudly demanding Billy Downing's head and saying that he was the one who had shot Billy and been primarily responsible for rescuing his beloved daughter, Travis was vehemently alleging that if Sandoval had not interfered, they would have gotten both women back safely, and Nan Tucker would not still be a prisoner of the outlaw band. Additionally, three of Sandoval's men had been badly injured in the fracas, and one of the men Travis had deputized had been shot.

"It's pure luck that no one was killed!" Travis claimed angrily.

Even as everyone celebrated Nola's return, they expressed concern for poor Nan Tucker. The dowdy little schoolteacher had been a favorite in Tumble. Now the gossip flew from one end of town to the other. Opinion was split, some siding with Travis and others condoning Sandoval's actions. Once again, Sam found herself caught in the middle of it all, an object of curiosity and censure.

To further confound matters, Elsie was no longer in residence as chaperone in Travis's house, and tongues wagged when it became apparent that Sam and Travis were now living alone together. Consumed with concern over Billy, Sam didn't really take too much notice, nor did she care what others might say or think. Her brother had taken a bullet in his upper chest, and for several days, his life hung precariously in the balance. Billy's health was foremost on her mind, pushing all else aside.

Three long, agonizing days passed before Doc Purdy could assure them that Billy would live. During that time, Sam spent almost every waking moment at the jail. This suited Travis fine, since it allowed him to keep an eye on her and still see to his duties. Without Elsie, it fell to Travis to keep track of Sam's whereabouts.

No sooner had it been determined that Billy would survive his wound, than Rafe Sandoval began harping for a hanging, with or without a trial. The man came to town at least every other day, always making it a point to stop by the jail and ruffle a few feathers. He would rail at Billy, glare holes through Sam, and alternately cajole and threaten Travis.

"If you want Downing to have a trial, then you'd better see to it that it's soon," he warned. "I want the man hanged and buried, so my little girl can put all this nastiness behind her and get on with her life. It's very hard on her right now, you know, with her name being bandied about by every gossip in town. The sooner this matter is settled, the better—and if you don't have the stomach for it, I'll hang the buzzard myself!"

Travis ignored him, while Sam gritted her teeth to powder! She would have liked nothing better than to give the pompous ass a swift kick in the britches or a good punch in the mouth. If she thought Lou would accept a bribe, she'd have asked him to yank out all of Sandoval's teeth the next time he came in for a haircut. Because the rancher owned one of the largest cattle ranches in Texas, he thought he was God!

The funny thing was, Nola had taken to coming into town even more often than her father, and she, too, always stopped by the jail. While Rafe was painting her out to be so shaken by her terrible kidnapping, Nola did not seem all that upset, though she was acting a bit strangely these days. Ostensibly, Nola came to see Travis.

This made Sam seethe with jealousy, though she tried to hide it from everyone, especially Travis. In fact, she could not understand herself these days. Though Travis had held a gun to her head, and she was almost certain he would have pulled the trigger if he'd had to, Sam was still attracted to him, more now than ever.

For the most part, Nola ignored Sam, and vice

versa, and for this Sam was heartily grateful. At least the woman was not continually griping at her or telling her to sit up straight. The deportment lessons, it seemed, were over, at least for the time being. Far be it from Sam to remind anyone!

Still, it seemed odd that Nola would be willing to spend so much time in such close proximity to one of the men who had kidnapped her. Billy's jail cell was open to the main part of the office, partitioned only by the bars that imprisoned him. He was in plain sight of everyone who entered, and Nola seemed unbothered by his presence. In fact, the more Sam mulled it over in her mind, the more she became convinced that Nola's visits served a dual purpose. The beauty could now preen before not one man, but two! And preen, she did!

In some strange way which Sam could not fathom, Nola seemed drawn to Billy. He seemed to fascinate her, as some people are drawn against their will toward that which is evil or forbidden.

When Sam dared to mention this to Travis, he scoffed at her: "That's sick, Sam! It's just plain crazy! I don't know where you come up with these outlandish ideas of yours!"

"I should have known you'd get your nose bent out of shape over the fair Nola showin' an interest in another man!" Sam huffed.

"You think I'm jealous!" Travis exclaimed in surprise.

Groaning inwardly, Sam refuted this. "I just think you're stupid not to see what's right in front of your face."

"It's too ridiculous to consider," he countered.

"Yeah," she conceded, sending him a mocking look. "About as ridiculous as you and me bein' attracted to each other, huh?"

Once Billy was no longer considered critical, Travis decided to limit Sam's visits with her brother. When she complained long and loudly, he arched his bushy brow at her. "I'm not about to have the two of you putting your heads together to figure ways to escape. You can see him twice a day and only while I am there."

"Not very likely, Kincaid. Billy's too weak to walk, let alone run or ride. And it's not fair to leave Nola alone with him in your office and not let me talk privately with my own brother."

"Nola is not going to try to help him get away," Travis was quick to point out. "As far as her being alone with Billy, she was waiting for me those two times we found her there."

"Talkin' to Billy, like the two of them was, er, were best friends." Even with Nan Tucker gone, it had become almost habit for Sam to continue to correct her own speech now. The schoolteacher's lessons had taken root in Sam's fertile mind.

"Nola comes to see me."

Sam gave an elaborate shrug. "Think what you want, Marshal. I see it different."

Now Travis corrected her, as was becoming his habit. "Differently."

She just smiled. "My way," she said.

Now that Sam was spending less time at the jail, Travis had to enlist several other people to help watch her. Lou Sprit was first in line as an enthusiastic volunteer. Sitting in his barbershop, Sam watched him trim so many heads and beards and mustaches, that she swore she had learned a new trade and could do as well herself.

When she mentioned this to Travis, suggesting that he let her try her skills on him, he flatly refused. "Find someone else to experiment on, you little termagant. I wouldn't trust you within ten feet of my mustache with a pair of scissors!"

"'Fraidy-cat!" she taunted.

"Not afraid, Sam. Just cautious. You've threatened to rip the thing off enough times to make me wary."

If teas and quilting bees were centers for women's gossip, Lou's barbershop was its equal for the men. By the time a week had passed, Sam knew just about everything that was going on in the entire town. Old Mr. Burns had caught his foot in a bear trap, shearing off three toes. Nate Ogle's cow had birthed triplets for a second time, which was some kind of record, according to the men. Harry's newest boarder at the hotel had set fire to his bed while smoking and almost sent the place up in flames. Fred James's wife was due to give birth to their seventh child any day now. Personally, Sam thought Mrs. James ought to send Fred out fishin' more often at night.

Though Sam was privy to most of the local gossip, from the men's point of view, rarely did anyone mention her brother while in the barbershop or in her hearing. Far from being polite, Sam thought that Lou must have given fair warning against such talk, and Lou was much too big for anyone with any sense to want to argue with. Even so, she knew most folks thought Billy should hang for his crimes, and it hurt Sam to even think of such a thing happening to him. She loved Billy; she loved all of them.

To help while away the hours in Lou's shop, Sam started sitting in on the poker games the men started up while waiting their turn in the chair. It was sort of a revolving game, with players coming and going and constantly changing, but it was fun. At the start Lou had a fit when Sam first proposed to play, as did a few of his patrons. It took Sam all of fifteen minutes to convince Lou to stake her.

From then on, Sam was never without pocket change. Though she never out-and-out fleeced anyone, Sam had a few tricks up her sleeve and was not above using them when she saw fit. She won consistently, and word spread like wildfire. Men started flocking into Lou's establishment, tripling Lou's business in short order. The big barber set up one firm rule: Anyone coming in didn't leave without a trim, a shave, or dental treatment. While he raked in the money on his end, Sam raked it in on hers.

When Travis finally got wind of all this, he was livid! He stormed into the crowded barbershop with fire in his eyes. "You big, dumb ox!" he yelled at Lou. "What the devil do you mean by allowing Sam to gamble in here? Do you know what you've done?"

"Yeah," Lou said with a smug grin. "I've done more business than you can shake a stick at! That little gal's a gold mine!"

"In one week, you've managed to undo all the fine lessons it's taken us all to teach her, you mush-head! For Pete's sake, she might as well be dealing cards at the Silver Nugget! You should hear the talk going around town!"

"Hey! Pipe down, will you, Kincaid?" Sam muttered past the cigarette dangling between her lips. "We're tryin' to concentrate on our game."

"Yeah, Marshal," another player put in. "I think I might finally win a pot here."

"Don't bet your britches on it," another man grumbled. "If I didn't know better, I'd swear Sam was cheatin'. I've never seen anybody win at cards the way she does."

"I don't cheat, Charlie," Sam said with a sly grin. "I don't have to when you're playin'."

This brought a hearty round of laughter from everyone but Travis. He stood there glaring at all of them, but especially at Sam. Marching over to the table, he snatched the cigarette from her mouth, tossing it to the floor and grinding it out with his boot heel. Ripping the cards from one hand, he tossed them on the table. From the other, he pried loose her half-filled glass of whiskey. "C'mon!" he commanded, grabbing her arms and hauling her out of her chair. "You're coming with me!"

"Damn you, Kincaid!" she shrieked, kicking at him as he pulled her toward the door. "I was holdin' four aces!"

"I don't care if you were holding a royal straight flush! Your gambling days are over! If I can't trust Lou to keep you out of trouble, I'll find someone who can! And if I ever catch you drinking again, I'll tan your bottom so hard you won't sit for a month!"

"You and whose army?" she screeched, the toe of her boot finally connecting with his ankle bone. "It's sure as hell gonna take a bigger man than you!"

"Yeow! Stop that, you little fury! By God, when I get you home, I'll show you who's big enough!"

Tumble hadn't seen this good a show in years. Later, the men watching would swear it was better than any play or comedy that had ever found its way to town. As their marshal wrestled the spitting redhead through the door and down the street, snickers followed them.

"Wonder what's really gonna happen when he gets her home?" one fellow commented with a suggestive wink.

"Yeah, well I'd like to know if he really is big enough to handle the little spitfire," another chuckled. "It's gonna take a heck of a man to tame that wild filly."

Within ten minutes of losing his cardsharp, Lou had a new money-maker going. He was making book on how long it would take Travis to bring his pretty prisoner to heel or the other way around. Everyone was making bets, and by the end of the day, the odds were in Sam's favor two to one.

"What have ya done to put the marshal into such a sour mood?" Billy asked her.

"Just breathin' does that!" Sam told him with a sigh, shooting a glare over her shoulder at Travis.

He was sitting behind his desk, watching her every move. Now he said, "Speak up, you two, so I know you aren't planning something."

Sam stuck her tongue out at him. "Go suck a rotten egg, Kincaid! And while you're at it, quit starin' at me all the time, like you was—uh—were expectin' me to slip Billy a gun or somethin'."

"If you had one, I'm sure you would." When the

ransom trade had failed, and Sam had come back to town with him, Travis had taken possession of her guns once more. "These days, there isn't much I'd put past you."

At Billy's questioning glance, Sam explained. "He caught me gamblin' at Lou's."

"And drinking and smoking," Travis added for good measure.

Her brother's face showed his confusion. "Is that all? That's what has him so riled? Geez, I thought ya'd set fire to his house, at least!"

Sam shrugged. "He's got it into his head to reform me. Thinks it's his Christian duty or somethin', I guess. Now, enough of him," she added with a grimace in Travis's direction. "I came to see how you're doin', not jaw all day about the marshal. How you feelin', Billy? You're still a mite pale."

"I'm feelin' better, I guess. Still as weak as a newborn kitten, though."

"I guess that's to be expected. You sure lost a lot of blood b'fore we got you back to town. I thought sure you were gonna up and die on me, Billy. Scared the liver out o' me."

"Didn't do much for me, neither," Billy said.

"Either," Sam corrected before she even thought twice.

Travis's hoot of laughter almost drowned out Billy's perplexed, "Huh?"

"Your sister has been learning how to speak correctly while she's been here," Travis explained with a chuckle. "She's also been learning to read and write."

"Well, I'll be a horned toad!" Billy sounded not only surprised, but impressed. "Wait till Pa hears that! And Tom'll be mad as heck when he finds out he's not the only one with book learnin' now. Maybe he'll stop lordin' it over all the rest of us." Then Billy's face fell. "'Course, I might not be around by then to see none of it."

Tears sprang to Sam's eyes. "Don't, Billy," she begged, her big, sad eyes pleading with him. "Don't even think it."

"Sam, I'm sorry, but it's the truth. We both know they're just gettin' me well again so's they can hang me." Billy's face mirrored her own dismay. "Don't know why they bothered fixin' me up. They should'a jest let me bleed to death an' saved us all the trouble."

Sam was almost choking on her sobs by now. If Billy died, she didn't know what she would do. Brushing the tears from her cheeks, she stiffened her backbone and tried to pull herself together. Right now, Billy needed encouragement, not a weeping sister. "We'll find a way, Billy. They won't hang you if I have anything to do with it. I promise."

Travis had seen her shoulders shaking and heard the tell-tale tears in her voice. "There's nothing you can do, Sam," he told them quietly. "All we can do is try to see that he gets a fair trial. The rest will be up to the judge to decide."

Ignoring him, Sam forced a wobbly smile for her brother. "We'll both see Pa and the boys again. Don't you worry none, Billy." On a lighter note, she said, "Maybe by then Miss Tucker will have taught all of them how to read. Now, wouldn't that be a hoot? Then we could all go somewhere and start a store or somethin'."

"Sure, Sammie," Billy agreed with a weary

smile. "Sounds nice. What kind o' store do ya want?" he asked, willing to indulge her fantasy to make her feel better.

"Oh, a general store maybe, or a little place to serve food and drinks. I'm gettin' to be a fair cook now."

"Sure, but we'll need some money to start it," Billy reminded her.

"Thinking of robbing a few more trains and banks already?" Travis asked wryly, his arms folded over his chest.

"I could get it without havin' to do that," Sam boasted. "I got a fair start playin' cards in Lou's place. I figure a good, solid month of gamblin' and I could buy us a store, all right."

"But your gambling days are over, sweetheart," Travis reminded her with a hateful grin.

She ignored his endearment. "Not by a long shot, Kincaid. Just postponed a while."

Billy's eyebrows had shot up. In a whisper, he asked, "Sammie, what's goin' on between you an' the marshal? He sweet on ya or somethin'?"

"Guess you could say it's the 'or somethin' part," she admitted with a shrug, trying unsuccessfully to hide the wild blush creeping into her face.

One look at her flushed cheeks, and Billy was doubly suspicious. "He your lover, Sam?"

Her head hanging, her teeth biting at her lower lip, Sam nodded. "Yeah, Billy, for all the good it's doin' any of us."

"Ya love him?" he asked incredulously.

Again she nodded miserably. "Don't let on to him, will you? It's bad enough as it is. B'sides, I figure once we're free of here, I'll forget him soon enough, just like he won't give me a thought when we're gone."

"I told you two not to whisper!" Travis growled, irritated that he'd not been able to hear this last exchange.

"Go sit on a cactus!" Sam snapped. "I swear, a body can't have a minute's privacy with you around!"

A short while later, Doc Purdy, her current keeper now that Lou Sprit had lost favor, came to collect her. Billy still had a thoughtful look on his face. Whatever he was thinking was bothering him. "Tell you what, Billy," she said in an effort to cheer him, "when I come to visit you tomorrow, I'll bring you an apple pie. I'll bake it myself, so you can see what a good cook I'm gettin' to be."

Billy rewarded her with a grin. "You do that, Sam, 'cause I'm gonna have to taste it to believe it. Last I knew, ya couldn't boil water without burnin' it." He gave a rueful laugh. "Guess poisonin' can't be any worse than hangin', an' anything'll beat jest sittin' here waitin'."

Chapter 17

If Sam seemed unconcerned about the town's gossip about her and the marshal, Travis was very upset and aware of it. Since the day they had returned to town to discover that Nan and Nola had been kidnapped, he and Sam had waltzed around one another as if trying to dance with a porcupine. Neither had mentioned his suggestion of marriage or their single night of shared passion, though the memories lay constantly between them like lingering shadows. It seemed the more they avoided these issues, the more aware of them they became, and the more irritable with one another.

For the first few days, it wasn't so very difficult, for Sam was so worried over Billy's survival that she had little emotion left for anything else. Those days were hectic for Travis as well. While Billy was too weak to move, and Sam refused to leave her brother's sickbed and was so preoccupied that she scarcely realized that Travis was gone, the marshal searched the countryside surrounding Tumble. Each day, he rode until there was nowhere left to look but returned after finding no trace of the Downings or their lady hostage.

At last admitting that finding them now was highly unlikely, he temporarily dismissed the idea and concentrated instead on trying to get Billy to talk. If anything, Billy was even more close-mouthed than his stubborn sister. Travis couldn't seem to get an ounce of information out of the two of them put together.

All of this put Travis thoroughly out of sorts. Then, to have to share his bedroom with Sam made matters worse. By exercising extreme will, he managed to keep his hands off her, if only to quiet his own conscience. Abstinence did nothing for his sense of humor, making him even more of a grouch. He wanted her more than ever now, having once tasted her sweet, hot passionate responses, and it was hell having to deny himself. But if Sam didn't want to marry him, the least he could do was control himself and try not to complicate their lives any further.

Luckily, Sam seemed to be of a similar mind, if her angry attitude was any indication. Each night, she turned her back to him as soon as they were both abed, Travis on his mattress on the floor. In silence and with exchanged glares, they would awake and dress and usually spend the remainder of the day sniping at one another, only to repeat the entire process day after miserable day.

In truth, Sam was angry with Travis for a number of reasons. First, he seemed to be reveling in the attention Nola Sandoval was showing him, not to mention the fact that he'd done nothing to Rafe Sandoval for messing up the exchange of hostages. He had limited Sam's visits to her brother, and now that Billy was well enough to be questioned, Travis was literally hounding the poor man about their family. Now he had put a halt to her only money-making project at Lou's, instead of being proud of the fact that she had found a way to prosper without stealing.

At the very top of Sam's list of grievances against him was the fact that though he'd mentioned marriage before, now Travis seemed perfectly content to sleep near her each night and not show the slightest sign of desire for her. It was thoroughly confusing, absolutely irritating, and totally exasperating. But then, so were Sam's feelings toward Travis. She had yet to forget or to forgive his holding that gun on her, yet she still desired him, still loved him. Would he have shot her? She tried to tell herself that he wouldn't have, that it had all been a bluff, but was she fooling herself, blinded by her own love for him?

Not that Sam wanted to marry the man, but it would have done wonders for her feminine esteem to know that he still desired her. But no! The man acted as if she were an old pair of bedroom slippers he no longer had use for! Upon first seeing him each morning, Sam's first reaction was one of intense desire. Then common sense would reassert itself, and Sam would remember how hateful he was toward her each day, and she had to fight the urge to throw something satisfyingly hard and heavy at him!

Unaware that Sam was fighting the same raging desires and actually craving his attention, Travis stuck to his plan—right up to the time it exploded in his face. Doc Purdy and Chas had been alternately watching over Sam when Travis was too busy to do so. At least with them, he didn't have to worry whether she was drinking or playing poker with every man in Tumble. Chas even found time to escort her to Alma Aldrich's for Sam's singing lessons.

This particular day, the last day of June, was hot and miserably muggy. Having finished with her singing lesson, which had sent poor Parson Aldrich seeking solitude elsewhere, Sam was being escorted back to the jail for her visit with Billy. She and Chas were walking slowly along the street and had come opposite the Silver Nugget when Sam happened to glance up and notice Molly Winfrow watching them from a second-story window in the saloon.

"Oh, look, Chas! There's Molly!" Sam exclaimed, waving and smiling at the other woman. Chas colored but nodded, a slight smile curving his lips.

Molly returned the greeting with a short wave, then hastily dropped the sheer curtain back over the window, shielding herself from view.

"C'mon, Chas," Sam said, tugging at his arm and guiding him into the street. "Let's go have a chat with Molly. I got me a few questions I'd like to ask her." As he balked, she dropped his arm and hurried toward the saloon on her own. Over her shoulder she called, "You can wait for me if you want, maybe have a beer. I won't be but just a few minutes."

"Sam!" Chas came out of his stupor with a jerk. "Sam! Come back here! Travis will skin me alive if ya go in there!" He loped after her, ignoring the heads turning his way in avid interest.

He'd been talking to himself. Without those awful shoes to hinder her, Sam bounded into the saloon, the bat-wing doors banging in her wake. Never breaking stride, she strode swiftly past the gaping bartender and several men who had stopped playing cards and were staring open-mouthed at her. Her boots rang loudly as she took the stairs two at a time. Behind her, she disregarded Chas's frantic cries, joined now by the bartender's.

Curious over all the commotion, several doors along the upper hallway popped open. Sam spotted several scantily-clad women, some yawning widely, before she recognized Molly. "Hi ya, Molly!" she called out with a grin. "You got time to talk with me a spell?"

"Uh, uh," Molly hesitated. "I'm not sure you should be here, Samantha."

"Oh, call me Sam. Everybody does!"

Before Molly, who was adroit at steering customers in and out of her door with finesse, realized it, she and Sam were inside her room with the door closed. Rounding on the saloon girl, Sam became serious. "Molly, I need your help."

At a loss and thinking the worst, Molly blurted, "I can't help you escape, Sam! Travis would run me out of town, and then only if I was lucky enough not to be tarred and feathered! Worse than that, Chas would hate me forever!"

Waving a dismissing hand in the air, Sam said, "Don't worry, Molly. That's not what I need your help with."

"You're expectin'?" the woman asked.

"Expectin'?" Sam echoed, her brow furrowed in confusion. "Oh! That!" she cried, as she finally realized what Molly meant. "No. Well, at least I don't think so."

"Then I don't understand," Molly confessed, shaking her head.

A calculating gleam glittered in Sam's dark eyes. "You know a lot about men and what they like, Molly. I want you to teach me what I need to know to make Travis want me again."

"Again?"

"Uh-huh," Sam nodded, grinning. "Again. I want that man so on fire for me, he'll have to check in the mirror to see if his hair is burnin'!"

With a wicked smile, Molly nodded. "Honey, you've come to the right place!"

Half an hour later, Chas was dragging Sam down the street, berating her with every step. "If Travis finds out where ya were, my ears will be ringin' for a week! What's in that package Molly gave ya? More trouble?"

"That's none o' your business, Chas Brown!" she told him with a stern glower. "And Travis won't notice it and ask embarrassin' questions if you keep your lip buttoned. In fact, he won't know any of this, if you don't say anything."

He gave her an incredulous look. "In this town? Heck, he probably already knows! Someone's bound to have told him."

"Shoot! He didn't know about my gambling for a whole week! Listen, Chas, I promise you that by the time he learns about this, it won't matter." Behind her back, Sam crossed her fingers and hoped she was right. If only Travis didn't catch on until tonight and ruin all her plans!

"Just swear to me that you're not plannin' to escape again."

"Not this time, Chas. You have my word. Not this time."

Travis frowned and turned his eyes toward the parlor ceiling. What the devil was going on upstairs in his bedroom? Sam had bathed and gone up a half-hour ago, and since then he'd heard all kinds of racket. For the past ten minutes it had sounded as if a woodpecker was trapped up there with her, but at least with all the noise he knew she was still there and not trying to escape again.

Again it came, that peculiar tap-tap, clip-clop knocking sound, traveling the length of the room from one side to the other and back again. That did it! She was either nailing all his socks to the floor, or she was training a miniature pony for the circus! Regardless, his curiosity was running rampant. He couldn't stand it a moment longer. He had to find out what she was doing up there!

Opening the door to his room, Travis got the shock of his life! There stood Sam, her head down and bent over from the waist, smoothing the long, black net stockings that covered her legs! Clad in a fancy, red satin corset that fit like a second skin, she was weaving slightly as she tottered on black, strapped high-heeled shoes. Mesmerized, Travis stared, agog.

Heat flared through him, and he had difficulty

swallowing as he watched her straighten. In those shoes and the alluring stockings, topped by lacy garters, her legs seemed to go on forever! Even standing perfectly upright, her breasts thrust impudently forward, seemingly ready to pop out over the black-laced rim of the bodice. Her flowing mane of red-gold hair scarcely veiled the charms so readily evident in the brief costume.

He must have made some noise, though he stood rooted to the spot, for she turned toward him. Travis gulped again. The glow in her black eyes was a blatant invitation. "Where?" His voice came out gruff, and he had to clear his throat and try again. "Where did you get that outfit?"

She countered his inquiry with one of her own. "Do you like it, Travis?" she purred. Tossing her hair back over her shoulder, she walked slowly toward him, the tap-tap of her heels revealing the sound he'd wondered about. "I thought at first the color would clash with my hair, but it doesn't, does it?"

That slightly husky tone of her voice was like having warm honey poured over him. With a will of its own, his body responded to it, and to her. "No, it doesn't," he croaked out, suddenly feeling like a schoolboy faced with his first woman.

"Sam, do you know what you're doing?"

"I wish you'd quit askin' me that. In fact, it'd suit me just fine if you didn't say another word for a while." She sidled up to him, her high heels bringing her lips to a more accessible level with his. Reaching out, she took his hands and placed them on the swell of her bosom. "Let's not fight, Travis, when there are so many things we can do that are so much more fun." Wrapping her arms about his neck, she tilted his mouth toward hers. "Kiss me, lawman," she sighed against his lips. "I promise to be a very willing prisoner tonight—a full surrender! Take me and make me yours."

Her perfume wafted about him, adding to the exotic spell she was weaving. Of their own, his hands fondled her breasts, finding the erect nipples sheathed in sleek satin. "Oh, God!" he groaned as her tongue traced the shape of his lips with hot, languid strokes. His fingers splayed out, spanning her ribcage as he pulled her lithe body against him, letting her feel his hard arousal.

He'd wanted her for so long, tormented by the memory of their lovemaking. He'd denied himself and her for as long as he could, and now his will, his sense of what was right and proper, was crumbling like a wind-blown sandcastle. She was here, she was enchanting, and offering herself to him. She was his for the taking, and Travis knew he'd be the biggest fool who'd ever lived if he did not accept her bewitching gift.

"There is a saying, Sam, about being careful what you ask for, because you just might get it," he growled, picking her up in his arms and striding toward the bed. He held her aloft, gazing into her deep, dark eyes, his own ablaze with yearning. "When morning comes, don't say I didn't warn you, my beautiful, brazen bandit!"

"Just love me, Travis," she begged, paying no heed to his warning. "Love me until I have stars dancing in my head!"

She awoke to the feel of his lips nuzzling her nipple. His warm breath washed her breast, his mustache sending tingles over her skin, like sizzling goosebumps. "Travis!" she sighed, arching lazily into him with a cat-like stretch. She felt so good! So marvelously content awakening to his loving touch.

His hand, which had been resting on the curve of her hip, now stroked a languid path from her breast to her thigh, strokes so light, yet strangely possessive. When his fingers wandered teasingly along her inner thigh, his calloused thumb brushing the fiery curls at the apex, Sam gave a delicate shiver. A tiny, sleepy moan of delight escaped her lips.

Travis chuckled low. "You remind me of a lazy, orange tabby cat, stretching and purring in the sun."

A serene smile etched her lips, though she had yet to open her eyes, content to let herself drift with the feelings Travis was eliciting. "The cat that got the cream," she murmured, savoring the delicious feel of his lips, which were now nibbling along her shoulder. "One who likes bein' petted."

He laughed again, low and soft. "I've noticed. I think I've finally found the way to tame the wildcat in you, my little feline."

Sam didn't bother to correct him; she didn't want to, for now his lips and tongue were tracing a wet, tingling path down across her chest. As his tongue delved into her navel, making moist swirls, she gasped. Sleep fled on swift wings, replaced by a fire that blazed high and bright. The soft bristles of his mustache tickled her lower stomach as his mouth lovingly outlined the ridges of her pelvic bones.

Her fingers curled into fists at her sides, then came swiftly up to tangle in his bright hair as his hands parted her thighs and his head lowered. His tongue was playing cat and mouse with that most sensitive nub of sensuality, darting and lapping until Sam almost screamed at the sweet, wild sensations streaming through her. Sucking in a sharp breath, she gasped, "Travis! Oooh, Travis! S–S–Stop!"

He didn't stop. Quite the contrary. His nimble tongue flicked out faster, harder, making her writhe in ecstatic agony beneath him, as he adored her most feminine secrets. Giving no quarter, he plundered her with lips and tongue, sucking and licking until she was nearly mindless with desire, climbing higher and higher on that spiral of rapture. Alternately her quivering muscles strained and relaxed as he held her just short of that glorious peak, teasing and tormenting her until tears of passion ran down her face and she pleaded with him to please, please release her from this exquisite madness.

Knowing she was at her most vulnerable, he asked thickly, "What will you give me in return, sweetheart?"

Delirious with delicious desire, she panted helplessly, "Myself. Anythin'! Everythin'! Just please, Travis, please!"

Only then did he give her that which she sought most at this moment. His fingers and mouth skillfully brought her to that pinnacle of pleasure, then held her closely as she cried out, shimmering and shaking beneath his touch. Spasms still racked her as he raised himself over her, plunging his throbbing shaft into her hot, wet depths. Their cries blended as his lips covered hers.

As they moved together, their mouths mimicked

their lower bodies, his tongue lashing into her mouth, her lips sucking and pulling at his tongue. Their pulses pounded in an untamed rhythm, their bodies gliding slickly as they strove together to touch new heights. He took her with powerful thrusts without restraint. She gave herself fully, gladly, meeting him stroke for silken stroke.

Then the fiery dam burst, sending molten lava streaming through them, hurtling them skyward like a flaming comet. Spinning through the heavens, they clutched at one another. Crying out, her head flung back in ecstasy, Sam's nails dug narrow furrows in his back, but neither of them noticed. They were too entranced to care.

Long minutes later, they lay sated in one another's embrace, breathing hard. Sam felt boneless, as if she had run a hundred miles flat out, her thighs still quivering. Travis had never felt so absolutely relaxed and so tremendously exhilarated at the same time. Lying there with his head nestled against Sam's soft breast, he never wanted to move from this spot. He wished he could freeze time at this moment and stay like this throughout eternity.

All too soon, however, the real world claimed them, and it was time to face the consequences of their actions. Travis's first words shattered the fragile illusion of bliss. "Unless you really want the gown and the whole rigmarole, I'd prefer a private ceremony—the sooner the better."

"Ceremony?" she questioned stupidly, her mind still fuzzy from their lovemaking.

"Our wedding, Sam. You don't really want a big to-do, do you? We can always have a party to celebrate later, when things are more settled."

Struggling upright in the bed, and shoving him from his perch on her chest, Sam glared at him. "We're not gonna get into that again, are we, Kincaid? I told you I'm not marryin' you, and that's that!"

"Oh, but you promised, Sam, my love," he crooned, returning her glare with a devilish grin. "And you always keep your word, don't you?"

"I never!" she huffed.

"Sure you did, honey." His smile widened, his hand reaching out to brush lightly over a sensitive nipple. "Remember when you were pleading so prettily for your pleasure? You promised me anything I wanted, and I want you—forever—as my wife, all nice and legal."

She stared at him, her eyes wide, glittering with emotion. "That's not fair, Travis! Surely you don't mean to hold me to that! God in heaven, I'd have promised almost anythin' then, and you know it!" Again, if Travis had mentioned loving her, Sam might have considered the idea, but the words she longed to hear had yet to pass his lips.

"Fair or not, that's the way it is, darlin'. Make up your mind to it. You and I are going to be married —soon."

"No! I won't do it, and you can't make me!" She slapped his pesky hand away from her breast.

One eyebrow rose high. "Can't I? Well, Samantha, we'll just see about that."

It should have been a warning when he called her Samantha, but Sam was too irate to notice. Caught up in her own anger, she dismissed his claim as ludicrous. There was absolutely no way he could force her to marry him if she didn't agree. She'd simply ignore him, like she had the last time

235

he'd mentioned marriage, and he'd forget the whole thing before long, she was sure. Her course of action decided, Sam shoved it from her mind. She had better, or worse, things to worry about than Travis's lukewarm proposals.

CHAPTER 18

"Why, my dear!" Alma Aldrich exclaimed, her hand to her ample chest. "I was just so thrilled and amazed to hear! And you never said a word!"

Sam stood next to the bars of Billy's cell and stared stupidly at the parson's wife. The giddy lady and her husband had just entered the jail behind a smugly grinning Travis, and Sam had no idea what the woman was going on about so breathlessly. Sam had come for a visit with Billy, and Chas had been left to guard them both until Travis got back.

"I beg your pardon, ma'am?" Sam asked hesitantly. "What didn't you know?"

"Why, that you and Travis were thinking of getting married, of course!" Alma gushed. "You could have knocked me over with a feather when Travis told us this morning."

"I know exactly how you felt!" Sam muttered, shooting a hateful glare in Travis's direction. In fact, Sam was feeling a bit disconcerted herself at this moment.

"Sam?" Billy's voice sounded behind her, and she turned to find him wagging his head in bafflement. "What's goin' on here?"

"We're about to have a wedding, Billy," Travis announced before Sam could get a word past her constricting throat. Chills of dread were working their way up her backbone, and she felt as if she had fallen into a nightmare from which she might never awaken. The snake had actually gone and done it! He'd talked with Parson Aldrich! The preacher and his wife were not here to visit with Billy, as Sam had first supposed when they'd walked into the jail. They really thought they were here for her wedding!

Billy voiced the thought foremost in Sam's muddled mind. "Here? Now?"

"Well, we would have had the parson perform the ceremony in the church, under normal circumstances," Travis informed them, "but I thought Sam would prefer to have at least one member of her family witness her wedding. Besides, as her older brother, who better to give the bride away?" As he spoke, Travis sauntered to Sam's side, his arm going about her waist.

Sam broke free of her stupor. "This isn't funny, Kincaid, and it's gone far enough. I'm not gon . . . na . . ." Sam stuttered to a halt and ceased trying to wriggle away from him. To her shock, she suddenly felt the barrel of a gun pressed against her back, where no one could see it and no one but she and Travis knew it was there.

"You were saying, Sam?" Travis asked in his most solicitous tone.

"N—nothin'." She swayed slightly, but Travis's other hand came up to grab her arm and steady her. As she stared up at him, the look in his turquoise eyes was relentless enough to make her truly wonder if he would pull the trigger if she dared defy him. Surely not! Oh, surely not in front of the Aldriches.

As if he'd read her mind, Travis leaned his head close to hers, his eyes hard and piercing. "I wouldn't bet my life on it, Sam," he whispered low.

Her face went paper-white, dots of perspiration popping out on her brow as she silently begged him not to do this. Her plea went unheeded as Travis turned a smile on the parson. "We're ready to begin any time you are, Parson. Chas, close the door and lock it, so we won't be interrupted, please. Then you can stand in as a witness with Mrs. Aldrich."

The next few minutes were the longest, most unbelievable Sam had ever experienced. Why didn't anyone realize that she was being held at gunpoint, literally forced into this? An hysterical giggle rose to her throat. She'd heard of shotgun weddings, but this was ridiculous! Never had she heard of the bride being forced into marriage like this; it was usually the reluctant groom being not-so-gently coerced by an enraged father!

There stood Parson Aldrich, calmly reading from his book, his eyeglasses sliding to the end of his nose in the stifling heat of the office. Billy had already done his part by saying he was giving her over to Travis's care, and Mrs. Aldrich was standing to one side with a silly grin on her face, fanning herself with her handkerchief. Chas was looking pleased and attentive. Sam couldn't bring herself to look up into Travis's face, afraid of what she might see there.

A sharp jab in her side brought her attention back to the proceedings. "Answer the man, Sam," Travis insisted.

"Uh . . . uh . . ."

"The proper response is, 'I do,' my dear," he prompted again. To the others, he said with a slight laugh, "My bride's a bit nervous, I think."

Again he prodded her with the gun barrel. "I—I d–do!" Sam blurted, starting to shake from head to toe.

Somehow, she managed to stumble through the rest of her recital. Travis repeated his part in a steady voice, rich and smooth and without hesitation. Then, before she knew what was happening, Travis was holding her hand in his, wedging a shiny gold band onto her finger, and Parson Aldrich was intoning those fatal, final words, "I now pronounce you man and wife. Travis, you may kiss your bride."

Knowing she was about to protest the wedding again, Travis sealed her lips with his in a long kiss. To those watching it seemed terribly romantic, if a bit unorthodox, the way the groom pulled his bride close and kissed her passionately. For Sam it was the final, bittersweet torment. His lips punished hers, his arms crushing the breath from her lungs. Already frighteningly short of breath, it seemed his intent was to suck the rest of the breath from her body. The world seemed to tilt sickeningly, her knees giving way beneath her until only Travis's arms about her kept her standing.

When he finally lifted his lips from hers, Sam wilted against him, gasping. Her hands clung to his arms as her head swam dizzily. "I think my bride has become over-excited," she heard Travis say, as if from within a tunnel. "That and the heat have undoubtedly exhausted her."

When she tried to raise her head and look at him, her eyes refused to focus. Suddenly she felt herself falling. Vaguely, on the fringes of her consciousness, Sam felt Travis's strong arms come about her back and knees as he lifted her into his arms. Then, to everyone's amazement, not the least of all hers, Sam fainted.

Slowly swimming up through layers of swirling fog, Sam finally opened her eyes to find herself lying in Travis's bed. Her new husband sat propped on pillows next to her, calmly puffing on his cigarette and watching her through the exhaled smoke. "I was beginning to wonder if you were going to sleep right through the day and into our wedding night," he drawled. "You know, of course, that the entire town is going to be counting the months between now and the time our first child is born."

Sam attempted to sit up, but her head began to spin alarmingly, so she quickly discarded that idea. Rolling her head carefully toward him, she asked weakly, "Why should they?"

"Well," he informed her, "it's not every bride who faints dead away at her own wedding, to be carried home through a crowded town in the arms of her groom."

Sam groaned and closed her eyes again. "I can't believe I did that!" she wailed. "And you, you coyote! You deliberately tried to squeeze the life out of me!"

He laughed. "Of course," he agreed pleasantly, "and you played your part to perfection afterward, too. Quite a performance, Sam. Sorry you had to miss the last part. Eyes were popping out all along Main Street, especially with Alma Aldrich hustling along behind us telling everyone with ears that we'd just been married. By now, the entire territory knows our happy news."

"Happy news, my bloomers!" Sam retorted furiously, her dark eyes snapping fire at him. "You had a gun stuck in my side, or we'd never be married now!"

Travis shrugged. "It got the job done. That's all I wanted." When she continued to glare at him, he exclaimed in exasperation, "Sam! You can't tell me you really believed I'd shoot you!"

"Danged tootin', I did!" she shrieked, tears swimming in her eyes. "You gave me a look that would've frozen a lake in the middle of the desert! You were gonna shoot me, or my name ain't Samantha Downin'!"

"But it's not, Sam. You're Samantha Kincaid now, honey." He leaned closer, that same determined glint in his pale eyes. "Now and always, till death do us part. You belong to me, Sam, body and soul, for all time."

"If it's death you're wantin', give me a gun and I'll gladly oblige you!" she yelled back.

"Oh, no!" he chuckled. "Getting hitched didn't addle my brains, love. It's you who's going to have to learn how to be a dutiful little wife from now on. You do recall promising to obey me when you repeated your vows, don't you?"

Very vaguely, she did remember pledging something to that effect. "That weddin' was a farce, and you know it, Kincaid! It can't be legal!"

"Oh, but it is, *Kincaid*," he returned with a mocking grin. "You and I are well and truly wedded, and as soon as I can get you out of that dress, you're going to be well and truly bedded by your new husband."

"You lay one finger on me and I'll scratch your face off!"

"Then it'll match my back, won't it?" he taunted, reaching for her as she scooted away from him. "I've never seen a woman who can lose herself as passionately or completely as you do. Mind you, I'm not complaining, Sam. I love it when you burn for me like that, all hot and wild."

She tried to push his hands away, but suddenly it seemed he had twice the usual number of arms and legs. With hardly any effort at all, he had her pinned under him, her skirts askew about her waist. "I don't want you, Travis!" she hissed.

"Tell me that in a few minutes, if you can, Sam," he taunted, nibbling his way up the slim column of her neck to her ear.

She told herself if she wasn't still so dizzy, she could have fought him. Maybe if her skirts weren't hindering her, she could dislodge him. Perhaps, if he wasn't kissing her with such passion, she wouldn't feel so weak. If only. . . .

Sam ceased making excuses, her mind drifting among clouds of desire. The bare truth was, she loved him. All he had to do was touch her, and she wanted him with a desperation that was frightening. Within moments of trying to deny him, she was aiding him in divesting her of her clothing, and

Travis of his, practically ripping the shirt from his back.

Her sharp teeth nipped at the muscled flesh of his shoulder, urging him to hurry. Her tongue found his nipples, hiding in the downy hair of his golden chest. Her hands caressed him and drew him down to her, their bodies melding into one. A wild wind roared in her ears; her blood thundered through her veins; and Sam gloried in his magnificent possession of her, claiming her fair share in turn.

By the time they had spent themselves, she was his, her heart lost to him completely, and deep within her heart, Sam rejoiced. No more running, no more hiding. She had found a home at last in Travis's arms.

If there was one sour note to Sam's marriage, it was that Travis and her family were still on opposite sides of the law. There was no help for it, or any changing the way things stood. As a U.S. Marshal, Travis was bound to uphold the law and to stop those who broke it. Billy was still his prisoner, as well as his brother-in-law, and would have to stand trial for his crimes. In fact, despite their marriage, Sam had to go before the circuit judge when he arrived in Tumble.

"I'm sure we can convince him that you've reformed, Sam," Travis told her solemnly. "Chas and I, Elsie and the Aldriches will all testify on your behalf. Since we're married, he'll probably release you into my custody and forget your part in those robberies. Of course, your main defense will be that you were only twelve when your family dragged you into that life of crime, and you really weren't responsible for your own actions. Don't worry, sweetheart. You're not going to jail or going to hang."

"I'm not so worried for myself as I am for Billy," she confessed. "He's my brother, Travis! I love him! Isn't there some way you can help him, too?"

Drying her tears with his lips, he vowed, "I'll try, Sam. I'll do all I can but I'm not sure it will be enough. A lot will depend on the judge and how much Billy decides to cooperate. I wish I could promise you it will all turn out all right, darlin', but I'd be lying to you. It's best if you're prepared for the worst, just in case."

He pulled her close, cradling her head on his chest. "Either way, I'll be here for you, Sam. If it helps at all, I'm sorry. I see you hurting and I feel your pain. If there were any way I could make it easier, I would, gladly. All I can do is share your pain and dry your tears, and try to take your mind from your troubles at least some of the time."

"Now that we're married, how will you get Nan Tucker back? Do you still intend to trade me for her?"

"When hell freezes over!" he exploded, turning her face up to his. His eyes were fierce to behold. "You're mine! All of you will just have to accept that fact and learn to live with it, especially you, Sam! The sooner you do, the better off you'll be. I'll never give you up to anyone!"

His attitude irritated her, but she calmed herself by telling herself he wouldn't be so possessive if he didn't care for her at least a little. So instead of arguing, she simply asked, "Then how are you goin' to get Miss Tucker back?"

"I'll think of something, if we ever hear from

that father of yours again. The longer this goes on, the more worried I get for Nan. Where in blazes are they, and why haven't they made any more demands?"

"I don't know, Travis. Maybe they're waitin' for Billy to get well. All I can tell you is, none of them will hurt her. I know my pa and brothers, Travis. They'd never harm a defenseless lady."

Every year since Texas had entered the Union in 1845, Tumble had celebrated the Fourth of July in grand fashion. This year was no exception. Tumble and its entire population went crazy, or so it seemed to Sam. The whole town literally rolled up the carpet, threw up its heels, and put on the biggest, noisiest shindig she'd ever seen! Even its most straight-laced citizens seemed to shed their inhibitions for this one day.

From early morning, the town was buzzing with activity, and the entire day was to be one long party. Down at the schoolyard, tables had been set up, and lanterns strung for the picnic lunch and the dancing later that night. There were even fireworks planned for after dark!

Inside the schoolhouse, booths had been erected by stringing blankets on lines, and all manner of merchandise was on display for judging and for sale afterward. Quilts and fine needlework vied with woodcarvings and drawings. There were jars upon jars of pickles and canned fruits and vegetables, miles of pies and cakes and cookies and candies, and any type of mouth-watering confection imaginable. Inside a tent near the outside tables, food and drink of all kinds were tempting the revelers to spend their coin, the enticing aromas drifting on the summer air.

No matter what the age, there were games and prizes to be won. Foot races were planned, and sack races, and contests. There was the annual horse race, of course, as well as the armadillo races. Upon seeing Travis's woebegone face, Sam truly regretted having killed poor Army, but what was done was done, and she couldn't go back and undo it. Still, she felt terrible about it. Maybe Travis would win the turkey shoot or the knife-throwing or hatchet-tossing contests—anything to cheer him up!

Ordinarily, Travis's major concern was keeping an eye out for anyone who became too drunk and decided to pick a fight. July fifth usually found his three jail cells filled to overflowing with drunks with black eyes and bruises, but rarely anything more serious. Today was different. Travis already had a prisoner to watch, and today of all days, he needed to keep a sharp eye peeled. If the Downings were ever to try to spring Billy, this would be their best chance with the entire town in mass confusion. Instead of wandering the town, enjoying and participating in the activities, Travis would have to spend most of his time in his office.

Realizing that this would not be fair to his bride of three short days, yet not feeling confident enough in her to allow her to roam about under anyone else's care all day, Travis and Chas struck up a deal. Every two hours, they would change places. First, Chas would tour the town, keeping alert to any problems arising. Then he would return to the marshal's office and relieve Travis. If either of them needed help, it was arranged that Lou and Harry and a few other reliable men would respond to the signal of three rifle shots fired into the air. It wasn't the most foolproof plan, but it was the best Travis could come up with.

The day started out calmly enough, all things considered, though it seemed to Sam that the population of Tumble had swelled threefold overnight! She'd never seen so many people in one place, all dashing here and there, crowding the boardwalks and choking the streets. It was impossible to hurry anywhere but fascinating to watch!

When Chas finally came to relieve Travis for the first time, Sam was itching to get out and join the commotion. Travis did not disappoint her, and everywhere they went, they met with congratulations on their marriage. By now, Sam had met a good number of Tumble's citizens, mostly from attending church on Sundays, but scores of strangers also added their best wishes to the newlyweds. Within an hour, her head was swimming with new names and faces.

They wandered the streets and stalls as Travis slowly made his rounds. Together, they watched the horse race, betting against one another's choices for winner. Sam's horse came in first, and Travis would be doing the supper dishes for the next week! By unspoken agreement, they avoided the armadillo races. Travis won the turkey-shoot which surprised no one. Though not the fastest on the draw, his was a deadly aim once his gun cleared its holster. Sam was inordinately proud of him, though she limited her praise to a few, well-chosen words.

At the ring-toss, Travis won Sam a rag doll. She was so touched when he presented it to her, that tears flooded her eyes. "Oh, Travis!" she cried softly, clutching the doll to her breast. "I can't remember when I last had a doll! Thank you!"

Her heartfelt words sent a lump to Travis's throat. He kept forgetting how unusual most of her childhood had been. "Maybe by this time next year, you'll be holding a real child to your breast, Sam," he leaned down to whisper. "Yours and mine. Would you like that?"

She blushed wildly under his vivid gaze. "I don't know," she murmured softly. "I don't know much about carin' for babies."

A tender smile touched his lips and lit his eyes even more brightly. "You'll learn, sweetheart."

On their wanderings, they even found time to sit for a wedding portrait, taken by a traveling photographer who had come to town for the day. "I've never had my picture taken before," she confessed nervously.

"Not even as a baby?" Travis asked with open curiosity.

"Maybe then, but all our pictures got burned along with the house when Quantrill's raiders came through. After that, we never had anymore taken, I guess."

"Well, I have to admit, I like the idea of your face in a wedding picture a darn sight better than on a wanted poster," he said seriously. "Now, smile, and look beautiful, so we can show this to our grandchildren someday. We don't want them to think I married some old sourpuss!"

Though they had to take their picnic lunch back to the jailhouse and eat it there, Sam really didn't mind. They shared their food with Billy and it gave her an extra opportunity to chat with him. She felt guilty about enjoying herself so, while he sat couped up behind bars, contemplating his fate.

All in all, the day seemed to fly by, and by the time the sun began to set, Sam was eager to join the dancing that would begin soon. Travis had promised her they would go as soon as Chas and Molly took their turn. She was also very nervous, never having learned to dance properly. All she and her brothers had ever done was hop about in an imitation of a miner's jig. She'd never danced in a dress before, never waltzed in a man's arms, never dreamed she would.

"I'll teach you, Sam," Travis assured her. Then he grinned that crooked grin of his. "All you have to do is follow my lead—which ought to be a new experience for you!"

"And for you, I suppose," she shot back, softening her words with a teasing smile. "Bet you never danced with a girl in boots before!"

They never made it to the dance. As Chas arrived back at the jail and Sam and Travis were preparing to leave, several riders thundered up outside the jail. At first, Travis thought it might be the Downings. Sam had the same thought until she realized there were too many riders out there for it to be her pa and brothers. At least a dozen men were shouting and shooting, most of them sounding as if they'd downed more than their share of whiskey, a few waving lit torches about their heads.

The mystery was soon cleared up when Rafe Sandoval's voice called out above the clamor. "Kincaid! We've come for Downing! Give him up peacefully, and no one will be hurt. And send out that pretty little outlaw sister of his, too! We're gonna have us a party—a lynchin' party!"

CHAPTER 19

Sam's blood pooled in her toes then rushed to her head. This was her worst nightmare come true! A lynch mob! A wild, drunken lynch mob! They meant to hang her and Billy, and the only help Travis had on hand was Chas. Two men against a dozen or more!

Travis must have been thinking along the same lines, for he said grimly, "With all the noise from the fireworks, it won't do much good to try to signal for help."

When Sam's wide brown eyes met Billy's, she found him frowning, his gaze flitting nervously toward the raised voices in the street outside the office. Molly looked truly frightened; Chas appeared anxious. Coming full circle, Sam met Travis's look. "Give me a gun, Travis," she said quietly, straightening her sagging shoulders and holding out her hand toward him.

On a short, humorless spurt of laughter, he replied, "Not on your life, Sam."

"This *is* my life we're talkin' about, Kincaid," she reminded him. "Mine and Billy's. If you think I'm just gonna stand by and let them drag my brother out of here and hang him, you've got another think comin'!"

"I'm not going to let that happen, Sam, and I'll see to it that no harm comes to you, either. You're my wife, Sam, and I'll take care of you."

It was Sam's turn to give a brusque laugh. "I've got news for you, Travis. That badge you're wearin' ain't big enough to cover your own sweet arse, let alone defend mine, too! Not against this mob! No matter how good you are, or think you are, right now you need help, more help than Chas can give you. Now, quit tryin' to be such a glorified hero and give me a gun, or do you consider yourself too much of a man to accept help from a woman?"

His answering stare was intense and measuring. It all boiled down to whether he could trust her. Both of them knew it as he continued to watch her. "I'll need your promise, Sam, that you won't try to escape or help your brother escape, that after we get this mob settled down and dispersed, you'll hand the gun over without a fuss."

For a few, tense seconds, Sam hesitated. Damn! This could be her one and only chance of saving Billy's life! Travis knew her too well. He knew that if she gave her word, she would be obliged to honor it. Sam's worried gaze went from Travis's face to Billy's, and back again. With a sigh, she agreed, "All right. You have my word."

Turning back to the business at hand, Travis peered out the window. "Give Sam her rifle, Chas, and her revolver. Molly, you and Sam get some ammunition laid out, so we'll have it close at hand. Then douse that lamp. Billy, stay away from that window. Hug the wall, where they can't get a good shot at you. I'm hoping things won't get that ugly, but these men are pretty drunk."

"I'd feel a darn sight better with a gun of my own," Billy lamented, but Travis shook his head. He was taking enough of a chance by arming Sam.

When the lamp had been extinguished, Travis went to the door. He opened it about twelve inches, holding it steady with his foot. Chas and Sam stationed themselves at the windows on either side of the door, while Molly hunched down near Travis's desk, ready to pass the ammunition to them. With his gun drawn and ready, Travis called out, "Go home, Sandoval, and sleep it off. You're not thinking clearly now. We'll talk again tomorrow."

"Isn't anything to talk about!" the man shouted back. "We want Downing. Send him out here!"

"I can't do that, Rafe. You know that. It's against the law. In fact, if you don't stop this foolishness, I'll probably have to arrest the whole lot of you."

Drunken laughter came in reply to this. "You're good, Marshal, but you ain't good enough to take out all of us. We know you've only got that deputy of yours in there with you, and that ain't enough fire power to stop us from taking Downing."

"Wrong!" Sam called, before Travis could respond to Sandoval's challenge. "He's got me, too, and if you want to live to see the sun rise tomorrow, you'd better high-tail it out of here, Sandoval.

I've got a gun barrel leveled right at your head, and what I aim at, I don't miss. You take one step out o' that saddle, and I'm gonna part your hair right down the middle!"

Sandoval's gaze swung toward the window Sam was guarding. "Well, now," he drawled drunkenly, urged on by the laughing comments of his cronies. "If it isn't Little Miss Outlaw, herself! Why, honey, I'm just scared spitless of you!" he jeered.

"That's Mrs. Kincaid to you, Sandoval!" she corrected with unconscious pride in her voice, unknowingly earning a strange look from Travis, and a more curious stare from Billy.

"That wasn't real smart, Marshal," Sandoval said, squinting to see Travis's shadowy form in the darkened doorway. "If you'd have played your cards right, you could've had Nola and the ranch someday. My baby was real sweet on you."

"And where is she now, when she could do the most good?" Travis heard Sam mutter under her breath, not loud enough for Sandoval to hear. "Does she know what her daddy's up to right now?"

Privately, Travis wondered the same thing. If anyone could talk Sandoval out of this stupidity he seemed bent on, it would be Nola.

Tired of talking and stalling, Sandoval signaled his men. His right foot had barely cleared the stirrup, his leg starting its rise toward dismounting, when a shot rang out. Four more shots echoed the first, whistling past several heads, as Travis and Chas added their own warnings to Sam's. One and all, the wary men swiftly reseated themselves in their saddles.

Sandoval's startled yelp of pain turned all eyes toward him. At first no one was sure exactly what was wrong with him, where he might have been hit. Then a thin line of blood streamed out from beneath his tan stetson. Clutching at his head, Sandoval clumsily knocked the hat off. There, as plain as day, was a wide, bloody strip creasing his scalp—straight through the center of his dark hair! Sam had made good her boast, without even dislodging the hat on his head!

Loud murmurs rose around the rancher. "Shee –it!" one fellow exclaimed excitedly.

The man next to Sandoval slowly bent to retrieve the hat, not wanting anyone to take his actions as threatening. When he straightened and examined the stetson, he let out a low whistle. "I'll be hog-tied and rubbed raw! There ain't even a hole in this hat! Nary a nick!"

Fire was shooting from Sandoval's eyes as he stared toward Sam. "You bitch! Hell's the only place for a she-devil like you!" His hand tightened on his rifle as he prepared to raise it toward her.

"Try it, Sandoval, and you'll be wearin' that pommel in your belly button next," Sam growled in warning. After her previous threat, every man there wondered if she couldn't actually do it, too! That was some fancy-shootin' little gal the marshal had married!

"Go home, Sandoval," Travis repeated. "Take your men and go before someone really gets hurt. I've known most of you for a long time now and I'd hate like hell to have to shoot any of you, but I will if I have to. Billy Downing is my prisoner and he's going to stay my prisoner until the circuit judge says otherwise. And Samantha is my wife now, so I'd advise you all to tread lightly with your threats against her."

Several men shifted uncomfortably in their saddles. A few turned questioning looks toward Sandoval. Still others refused to look in his direction. Then, one by one, Sandoval's men began to back away, melting into the darkness.

"Hey, you yellow-livered cowards!" Sandoval hollered after them, his face flushed with rage. "You gonna let this two-bit tin star and his mouthy little wife scare you off like this?" Totally ignored, he bellowed, "Get back here, you hear? I'll see to it you don't work within a thousand miles of here if you don't! You ride off, then just keep movin', and don't come to me for wages due, either!"

Within minutes, only Sandoval and two of his men remained outside the jailhouse. "Well, Sandoval? What's it gonna be?" Travis asked tersely, stepping out onto the boardwalk outside the office door.

For several moments the two men glared at one another, Travis's eyes literally freezing the older man in his saddle. Finally Sandoval grumbled, "Okay, Kincaid. I'm going, but you'd better make damned sure that prisoner of yours doesn't escape before the judge makes it to town. You hear me? I wouldn't put it past you," he sneered. "After all, he's your brother-in-law now, isn't he?"

"Billy will be here," Travis replied, glaring at the man who might have been his father-in-law if he had married Nola instead of Sam. After seeing what the man was capable of, Travis considered himself fortunate not to be related to the arrogant rancher.

Travis watched until Sandoval had ridden out of sight. Then, with a heavy sigh of relief, he entered his office again. Calmly, he relit the lamp, then turned to Sam. Holding out his hand, he said, "I'll take your weapons now, Sam."

She stood rooted to the spot, not moving, just staring at him with those black-brown eyes of hers. Travis was waiting for her to turn her guns over to him, his own eyes like shards of turquoise ice. Chas and Molly stood silently watching, reluctant witnesses to this private drama between husband and wife.

As if sensing his sister's weakness, Billy thrust both hands through the bars toward her. "Don't do it, Sammie," he compelled softly. "Ya know you're my only chance of gettin' out o' here alive. I'm your brother, Sam. Pa wouldn't like your turnin' your back on your own kin." His voice turned sly, knowing. "Ya can't do it, can ya, Sis? All ya have to do now is walk over here an' hand me your rifle. I'll do the rest. Come on, Sammie. Give me the gun."

All the while Billy's imploring words swirled about her, Travis's eyes held her trapped. He made no move to draw his own gun, which he'd holstered before re-entering the room. He simply stood there and waited, his hand outstretched.

Sam was torn. Never in her life had she given her word then gone back on it. Pa had drilled that sense of honor into her, even as he'd taught her to ride and shoot. Yet, Billy needed her help. How could she not aid her own brother, when he might hang if she didn't help him escape? Then again, how could she break her vow to Travis? He'd trusted her enough to give her the gun, trusting her to return it as she had promised.

Pain twisted her features as she weighed her options. Agony glowed in her dark eyes. Her heart was breaking. Either way she chose, she would be hurting someone she loved; either way, she would lose, and someone she cared for would pay the price of her decision.

Sam was sure that, if she truly wanted to, she could shoot Travis and level a bead on Chas before either of them could draw their guns from their holsters. She was faster on the draw than either of them, and her revolver was already in her hand. It would be a simple matter to toss the rifle to Billy and set him free. But could she do that to Travis? Her aching heart told her no, but her tears were for Billy as she slowly reached out to hand her weapons to Travis.

"No, girl! Dammit! No!" Billy wailed.

"I gave my word, Billy," she said in a choking voice that begged his forgiveness. "I gave my word!" With that, she practically hurled the guns at Travis and fled from the room.

Travis caught up with her a short distance from the office. "You shouldn't be walking home alone, Sam. Not after the trouble we've had tonight."

Sam ignored him, swiping angrily at her tears.

"I was proud of you tonight," he ventured again. "I've never seen anyone shoot the way you do."

"I could have shot you, you know," she responded belligerently, sniffling. "Billy could be free now, if I hadn't made that stupid promise."

"I know that, Sam, and I know how hard it was for you to hand me those guns but I'm glad you did. Thank you."

Shaking her head sadly, Sam said regretfully, "I can't say as you're welcome. Billy might hang because of what I did tonight."

Catching her arm, he pulled her to a halt, turning her to face him. His fingers cupped her chin and tipped her face up to meet his gaze. "No, darlin'," he corrected softly. "If Billy hangs, it will be for crimes he's committed, not for anything you did or didn't do to help him. Remember that, Samantha Downing Kincaid," he instructed firmly. "Each person is responsible for his own actions in this world, and accountable for his own deeds in his lifetime. He'll either reap the rewards or pay the penalties, but the pride and the guilt rest solely upon his shoulders. They don't belong to anyone else."

"That's easy to say, but if he hangs, I'll never forgive myself, Travis. I'll carry that burden with me for the rest of my life, and I'll never be able to look Pa or Hank or Tom in the face again."

"You did what you had to do, Sam—what was right."

"That don't make it settle any better," she told him flatly, her feet dragging wearily with each step as she started once more for home. "It's poor comfort for turnin' your back on your own brother."

Nothing Travis could say would dispute that or make Sam feel any better, and Travis's own heart ached for her. He would have hated to have had to make the choice she did tonight. For a few moments, he had held his breath in suspense, thinking she might turn on him with her gun. Even now, he couldn't be sure why she'd made the choice she had. Was it simply because she had given her word as she'd told Billy? Or was it something more? Could it be that Sam could not bring herself to level her weapon at him? Could it be that she had come to care for him, just a little? Or was it out of a growing sense of respect for him and the law he represented?

Whatever the real reason, Travis had breathed a silent, heartfelt sigh of relief when Sam had refused Billy's pleas. It had been the first real test of their new marriage, the first trial of Sam's loyalty, and whether her choice had had anything to do with him personally or not, consciously or unconsciously, Sam had passed it with flying colors. Travis's pride in her knew no bounds. It gave him hope that their marriage really did stand a chance of succeeding, despite all the odds and all the problems that faced them. Good Lord, but he did love this brave and beautiful woman to whom honor meant all!

The more Sam thought about it, the angrier she became. "You should have arrested Sandoval and every one of those men!" she railed at Travis. "What makes him any better than the rest of us? Just because he owns practically every acre of land from here to Dallas, doesn't mean he should be able to get away with murder!"

"No one was murdered," Travis reminded her so calmly that she wanted to hit him over the head.

"No, but they would have, if they could have gotten their hands on me and Billy. Lynchin's usually end in death, Travis. When you can't breathe, you die!"

For days, they argued over this, again and again. Sam wanted Sandoval arrested. Travis refused, saying the men involved would never have done what they had if they hadn't all been drunk.

"So!" Sam reasoned spitefully. "A poor excuse is better than none, at least in your opinion, huh? Or is it because he's your old sweetheart's father?"

Travis grinned that crooked, devilish grin. "Jealous, Sam?"

"When jackasses sprout wings!" she lied. "Let me know when you can fly."

Sam wasn't the only person who was angry. After watching Sam throw away his only chance of escape, Billy wouldn't even speak with her. When she came to the jail to visit with him, he turned his back to her or flatly told her to go away. His temper was every bit as volatile as hers, and they'd both inherited the same stubborn streak. Billy was not about to forgive her anytime too soon, no matter how sweetly she begged, or how convincing her excuses, or how many pies and cookies she tempted him with.

One morning, in an effort to appease his new bride, Travis asked her, "Do you think you could teach me how to fast draw, Sam? As accurate as I am after drawing my Colt, I've never quite gotten the hang of the fast draw. Maybe I'm just not naturally inclined to such things, or maybe there's some trick to it that I've never caught on to. What do you think?"

She eyed him skeptically. "Well, we could try, I reckon. You sure you're ready to trust me with a gun in my hands again? Maybe this time I'll just shoot you and set Billy free and go with him."

With a level look, and a sly grin to follow, Travis drawled, "I'll take my chances."

Even knowing that these so-called lessons were,

in large part, Travis's way of trying to smooth her ruffled feathers, Sam agreed. In a way, it was fun to be doing something like this together, to have Travis actually accept this part of her for a change, instead of berating her for her unladylike talents.

As far as target practice was concerned, Travis needed lessons like a duck had to be taught to swim! He was naturally gifted with keen sight, a steady hand, and a supremely accurate aim. However, when it came to drawing his revolver from his holster, he was as slow as molasses in January. Here, he definitely needed Sam's expert advice.

First they worked on his holster, oiling, working, and waxing the leather until it was as slick and smooth as a new baby's bottom. Though Travis always took excellent care of his six-shooter, he watched with amused fascination as Sam meticulously dismantled his Colt .45, cleaned it, reblued it, oiled it until it gleamed. Then she did the same with her own. When she was done, the weapons slid in and out of their respective holsters like butter on a hot plate.

"Slippery" was Sam's term for it. "And that's just the start," she told him with an exaggerated wink.

What had begun as a lark, soon turned into serious business as Sam took Travis in hand. She knew all the tricks. "You never tie down the holster guard strap over your gun when you think you might need to draw in a hurry. In the time it takes to free your hammer, you could be dead six times over," she told him. "And always tie down the leg strap, so the holster rides firmly against your thigh. No floppin' against your leg, no fumblin' for the grip. One fast, smooth draw when you need it most."

Also, according to Sam, Travis was wearing his holster much too high on his hip. "But I'm used to it like that," he objected, when she insisted he lower it. "It feels right. I'm comfortable with it there."

"You'll be comfortably dead one of these days if you don't mind what I'm tellin' you. Look how high you have to raise your hand, how much your elbow and arm have to bend to reach the butt. Wasted motion, Travis." She demonstrated the difference for him, her own holster tied low, the butt of her Colt riding even with her fingers when her arm hung extended at her side. In an amazing blur of motion, she had the gun drawn and leveled, the hammer back, and her finger on the trigger.

Travis was impressed. Still, he felt the need to point out to her, "You're not leaving any time to aim properly, Sam. Now, I know there are men who can draw fast and shoot straight almost consistently, but—"

"Look, Travis," she interrupted with a sigh. "It's not really that hard to figure out. The average man stands about six foot, give or take an inch. His heart is about fifteen to sixteen inches below the top of his head. That's right about here, from twenty feet away." Once more she drew her Colt, her arm coming to a certain level and stopping as if with a mind of its own. She didn't even bother to check her aim. "You learn to judge, to allow for different distances. It's no different, really, than learnin' to lead a movin' target, once you get used to it."

As he continued to eye her skeptically, she turned toward a stand of trees. "That big one on the left," she said. "We'll pretend that's a man."

Again she drew the gun, so fast that Travis could scarcely believe it, her thumb pulling the hammer back even before the barrel cleared leather. Her finger was squeezing the trigger even as her arm stopped. She fired, and chips of bark flew from the tree trunk. When Travis walked to the tree and measured the height of the bullet hole, it was exactly where a man's heart would be.

"All it takes is practice, a steady hand, and a good eye," she told him. "You've got the eye and the hand—now, practice."

She helped him, she counseled, she guided and goaded. She praised his progress and encouraged him when he felt like giving up. She challenged and tested him until he rued the day he'd suggested this. Yet, as the days passed, Travis had to admit that his draw was becoming a lot smoother, much more controlled, noticeably faster. And the more he practiced, the faster and more accurate he became with the quick draw, and correspondingly more comfortable and confident with it.

If he could become really proficient, it would be such a relief not to have to have his gun already drawn before he could be sure of an accurate shot. That, if anything, had been his main drawback in the past. There had already been a few times when it had almost cost him his life. He'd been lucky, but luck would only take him so far.

Yes, Travis had to admit it. In the short time he'd known Sam, the little outlaw had taught him a good many things—most of them surprising, some even shocking, a few of them actually useful! The years ahead, with Sam as his wife, should be anything but dull!

CHAPTER 20

The days seemed to crawl by, yet at the same time, to fly. Any day now, the circuit judge would ride into Tumble; any day now, Billy could be sentenced to hang. Sam had finally cajoled him into speaking to her again, but their relationship was still strained. More than that, Sam was sure Billy was up to something. Though she couldn't put her finger on exactly what was wrong, she felt certain that Billy knew something important and was deliberately not telling her. Didn't he trust her anymore, since the near-disaster of July fourth, or was it primarily because she was Travis's wife now?

To add to Sam's irritation, Nola Sandoval was still hanging around the jail, as if it were her right to be there. The woman was a thorn in Sam's side, and a constant bone of contention between her and Travis. Every time Nola's name was mentioned, Sam and Travis exchanged heated words.

"Why in tarnation is she still hangin' around you, like an ant around a honeypot?" Sam grumbled.

"She's just a friend, Sam. Stop trying to make something out of it. If you'd give her a chance, maybe the two of you would become friends, too. Nola really is a nice person, once you get to know her."

"I'd druther be friends with a family of skunks! Come to think of it, I'd probably trust 'em a lot further than I do her, too!"

With a frown, Travis said, "This jealous attitude of yours is getting tiresome, Sam."

"I'm not jealous!" she retorted smartly. "If I were, I'd of shot her by now. She sure doesn't seem put off none by your bein' married, though, does she?"

"Now, be fair, Sam. She's been nice enough to offer congratulations and still want to be friends. I'd say that says a lot for her as a person. And she also apologized for the way her father has behaved. Nola is thoroughly embarrassed about that, you know."

"I ain't . . . er . . . haven't seen her apologizin' to me," Sam hastened to point out. "And she hasn't bothered to congratulate me on our weddin', in case you haven't noticed. Seems she only bothers herself to talk to you."

Indeed, Nola still frequented the jail but she was also there when Travis was busy elsewhere. The woman managed to turn up at least three times a week, sometimes more. On those occasions when Travis was not there, she visited with Chas and even spoke a bit with Billy now and then.

These visits seemed to cheer Billy some, even more than those with Sam. If Sam was to bet her last dollar, she'd swear her brother was actually getting sweet on the girl. When she tried to ask him about it, however, Billy refused to discuss Nola with her.

That wasn't the only secret Billy was keeping these days. One night, after Travis had gone home for the evening, leaving Chas in charge of their prisoner, Billy had a surprise visitor. As Billy was sitting in his cell, sullenly cheating at solitaire and listening to Chas snore in his chair a few feet away, he thought he heard something outside the cell window. Cocking his head to one side and silently edging his way toward the outer wall, he listened. Again, he heard the sound.

"Psst! Psst! Billy!"

"Hank?" Billy answered softly, peering nervously at Chas.

"Yeah! You awright, Billy?"

Billy smiled. Hank was loyal, but not the brightest thing around. "Keep your voice down, Hank," he warned his younger brother. "The deputy's sleepin' sort of light in here. Are Tom and Pa with ya?"

Outside the cell, Hank shook his head. It took him several seconds, and a verbal prompting from Billy, before Hank realized that his brother could not see him. Neither could Billy hear him shaking his head. "Naw," he answered at last. "Pa's still layin' low. That shoulder wound's still givin' him trouble. Doesn't seem to want to heal proper since it busted open the last time.''

That worried Billy. He frowned and asked, ''Where's Tom?''

''Tom's back at camp, lookin' after Pa an' keepin' an eye on Miss Tucker.''

When no further information was forthcoming, Billy prompted, ''They fixin' to try an' spring me soon, Hank? That judge is gonna be here any day now. My time's runnin' out fast.''

''I know. That's why Pa sent me to see how you're holdin' up. He's doin' poorly, Billy. Tom an' I are gettin' real worried over him. Tom wants to take him down to Mexico, where we can git him some doctorin' without gettin' ourselves caught.''

His breath hissed between Billy's teeth. ''Pa's that bad?''

''Yeah, but he tries not to complain much, an' he doesn't want to go south without you and Sam.''

''Forget Sam,'' Billy growled disgustedly. ''She went an' got herself hitched to that marshal.''

''She what?'' Hank bellowed.

Chas stirred in his chair, his snore cut short, and Billy froze against the wall. He could only pray that Hank would have enough sense to remain quiet for a minute. Seconds ticked by as Billy held his breath, waiting. Several painful heartbeats later, Chas resumed snoring, and Billy finally dared to breathe again.

''Sam an' the lawman are married, Hank,'' he repeated in a whisper.

''How'd that happen?''

''I ain't real sure how it came about. All I know is, we can't count on Sam's help no more.'' In as few words as possible, Billy related what had happened on the Fourth of July, and how Sam had let him down.

"But, Billy, if Sam gave her word, there weren't anythin' else she could do," Hank said, supporting their baby sister.

"I should of known you'd take up for her," Billy hissed. "The two of ya always was as close as two peas in a pod. Meantime, I'm still sittin' here waitin' for them to measure my neck for a rope, no thanks to any of ya."

"Ain't nothin' we kin do," Hank whined. "Tom an' I been takin' turns watchin' the jail when we kin, but someone's always guardin' ya, an' Pa's ailin' too bad to help. We talked about tryin' to trade Miss Tucker again for you and Sam, but after what happened the last time, Pa don't want to chance anyone else gettin' hurt."

Hank paused, then asked, "Ya healin' awright, Billy? Ya fit to ride, yet? Gawd, did ya give us a scare. We thought for sure ya was dead!"

"Healed or not, if I git the chance, I'm bustin' out o' here!" Billy told him. "I'm still sore, an' I don't know how I'll sit a horse, but I kin walk around some now. I'm gittin' stronger every day, so anytime you an' Tom kin fix it, I'm ready an' waitin'."

"We was kinda hopin' you and Sam could do somethin' between ya," Hank admitted softly. "Tom says if we don't git started for Mexico soon, Pa'll never make the ride."

Billy closed his eyes, pain for himself and his father washing through him. "Then, go, Hank. You an' Tom take Pa to Mexico before it's too late."

"What about you?"

"Don't worry about me. Tell Pa I said I'll find a way to git loose. Tell him I'll meet ya in Mexico. Maybe I kin still git Sam to help or someone else, maybe. Where ya headin' down there?"

Hank mentioned a little town not far from the border, where they had stopped a couple of times before. "Ya sure, Billy? Pa ain't gonna want to leave unless he thinks you'll get free."

At this point Billy wasn't sure of anything but he tried to reassure his younger brother. "If that judge will hold off long enough for me to work a few things out, an' give me time to heal enough to ride, it'll help. 'Course, it'd help a darn sight more if I could git my hands on a gun. Breakin' out o' here without one's gonna be a sight tricky."

On the other side of the wall, Hank blushed. "That's one of the reasons Pa sent me," he admitted sheepishly. "But how am I supposed to give it to ya?" He eyed the bars on the window in dismay. Not only were there bars across it horizontally, but vertically as well, criss-crossed so tightly that fitting a gun through was an impossibility. "Maybe I kin sneak it to Sam somehow, an' she can get it to ya."

Inside the cell, Billy stood shaking his head at his brother's reasoning. Hank wasn't going to win any prizes for brains any time soon. Knowing this, Billy surely wasn't going to suggest that Hank try blasting him out with dynamite or anything else life-threatening. "Yeah, Hank," he snorted disgustedly. "Whacha gonna do? Walk up an' knock on the door and ask Kincaid to have Sam deliver it to me?"

"No," Hank replied with a huff. "I ain't that dumb! I was gonna try to knock on her bedroom window like the last time. If they're married, the marshal might not keep her windows nailed shut no more."

Billy couldn't believe what he was hearing. "You dunce!" he hissed. "Ain't ya got the brains God gave a goat? Think, Hank! They're married, you fool! That means they're sharin' the same bed! You go knockin' on Sam's window, an' you gonna come face to face with Kincaid's Colt!"

If Hank had blushed before, it was nothing compared to the heat that flooded his face now. "Oh. Reckon I hadn't considered that," he conceded.

"I reckon ya didn't," Billy agreed dryly.

"Then what we gonna do?"

"Like I said, you go back an' tell Tom to get Pa to Mexico, an' I'll do the best I kin for myself. I got me an idea that might work."

"What about Sammie?"

"I don't know. I'll jest have to see how things go. If I kin bring her with me, I will, Hank, but if she wants to stay with Kincaid, there ain't much I kin do about it. Besides, she's not in the same trouble I'm in, an' I got to look out for myself first. Jest tell Pa not to worry."

"An' Tom?"

"Tell him to worry. An' since he's the one who once thought he'd like to be a preacher, tell him to practice some prayin', if he kin recollect how."

For the first time in her life, Sam's days began to fall into a pattern, a comfortable routine. It was strange; it was nice. After all the endless months and years of running and hiding, it was odd to be living a normal life like almost every other person in the world. Each day began and ended the same way, in the same bed, in Travis's arms.

On Sunday mornings, they went to church; on Mondays, Sam washed their laundry; and on Tuesdays, she ironed and mended their clean clothing. Each Tuesday and Friday, she baked fresh bread and pies for the weekend. Wednesdays, she churned butter and caught up on odd chores. On Thursdays, Sam cleaned the house from top to bottom, and Saturdays were set aside for shopping.

Likewise, the hours of her days were much the same. Breakfast, dinner, and supper never varied more than half an hour on any given day. Though the variety of the menu was limited by Sam's cooking skills, what she did manage to fix was much more edible. Before long, Travis knew without thinking that on Mondays they would be eating beef stew; Tuesday meant ham and beans; Wednesday night was meatloaf and baked potatoes; Sunday either a roast or fried chicken, depending on what struck Sam's fancy at the butcher's the previous day. Rarely did Sam become daring enough to try her hand at a new dish and only once did she dare to set fried liver before him for dinner.

They arose at the same hour each day, they ate at the same time. Billy could almost time Sam's visits to the minute. He could almost bet money on which dress she was likely to wear on which day of the week. She was settling into a routine, but rather than being perturbed by it, Sam seemed to thrive on it. She smiled a lot these days, and Travis often came home to find her humming contentedly as she went about her housework.

Since Elsie was still recovering from her fall, unable to resume her housekeeping duties for

Travis, the cooking and household chores had fallen to Sam. Of course, as his wife, it was expected that she do these things about the house. However, as both Sam and Travis knew, theirs was not the usual marriage. Nor was she the usual wife. There was so much Sam did not know how to do.

While her cooking was improving and cleaning was no problem as a rule, small things often stumped her. Travis was the one who had to show her how to make the bed properly when she had stripped the sheets to wash them. He swallowed sharp words and calmly resigned three of his favorite shirts to the rag bag before she finally learned not to let the hot iron lay on the cloth too long. It was longer still before she caught on to the proper manner of pressing their clothing without ironing wrinkles into the fabric. He bit his tongue and tried not to complain, but when she starched his underdrawers, it was simply more than he could take and still remain silent! A man could only put up with so much, after all!

Of necessity, Travis was forced to leave Sam unattended much of the time. If they were to have meals on time and clean clothes and house, Sam needed time to accomplish her chores, and Travis could not be with her constantly. He had his own job to do. Not certain how far he could trust her yet, Travis spent the first few weeks constantly wary. It seemed to him that he was holding his breath from the time he left the house in the morning until the time he returned at night. Every time he walked into the house, he dreaded finding her gone. Each time he walked in and couldn't find her immediately, he panicked. Each time he arrived to find her puttering around in the kitchen or hear her off-key singing floating down the stair-case, he heaved a heartfelt sigh of relief.

During this time, if Travis could have looked into Sam's mind, he would have relaxed a lot sooner than he did. Even with her worries about her family, Billy in particular, Sam was enjoying her-self. It came as a pleasant surprise to find that she did not detest the household chores as much as she had anticipated. While she often missed Elsie's supervision and the older woman's advice, Sam found she enjoyed having the house to herself so much of the time.

The house felt more like hers now, and Sam felt less and less like an intruder. She was free to roam about and investigate. Within days, she had rear-ranged the kitchen cupboards to suit herself, put-ting things where they were more convenient for her. She could also arrange her days and her schedule to suit herself as long as it did not interfere with Travis's needs. If she felt like clean-ing the house from the bottom up instead of beginning with the upstairs bedrooms, she could do so. She could launder the clothes in any order she chose rather than adhere to Elsie's set pattern of always washing the sheets first. If she wanted to wait until after supper to wash the pots and pans she'd dirtied in preparing the meal, there was no one to tell her differently.

Sam found a certain freedom in all this that came as a pleasant surprise. It shocked her a little to find that she enjoyed looking after the house and her new husband. Daily, she learned countless little things about him, like the fact that he never failed to remove his socks without leaving them turned inside out, and he had a habit of taking off his shirts in such a manner that one sleeve was always caught half within itself, remaining that way until she did the laundry. Without fail, he read his paper from back to front, he insisted on taking the left side of the bed, and only snored when he was dead tired and flat on his back. He drank his coffee black, preferred fried eggs to scrambled, had a passion for catsup, and absolutely detested cooked cabbage or fried liver—and starch in his underwear!

There were times, when Sam thought about it, that her newfound contentment scared her spitless! Why, she was becoming as domesticated as a lazy old housecat! She found herself actually mooning over Travis's laundry, lovingly stroking his shirts and matching his socks. She caught herself snuggling his pillow to her chest, sniffing at it to catch the smell of him as she made the bed in the morning.

At moments like this, she couldn't believe she was really acting this moon-struck over the man! Not her! Not Sam Downing! It made her wonder about her own sanity sometimes, wonder if some other woman had invaded her body. Surely, the old Sam would have pitched a fit before willingly donning a petticoat and dress! The old Sam would never have been caught baking oatmeal cookies, which she detested, just because they were someone else's favorite, or daydreaming about making new kitchen curtains merely because she'd seen fabric the exact color of Travis's eyes!

When she caught herself acting silly like this, she consoled herself with the fact that she still wore boots much of the time, even with her dresses, except on Sundays. Only then, with her fancier dresses, did she wear those dratted shoes that pinched her feet so dreadfully! And she had yet to wear a corset, thank heavens! It would take more muscle than even Travis had to get her into one of those torturous contraptions!

And she still got to wear trousers from time to time, like when she and Travis were target practicing. There just wasn't any way to strap on a gunbelt around yards of billowing skirt. Travis might frown at her pants but he refrained from saying anything, and Sam almost laughed when she caught him eyeing her behind, snuggly outlined by the form-fitting britches, a tell-tale gleam lighting his turquoise gaze.

If Sam found comfort in the steady routine of managing her own home, of having order to her days for the first time in her life, she delighted in the nights, long, dark nights spent snuggled securely in Travis's embrace. That was only one reason among many why she resisted all thoughts of running, aside from the fact that Billy was not yet well enough to attempt an escape. When Travis pulled her into his arms, his warm lips drugging her with insistent kisses, his hands roaming enticingly over her body, fleeing from him was the last thing on earth she wanted.

The house with its walls of wood and plaster and its rooms full of furnishings was only a building, after all. Travis, with his strong arms and blazing eyes, was her home, the place where her heart beat wild and free. He'd managed to capture her heart, and Sam had never felt so safe, so secure, so ridiculously happy. Though she'd lost the freedom she had so treasured, she knew she'd rather be imprisoned by him forever than ever to leave his side.

Once she finally admitted this to herself, Sam knew her heart had long ago made the choice her mind was finally accepting. How her family would react, she did not know. Pa would be hurt. Billy was already angry with her. Tom might understand. Of all of them, Hank would certainly forgive her most readily. Being the youngest of the boys, he was closest to her. However, regardless of their feelings, regardless of any lingering regrets, Sam had made her choice.

Now all she had to do was to convince Travis of the fact, without making herself appear a lovestruck fool. Words alone would not allay his suspicions or bring his trust. Time and love would have to do it, and Sam could not bring herself to tell him that she loved him. Somewhere deep inside her heart, she yearned to hear those words from him first, to have him declare his love for her. Would that day ever come, she wondered? Though he desired her, would he ever come to really love her? Given their circumstances, would he ever even come to trust her, let alone give her his heart? The passion between them was magnificent, but Sam craved his love.

A few days later, as Sam was leaving the church after her singing lesson with Alma Aldrich, Parson Aldrich called to her. "Samantha! Can I see you for a moment in my study, dear? I really hate to delay you, but this is important."

Flashing him a smile, Sam couldn't help but tease, "You fixin' to try and talk me out of these singin' lessons, Parson? And here I thought I was doin' so good!"

The poor man almost cringed. "Well," he hedged, "you are improving some, I'd say, but this is something entirely different."

Guiding her into his study, he went to his desk and pulled out a paper. "It crossed my mind the other night that you had never signed your marriage certificate. When you fainted after the ceremony, I guess nobody thought of it in all the excitement. Travis signed it, of course, but then I forgot to give it to him. I'm glad I did now, or I may never have caught my error. I'm surprised he hasn't asked me for it before now, but I feel like such an old fool. How could I have forgotten something so important?" He stood shaking his head at himself in bewilderment.

Sam stared in stunned bemusement, her eyes going from the pastor to the paper on his desk. "Does this mean Travis and I aren't married?" she asked weakly, a sick feeling in the pit of her stomach.

"Oh, no, my dear!" he assured her, not wanting the woman to think she'd been living in sin these past weeks. "I assure you, that in the sight of God, you've been married since you spoke your vows. However, the laws require that both the bride and groom sign the certificate, and we certainly don't want any legal problems to crop up later because of a silly oversight now, do we?" He handed her a pen and directed her hand toward the proper line on the document. "Just sign here, Sam, and everything will be right as rain."

Her hand hovered over the paper, the pen a scant inch away from it. What if she refused? What would happen then? Would that mean that legally, she could not be held to her vows? All these thoughts and more raced through Sam's mind as she hesitated. It certainly would pay Travis back for holding a gun on her in the first place, now wouldn't it? How would he react, knowing that her pledge was worth nothing if she refused to sign this paper? All his efforts gone to waste!

Then she shook her head to herself. No, she couldn't do that to him. She couldn't do that to herself. She wanted to be married to him, to belong to him and have him belong to her. She loved him, with all her heart and soul, and hadn't she just been wondering what she might do to prove herself to him? Of course, if she had her way, Travis would never know of this oversight. But she would know that she had done the right thing, that she had honored her vows to him. No more hedging, no more doubts, no more anger over the fact that she'd had no choice in her marriage to him. This time it was her choice, done willingly and with a loving heart.

With a wobbly smile and a soft sigh of relief at having won this small battle with her own conscience, Sam put her name to the paper, scrawling her signature in bold letters below Travis's.

CHAPTER 21

Pushing the hair from her eyes, Sam leaned weakly against the kitchen counter. She was trying to fix breakfast for her and Travis, but the heat was already almost too much to bear. It was making her dizzy, and the smells of coffee brewing and the bacon sizzling in the skillet were causing her stomach to turn. As Travis walked into the kitchen, the sight of those eggs, staring up at her like big yellow eyes, was enough to push Sam over the edge. With a strangled cry of alarm, she dashed for the back door.

Several agonizing minutes later, she returned to the kitchen, sending him a sheepish look. Travis had rescued their meal from charring and was setting the plates on the table. "I guess I'm not used to cookin' in this heat," she told him lamely.

"Are you sure that's all it is?" he asked. "Maybe you'd better see Doc Purdy. You could be coming down with something."

But Sam was sure it was this late-July weather. For the last week and a half, they'd been having the worst hot spell Texans could recall in years. By mid-morning, the temperature would soar, and by mid-afternoon everything and everyone was wilted. Just breathing was a monumental effort. At night, heat lightning would light up the sky, bringing nothing but empty promises and no rain. Even then, what chance breeze happened along was stifling.

The flowers had all shriveled and died, the gardens had dried up, and green grass was only a memory now. Dry winds blew tumbleweed around and kicked up dust devils everywhere. The creek was low and sluggish, and everyone feared if they didn't get some rain soon, wells would start to go dry.

Still, when the dizziness and nausea continued to plague her, when her normal energy did not return, Sam finally relented. Maybe Travis was right; maybe it was something more than the heat. While she'd rarely been sick a day in her life, there was no sense taking chances. Lord only knew what that dry wind was carrying with it. If nothing else, perhaps Doc Purdy could give her something to perk her up again.

As Sam sat on the edge of the examining table, buttoning up her dress, Doc Purdy grinned at her. "Well, Sam, there's nothing wrong with you that about seven more months won't cure."

"Seven months?" she echoed stupidly, frowning at him.

He nodded. "I figure the baby's due about the first of March sometime."

"Baby?" she squeaked.

She looked so thoroughly astounded, so absolutely dumbfounded, that Purdy could not help but laugh at her. "Yeah, Sam," he chuckled, teasing her. "It comes from all that cavortin' around you and Travis do in bed at night, you know. That's how babies are made."

"But a baby!" she said, her voice filled with wonder. Her huge brown eyes filled her face, and her hands fluttered lightly over her stomach. "Great Gertie's garters! A baby!"

Ten minutes later, Sam was wandering dreamily along the street toward Travis's office. She could hardly remember a word Doc Purdy had said afterward. Suddenly she stopped dead in her tracks, almost causing a cowboy to tumble over her as he nearly barreled into her back. Again, her hands went to her still-flat tummy. "A baby!" she murmured in awe, unable to fathom the news fully.

She almost floated into Travis's office on a cloud of wonder. One look at her face, and Travis, who was discussing something with Chas, stopped in mid-sentence. "Sam?" he questioned, rising from his chair and going to her side. She stood there, gazing up at him with a grin curling her lips. Taking her arm, he led her to his chair and set her down into it. She followed like someone in a trance. "Sam? What is it?" he asked again.

"A baby," she said softly, her eyes round and dreamy. "Travis, we're gonna have a baby!"

285

Travis's knees went weak and he clutched the edge of the desk. For a minute, he felt as if he'd been hit with a two-by-four. Then, with a silly grin to match Sam's, he almost whispered, "A baby? You sure?"

"Doc Purdy told me," she said with a wobbly nod. "In March. I was so surprised, I don't recall much else he said. Reckon I'll have to ask him again later."

For several seconds, they stared at one another. Then a wide smile curved his mouth, and Travis let out a whoop of joy that nearly took the roof off the jailhouse. Scooping Sam up out of the chair, he twirled her round and around, until they were both laughing breathlessly. Even Chas got into the act as he tried to thump Travis on the back on each turn, gleefully congratulating them both.

By the time they stopped, they were both dizzy and laughing hilariously, tears of joy streaming down Sam's cheeks. Chas stood chuckling, sharing their delight. Only Billy, staring out from between the bars of his cell, wore a sullen frown. "Guess this means you'll be stayin', huh, Sam?" he asked quietly. "No more ridin' with Pa an' the boys."

His question sobered her. "Yeah, Billy," she answered softly, easing out of Travis's arms and going to stand before her brother. "That's what it means. I'm gonna have to learn to be a mama now, and I can't be roamin' all over the countryside. I've got a home, and a husband, and a baby on the way, and it's time I settled in one place. It's what I want, what I've wanted for a long time now, somewhere deep inside of me."

"Then I'm glad for ya," he said with a sad smile.

"It's high time one of us got what we've been wantin'." His smile grew a little wider as he tried to share her happiness, but the smile never quite reached his eyes as he added with false joviality, "Hey! I guess that means I'm gonna be an uncle! Never thought I'd see the day!"

Left unspoken was the awful fact that, if he were hung, Billy wouldn't live to see the day Sam's child was born. This thought further dampered Sam's joy, and a lump caught in her throat. Blinking back her tears, she managed a trembling smile. "And Pa will be a grandpa. How does that boggle your brain?"

"I'd like to see the look on his face when he hears," Billy said wistfully. "I think once the shock wears off, he'll be pleased, though."

"You think so?" Sam's voice quavered and broke.

Billy grabbed Sam's hand and squeezed her fingers tightly in his, fighting tears of his own. "Baby sister, I know so."

The woman stopped inside the cantina, waiting for her eyes to adjust to the dim interior after the blinding glare of the Mexican summer sun. Her hazel gaze roamed the room until she found the man she sought. As she walked toward him, her bright blue skirt swirled gently about her legs, her breasts jiggling slightly beneath the gathered cotton top. Her unbound hair swayed across her shoulders in waves of mink brown.

Sinking into a chair at his table, she reached out and clasped both of his hands in hers, her face a mask of sympathy. "Tom," she sighed.

The man raised anguished eyes to hers, afraid to hear what she might say, but at the same time afraid not to. "What did the doctor say, Nan?"

She shook her head. "It's not good, darling. There was a piece of lead still in the wound, I guess, and that's why it has never healed properly. The doctor found it, but the poison is all through your father's system now. It's just a matter of time before he dies, sweetheart. There's no hope that he's going to get better. I'm sorry."

Swallowing the lump in his throat, Tom asked gruffly. "How long?"

"The doctor couldn't say for sure. Maybe weeks, maybe a couple of months. Not long."

"Does Pa know?"

She nodded, wiping at the tears that trickled down her cheeks. "He insisted on knowing, Tom."

"What does he want to do now?"

"He hasn't said, but I really don't think he has much of a choice. He's too weak now to travel and he's not going to be getting any stronger in the days to come."

"Did he say anythin' at all when the doctor told him?"

"He said he's tired, love. He said he'll be happy to rest and to see your mother again. And he said he's glad that Sam has a life of her own now and is settled, that she isn't going to be here to see him die like this." A sob caught in Nan's throat, and she could speak no more.

"Yeah, I'm glad, too," Tom said, swallowing hard. "At least Pa won't be frettin' about Sammie, wonderin' how she is or if she's gonna hang. I wish we could say the same about Billy. It's been two weeks now an' not a word. If he was gonna be able to bust free, he would've done it by now. I'm startin' to worry, honey. Maybe we shouldn't have left him."

"There wasn't anything else we could do unless you wanted to take the chance on all of you getting caught. At least this way your pa will die a free man, with some dignity."

"And Billy? Will he?" Tom asked, turning tormented eyes to hers, seeking the comfort only she could give him.

"He'll come, Tom. Have faith and a bit of patience. He'll come, yet."

"I jest hope if he does, that he gits here before Pa dies. Sort of set Pa's mind at ease, ya know?"

For all their sakes, Tom's included, Nan hoped Billy would come soon. Rising, she tugged at Tom's arm. "Come on, darling. Let's go up to our room for a while. Hank's sitting with your father, and you need rest more than you need that whiskey you've been trying to drown yourself in."

Their eyes met, exchanging a sad look. "I need you more than I need anythin' right now," he admitted softly.

"I'm here, Tom. I'll always be here."

"Then marry me."

Nan's eyes went wide. "Do you mean it, or is it the whiskey talking?"

"I mean it. I want to marry ya."

"When? Where?"

"Here. Now. As soon as possible."

"What about your father?" With a frown, Nan asked the question that was bothering her the most. "Are you sure you're not just feeling low right now, with your pa dying? Your emotions are in turmoil, Tom. Maybe you aren't thinking too clearly right now. Perhaps we should wait awhile."

"I'm not one of those children ya teach, Nan," he grumbled. "I'm a grown man an' I know what I want. I want a life with ya. I want ya to be my wife. After Pa is gone, I want to go somewhere where nobody's ever heard of the Downing clan an' I want a home and a family with ya. I'm so damned tired of runnin'."

"What will you do?"

"For a livin'?" he asked.

She nodded, hope and love lighting her features, making her plain face pretty.

"If I could do it somehow, I'd like to preach," he said with a shy smile. "Don't ask me why, but that's what I've always wanted to do ever since I was a kid. Pa never cottoned to the idea much, but Ma liked it. She used to take me up on her lap an' read to me from the Bible an' then she taught me to read for myself. Billy didn't want to learn, but she taught him some anyway, an' Hank never did catch on, bein' as slow as he is. Ma died before she could teach Sam. That's why I was so glad when ya told me you'd been teachin' her to read. Now that you're gone, I hope she doesn't give up learnin'."

"She won't. Travis won't let her." She tried to reassure him once more. "She'll be fine, Tom. Travis is a good man. He'll treat her with love and care."

"Sounds like Sam's got her a good husband," Tom concluded. "Now, what about you? Are you gonna get ya one, too? Ya gonna marry me, woman? Or do ya jest want to live together in sin forever? People tend to frown on preachers who do that. Don't ya want to make an honest man of me?''

Despite their problems, Nan laughed softly. "Yes, I'd love to marry you and make an honest man of you, Tom Downing, but I think tomorrow will be soon enough." Leading him toward the door, she whispered. "I'd like just one more night of wallowing in sin with you in that nice, soft bed, if you don't mind too much. Tonight I want to lust after your body, and let you ravish me to my heart's delight."

He gave her a sly wink. "Suits me fine, honey, but are ya gonna be this wicked when ya get to be a preacher's wife?"

"Only behind a closed bedroom door, sweetheart. Closed and locked!"

Sam walked on air for days, after learning she was to bear Travis's child. Even being sick every morning didn't dim her joy, but to add to it, Nola Sandoval had left Tumble. She had gone to visit her aunt in Minnesota to escape the dreadful heat of Texas for a while. She was to be gone for several weeks, and during that time, Sam would not have to see her or even think about her. No longer would she be popping in at the jail, a temptation to Travis.

Sam's contentment was nearly complete. The only fly in the ointment was her worry over Billy and her family. Now that she was expecting a child, she wanted to share her joy with them. She saw Billy every day, but it wasn't the same as if he were free, and it seemed she missed the others more now than she had when she'd first been captured.

If she could see them for a few minutes, just to say hello, just to tell them about the baby, just to say good-bye!

It wasn't enough to run to Elsie with the glad tidings, or send word to Molly, or even to whisper and dream with Travis in the middle of the night. It wasn't enough to imagine what her child would look like, or how it would feel in her arms, or to try to choose the right name for a boy or a girl. She wanted to have Pa and her brothers nearby. She wanted to run into her father's arms, and feel him hug her close to him and tell her how thrilled he was, and how he hoped that she'd have a baby girl as sweet and beautiful as she was, as wonderful as her mother had been. She wanted Billy to be free. She wanted Tom and Hank there to give her child a sense of family, to take their places as favored uncles, ready and willing to help spoil her baby rotten, and to teach it how to laugh.

Sam wanted what she could not have—a miracle—the impossible.

"What I can't figure out is how you managed it!" Travis roared, dragging his fingers through his rumpled blond hair. "How, Sam? Tell me!" His brilliant eyes were like jeweled daggers aimed at her as he towered over her chair. Even his mustache was quivering in righteous anger.

"I didn't, I tell you! I didn't do it! I can do a lot of things, Travis. I can ride and play poker and shoot a hole through a nickel but I can't be two places at the same time! Damn it, I didn't help Billy escape!"

"Then who did, pray tell me?" he bellowed back at her. "Who else cared enough about him to see that he managed to escape a week before the circuit judge is due to arrive? You read that telegram I got yesterday. You knew the judge was coming!"

"So did half this blasted town, you idiot!" she screamed. "Even if I didn't know he was comin' next week, everyone knew he'd be comin' soon."

"Yes, but you knew that Billy was well enough now to try it. You're the one who had ample opportunity to talk with him, to plan something! Now I've got a deputy with a goose egg the size of Texas on the back of his head, and no prisoner—and Rafe Sandoval breathing down my neck!"

"Poor Travis!" she mocked, her own eyes blazing. "Maybe if you'd stop badgerin' me long enough, you'd have time to organize a posse and go after Billy. On the other hand, stand there and holler at me all you want. It'll give Billy a better chance!"

"You'd like that, wouldn't you? You'd get a thrill out of making an even bigger fool of me than you already have!"

"You're doin' a fine job of that all by yourself, Kincaid! And, yes, I do hope Billy gets away! Why shouldn't I? He's my brother!"

"And I'm your husband!" he reminded her loudly.

"A fact I'm regrettin' more by the minute!" she shot back angrily.

Travis ignored that last remark. Instead, he bent down and trapped her in her chair by placing a hand on either side of her. His nose nearly touched hers as he snarled, "Where is he headed, Sam?"

"I wouldn't tell you if I knew!" she snapped. "But you tell me somethin', Marshal. How in tarnation am I supposed to have helped Billy escape when I was right there in bed beside you all night?"

"That's what's had me chasing my own tail all morning!" he yelled in exasperation. "How in hell did you do it?"

"I didn't, that's how!"

"Oh, God!" Travis moaned, dropping his chin to his chest. Finally he sighed and pushed himself away from her. "You know, I almost believe you. That's what worries me most, I think."

She gave him a very unsympathetic shrug. "You have to admit, it would have been a little difficult for me to crawl out of bed, get dressed, sneak out of the house—with a gun, mind you—and clobber Chas over the head. Then let Billy loose, come back here, and undress and get back into bed with you, and never be seen or heard by anyone in this town, let alone expect you to sleep through the entire thing. The whole idea is really ridiculous, Travis! Now, if you'd quit tryin' to pin the blame on me, maybe you could figure out who really did it. Besides, where did I get the gun I was supposed to hit Chas with? You keep all of them under lock and key all the time, except when we're practicin'."

Travis was beginning to think Chas's headache was insignificant compared with the one he was getting. "Okay, Sam. You've made your point."

"Good. How kind of you to notice!" she snipped.

"I suppose it could have been your father and brothers," Travis said thoughtfully.

"Or Nola," Sam added.

"Nola? Now, Sam, you're really stretching things too far this time. Nola's in Minnesota with her aunt by now."

Sam arched a brow at him. "Is she?"

"Of course, she is! Where else would she be? And why on earth would she want to help Billy get free in the first place?"

"Because she's fascinated by him to the point where she is almost obsessed. And don't go yellin' at me again, Travis Kincaid!" Sam shook a warning finger at him, like a mother scolding her son. "You go and check on her whereabouts before you start accusin' me of anything else! Send a telegram to that aunt of hers, and when you get an answer, then you come and show it to me, and if I'm wrong, I'll apologize. But if I'm right, at least you'll be able to tell Rafe Sandoval that his own darlin' daughter is at fault this time around! Maybe that'll take some of the hot air out o' that big bag o' wind!"

Travis sent the telegram before he left town with his posse that morning. He didn't wait for a reply. He'd wasted too much time already trying to get a confession or some sort of information out of Sam. As soon as he'd rounded up his men, including Sandoval, who insisted on coming along, and made Lou Sprit temporary deputy, since Chas was out of commission for now, Travis rode out to try to find some trace of his escaped prisoner.

To Sam's mortification and dismay, Travis asked Elsie, who was now recovered, to stay at the house with Sam until he got back. It hurt Sam more than he would ever know to find that Travis still did not trust her in the least. He honestly thought that she'd had something to do with Billy's escape, though he had yet to prove it or figure out how. Evidently, he didn't even trust her not to try to run away while he was gone, even though she was now his wife and carrying his child. They were right back where they'd started, with Sam feeling like a prisoner and Elsie set to guard her!

Would that stubborn man never learn? How long would it take before he really saw her for the woman she had become, the woman he'd helped create?

Sam wasn't the only one suffering trampled feelings. As he rode with his posse, trying to track Sam's brother, Travis felt mortally wounded. God! He'd actually begun to trust her, to believe in her! How could Sam have done such a thing? More than just his pride was stung. It felt as if his heart were shattered in his chest. He was one big emotional ache!

What was he supposed to do now? Yes, he had to find Billy, but that was just the start of his problems. The circuit judge was due to arrive next week, and it was going to be real cute trying to explain that the town marshal's own wife had released the prisoner! Lord, Travis would consider himself lucky if the good citizens of Tumble didn't run him out of town on a rail. At the very least, he was sure to lose his job!

Grumbling to himself, Travis was mad enough to spit nails. Damn that lying little baggage! Was this all the thanks he got for all his efforts? He'd done his darndest to turn her into a lady, to prove to everyone in town that Sam had reformed. In one night, she'd managed to shoot holes in all his plans to get the judge to pardon her for her part in the Downing robberies. There might have been a good chance of that before, but now there was no way the judge was going to overlook this latest crime of hers!

What was he going to do? She was carrying his child, for pity's sake. Disregarding his own crumbled pride, his love for the spiteful wench, and all else, Travis certainly did not want his child born in prison! *Why, Sam?* he asked himself for the thousandth time. *Why did you do it?*

CHAPTER 22

Sam was in the midst of the most delightful dream! Travis was whispering sultry words of love in her ear, nibbling on her earlobe, sliding his warm lips down her neck. Oooh, but it felt delicious! She shivered with delight as his fingers found a burgeoning nipple and fondled it to ripeness. As his tongue lapped at its twin, she arched into him, and when his hand slipped between her thighs and urged them apart, she moaned softly in anticipation. Linking her arms about his neck, she pulled him down to her. "Travis!" she sighed. "Hurry, Travis!"

Above her, he chuckled softly. "Open your eyes, honey. Look at me."

Shaking her head, she moaned. "No. Make love to me. Now."

"Not until you look at me," he said. "I want to know that you're awake enough to enjoy this."

Again she shook her head. "If I open my eyes, I'll wake up and you'll be gone," she muttered agitatedly.

He laughed and kissed her lightly on the lips. "No, I won't. I'll be right here. Now do as I say. Open your eyes."

Slowly, reluctantly, Sam's lashes fluttered open. Then she sighed languorously. "You're still here." He'd been gone for five days and now he was back.

He rewarded her with another kiss, this one longer and much more devastating. It sent her emotions whirling once more, her blood shimmering through her veins. His hands traveled the warm, naked length of her, awakening her senses and making her flesh tingle. Even as his hands caressed her, his body slid temptingly along hers, and she felt his bold, swollen masculinity prodding against her. When he finally broke off the kiss, she came up gasping for air.

"Look at me, Sam," he urged again. As her eyes slid open, he murmured huskily, "I want to see the desire flare in your eyes as I come into you. I want you to see the wonder in mine as we become one. Share the passion with me, sweetheart—all the way!"

Slowly, inch by teasing inch, he entered her, his eyes holding hers. Spellbound, even as his passion claimed her soul, she saw his pupils dilate, saw his eyes darken, and the muscles of his face contract with intense pleasure. "You're so warm, so smooth!" he rasped. "It's like being wrapped in silken flames. When I'm deep within you, I can feel you quiver inside. Did you know that? It almost makes me lose my mind, but it's a madness I crave, over and over again."

His brazen words, his bold eyes, his body stroking powerfully within hers sent hot slivers of raw need spearing through her. Her fingers clenched into his broad back as she strained toward him, wanting more—more.

"Tell me what you're feeling," he whispered hoarsely. "Tell me."

"Oh, God, Travis!" she groaned. "I can't!"

"Tell me!"

"I can't begin to describe it!" she whimpered shakily. "I'm on fire! I'm full and I'm hungry and . . . I ache! I . . . I want!"

"What is it you want?" Even as he asked, he plunged into her again and again, giving her pleasure, taking it, fanning her fires of desire.

"You!" she gasped out, her body writhing. "You! More! Now!"

His hard, calloused hands cupped her buttocks, bringing her up and into him and he lunged even deeper, more completely, until Sam could no longer tell where his body left off and hers began. It was glorious! They began a mad spiral into rapture's realm, a wild whirlpool that spun faster and faster, like a carousel gone out of control.

Sam's breath came in gulps and spurts as she watched Travis's face above hers, saw his eyes narrow into blazing slits, his jaw clenched against the almost unbearable pleasure that held them in its relentless grasp. Faster, harder, together they reached for that ultimate peak of passion. Dizzy with desire, her own face a strained mask of sensuality, Sam felt the shimmering waves about to crash over her. Unable to bear it, she shut her eyes, her teeth literally grinding against one another as she prepared for that final moment of ecstasy.

But even now, Travis would have his way. His fingers dug deeply into her shoulders in a silent command, and her eyes flew open again to meet his at the very moment when splendor carried them both spinning over the brink, into a fathomless well of glory. Her eyes now wide with wonder, Sam caught a glimpse of heaven in Travis's exultant gaze, viewed her own awe-filled emotions etched across his taut features as their bodies began to shudder with spasms of pure pleasure. His glad shout of joy blended with hers as they surrendered to the wild, sweet fury of love.

Too replete, too bonelessly satiated to do anything but drift off to sleep in the comfort of Travis's embrace, Sam did not think to question him until the next morning. Upon waking, her first question after five days of wondering and worrying was, "Did you find Billy?"

"No."

"I'm glad."

Slanting her a look as he buttoned his shirt, Travis smiled wearily and shook his head. "I don't think you're going to be singing such a glad tune next week, Sam. When the judge arrives and learns what you've done, we'll play hell trying to keep you out of jail, or haven't you thought that far?"

Her brows drew together in a frown as she accused, "You still think I helped him escape, don't you?" Then she sighed, turning away from him. "Somehow, after last night, I thought maybe you believed me now."

"I want to, Sam. I keep telling myself your

brothers and father might have done it. In fact, if I wasn't the marshal here and didn't have a responsibility to this town and its people, I might not even care if you did let Billy loose. I understand how much you love him but when I think that because of you our child might be born in jail, I could horsewhip you! How could you jeopardize all our lives this way?''

When she failed to answer him, he reached out and grabbed her shoulder, spinning her about to face him. Her tears caught him by surprise, the open agony on her face sending shafts of pain through him. "Oh, Sam! What are we going to do now?" he murmured, drawing her toward him.

For a moment, Sam allowed herself the luxury of leaning her face into the hollow of his shoulder, as if to draw strength from him. Then, abruptly, she stiffened and pushed away. Brushing angrily at her tears, she pulled her pride about her like a shield. "I don't care what you do, Travis," she told him coldly. "I've tried my best and if that's not enough for you, then I don't know what else to do. You do what you have to, Marshal Kincaid. I just don't care anymore."

For two long, agonizing days, Sam's pride and Travis's anger lay between them in a silence so thick they almost choked on it. While he buried himself in his job, trying to cope with Rafe Sandoval's threats, and searching desperately for stray clues to account for Billy's mysterious escape, Sam moped about the house under Elsie's watchful eye. So great was Sam's heartache that she didn't know how she could bear much more. Never had she felt more bereft, more betrayed. The joy had gone out of her life. Even the thought of her unborn child failed to cheer her. How could she rejoice, when her baby's father had failed her so?

Each day seemed a lifetime; each hour a bleak eternity. After sharing two endless, silent meals with her, Travis chose to eat in a restaurant down the street from the jail rather than face her across the table. Though she waited anxiously to hear his footsteps on the stairs at night, he stayed away until he was certain she would be asleep. Only then did he return home to spend a restless night alone in Sam's old room. Sam told herself she was glad, knowing it would tear her heart out if he were to come to her now, making a travesty of their lovemaking.

By the third day, Sam and Travis both looked like death warmed over with dark circles testifying to their lack of sleep and their despair. Elsie began to wonder if either of them remembered how to smile, and found herself longing wistfully for the return of days past when the two of them would rant and rave at one another. Even that was preferable by far to this awful, nerve-racking pall that hung over them. She even tried badgering them into a full-blown fight, but neither of them bothered to take the bait. It was as if they'd both just given up, and Elsie wanted to weep for them.

Then, that afternoon, as Elsie was trying to talk Sam into visiting Alma Aldrich, to get her out of the house for a while, Travis suddenly burst through the front door. Spotting them in the parlor, he skidded to a halt. A multitude of emotions flitted across his face as he stared longingly at Sam, as if not sure what to do or say first. Finally he began to walk slowly toward her, stopping in front of her and dropping to his knees. Taking her cold hands into his, he said shakily, his heart in his eyes as he gazed imploringly into her face, "Sam, I'm sorry. Oh, dear God, honey, can you ever forgive me?"

Sam's first thoughts were of Billy, and she feared the worst. Her hands clenched Travis's in a bone-crunching grip. "Is it Billy?" she cried out, terror clawing at her. "Is he dead?"

"No! Oh, no, Sam! Damn me for scaring you like this! It's nothing like that! Darlin', I'm such an idiot!"

As color returned to her face, she frowned down at him. "What is it then?"

"You were right all along, and I was just too blasted blind to see it. A mislaid telegram from Nola's aunt in Minnesota has finally arrived. Nola never planned any visit. Once I found this out, I questioned the conductor on the morning run to Dallas, and he remembered that she got off the train in Dallas. Chas took this morning's train and wired back the information a few minutes ago. It seems a girl matching Nola's description purchased supplies and two horses at one of the livery stables. She left and hasn't been seen since the day before Billy's escape."

Sam started to shake. Slow, hot tears trickled down her cheeks as she sat staring at him, but still she said nothing. She sat there like a weeping statue. "Sam, please!" Travis begged. "Scream at me! Hit me, if you want! Tell me what a stupid fool I am! Just don't sit there and stare at me with those dark, condemning eyes of yours! Honey, I'm sorry. I'm so damned sorry for not believing you. If I live to be a hundred, I'll never forgive myself for all I've put you through these last few days, but if you care for me and the baby at all, please say you understand. Tell me you don't hate me."

When she spoke, her voice was so low and trembling that he had to strain to hear her words. "I don't hate you, Travis, but you've hurt me very badly. I'd thought you were comin' to trust me, that we trusted each other. Didn't you see that I'd given up runnin' and quit fightin' you? Couldn't you tell how happy I was about the baby?"

"Yes," he admitted, "but I also saw how desperately you wished that Billy were free. Knowing that, you were the first one I blamed when he escaped. I was wrong and I'll regret that as long as I live. I didn't mean to hurt you, Sam, but I was hurting, too. When I thought you were guilty, it was eating me up inside."

"Oh, Travis! How do we stop all this?" Her eyes resembled those of a wounded fawn as she gazed into his face. "The truth is, I wanted Billy free, and maybe if Nola hadn't gotten there first, I might have tried somethin' myself. I really don't know. I reckon we'll never really know now. All I know is, it would have killed me to see him hang."

She took a deep breath, as if to steel herself for what she had to say next. A weak smile trembled over her lips. "We started out all wrong, you and me," she told him hesitantly, her eyes shying away from his, then coming back almost against her will. "Maybe now's not the right time to say this, but as long as I'm sittin' here admittin' the worst, I might as well confess somethin' else." She hesitated for a heartbeat, a flicker of uncertainty crossing her face, while Travis mentally braced himself against whatever she might say. Then, quietly, almost fearfully, she said, "I love you, Travis."

The breath whooshed out of Travis's lungs on a giant wave of relief and shock, relief that Sam hadn't confessed something dreadful, shock that she'd actually said she loved him. Behind him, Elsie sank heavily into a chair, a prayer of thanks on her lips, but neither Sam nor Travis took note. They had eyes and ears only for one another at this moment.

Still on his knees before her, Travis gripped Sam's hands in his, squeezing tightly, almost afraid to believe he'd heard her correctly. "Sam!" he murmured. "Oh, sweetheart! Do you really mean that? Because if you do, you've just made me the happiest man in all of Texas, maybe all the world!"

All she could do was nod, but that was enough confirmation for Travis. Drawing her down onto the floor with him, he pulled her gently into a heartfelt embrace, rocking her back and forth in his arms. "I know I forced you to marry me when you didn't want to. Since that very first day, I've made you do so many things you didn't want to do, but I didn't know how to make you love me. I've wanted you from the start, Sam, and somewhere along the way, I fell in love with you but I was afraid to tell you how I felt. I couldn't risk having you laugh at me, or worse yet, tell me you didn't care."

His hands came up to frame her face, and he laughed and kissed her tenderly. "Thank God, you've got more courage than I do, my love! Now

I'll tell you every chance I get. I love you, Samantha Kincaid. With all my heart and being, I love you, and Lord help you, if you ever change your mind about loving me back, because I'll never let you go now."

Love shone from her face, and she laughed back at him, softly. "Marshal, you couldn't get rid of me if you tried!"

In the next couple of days, Travis gathered more information, all of it pointing toward Nola as the one person who had helped Billy escape. She had taken a pistol and a rifle from the ranch, along with several hundred dollars of her father's money. There were at least two witnesses who claimed to have seen her outside of Tumble on the day of the escape, plus the fact that neither Billy nor Nola had been seen since.

When Rafe Sandoval learned of his daughter's involvement, he was fit to be tied. At first, he refused to believe it, preferring to think that Travis was inventing this tall tale to save his own neck and Sam's. Then, when he could deny it no longer, he chose to believe that Billy had somehow forced Nola into helping him and then taken the girl hostage again. At last, with the truth of the matter staring him straight in the face, he threatened everything imaginable on Billy's head. Thoroughly distraught, he swore that if he ever saw his daughter again, he would beat her senseless and then send her to the most remote convent he could find. Finally, he hid himself away at his ranch, confused, hurt, ashamed, and absolutely miserable.

The following week, Judge Andrews arrived on

the Thursday afternoon stage and still there was no sign of Billy or Nola. Though their primary prisoner had escaped, there were numerous smaller cases to be heard and decided, and the judge decided to wait until Monday to hold court. That gave Andrews time to review the cases, and Sam the entire weekend to fret herself into a dither. On Monday, the judge would hear testimony on her behalf, and decide what should be done about her.

"My entire life is in that man's hands!" she wailed anxiously, finally realizing the severity of things. "What if he's so mad about Billy bein' gone that he decides I should hang?" Throwing herself into Travis's arms, she clung to him in fright. "Oh, Travis! Tell me they won't hang me! At least not until I have the baby!"

It was only Saturday night, and Sam was coming as unsprung as a shattered watch. Elsie had tried to tell Travis that Sam's condition was making her more emotional than usual, but Travis was beginning to fear for her sanity. Monday and Judge Andrews's decision couldn't come soon enough to suit him. Meanwhile, he did his best to comfort and reassure her. "Honey, I won't let them hang you," he crooned, stroking her back with his big hands.

Silent sobs shook her as she snuggled closer, trying to absorb enough of his heat to drive the fear away. "But—but what if they put me in jail?" she whimpered. "What if they lock me away somewhere in some dark prison and I never get to see you again?"

"We won't let them do that, Sam." Gently he brushed the tears from her face. "Sweetheart, listen to me. We have Chas and Elsie and the Aldriches to testify on your behalf. You have to stop worrying yourself sick like this. It can't be good for the baby, darlin'. You have to believe that Judge Andrews will see things our way and decide in our favor. Sam, I know him. He's not an unreasonable man.''

She finally fell asleep in his arms, but it was a restless night for both of them. Sunday morning found them sitting in their customary church pew, staring at the back of Judge Andrews's head in the pew in front of them. Seeing him there almost sent Sam into nervous spasms. When she tried to sing, her voice came out in a strangled croak, worse even than her usual singing. From the pulpit, Parson Aldrich sent her a pained, but understanding, look. Alma smiled sympathetically and shook her fuzzy gray head. Sam clamped her hand over her mouth, pushed Travis roughly aside, and bolted down the aisle. In the process, she managed to knock Judge Andrews in the head with her hymnal.

Following, Travis held her while she was sick. Then he gently wiped her face with his handkerchief and pulled her down to sit with him in the shade of a nearby tree. Though she finally calmed, her face remained so pale that Travis could count each of the freckles sprinkled across her nose. They stood out like flecks of cinnamon in a bowl of sugar. With an aching heart, he tenderly kissed each one.

"It will be all right, Sam. I promise you. Even if the worst should happen, I'd personally break you out of jail, and Chas and Lou would help me do it. I swear, I'd take you away to some island somewhere, and the two of us would live on love and coconuts for the rest of our lives."

This brought a wobbly smile to her lips. "You'd really do that for me?" she asked, reaching up to stroke a trembling finger over his mustache.

He nodded. "In the blink of an eye. But I really don't think it will come to that. Of course, you shouldn't have clobbered Andrews with that hymnal, you know."

She groaned and closed her eyes. Then she started to giggle. "I love you, Travis Kincaid, and I need you more than anything in this world, but right now what I want most is a cigarette and a tall glass of straight whiskey. If I could just get so stinkin' drunk that I wouldn't know anythin' until after tomorrow's hearin', I'd be so blessedly thankful!"

"I have something that'll work even better," he vowed. Drawing her to her feet, he led her home. Once there, he carried her upstairs to their bedroom. With the utmost care, he proceeded to undress her. He brought her a snifter of brandy to help relax her, gave her a few puffs from his own cigarette, and then he gave her the most bone-melting massage she could ever have imagined. By the time he'd finished, she was as limp as a rag doll without its stuffing, drifting gently into dreamless slumber.

When she awakened later in the day, he fed her hot soup, spooning it into her mouth himself. Afterward, he made glorious love to her, taking her out of herself time and again, refusing to allow her a moment to contemplate her problems. With kisses and caresses, he brought her solace and beauty, until at last she slept again, curled into the curve of his big, protective body. When she awoke trembling in the night, he was there to soothe her with words and more.

Together, they watched the sun rise on the new day, its soft, pastel colors washing the eastern sky with warm promise.

Sam's case was the first of the morning, and she wasn't sure if she were grateful or not. One look at the judge and she started to shake. He really looked grumpy and out of sorts this morning. To make things worse, he looked at her and frowned. "Aren't you the young woman who bashed me with the hymnal yesterday?" he growled.

To Sam's amazement, Travis actually laughed! "Your Honor," he said, offering his hand to the man, "may I introduce my wife, Samantha Downing Kincaid. We're sorry if Sam gave you a headache, but carrying this baby doesn't always agree with her, you see, especially in the morning."

The judge grunted and smiled wryly. "I suppose I should be grateful then that I merely got whacked with a book."

"Yes, sir," Travis agreed with an answering grin.

From there everything went fairly smoothly, though it took quite some time for all the testimony to be heard from the various witnesses. Even Travis was required to give his sworn testimony. When Judge Andrews proceeded to question Sam about her childhood and her own involvement in the Downing robberies, she answered truthfully in a low, trembling voice.

But when his queries turned more toward her father and brothers, Sam flatly refused to answer. She told him in bold terms that she would never aid in their capture. Travis listened with a mixture of pride and dismay as she said defiantly, "This is my family we're talkin' about, Judge, and regardless of what they've done, I still love them and I owe them my loyalty. I don't care what you threaten me with, I won't betray them. I can't—not if I want to live with myself. I've given my word that I won't ever be a part of any lawless dealin's with them again, but I won't help you hang them, either."

"You know you're not being very cooperative, don't you?" Andrews said.

Sam nodded silently, her chin jutting out at him.

Sam and the judge stared long and hard at one another, neither of them backing down at all, while Travis and all their friends held their breath. Finally, Judge Andrews nodded. "All right, young woman. While I wish you would tell us more, I can understand your feeling the way you do. I can even respect your loyalty to your family.

"But now your loyalty is to your husband. He and your friends have convinced me that you have reformed your ways, even if you aren't properly repentant of your past deeds. Because of this, and taking into consideration your tender age when you entered into your life of crime, I am going to release you into your husband's care. You are free to go."

At his words, the entire courtroom erupted in cheers. Tears of joy streamed down Sam's face as she threw herself into Travis's arms with a huge sigh of relief. It was some time before order was restored and court business could resume.

Two days later, Sam found herself entertaining Judge Andrews in her home. It was his last night in town, and she and Travis had impulsively asked him to come to dinner, to show their heartfelt gratitude for his leniency. She and Elsie had put the steaming dishes on the table, and they were just sitting down to eat, when there was a knock at the door.

Frowning, Sam asked, "Now who could that be? Travis, did you invite someone else to dinner and forget to tell me?"

"No, but I'll see who it is." He started to rise.

With a pat on his arm, she urged him to sit. "You stay here and talk with Judge Andrews. I'll answer it."

Walking into the hall, Sam took a moment to check her appearance in the hall mirror, patting a stray strand of hair into place. Then she calmly opened the door to find herself face to face with her youngest brother.

"Hank!"

CHAPTER 23

"**H**ank! What on earth are you doin' here?" In her initial surprise, Sam didn't even think to lower her voice. It came out in a loud shriek. By the time she realized what she had done, she heard Travis's footsteps crossing toward the hallway.

"Sam? What's going on?"

Then he was there beside her, his big hand clamped about her waist as if he knew how unsteady she was at this moment. His piercing eyes were trained on the young man waiting on the porch. There was something oddly familiar about the fellow, though Travis could not quite place what it was, perhaps something about the eyes or the proud lift of his jaw. Suddenly it came to Travis. With arched brow, he drawled, "Another of your brothers, Sam?"

Before that stabbing stare, Hank shifted nervously and cleared his throat. "Marshal Kincaid, I'm Sammie's brother, Hank. I come to give myself up but first I'd like a word with my sister, if that'd be all right with ya."

Travis didn't know what he had expected, but it certainly wasn't this. For a full minute, he continued to stare at Hank. Then, with a wry shake of his head, he waved his arm inward. "You might as well come on in, Hank."

As Hank stepped over the threshold, Sam came out of her stuppor. "Hank! What's goin' on?" Then she groaned and seemed to wilt a little. "Oh, Lord, Hank! Of all the times to show up here, you couldn't have picked a worse time if you'd tried! There's a judge sittin' at my dinner table right this minute! And whatever possessed you to walk up and knock on the front door like this?" Her eyes searched his face, noting the weariness that etched his features, the pallor lurking beneath his tan.

"I had to come, Sammie," he said almost apologetically, his eyes skittering away from hers and locking on those of the marshal. With a slight grimace, he unbuckled his gunbelt and handed it to Travis. "Reckon you'll be wantin' this."

Accepting the weapon, Travis nodded in the direction of the parlor with its connecting dining room. "You're going to have to meet Judge Andrews sooner or later. It might as well be now."

"I–uh–I gotta talk to Sammie first, Marshal," Hank stuttered, walking slowly into the parlor. Once more his weary gaze sought Sam's. "It's somethin' best not put off."

A feeling of icy dread worked its way up Sam's spine, and for the first time she realized that Hank wasn't just tired. A soul-deep sorrow lingered in his dark eyes, calling out to her. Blindly, she felt for Travis's hand, instinctively knowing the news was bad. "What is it, Hank?" she murmured, wanting desperately to cover her ears with her hands, to keep herself from hearing his answering words.

Hank's gaze shifted from hers to Travis's, as if to prepare them both, then settled on his sister's face. "It's Pa, Sammie. He's dead. We buried him four days ago."

For a long minute, she froze, not even drawing breath. Then, as pain clawed its way through her, a high, keening wail issued from the depths of her soul. Travis caught her tightly to him as her knees collapsed beneath her. "Nooo! Nooo!" Tears raced down her twisted face, unheeded, as her hands clenched into fists and she beat at Travis's chest in violent denial. "No! He can't be dead! Travis, Hank's lyin' to me, isn't he? Pa ain't dead!"

She was totally unaware of Elsie dashing into the room to discover what was wrong, or of Travis leading her to the divan and gently setting her down upon it, or of Hank hovering nearby with tears sparkling in his own dark eyes. Nor did she see Judge Andrews standing in the doorway, curiously surveying the scene. She heard only her own terrified heartbeat, and Hank's awful words echoing over and over again in her ears. "Pa!" she whimpered, the sound like that of a wounded animal. "Pa! Oh, Pa!"

It could have been merely minutes or long hours later when Sam's wild sobbing eased to painful hiccups. The first thing, outside of her own pain, she felt were Travis's hands running soothingly up and down her spine. She clung to the sound of his deep voice, murmuring comforting words of love to her as he cradled her close to his heart. The urge to bury herself in his arms forever and hide there from the hurt was great. But questions were already forming in her mind, and she knew she could not avoid hearing the answers much longer. Slowly, fearfully, she loosened her hold on him, turning her head in search of her brother.

Hank was kneeling near her knees. Hovering nearby, Elsie stood uncertainly, a glass of brandy in her hand, her face a mask of sympathy. "Here, honey," she said, holding out the liquor. "This'll brace you some."

As Sam reached out with trembling fingers to take the glass, the brandy sloshed over the rim. With Travis's help, she managed a huge gulp of the fiery liquid, then gasped for breath. "How, Hank?" she wheezed, her eyes begging her brother. "Tell me."

"It was that old shoulder wound. It didn't seem to want to heal right an' it kept gettin' worse an' worse. The doc said Pa had a piece of lead still in there, after all this time. He dug it out, but it was too late. The poison was all through him, Sam. There wasn't nothin' the doctor could do to save him."

If anything, Sam paled even more upon hearing this. "Oh, God, Hank! I killed him! I killed him! It was all my fault!"

"No, Sammie! No! Ya can't think that!" Hank grabbed her hands and squeezed tightly.

"But, it's true!" she gasped. "I missed a piece of that bullet when I dug it out of Pa's shoulder. It's my fault! I should've seen it!"

"Sammie, stop it!" Hank's voice was gruff with

sorrow and pain. "Ya did your best. Ya ain't no doctor, Sammie. Ya did the best ya could."

"Well," she said, with a humorless laugh, "it wasn't good enough, was it? Pa trusted me, Hank, and I let him down. Because of me, Pa's dead!" Fresh tears stained her tortured face.

"Pa didn't feel that way, Sammie," Hank said quietly. "He figured ya might think like ya do, an' he wanted us to tell ya not to blame yourself, 'cause he didn't. He said to tell ya it was his own darned fault an' nobody else's. It was his own carelessness that got him shot in the first place, he said. It was that bullet, fired by a stranger, that killed him, Sammie—not you. Pa didn't blame ya. He loved ya, right up to the end."

As Hank drew his sister into a shared embrace, Travis eased away, letting them comfort one another. Quietly, he went to stand next to Judge Andrews who was still standing just inside the parlor with an uncomfortable look on his stern face. "Sorry about that dinner, Judge Andrews," Travis told him.

"It's all right, Travis. It couldn't be helped. Maybe I should just tiptoe out of here and let you deal with this now. This is family business and I'm intruding."

"No, Judge," Travis answered, shaking his head. "I think you'd better stay awhile, if you will. You see, that's Sam's brother Hank, and he's one of the Downing gang, too. He came to tell Sam about their father's death, but he also came to turn himself in, or so he says. Looks like we lost one prisoner only to have another one land on our doorstep, and I'd really like your help in dealing with this."

The judge sighed heavily. "Guess I won't be on that stage tomorrow after all," he commented, almost to himself.

Across the room, Hank was consoling Sam. "He didn't suffer too bad, Sammie. Really. It could've been a lot worse. It could've gone on a lot longer, maybe. At least Billy got there to see him before he died, an' that helped some."

At this, Travis's ears perked up. He listened attentively as Sam asked, "Billy got there? Billy's okay?"

Nodding, Hank told her, "He's fine as frog's hair. Miss Nola, too. Pa was much relieved to see him an' know that Billy wasn't gonna hang. An' when Billy told him about ya, an' how you're gonna have a baby an' all, why Pa's face lit up like Christmas! He liked hearin' that, Sammie, an' knowin' you're settled and happy. It took a heap of worry off his mind to know ya got someone like the marshal lookin' out for ya."

"And Tom? What about him?"

For the first time, Hank smiled, a wide smile that lit his dark eyes. "Guess I forgot ya didn't have no way of knowin' the good news, neither. Tom an' Nan went an' got themselves hitched! Had one of them Mexican priests marry 'em right there in Pa's sickroom, so Pa wouldn't miss none of it!"

Sam was speechless, but if she was dumbfounded, Travis was flabbergasted!

"Married?" Travis repeated loudly.

"Tom and Nan Tucker?" Sam shrieked, finally finding her voice.

"Our Nan Tucker?" Elsie echoed with wonder. Then the portly housekeeper started shaking with laughter. "Well, I must say, that dowdy little schoolteacher had more to her than most of us might have thought! Imagine that! Nan Tucker married to an outlaw!"

Shooting Elsie a dire look, Sam reminded her, "It's not all that different from me marryin' Travis, Elsie."

Still laughing, Elsie waved a hand in the air. "Oh, don't mind me, Sam. It just struck my funny bone, Nan gettin' her a man after all this time. Now," she said slyly, with a glance at Travis, "the question is, will the marshal get his?"

This served to sober everyone again and to remind them that, while Billy and Tom were free, Hank was not. Since the moment he'd appeared at the door and turned himself over to Travis, he'd officially become a prisoner. With a great deal of regret, Travis faced his wife. "Darlin', I'm sorry, but I'm going to have to question Hank, and I've asked the judge to stay and hear it. Now, we can either do it here, or I can take Hank down to the jail, whichever you'd rather."

Suddenly, for the first time since Hank's arrival, Sam thought of Judge Andrews. "Oh, my goodness!" she exclaimed, her hands flying to her face. "Judge Andrews!" Her eyes searched and found him standing nearby. "I'm so sorry! I forgot about dinner! I forgot about you!"

"Quite understandable, young lady, under the circumstances."

"But you must be starvin', and the food has all gone cold, I suppose."

"When I saw what was happening, I put the food back in the oven to stay warm," Elsie assured her. "And I don't think any of us are starving, except maybe your brother, here," she went on to point out. "How long has it been since you've had a decent meal, boy?"

Shifting nervously, Hank murmured, "Quite a while, I reckon."

"Then let's get some food into you." As she headed toward the kitchen, Elsie called back over her shoulder. "Travis, Judge Andrews, you can ask your questions over dinner as well as anywhere else, so get yourselves to the table. Sam, set another place for your brother, before the poor boy faints dead away from hunger."

Amused, Judge Andrews caught Travis's eye. "Is your housekeeper always this bossy?"

"No," came the wry answer. "Sometimes she's worse—and now she's teaching Sam all her tricks!"

Over dinner, Sam just pushed her food around on her plate. Her grief was too fresh for her to have an appetite. However, from the looks of things, Hank had no such problem. He was tucking into his meal as if it might disappear before he got his fill. It made Sam wonder how long it had been since Hank had last eaten.

Across the table from her, Travis was thinking the same thing. Had Hank ridden all the way from God knew where in Mexico without provisions? As he watched Hank literally attack his food, shoveling it into his mouth with total lack of concern for manners, Travis was reminded of a time when he'd watched Sam do the same thing not so very long ago. It made him realize how far Sam had come since then, how hard she had worked to improve herself—for him? While the thought warmed him, he found himself hoping that most of her growth had been for her own benefit as well.

Drawing himself back to present problems, Travis asked something he'd been wondering about since Hank had first mentioned it. "How did Billy know where to find you in Mexico, Hank?"

Hank swallowed and wiped his mouth on his shirt sleeve. "'Cause I told him where we'd be."

"When?" Travis questioned with a frown.

"When I snuck into town an' out back of the jail late one night about a month or so ago. Billy told me you an' Sam were married, an' I told him we was gonna have to head down to Mexico to get Pa to a doctor. He said he'd find some way to escape without our help, an' for us to get Pa to a doctor as quick as we could an' not to worry none about him or Sam."

"Sam? Did you know anything about all this?" Travis's frown deepened as his sharp gaze swung in her direction.

"Billy didn't say a word, Travis. I swear it. But now that I think back on it, he was actin' strangely, like he was hidin' somethin' from me."

"Where are your brothers now?" Judge Andrews asked.

A particularly pained look crossed Hank's face, his worried gaze cutting to Sam's, as if silently asking her advice.

"Hank," the judge continued softly, "you know there's going to have to be a trial, and the more you cooperate, the better things will go for you."

Still Hank hesitated. "They're safe in Mexico," he muttered finally. "But I ain't tellin' ya exactly where in Mexico." In his own defense, he added,

Catherine Hart

"B'sides, they more 'n likely ain't there anymore, no how. They was talkin' about goin' somewhere an' ranchin' or somethin'. I don't know where."

"And they sent you back here to tell Sam about your father's death?" Travis questioned. "Why? Weren't they at all concerned that you'd land in jail, like Billy did, and maybe hang?"

"Travis! I'm sure Tom and Billy didn't instruct Hank to walk up and knock on the front door the way he did!" Sam exclaimed. "They probably expected him to get a message to me in secret!"

"No! It was my idea!" Hank blurted out. "We all knew we had to get word to Sammie, an' I sort of volunteered, I guess. B'sides, Tom's got Nan now, an' Billy has Miss Nola, an' I kinda felt like a fifth wheel on a wagon, if ya get my drift. Sam an' me, we always been closer than the rest of 'em, an' I wanted to be near her again. I figured if I come here an' give myself up, maybe things would work out somehow. I'm tired o' bein' on the run an' eatin' beans every day o' the week, an' I missed Sammie somethin' dreadful. Now with Pa gone, an' the boys gettin' tied up with the ladies, I couldn't figure what else to do. I jest wanted to be with Sammie, especially now that she's gonna make me an uncle."

The judge and Travis exchanged a look. Then, as he watched Hank delve blissfully into a huge slice of rhubarb pie, Judge Andrews said, "Travis, Samantha, I wonder if I might have a private word with the two of you, while Hank finishes his meal? I'm sure Mrs. Willow won't mind looking after your brother for a few minutes, would you?"

With a shake of her head, Elsie motioned them

toward Travis's study. "You go on, and I'll bring you some coffee along in a few minutes."

Once behind the closed door of the study, Judge Andrews eyed Sam speculatively. "Is Hank all right, Samantha? What I mean is . . ."

"Is Hank playin' with a full deck?" Samantha supplied ruefully.

Judge Andrews grimaced. "Well, I wouldn't have phrased it quite that way, but yes. By the way, how old is Hank?"

"He's four years older than I am, so I guess that'd make him twenty-one now, but he's always seemed more my age, if you take my meanin'. He's my youngest brother."

At the judge's nod, she explained further. "Hank's never been the brightest thing to walk ground, Judge Andrews, but he's got a heart as big as all outdoors, and he'd do almost anythin' for someone he cares for. We've all sort of had to look out for Hank, kind of lead him around, so to speak. He forgets things sometimes, and strangers seem to think he's slow in the head. Maybe he is, but he can't help it. We used to ask Pa if he or Mama dropped Hank on his head when he was a baby, but we just josh around sayin' that. None of us ever wanted to hurt Hank's feelin's or make him feel dumb. He's our brother, and we love him, so we just tuck him under our wings as best we can and go on like normal."

"But he is slow?" the man prompted.

"Now, what outlaw with all his bullets in the proper places would walk up to a marshal's house and knock on the front door?" Sam asked, rolling her eyes toward the ceiling and giving a sigh of dismay. "Hell's fire, when Hank tried and failed to rescue me from here a few months back, he even forgot to tell me where he and the others were hidin' out. Made me so mad I could've spit nails!"

"But he's basically harmless? Is that what you're trying to tell me?"

Sam nodded. "He's not a great thinker, Judge. On his own, Hank couldn't decide what to eat for supper, let alone what bank to rob. Pa always decided things like that and sometimes he'd ask Tom or Billy what they thought, or even me. But Hank just followed their lead, like a puppy at his master's heels. Oh, he's got a temper when he's riled, like the rest of us, but Hank's not mean. He'd never deliberately set out to hurt someone just for the fun of it. And he's not really stupid, just slower than most at thinkin' things out."

"Travis? What do you think of all this?" Judge Andrews asked.

"It's strange!" Travis exclaimed softly. "You could have knocked me down with a feather to find him standing on my porch, and then he handed his gun over before I even asked him for it." He shook his head in amazement. "He's got to know he's going to jail but then he sits down and eats like he hasn't got a care in the world! And another thing that bothers me. If he crept up to the back of the jail and talked with Billy, why didn't he try to break his brother out of jail then?" As he asked that, Travis looked to Sam for an explanation.

She shrugged. "I don't know. Maybe, knowin' Hank and the way he can bungle things, Pa and Tom thought it would be safer to tell him not to try anythin' other than talkin' to Billy."

After a few more minutes, they rejoined Hank at

the table, where he was still eating and talking with Elsie.

"Hank, I want to ask you something, and I want an honest answer," Judge Andrews told him solemnly. "Think about it before you tell me. If you could do anything at all with your life now, what would you do? Would you still choose to rob banks and such?"

A thoughtful look crossed Hank's face, and, again, he looked toward Sam for guidance.

"No, Hank," the judge admonished. "Don't look at Sam for answers. I want your answer, all on your own. What is it you would like to do for a living, now that your father is dead and your brothers are going their own ways?"

"Well, I . . . I don't rightly know. I kinda liked it when we all worked at those ranches a few years back, but I like workin' with horses better than cows all day. Cows is dumb critters, if ya know what I mean." Hank's face became animated as he began to get caught up in his thoughts. "Now, horses are real smart! They can tell right off if a person likes 'em or not. If ya get the right horse, ya can teach him lots of things. And he's real grateful when he's bein' treated right, ya know? Next to family, my horse is the best friend I've got, I reckon."

Suddenly, with a stricken look, Hank tossed down his fork. "Oh, my gosh! Here I sit, feedin' my face, an' old Target is still out there tied to the hitchin' post, saddle and all!" Pushing back his chair, he started to rise. "If y'all excuse me a while, I'd best see to him."

With a shake of his head and an odd look, Travis waved Hank back into his seat. Another strained look passed between Travis and Judge Andrews. "I'll see to your horse, Hank. Don't worry. As soon as we get things straightened out here, I'll see that he's stabled in the livery."

"That's mighty nice of you, Marshal. You'll see that he's rubbed down good an' grained an' all?"

Travis nodded, and Judge Andrews coughed to clear his throat. "So! You think you'd like to work with horses, Hank?"

Hank's head bobbed, and he answered around another bite of pie. "Yessir."

"What about all those robberies and hold-ups? Don't you think you'd miss all the excitement?"

"Naw." Hank shook his head. "Pa was the one big on that kind of thing. I'd be happy jest to be around Sammie. Even if I couldn't work around horses, I could help Sam out. I could cut wood for her an' haul water for her, maybe even hunt for meat now an' again. And after she has the baby, I can even look out after the little fella for her."

Closing his eyes for a moment, Judge Andrews rubbed at the bridge of his nose, as if to ease an oncoming headache. "Well, you know, don't you, that before you do anything else, you'll have to go to jail for a while? Then there will have to be a trial. Even your sister had to go through a hearing before my court. Things went fairly easy for her, mainly because she had a lot of the townspeople behind her, and because she has tried so hard to prove herself these past weeks.

"In your case, Hank, things will be more complicated, I'm afraid. The citizens of Tumble don't know you. They consider you a wanted outlaw and they are going to want to see justice done. Not only that, but they are still mad as hornets that your brother, Billy, managed to escape. I'll try my best to be fair, both to you and this town, but I can only do so much. We'll just have to see how things go during the trial."

"You're sayin' I could hang, aren't ya?" Hank asked, his fork clattering to the table and a frown creasing his brow.

"That or go to prison, maybe. Yes," Judge Andrews conceded truthfully.

Once more, Hank's eyes sought Sam's, and they shared a worried look. "Guess that's a chance I'm gonna have to take, then," Hank said softly. "I know I gotta pay for some o' the things we done but I sure do hope I git to see Sammie's baby when it comes. It's like Pa left an empty place in this world when he died, an' it won't be filled till this baby's born. I need to see Pa's place filled, ya know?"

Tears stung Sam's eyes, and she swallowed hard as she reached across the table to clasp Hank's hand tightly in her own. "I know, Hank. I know."

CHAPTER 24

Hank was in jail, awaiting trial. Tom and Billy were exiled in Mexico. Pa was dead as a result of a tiny piece of lead Sam had missed when dressing his wound. The stifling heat wave continued, and the baby was making Sam miserably nauseous and sleepy at odd times of the day.

Sam was thoroughly, deeply depressed. Each day, it was an extreme effort to open her eyes in the morning and gather enough energy to get out of bed. It was as if she'd been strong for as long as she could, and now her energy was depleted. Having Hank show up when he did and learning about her father's death had been the last straw. Sam was tired.

Day after day, she dragged listlessly about the house, her disinterest more than evident. Elsie was ready to pull her own hair out—or Sam's! "Will you please jerk yourself out from under that black cloud?" she complained loudly, her sympathies strained after an entire week of watching Sam mope about. "You're young, you're healthy, you have a wonderful husband and a baby on the way. A smile wouldn't kill you, you know!"

At Sam's irate scowl, she continued, "Sweetie, I know you're hurting over your father's death. You wouldn't be human if you weren't but you have to deal with it and go on. You can't bury yourself with him. From what you've said, he wouldn't want you to."

Dark, wounded eyes sparkled with fresh tears as Sam silently begged Elsie's indulgence. "I . . . I didn't get to say good-bye!" she said simply, gulping back a sob. "I should have been there, to hold his hand, to tell him how much I love him, like we did with Mama. I should have been there, Elsie! I should have been there to tell him how sorry I am that I made him get so sick, to tell him how much I'd miss him, to touch him and soothe him!"

By now sobs were quaking through her slender frame, and when Elsie gathered her into her arms, all Sam could do was cling and cry. "Let it go, Sam. Cry it all out."

The next day, Sam had a long talk with Parson Aldrich and an even longer talk with Hank. Reluctantly, painfully, her brother related to her every detail he could recall of Bill Downing's final days on earth, reliving them and sharing them with Sam. Fresh wounds were torn open and cleansed, and a healing process began for both of them.

Two days later, Sam received a letter and a small

package from Mexico. The letter was from Nan and Tom; the package contained a delicate locket. The note explained:

Dearest Samantha,

It is with the most heartfelt sorrow that we send this locket and our love to you. By now, surely, you have heard from Hank and learned of your father's death. We wanted you to know that the doctor eased his pain as much as possible, and that he did not suffer overmuch.

He spoke of you often and with love, and if you are blaming yourself for his death, then please don't. I know that it was his wish that you not blame yourself in any way. One of his last requests was that we send this locket to you with his love. Unfortunately, Hank forgot it when he left, but we hope it reaches you now. The locket belonged to your mother, and your father carried it with him always. Now it comes to you, and later to your son or daughter, as a treasured momento.

May it ease your heart to know that, at the end, he was at peace. On his last breath, he seemed to look up and smile, and then he sighed your mother's name. Tom and I like to believe that, in that moment, he saw your dear mother coming for him and that they were reunited at last.

He wished you happiness in your new life, dear sister, as both of us wish the same for you. Hank may have told you of our marriage, and though we wish we could share our joys and sorrows with you, that is not possible at this time.

Tom is trying to find a way to make a future for us here, and it is our fondest dream that somehow Tom can study to become a preacher, as he has always wanted to do. Billy and Nola hope to go into ranching. They, also, send greetings and hope that you understand and forgive their hasty departure.

Though we long to hear news of you and of Hank, all we can do is pray for the best. If it is within your power or Travis's, we know that you will do your best to see that no harm comes to Hank. We will send word to you when we can, though we know you cannot reply without endangering us all.

Perhaps someday everything will work out, and we will all see one another again. Until then, know that our hearts are with you. Be happy, Sam, with your coming child and your life with Travis. Give him our regards, and to Hank as well.

Always,
Nan and Tom

Through her tears, Sam clutched the locket to her breast, struggling laboriously through the words of Nan's letter. Twice she read it, savoring every precious word, aching with agony for herself and for them. The irony dawned on Sam that, without Nan's persistent guidance, she would never have been able to read this letter herself. Now

Nan was part of her family, her sister-in-law, writing to her from some unknown town in Mexico and offering solace for her grief. Perhaps Nan had been the one to hold her father's hand in Sam's stead, to smooth his fevered brow and give him ease. Sam hoped so, knowing that Nan would have done so with a compassionate and loving heart.

It was as if receiving the locket was a turning point of sorts for Sam, as if seeing those old pictures of her mother and father together and knowing they were now together in the hereafter, served to heal her immense grief. Once more, her lips turned upward in the smiles that Travis had grown to know and to love so well.

And perhaps the locket brought with it some kind of benevolence, for within the next few days, despite repeated protests from Rafe Sandoval, Judge Andrews held a hasty trial and handed down his verdict. Hank Downing would not hang. Neither would the young man spend the rest of his days in prison. As in Sam's case, Andrews took into consideration Hank's age when he'd first followed his family along their road to crime. Also, he stressed Hank's slight mental deficiency as added reason for his final decision.

Hank would spend the next three months behind bars right here in Tumble and under Travis's eagle eye. After that, he would be released into Travis's custody. He would live with Travis and Sam in their home and would be forbidden to leave Tumble, to consort with criminals, or to carry firearms for one year. It was arranged as part of the conditions of his release that Hank would work at the livery stable under strict supervision.

Though many people disagreed with Judge Andrews's decision, there wasn't much they could do about it. Time would tell how reliable and trustworthy Hank Downing turned out to be. Meanwhile, they would sit by and watch—warily.

Amid all the grumbling, Sam was thrilled beyond belief. Travis had his doubts but wisely kept his thoughts to himself. It had been some time since he'd seen Sam this happy, and he wasn't about to burst her bubble prematurely. Besides, maybe it would all work out all right after all.

Still, Travis's little house was about to become a bit crowded for his tastes. Six months ago, there had only been him with Elsie coming in to cook and to clean. Now Elsie lived in, and soon there would be four adults and a baby sharing the dinner table, the linens—everything—and Travis wasn't sure he really liked the idea. It would take some getting used to once Hank moved in, too. Travis and Sam had only been married a few precious weeks, and already privacy was but a fading dream. Only Sam's glowing face and his love for her made it all worth the sacrifice.

"What happened to the honeymoon?" he grumbled late one night, after Elsie had finally stopped bustling about in the bedroom next to theirs.

"The honeymoon?" Sam echoed.

"Yeah," he told her with a crooked grin that set her heart racing. "You know, that time together that newlyweds sometimes have to themselves, all peaceful and private? Seems like we haven't had much of that for ourselves with one of your brothers or the other popping up like weeds."

Sam could feel her hackles rising. "Now you look here, Travis Kincaid! It was you who insisted —no, *forced*—our weddin', while Billy was still in jail. If the timin' was wrong, that wasn't my choosin'! And when he escaped, it was you who insisted on havin' Elsie move back in here with us, so don't you go blamin' me for not havin' time alone together!"

"Okay, okay! Don't get your dander up!" he placated, holding his palms up as if to ward her off. "All I'm saying is, I wish we could have more time alone, all to ourselves. Once Hank is out of jail, he'll be living in with us, and then the baby will be here before we know it and taking up a lot of your time."

"We can always ask Elsie to move back to her place for a few weeks," Sam suggested, her brow furrowing with thought. "Hank's gonna be in jail for the next three months, and we'll have the house all to ourselves. I don't think Elsie would mind, if we ask her nicely."

Travis brightened a bit, and said hesitantly, "But don't you need her now? I know you haven't been feeling too well lately, and soon you'll be waddling around like a stuffed goose . . ." His teasing grin softened his words, but Sam rose to the bait.

"A stuffed goose!" she screeched. "Why you pompous ass! I didn't get this baby by myself, you beast! If it wasn't for you, I wouldn't be in this fix!" She pounded him about the head with her pillow as she continued to rail at him. "Seems to me you had a heck of a lot of fun creatin' this child, too, if I recall correctly!"

"And you didn't?" he queried with a chuckle, his

voice muffled by the pillow she had stuffed over his face.

"Welll," she conceded sheepishly, letting him push the pillow aside and roll her to her back. He lay over her now, laughing down at her. "Maybe a little."

Travis's lips hovered over hers. "Samantha Kincaid, you're a terrible little liar, but I love you, anyway."

One kiss led to another; one caress to many more. Soon Sam was writhing beneath him, trying to stifle her wild cries of delight. Later, with her head cradled upon Travis's shoulder, her body relaxed and content once more, she whispered, "I'll talk to Elsie tomorrow."

She felt his nod and his sigh. "All right. I guess that's better than nothing. I wish we could just lock ourselves away and pretend we weren't home for at least a week, maybe more. Even if we did, there would be dozens of people who would 'just have to see the marshal' for some reason or another."

"Can't you get Chas to take over for a little while?"

He shrugged. "As long as I'm in town, there are still those who would insist on bringing their problems to me."

"Then let's go away somewhere for a few days, or don't we have the money?" Travis always managed their finances, and Sam wasn't certain how much they could afford to spend.

"Depends on how we travel and where we go," he answered, the spark in her eyes creating an excitement that was infectious.

"Could we take the train to Arkansas, somewhere around Hot Springs?"

A smile grew on his lips. "I think we could manage that. What do you have in mind, darlin'? A dip in the mineral springs there?"

She shook her head and gave him an enigmatic smile. "You just get us to Hot Springs, and I'll take over from there," she told him. "I've got the perfect place in mind, nice and private. You'll love it! I promise!"

"Is this going to be a surprise?" he asked doubtfully. By now he knew Sam and her family well enough to be leery of any grand surprises she might cook up.

"Oh, Travis! Don't be such a worry wart! If I can arrange it, it will be perfect, but I can't tell you much about it now. It would be breakin' a trust to a good friend."

"Who?"

"I can't tell you that, either. He's an old friend of the family."

Travis groaned. "I don't know about this, Sam."

"I do. You arrange to have Chas cover for you for a while and get the train tickets. I've got a couple of telegrams to send."

Two days later, Travis was wondering what the devil he'd gotten himself into. If anyone would have told him he'd be docilely following Sam up a treacherous mountain trail, blindfolded, he would have told them they were out of their minds. Now he was wondering if *he* wasn't the one out of *his* mind.

In Hot Springs, they'd purchased supplies and obtained horses, and outside of town, Sam had produced the hankie to be tied about Travis's eyes. "Trust me, Travis," she'd told him with a sweet smile. "It's just that I promised not to let you know the exact location of the cabin."

The sound of falling rock brought Travis's thoughts to the present with a jerk. "Sam?" he called out. "This has gone far enough. I'm removing this blasted blindfold before you end up killing us both."

"Don't you dare, Travis Kincaid, or I'll never speak to you again!" she warned.

A wry smile curled Travis's lips. "If that's a promise, it might be one more reason to do it."

"That's real funny!" she retorted. Then she cajoled, "You've come this far, Travis. We've only got a couple of miles yet to go. Don't spoil things now."

Reluctantly, against his better judgement, he agreed. "Talk about the blind leading the blind," he muttered, wondering if he would survive another couple of miles. His lungs told him they were well up the mountain. Though he'd tried to determine their general direction, Sam had led them through so many switchbacks that Travis could not begin to guess where they might be now.

The only thing he was sure of was that he was a fool to be going along with this so calmly. Even now, his right pant leg was brushing against the rock wall along the trail, as his horse nudged closer to it. Travis got the distinct impression that the trail was extremely narrow here, and a shiver ran up his backbone as he heard pebbles falling like raindrops along the left side of the trail. They fell a long, long way, and he could only hope he and his horse would not soon follow suit.

"You can take the blindfold off now, Travis," Sam said an eternity later. "The trail gets a bit tricky here, and it's best you have control of your horse."

He tore the cloth from his eyes, reflexively catching the reins she tossed back to him. As his eyes adjusted to the late-afternoon sunlight, Travis gazed about in awed horror. "Sam, if I didn't love you so much, I swear I'd kill you!" They were following a crumbling, three-foot-wide ledge that wound about the mountain like a frayed ribbon. To the left was a severe drop into thin air, hundreds of feet straight down. Ahead, the trail veered sharply upward. To Travis, it looked as if only a mountain goat or maybe a cougar could traverse it success-fully.

"You've got to be kidding, Sam!" he groaned. "Hell, woman, if you wanted to kill me, did you have to bring me so far to do it? There's no way we can get up there!"

"Sure we can," she assured him blithely. "It's a little rough but it can be done."

Eyeing her with obvious disbelief, Travis asked, "According to who, Sam?"

"Accordin' to me. I've done it a couple of times before. All we have to do is let the horses rest a few minutes, then we take it all at once, all the way to the top, as fast as we can."

He shook his head. "It's suicide."

"It's not that hard, really. I'll go first. Let me get a runnin' start before you follow, but once you get goin', don't slow down!" With no further warning, Sam spurred her horse up the incline.

"Sam!" With his heart in his throat, Travis watched his wife tear up the steep slope, her slim body stretched forward along her horse's body. For a moment more he hesitated. Then, with a curse and a prayer, he spurred his own mount after hers.

Travis aged ten years before his horse finally found firm footing at the top of the ridge. A few yards away, Sam sat grinning at him. "See? What'd I tell you?" she boasted. "Easy as pie!"

His dark scowl promised retribution. "And how do we get down when we're ready to leave?" he asked with a growl. "Or do you plan on us living out the rest of our lives up here?"

Sam's grin widened. "Now, that's an idea that has a lot goin' for it," she teased. "As to gettin' back down, don't you worry none. I got you up here and I'll get you down again safe and sound."

Half an hour later, Sam guided them out of the trees into a large, flower-strewn clearing, and Travis got his first real glimpse of where he and Sam would be spending the next week. A lone cabin stood backed against a rocky ledge. To one side, a brook sang merrily on its way down the mountain. At the front of the cabin, about two hundred yards opposite the rock wall, was the most spectacular view Travis had ever seen. The small mountain meadow ended abruptly there, but beyond, he could see for miles and miles across hills and valleys to distant mountains. Small lakes and streams dotted the landscape with specks of blue amid varicolored greens.

For the first time in hours, Travis thought perhaps Sam's choice of honeymoon location wasn't so bad after all now that he'd lived through the hair-raising ride up here. Not only was it secluded and beautiful, it was a good deal cooler up here than back in Tumble.

"Isn't it the most beautiful place you've ever set

eyes on?" Sam breathed. "I fell in love with it the first time I saw it. Seems to me, heaven couldn't be much prettier than this."

"It is marvelous," Travis granted, "but who owns it? Why all the secrecy, Sam?"

"I told you it belongs to a friend." The sheepish look on her face made Travis warier.

"Does this friend have a name? Do I know him, by any chance?"

"Well," she hedged, fidgeting in her saddle, "I don't know if you know him or not, personally, that is, but I suppose you'd recognize his name."

"Which is?"

Her voice was small as she answered almost shyly, "Sam Bass."

"Sam Bass!" Travis's shout boomed across the little meadow and echoed back from the rocks. "How could you?" he groaned. "The man's a two-bit gambler-turned-robber! He's been holding up stagecoaches from here to Waco all summer! And now you 'borrow' his cabin for our honeymoon!"

Sam glared at him. "Bass is a good enough sort."

Travis glowered back. "Maybe according to your standards, but I don't particularly cotton to being beholden to an outlaw!"

"Don't get your drawers in a knot over it! You're not beholden to him for anything. Sam Bass owed the Downings a favor, and when I wired him, he was happy to even things up by lettin' us use the cabin. The only thing he asked was that I not give away its location to anyone. That's why I had to blindfold you."

"Great!" he fumed. "That's just great! Now I suppose if we stay here, I'll have to be looking over my shoulder for bandits popping up by the dozens! Well, I'm not spending my honeymoon consorting with criminals!" He reached for her reins. "Come on. We're leaving!"

Dancing her horse out of reach, Sam snapped, "You can leave if you want, Travis, but I'm stayin' right here. It's been a long ride, and I'm plumb tuckered out. Besides, it'll be gettin' dark soon, and the trail's too rough to ride at night."

His eyes were turquoise slits as he scowled at her, but Sam simply shrugged and kneed her horse toward the cabin. "By the way, Travis, I made sure we'd have the cabin all to ourselves when I made the arrangements with Bass. He won't be usin' it till after we leave, and neither will anyone else. It's part of the deal."

"And you believe him?" he sneered, following her lead.

"Yeah. I do. Sort of one outlaw to another, you know?" she answered cockily. "Haven't you ever heard of honor among thieves?" She let him mull that over for a couple of seconds, then added, "B'sides, Sam's seen me shoot. He knows better than to try and cross me—he likes breathin'."

CHAPTER 25

Two mornings later, Sam stepped out of the cabin, yawned, stretched contentedly, and went in search of Travis. She found him by the stream, a cane pole dangling lazily across his knee. He looked like she felt, relaxed and carefree.

"Fishin' for breakfast?" she asked.

He nodded, grinning at the picture she made, standing there dressed only in one of his shirts, which hung to her knees, her bright hair streaming every which way, her legs and feet bare. He patted the spot next to him, urging her to sit.

"Any luck yet?" she questioned, tucking her legs up under her and leaning against his shoulder for support.

"Not until you showed up." He bent his head and stole a quick kiss from her. "Mmmm, sweet!

Maybe I'll just let the worm fend for himself while I get myself a little morning delight right here on the bank.''

He rolled her onto her back in the thick green grass, his fingers finding the top button of the shirt and loosening it. His bold, teasing eyes gleamed down at her in challenge.

"We might starve," she teased back, wriggling seductively beneath him. The sparkle in her eyes more than matched his.

"We'll live on love," he countered gruffly, deftly loosening another button.

She giggled as he nibbled on her neck, making gooseflesh pepper her skin. "That doesn't sound very fillin'.''

His tongue snaked up to flick into her ear. With a squeal, she shivered in response. He laughed. "Shows how much you know! Give me a minute, and I'll prove just how filled you can get."

"Braggart!"

"Have you had any complaints yet?"

"No."

"I didn't think so."

Sam could feel the grin on his face as his mustache brushed over her lips as lightly as a butterfly's wings. Then, as her mouth sought his, the kiss deepened.

The sun had not yet burned off the dew, but Sam did not notice the dampness. Her flesh was aflame with desire. She knew only heat and want as Travis peeled back the two sides of the shirt, baring her perfect breasts to his touch. Morning sunlight bathed her body in a golden glow, lending an added sheen to her red-gold tresses.

Travis was entranced. Her flesh beckoned his

touch, and he gave it gladly. With her help, he was soon as naked as she. His lips sought her breasts, suckling deeply, delighting them both, building the desire. Her slender fingers twined through the crisp, tawny hair on his chest, finding and fondling the flat nipples hidden there.

A low growl of animal pleasure vibrated from him, and her sensual purr answered his love call. Within her eager, seeking hand, she stroked his throbbing shaft of silken, pulsating need. Beneath his skilled caresses, she writhed in glorious torment until she thought she might scream with unbearable yearning. Then he was over her, in her, filling her as he had promised, and she drew him deep within her, arching up to him, offering all to him.

It was heaven at its sweetest and hell at its hottest. Long, hard satin strokes sent them climbing rapture's rainbow. At the top, they clung for breathless, tingling moments in wild anticipation. Then together, they plunged over the peak, careening madly along a sun-sparkled slide of purest molten gold.

They lay spent, still entwined, gradually becoming aware of the world around them as the earth slowly ceased spinning. In the trees, the birds still sang their sweet songs. The sun shone brightly, a frog croaked, a cricket chirped. In the stream, a fish jumped, and the forgotten fishing pole lurched and slithered rapidly toward the water's edge.

"Oh, my gosh!" Sam yelped. "Travis! Get the pole! You've got a fish!"

Startled into action, Travis leaped up and began to chase the elusive pole along the bank. Naked as a jaybird, he ran after it but every time he made a grab for it, it jerked beyond his reach. Finally, in desperation, he lunged for it, grabbing hold of it as it disappeared into the water. In he went, pole and all, headlong into the chilly mountain stream.

Sam had never laughed so hard in all her life! Watching Travis chase after that pole was the funniest thing she'd ever witnessed. When he bobbed to the top, his teeth chattering, triumphantly waving the fishing rod, she collapsed in peals of laughter, her sides aching. When, seconds later, he clambered up the bank, a nice fat trout in tow, gales of mirth brought tears to her eyes.

Knowing what a sight he must have made, charging down the bank as naked as the day he was born, Travis couldn't help but laugh with her. With a gallant bow, he lay the flopping fish at her feet. "Your breakfast, madame!" he quipped with a smirk. "And if you dare tell another living soul about this, I'll deny it to my dying day!"

"Oh, but, Travis!" she wheezed, laughing up at him. "You don't know the best part of it! Before we left the house, I put a sign on the front door. It says, 'Gone Fishin'! If they only knew how!" Another round of giggles claimed her. In fact, all through the day at odd moments, she would catch his eye and set them both off into another spurt of uproarious laughter.

On their third day there, Sam guided Travis on a small tour through the rocks behind the cabin. For half an hour they climbed and clambered over boulders half the size of the average house. Finally they came to a small, bubbling spring. Steam rose from its surface, emitting a curious odor.

"A hot spring!" Travis exclaimed in obvious delight.

"Not just any old hot spring," Sam crowed. "Our own private hot spring. As far as anyone else knows, this one doesn't exist. Of course, it's a bit off the beaten path and harder than heck to find. With any luck, it'll remain hidden from the outside world for a while, along with the meadow and the cabin."

Travis was already shucking his clothes. "I hate to admit it, Sam, but right at this moment, I'm inclined to agree with you. As reluctant as I was, and still am, to accept Sam Bass's offer of this place, I'm glad I let you talk me into staying."

"So am I, Travis." Tossing her own clothes aside, Sam took his hand and let him help her into the churning water. "This place is the next thing to paradise. It'd be a shame not to take advantage of it. After all, it has everythin' we could want for a honeymoon—absolute privacy, a wonderful view, spectacular sunsets, a hot spring, a cozy cabin . . ."

"And you and me," Travis finished for her, drawing her firmly against him, their bodies rubbing sensuously beneath the water, causing more tingling bubbles to rise to the surface. "You can't have a honeymoon without the bride and groom."

"And lots of lovin'," she added, running her tongue below his mustache and nibbling at the corner of his lip.

"Yeah," he groaned, feeling another part of him spring vibrantly to life again. "Let's not forget lots and lots of loving."

They laughed, they loved, they talked about anything and everything. Sam heard dozens of tales about Travis's adventures as a marshal and as a Texas Ranger. She learned some of what he had been like as a boy, just as he learned more about her. They exchanged dreams and plans for their future together with their children. By the time their week was spent, they were both reluctant to give up the sweet seclusion and return to the real world. Their wedding trip had been perfect, a marvelous slice of heaven in a setting as beautiful and wanton as Eden must have been. With sighs of regret, they turned their backs and rode away from paradise.

To Travis's amazement, Sam led them away from the meadow in an entirely different direction from the way they had arrived. Again, after they'd ridden a short distance, she insisted that he wear the blindfold. "I promised Sam and I never go back on my word," she told him. "Don't worry, though. We're not goin' back down the trail the same way and we won't have to use that steep drop."

Though he couldn't see, his other senses told him when they entered the dark, damp cavern. The horses' hoofs echoed loudly, and he could hear trickles of water dripping down the rock walls. Sam's voice reverberated back to him as she told him when to duck for a low overhang. It seemed they'd gone quite some distance when Travis suddenly became aware that he was hearing a muted roaring sound. At first, he couldn't place it in his mind, but when they got closer to it, he realized that he was hearing falling water. They were nearing a waterfall.

"Okay, Travis. We're gonna get drenched some here," Sam warned. "Just hold tight and let your horse find his own footin'."

Drenched wasn't quite the word Travis would have used. Half-drowned came closer to describing it. One minute a few sprinkles dampened him, and the next tons of water were pounding down on him and his mount. His horse almost stumbled under the sudden deluge, but somehow managed to keep its feet. Then, when Travis was certain he would drown, they rode out into warm, welcoming sunlight. Half a dozen sloshing strides later, his horse bounded up onto dry land once more, and after a couple more miles of winding trail, Sam informed him that it was safe to remove the blindfold.

Their hidden haven was far behind, shielded in secrecy, its mysterious location guarded still. But their memories of their time alone there would live on forever, shimmering like a magical dream in their minds.

Tumble seemed miles and eons away from Hot Springs and their wondrous wedding trip. Life limped along at a familiar pace, catching Sam and Travis in its familiar rhythms. Though they had some privacy, with Elsie only coming in twice a week to help out as Sam's pregnancy advanced, they found themselves settling into everyday life once more.

Salvaging what they could of the garden vegetables, Elsie taught Sam how to can and preserve, putting up jar after jar of jams and jellies, peas and beans, corn, pickles, and beets. They made applesauce until Sam was sick of looking at it. They boiled tomatoes until she saw red in her sleep. Before they were done, fruits and vegetables danced merrily through her dreams.

When the last of the food was preserved for winter, Sam drew a deep breath of relief. But Elsie had new projects in mind now. There were candles to make and soap from ashes saved from last winter's fires.

"But we can buy all the soap and candles we want from the mercantile," Sam groaned in dismay. "Why do we have to make them?"

"Because you need to know how, that's why," Elsie pointed out stubbornly. "Convenience is no excuse for laziness or stupidity. Every young wife should know how to make her own soap and candles. You never can tell when such knowledge might come in handy. Besides, it's cheaper, and a woman needs to learn thrift, too."

Then, when the last cake of soap was done, and the last candle drying on its wick, Elsie proclaimed that it was high time Sam learned the fine art of quilting.

"Elsie, you know I can't sew any better than I can sing," Sam complained. "I'm havin' enough trouble just tryin' to make baby clothes."

Though Elsie agreed wholeheartedly, she said, "That's no reason to quit trying. The more you practice, the better you'll get. Besides, think how proud you'll be when you've got a quilt you've made with your own hands. Why, someday you might hand it down to your grandchildren. Wouldn't that be something?"

To Sam's thinking, it would be nothing short of a miracle! "I think my talents might run more to rag rugs," she grumbled. Still, more to shush Elsie than anything else, Sam took needle and thread in hand and bravely tackled the quilt. If it turned out as awful as she dreaded, she could always stuff it in a closet and burn it once Elsie had forgotten about it.

Now that Sam's pregnancy was beginning to show more, the coming birth of their child seemed more of a reality to both her and Travis. He started worrying more than ever about her health and the baby's. He'd even gone so far as to visit Doc Purdy, and he came home armed with advice on the proper care and nurturing of the mother-to-be. Nervous about being a mother to begin with, Sam was soon beside herself and ready to clobber Travis.

"Have you had your milk today?" he would ask. "You know Doc Purdy said you should drink milk."

"I hate milk, and you know it," she would grumble, only to find herself forcing a glass of it down a few minutes later just to shut Travis up. If she didn't, he would pester her mercilessly until she did.

He monitored her meals with the zeal of a fanatic, making certain she ate enough meats and vegetables and fruit. This, Sam didn't mind so much since she liked almost any kind of food, but when he began to limit her sweets, she pitched a fit.

"That's your second helping of peach cobbler, Sam," he'd say. "That'll make you fat, honey. It won't do the baby any good, you know. Why don't you eat a nice, juicy apple, instead."

"I happen to like peach cobbler," she'd tell him with a glare. "If I'm gonna look like an elephant, anyway, I might as well enjoy myself while I'm at it."

"But the apple would be better for you."

"I want the cobbler, Travis!"

She really got back at him when she developed a craving for licorice—black licorice. She whined and complained and wheedled late into the night, robbing him of any sleep he'd hoped to get. By morning he couldn't wait for the mercantile to open, and he came home laden with their entire stock of long black licorice whips.

"I hope this makes you happy," he snarled. Licorice in hand, Sam was in heaven.

"Why this?" he dared to ask, wrinkling his nose.

"Why ask me? Go ask your precious friend, the doctor," she snapped back at him. "Maybe it has somethin' to do with you makin' me quit smokin'. I don't know. At least it doesn't give me heartburn, like everythin' else does these days."

"You know," Elsie put in, trying to ease the tension, "they say when the mother has heartburn, the baby is going to have a head full of hair."

"Doc says that's just an old wives' tale," Travis informed them in that irritatingly superior tone he'd adopted lately.

"Yeah, well right now I wouldn't care if the kid was born with six toes on each foot and as bald as an egg," Sam retorted. "I'm sick of swillin' soda to get rid of the burnin'."

He eyed her disgustedly. "Lord only knows what all that licorice is going to do to the baby. Have you bothered to think about that?"

"Oh, Travis, darlin', I've thought of a lot of things lately," she drawled, sending him a sour smile.

"Mostly, I've been thinkin' how nice it'd be if you'd go to Alaska or China or somewhere and stop pesterin' the daylights out of me every minute of the day! I've also had wonderful visions of givin' you a swift kick in the pants!"

To both women's amazement, he laughed. "Honey, if that's what you have in mind, you'd better try it soon or give up the idea altogether. If you gain much more weight, you won't be able to get your foot that high!"

"I wouldn't bet on it!" she sneered. "But if that happens, I'll just have to settle for puttin' huge, bruised knots on your shins."

Travis only eased up on her when Sam told him he was making her terribly nervous. "I'm beyond irritated, Travis. Honest to God, you're givin' me the nervous jitters! If you don't stop botherin' me about things all the time, I'm gonna end up breakin' out in hives! Then it'll be all your fault when this baby's born lookin' like a red-spotted pup!"

That comment and another talk with Doc Purdy convinced Travis that it might be best not to aggravate her any more. "A calm mother is a happy mother, Travis," Purdy consoled. "And a happy mother makes for a happier father and baby. Just keep Sam away from the cigarettes and the liquor cabinet and don't worry so much about what else she eats. I'm sure, if she eats as she usually does, she'll do fine."

"But, Doc, black licorice?" Travis bemoaned. "Is that normal?"

Purdy laughed and shook his head. "Has anything about Sam been normal yet? But don't fret.

To my knowledge, there's nothing in licorice that could harm your child. Relax, Travis, or you're going to be the one I'm treating for hives."

They were eating supper one evening a few days later. Travis had just taken a big bite of chicken when across the table from him, Sam suddenly clutched her stomach and let out a strange moan. Startled, Travis half-rose from his chair, fear for her written clearly on his face.

Without thinking, he swallowed the entire mouthful without bothering to chew it. Promptly, it lodged in his throat, and he began to choke. In the next few seconds, he found himself wheezing, unable to get his breath, his throat working spasmodically to rid itself of the blockage. He reached for his coffee cup, his hand jerking violently with each racking cough, and succeeded only in toppling his coffee across the table top.

Forgetting her own problems, Sam rushed to his aid. By now, Travis's face was a dull red, tears streaming from his eyes. With one hand he was clutching his throat while the other grabbed at his chest, and she was positive that at any moment he was going to fall dead at her feet! Not knowing what else to do, she began thumping him heartily on the back. Within a few minutes, he was waving her aside, frantically nodding, but he was breathing again and his face was returning to its usual color.

Grabbing her glass of milk, Sam thrust it into his hand, watching anxiously as he half-gulped, half-choked it down. Guiding him back into his chair, Sam fell into hers with a heavy sigh. "God a'mighty, Travis! You scared the tar out of me!"

"Me?" he wheezed, glaring at her as he wiped his napkin over his damp face. "You're the one who groaned and grabbed your stomach!" Then he forgot his anger in renewed fear for her. "Are you all right? Are you in pain?"

"Yes! No!" she stammered. "Darn it all, I'm fine! All I had was a twinge of sorts! You're the one who almost choked to death! Are you all right?"

That menacing glower was back on his face, drawing his brows together and flattening his upper lip beneath his mustache. "I'll live, yes!" he rasped. "Now, what's this about a twinge?"

"Nothin' to get all upset about," she assured him. "It lasted the shortest time, but it made me feel so strange! It was like a bird's wing flutterin' inside, all light and feathery."

"It didn't hurt?"

"No, it felt odd, that's all." Suddenly her eyes widened. "Travis! There it goes again!" She grabbed for his hand, dragging it across to her stomach. "There! It was right there!"

Together they waited, and sure enough, it came again, the slightest of movements, like a breath of a breeze lightly stirring the leaves on a tree. Sam's wide black eyes locked with Travis's. "What is it?" she whispered.

His own brilliant eyes were sparkling now, with joy and wonder. "It's the baby, Sam," he murmured in an awe-filled voice that shook with emotion. "It's our baby moving inside you!"

CHAPTER 26

Autumn waned, and almost before they knew it, the Thanksgiving holiday was approaching. Hank would be released from jail in time to spend the holiday with them, and Sam had spent days getting his room ready. She'd done it gladly, knowing that this was the first time that Hank would have a room to call his own. Even as a young boy, he'd shared a bedroom with his brothers. It was also the first time in years that he would have a permanent home, and Sam wanted to make everything as nice as possible for him. She wanted him to be comfortable and happy and to feel wanted and truly a part of their little family.

By now she was more than halfway through her term, and her stomach was ballooning with each day or so it seemed to her. Each added pound appeared to go directly to her stomach, and the more weight she gained, the clumsier she became.

"You're like a two-wheeled cart with the load all in the front," Travis teased her. "Face it, honey, you're front-heavy. We'll have to watch that you don't tumble over on your face in the next couple of months!"

Sam was not amused. "You're a barrel of laughs, Travis!" she retorted sourly.

"Not me," he laughed, eyeing her burgeoning stomach, "but speaking of barrels, you're starting to look like you swallowed one."

"I wish, for a while, you could trade places with me," she answered with a glare. "I'm willin' to bet it wouldn't seem quite so funny to you then, if the shoe was on the other foot. B'sides, you seem to conveniently forget who put this baby here to begin with." Sam rubbed her swelling tummy to relieve the itch of stretching skin. "As much as I want this child, Travis, there are days when I'm not real thrilled with you."

"Aw, sweetheart, don't get mad," he said, hastening to placate her. "You know I'm just teasing you. I love you, you know, and I think you look real cute with your little tummy sticking out that way."

"Cute!" she sniffed. "Now there's a word I could grow to hate real quick!"

Despite her complaints, and her enlarging girth, Sam was happy. She was looking forward to the birth of their child, and often found herself daydreaming about what it might look like, whether it would be a boy or a girl. Either way, she was sure the baby would be active and healthy. It moved about inside her constantly now, kicking and poking about, and Sam never failed to thrill at the feeling.

At night, when she and Travis had retired to their bed, he would lay with his hand or his head over her tummy, sharing the joy and anticipation with her, and they would consider names for their child. Somehow, they always seemed to concentrate more on boys' names than girls'.

"What about Peter?" she suggested.

Travis shook his head. "That'd be almost as bad as Horace, to my mind. I guess it's because I knew a man named Peter when I was growing up, who was the most tight-fisted, thin-lipped miser you'd ever care to meet. How about Andrew?"

Sam's nose wrinkled. "Folks would call him Andy, which would be fine while he was young, but I can't picture a grown man with the name."

"Stewart?"

"No."

"Jeremiah?"

"Uh–uh."

"What about Douglas?"

"Well, that has possibilities, but what do you think of Bradley?"

On it went. Weeks later, they had settled on the name Trevor if the baby was a boy, but a girl's name eluded them. "We could always call her Little Who's It, I suppose," Travis said with a shrug.

Sam's look told him what she thought of that. "I'll think of somethin'," she promised, squelching a yawn. "Maybe tomorrow." With that, she curled up and drifted off to sleep, her stomach nestled into the curve of Travis's back. As if in retaliation for his awful selection of names, Little Who's It pounded Travis's back with energetic kicks long into the night. Sam was too tired to care, and Travis really didn't mind being pummeled at all. He eased into slumber with a smile curving his lips.

Three days before Thanksgiving, Hank was released from jail. Sam was ecstatic, and she showed him around the house as if it were the king's palace. "Look, Hank! There's even a pump in the kitchen, so we don't have to haul buckets in from outdoors."

Hank wasn't so appreciative of this as he was of his very own room. "This is real nice, Sammie," he said, looking about the bedroom and admiring the matching blue-and-brown curtains and bed cover. He sat on the bed, bounced experimentally on the mattress, and smiled. "This is a lot more comfortable than that jail cot. Thanks."

"I imagine anythin' would be more comfortable than that. Oh, Hank! I'm so happy to have you here!" She sat on the bed next to him, hugging him close to her, glad tears stinging her eyes.

"I'm happy, too, Sammie, an' I promise I won't be no trouble to you and Travis. I'll work hard, an' I'll pay for my keep, an' I'll stay out of trouble."

"And you'll go to church with us on Sunday mornin's when you don't have to work," Sam added.

Hank's look of dismay was almost comical. "Do I hafta?"

Sam nodded. "Yes, Hank, you have to. The judge thought it would be a good idea and a nice way for you to get to know the townsfolk, and Travis and I agree."

"But I'll get to meet a lot of 'em, anyway, workin' at the livery stable," he argued.

Sam nodded. "Yes, but by goin' to church, you'll be showin' them that you mean to do right, Hank. You've got to prove to them that you don't want to be an outlaw anymore, b'fore they'll really accept you."

"Is that what you did?"

"That, and a lot more b'sides. Anyway, you might like church, once you try it."

The next day, Hank started to work for Ed Howard. Ed had reluctantly agreed to the arrangement, only relenting under pressure from Judge Andrews and Travis. Despite Ed's rather sour, suspicious demeanor toward him, Hank enjoyed working with the animals. Without complaint, Hank spent his days mucking stalls, feeding, watering, and grooming the horses. The work was hard, the hours long, the pay little, but Hank settled into it as if he were born to it. Little by little, Ed's attitude toward Hank began to soften, especially when he saw how well the animals responded to Hank's gentle handling.

Sam wanted her first Thanksgiving with Travis to be perfect, a cordial celebration with friends as well as family. With Travis's wholehearted approval, she invited Chas and Molly to join them. She also invited Parson and Alma Aldrich, and was delighted when they accepted.

Elsie was spending the day with her own children and grandchildren at her daughter's house, but to Sam's immense relief, she offered to help Sam prepare her first holiday dinner. Long before her guests began to arrive, the house was gleaming, the pies were cooling, and the stuffed turkey was sending its tantalizing aroma throughout the house. The kitchen table almost groaned beneath the weight of the varied dishes.

Scurrying from the kitchen, Sam hurried to dress before her guests arrived. She'd made a new dress with Elsie's assistance, and disregarding the size of her stomach, she thought she looked quite attractive in it. From the glow in Travis's eyes, it was evident that he thought so, too. The dress was rust-colored, not a dull shade, but with the vibrance of an autumn leaf. A wide, snowy, hand-crocheted collar adorned the demure neckline and the cuffs of the long sleeves. A series of pleated tucks at the waist helped to disguise Sam's rounding figure, while the fitted bust drew still more attention from her stomach to her high, firm breasts.

Even her unruly hair had obeyed her hand today, falling in shining copper waves from the combs that held it up and back from her face.

"You look absolutely ravishing!" Travis complimented, his eyes traveling the length of her in avid admiration. "And tonight, after all our company is gone, I can promise you that you will look absolutely ravished before the evening is done."

"I'll hold you to your word, Marshal Kincaid," she countered with a come-hither smile, her sense of her own womanly charms much restored. "If I might return the compliment, you look mighty appealin' yourself."

Indeed, he did, in his brown corded trousers and coat. The color contrasted nicely with his sun-streaked blond hair and his freshly-trimmed mustache. A matching string tie banded the collar above his crisp white shirt. In honor of the occasion, his boots were polished to an extraordinarily high gleam. He looked especially handsome to Sam today.

The day went very well, and Sam was pleased with herself. This was the first time she'd had more than one or two people for dinner, and she had been nervous about it, but everything turned out wonderfully. The turkey was done to perfection; the dinner rolls were soft and flaky; the pies weren't runny; and miracle of miracles, she managed to make the gravy without lumps, all on her own!

Everyone assured her that the meal was grand and lauded her lavishly on her culinary skills until Sam became quite embarrassed. "Elsie helped out quite a bit," she admitted graciously. "Much of the credit should be hers."

"Oh, but you did most of it by yourself, Sam. I'm very proud of you," Travis said, making her blush even more.

Hank could scarcely believe his luck. "Sammie, Pa would never believe ya could learn to cook this good! Billy said somethin' about missing your pies, but we all thought he was joshin' us. Why, I can recollect when ya couldn't heat a can of beans without burnin' 'em! I think I'm really gonna like livin' here, if ya keep cookin' like this!"

Mopping up his gravy with his roll, Hank stuffed it into his mouth whole, but Sam was too pleased with his praise to berate him for his table manners now. There would be plenty of time for all of that later when she and Travis and Elsie would take

Hank in hand, as they had done with her a few short months ago. For now, Sam merely basked in the welcome glow of their kind words.

The women had cleared the table, and they were all lingering over huge slices of pumpkin pie topped with frothy whipped cream, when Chas cleared his throat noisily and caught Molly's eye. As the others, their attention caught, looked on, he arched a brow in Molly's direction. She answered with a shy nod, her teeth worrying nervously at her bottom lip.

"Molly and I have an announcement to make, and we sort of wanted to share it here and now with our best friends, if y'all don't mind," Chas said. At their curious looks, he continued in a rush, "I've asked Molly to marry me, and she's said yes."

Alma was the first to react with a squeal of delight. Much to Sam's relief, Mrs. Aldrich had not objected to sharing a table with Molly today. Rather, the parson's wife had gone out of her way to be pleasant to her. Her husband had done likewise, and the gathering had not been in the least the strained affair that Sam had feared when she first discussed her guest list with Travis. Both Hank and Molly were outcasts, but Sam had hoped that the Christian couple would be the ones to make them feel more comfortable. She was not disappointed now.

Following his wife's lead, Parson Aldrich peered over his sliding octagonal glasses and smiled benignly at Chas's announcement. Travis was a bit more enthusiastic, leaping from his chair to thump his friend on the back in hearty congratulations. Walking swiftly around the table, he kissed the blushing bride-to-be on the cheek. "Congratulations, you two!" he exclaimed. "I think that's just grand! Don't you, Sam?"

All heads turned her way. Sam sat primly in her chair, her arms folded across her chest in a stern manner. Her lips were curled slightly into a smirk, the glitter in her dark eyes not easily read. She looked from Chas to Molly, letting the silence in the room settle and drag out. Then she announced in a dry tone, "Well, it's about time you finally got up the nerve to ask her, Chas Brown!"

Only then did Sam smile, a wide, warm smile that lit her whole face and proved her joy for both of them. "I think it's fantastic! Now, I just hope it doesn't take as long to get you to the altar as it did to get you to propose! When's the weddin'?"

By now, Chas had turned a dull red at her teasing, and Sam almost regretted doing it. Chas was so painfully shy at times! But he took their ribbing good-naturedly. "Well, Molly and I talked about gettin' married around Christmas sometime, if Parson Aldrich will agree to marry us."

Every gaze now centered questioningly on the pastor. "Of course, I will, son," the man answered. "You and your lady pick the date, and I'll be more than happy to conduct the ceremony."

"Will you be my best man?" Chas asked Travis.

"I'd be hurt if you chose anyone else."

For the first time, Molly spoke up. "Sam, would you be my matron of honor?"

Thinking of the sight she would make with her belly sticking out, Sam grimaced. As Molly's face fell, she hastened to say, "I'd be honored, Molly. Honestly. I just wish I wasn't goin' to be so blasted fat by then! My one chance to have a really fancy dress and I'm gonna look like a cow!"

Everyone laughed, and for the next hour, they discussed plans for a Christmas wedding. Even Hank was included in the talk, assured that he was also invited to the wedding. Alma agreed to play the organ.

"How many guests will you be inviting?" the parson's wife asked, unwittingly bringing up a touchy subject that everyone had so far avoided.

"Uh, well, under the circumstances, we thought it be best to keep it small," Molly stammered, her fingers nervously pleating her napkin. "About the only friends I have in town all work at the Silver Nugget."

Now it was Alma's turn to be embarrassed. "Oh, dear! I'm so sorry! I should have realized, of course!"

Struggling against his shyness, Chas blurted, "That's one of the reasons we decided on a Christmas wedding, though, ya see. We figured, with everyone in the spirit of the season and all, maybe there wouldn't be as much of a fuss set up when everyone finds out that Molly and I are going to get married. They might be in more of a mood to accept it, and us, then."

"Quite right," Parson Aldrich agreed with a nod. "At Christmastime, everyone seems to be a bit more mellow, more giving and forgiving. It's a shame they can't extend all that gracious sentiment to the rest of the year."

"Well, let's think about this a moment," Alma said, considering. "We always have added services around Christmas, you know. There is the pageant, for one thing." Her face took on a calculating expression that amazed them all. "Now, if we were to schedule the wedding after the pageant or directly following the Christmas Eve service, while everyone is still in attendance, what could anyone do? Especially if they didn't know about it until we sprang it upon them that very evening? What do you think, Mr. Aldrich?"

Her husband smiled across at her gently. "I think you are a devious and brilliant woman, my dear. We would have them penned like sheep at a shearing!"

"And not one of them could utter a word of objection if some of Molly's friends decided to attend the Christmas Eve service, could they?" Alma continued. "After all, what Christian person would deny anyone the right to hear the word of God on such a holy night? Surely, we could not turn anyone away from the church on the celebration of our Lord's birth!"

With a deep chuckle, Travis tipped an imaginary hat in Alma's direction. "Mrs. Aldrich, I commend you. You have a cunning mind, matched only by the gentleness of your heart. Between you and Sam, I'm beginning to wonder why women don't rule the world instead of men."

Alma smiled serenely. "But we do, dear boy. From behind the scenes."

With Thanksgiving behind them, Sam found herself focusing now on the upcoming Christmas season and Chas and Molly's wedding. By some odd happenstance, the quilt she was working on was turning out quite nicely, and Sam decided that it would make an acceptable wedding gift, if she could finish it in time. However, she also had to come up with Christmas gifts for Travis, Hank, Elsie, and several friends. Now she was glad she'd never spent any of her winnings from those poker games she'd participated in at Lou's barbershop. At least she had a little money of her own with which to purchase gifts, and Travis need never know how much she might spend on him.

Since there was so much more to do now, getting ready for the holiday season, Elsie voluntarily put in more time. Together they baked cookies and rum cakes, decorated the house with red ribbon bows and fragrant pine boughs, and began sewing a new dress for Sam to wear to the Christmas Eve service and the wedding to follow.

Elsie had been taken into their confidence about the wedding plans and sworn to secrecy. Having gotten to know Molly a little better in the preceding months, and finding that she liked the woman despite her shady occupation, Elsie readily agreed. "You know," she commented idly one day, as she and Sam were rolling out salted dough with which to make tree decorations, "it's a real shame Molly won't be having a bridal party like most women do before they get married."

"A bridal party?" Sam echoed in confusion. "What's that?"

A surprised look came over Elsie's face. "Oh, I'm sorry, Sam. You and Travis got married so quickly, I forgot that you never had one, either. I guess I never realized you might not know about such things."

She went on to explain. "A bridal party is where all the bride's women friends get together a few days before the wedding and throw a party for the bride-to-be. They bring gifts for the bride, and they sit around and drink tea or punch and eat cookies and such. Sometimes they play foolish games, but mostly they trade stories about their own weddings and the joys and trials of preparing the wedding and living together with their husbands in those first months afterward. Usually, it's a lot of fun."

Now Elsie sighed and shook her head. "Somehow, I can't see the proud and proper women of Tumble getting together to throw a bridal party for Molly, though. Most of them wouldn't spit on her if she was on fire. It's a shame, all right, but there's nothing for it, I guess. It'll be enough to get them to sit still for the wedding they're all about to get shanghaied into witnessing, and maybe to speak to her on the street afterward. Something tells me poor Molly is going to have a harder time being accepted than you ever did."

"Why?"

"Mostly because you didn't sell your body. Somehow, robbery is an easier pill to swallow than being a harlot, even if Molly didn't have much choice." By now, both Elsie and Sam had heard Molly's sad tale and knew that Molly had been orphaned at the tender age of thirteen. With little education and no one to look after her, Molly had turned to prostitution to survive.

"No," Sam corrected, "I didn't mean why won't Molly be accepted. I meant, why can't Molly still have a bridal party?"

Exasperation creased Elsie's features. "Haven't you heard a thing I've said? Is your hearing going along with your waistline, Sam?"

"Now, don't go gettin' nasty, Elsie," Sam warned, "or I'll claim a cramp and leave you to make these decorations all on your own."

"Well, what are you getting at then?"

"I was wonderin' why we couldn't give Molly a

party. Travis and Lou are planning a shindig for Chas the night before the weddin'. As Travis explained it to me, all of Chas's friends are gonna get together to celebrate his last night as a free man." Sam's nose wrinkled in disgust. "I took that to mean they're all gonna sit around and cry in their beer and come home stinkin' drunk!"

Elsie laughed. "You figured right. Still, back to your idea for Molly. It wouldn't do much good to throw a party and have no one to invite, now would it?"

"Oh, we'd have plenty of women to invite!" Sam's eyes took on an unholy twinkle that forewarned of trouble. "And at the same time, we'd be makin' sure all those drunken men would be behavin' themselves while they celebrate Chas's good fortune—or misfortune, whichever way they see it."

"What sort of mischief do you have up your sleeve now, may I ask? Why, your eyes are fairly brimming with it!"

"Nothin' that awful, I assure you," Sam said with a grin. "I thought we might invite some of Molly's own friends to a private party. I'm sure they'd just love to help celebrate Molly's gettin' married, and we can hold the party here on the very night the men take Chas out to his groom's party. No one else need know. We can certainly keep the news of it from spreadin' about town to all those so-called proper ladies, can't we?"

Elsie gasped so loudly and deeply, that Sam feared the housekeeper might swallow her own tongue. "You're talkin' about inviting harlots into this house? Samantha Kincaid! Travis would have a conniption fit, if he could hear what you've just suggested! Why, he'd lock you in your room for a week if you dared think of actually doing such a thing!"

"Oh, for Pete's sake!" Sam sighed in annoyance. "We're talkin' about an innocent little party attended entirely by women in honor of Molly's upcomin' weddin'. It's not as if I'd suggested that Molly's friends bring their customers along or anythin'! What possible harm could come from it? What real trouble could we manage to get into?"

"With you behind it, there's no telling!" Elsie exclaimed with a dour expression. "My only consolation is that Travis would never, ever agree to such an idea, and you can rest assured that I'll be the first to tell him about it before it gets beyond the scheming stage in that twisted little mind of yours, Samantha."

"Oh, I plan to tell him all about it as soon as he comes home, Elsie, and I'll make you a wager, here and now, that we'll have that party for Molly, just as I want."

"Not in a million years. I'd bet a month's wages on it."

Sam gave the housekeeper a sly smile. "I'll cover that bet, Elsie, and raise you one full week of washin' dishes after supper. And if I win, you have to help me throw the party!"

"You're on!"

CHAPTER 27

On the evening of the twenty-third of December, ten of the loveliest "soiled doves" in Tumble gathered together at the home of Mrs. Samantha Kincaid. They were met at the door by their smiling hostess who took their wraps and handed them to a sour-faced older woman who answered to the name of Elsie.

"I still don't know how you managed it," Elsie grumbled aside to Sam.

With a wink and a smile, Sam replied in a whisper, "I promised him things you never would."

"That's cheating."

"Travis didn't think so."

Molly was thrilled to tears with her bridal party. "Sam, I'm so touched that you would think to do this for me! The girls and I were shocked that you would invite them into your home, but we're happy and grateful to be here. Thank you."

"No thanks are necessary," Sam assured her, giving Molly a friendly hug. "Just enjoy yourself tonight."

Molly frowned. "Does Travis know about this?" she asked hesitantly.

Nodding, Sam sent a smug grin in Elsie's direction. "Sure does. Don't worry. Just relax and have fun. And smile! You're the guest of honor, and in little more than twenty-four hours, you'll be Mrs. Chas Brown."

"I can hardly believe it!" Molly murmured. "Imagine me, of all people, getting married and settling down."

Sam's laughter rang clear. "That's what I thought about myself not so long ago. Now look at me!" she chuckled, patting her bulging tummy.

It took awhile for everyone to start to relax and to feel comfortable about the situation, especially with Elsie glowering over them, but Sam's outgoing friendliness soon set them at ease. Before long, they were all chattering like magpies, joking and teasing and offering advice to the bride-to-be. Things really began to warm up when Molly opened her gifts. Two of the girls had gone together to give her a red satin nightgown that was guaranteed to give Chas heart palpitations.

"Honey, you wear that, and Chas won't come up for air for a week!" Frannie predicted with a sultry chuckle.

Gazing in wonder at the shimmering gown, Sam

said, "Geez, Molly. I think I'm jealous!"

This brought a round of laughter from the others until Bettina announced on a wistful sigh, "So am I. To tell the truth, we all envy you your good luck in finding a man as wonderful and understanding as Chas, but we wish you the best of everything, too. You made it out, Molly, and we couldn't be happier for you."

After Bettina's pensive statement, Sam noticed that Elsie's nose came down out of the air a bit. She didn't seem half as condemning as she went about serving cake and holiday eggnog to their guests.

Sam's gift to Molly was a pink-checkered apron edged in eyelet lace. Molly adored it. "Now all I have to do is learn to cook as well as you have," Molly said.

As Molly opened the hand-knit pot holders Elsie had made for her, the housekeeper grumbled, "If you run into trouble, just give me a holler. If I could teach Sam here how to cook, I can teach anyone."

"This might help, too," another of the girls told her, holding out another present. When Molly unwrapped it, she found a brand-new cookbook.

"Now this," Rose said, pushing a gaily ribboned box into Molly's hands. "Bettina and Nell and I got this for you."

Molly sat frowning down into the opened box, not quite sure what to make of this latest gift. Nell giggled and earned herself a sharp jab in the ribs from Rose. Thoroughly puzzled, Molly drew forth a chipped dinner plate and a cup with the handle broken off. Still more pieces littered the bottom of the box. "Uh, girls," she began nervously, "I'd like to say thanks, but what am I supposed to do with all these broken dishes?"

Now the laughter rang free and clear as Molly's friends explained. "These are to throw at Chas when you get mad at him, so you don't end up havin' to break all the good dishes!"

Molly's laughter joined theirs. Even Elsie chuckled at this. "Best idea I've heard in a long time."

Then, immediately following their fun-filled gift, the three friends presented Molly with a new set of everyday crockery. "Wish it could have been good china," Rose offered with a shrug, "but the thought's still there. Hope you like them."

"Oh, I do!" Molly's eyes filled with emotional tears. "I don't need fancy china. Not when I have friends like you!"

The party might have wound down soon thereafter if one of the girls hadn't decided to spruce up Elsie's eggnog with a sizable douse of rum. It didn't take long before all of them were feeling very relaxed and sociable.

"We were supposed to play some kind of silly old parlor games now," Sam announced, shaking her head slightly as if to clear it. With a grin, she asked, "Who wants to play poker instead?"

On a chorus of agreement, they cleared the dining-room table and sat down to play. Elsie started to object then shrugged indifferently. Taking another sip of eggnog, she wondered why she was starting to feel so good, and when Sam offered to teach her how to play, she gamely agreed. "Why not?" she drawled with a lopsided smile.

Casting a critical eye at the housekeeper, and

pondering the sudden bouyance of her own spirits and everyone else's, Sam's suspicions rose. Did the eggnog have more of a punch than it had at the start? Not that it probably mattered all that much, but considering her condition and Doc Purdy's advice, and without a word to anyone else, Sam switched to weak tea for the rest of the evening. With a mental pat on the back for herself for being so good when she really did prefer the eggnog, she dealt the cards.

It wasn't until Travis and Hank came weaving through the door in the wee hours of the morning, that the party broke up. Waving her guests off with hushed good-byes, Sam then toddled wearily arm in arm up the stairs and into bed with her husband.

It was a very bleary-eyed group that met at the breakfast table the next morning. Despite her abstinence after discovering that the eggnog had been liberally laced with liquor, Sam was still not feeling quite her normal self. Neither was anyone else, it seemed, particularly Elsie.

Slamming the coffee pot down on the table, the housekeeper grabbed her head and gave a pitiful wail. "You!" she accused in a loud whisper, pointing a shaking finger at Sam. "You doctored my eggnog, didn't you?"

This Sam denied with a shake of her head. "Not me, Elsie. Someone else may be guilty of it, but I didn't touch it. I swear."

"Well, somebody did! My head's about to burst like a ripe melon!"

"Please, Elsie," Travis begged. "Don't even mention food to me until I've had about six more cups of black coffee."

Hank didn't say a word. He just made a sudden dash for the back door, his face as pale as Sam had ever seen it.

By evening, they had all recovered sufficiently to look forward to the Christmas Eve festivities. The twinkling Christmas candles mounted to the walls sent a soft, warm glow through the little church, as the pine boughs gave off their pungent fragrance. As Sam sat next to Travis in the church pew, listening to Parson Aldrich deliver a moving Christmas Eve sermon, he linked his fingers with hers and rested their entwined hands gently over her stomach. Their baby kicked, and they shared a tender smile between them.

During the closing prayer, Sam and Travis slipped quietly from their seats. While Sam joined Molly at the rear of the church, Travis went to stand near the front altar next to Chas. As people began to stir in their seats and reach for their coats, Parson Aldrich called for them to remain seated. "We have a special Christmas treat for you this evening, one we are sure you will not want to miss."

He nodded toward Alma, seated at the organ, and she began to play a soft, haunting melody. With a slight rustle of skirts, Sam started down the center aisle, curious eyes turning her way. Even in her new gown, Sam felt ungainly, and a blush stained her cheeks as she made her way toward the front of the church. When she made it there without stumbling, she drew a shaky breath and stepped to the side. Her huge brown eyes found Travis's and gained strength from them, then she turned to watch as Molly began her lone march down the aisle.

Dressed in a pale blue gown that made her look like a Christmas angel, Molly walked slowly forward. Her fingers trembled slightly as they clasped the Bible before her, her eyes wide and bright as they sought Chas's. He sent her a nervous smile, and Molly's lips curved a bit.

By now everyone was aware that they were about to witness a wedding. Low murmurs rose from the pews, but no one rose to leave. Even if they wished to, Parson Aldrich's unwavering look kept them fixed in their seats. As Chas reached out to clasp his bride's hand in his, everyone settled back to watch.

As the words of the solemn ceremony enveloped her, Sam's eyes again caught Travis's. They stood apart from one another, on either side of the bride and groom, yet somehow together. A warmth stole through her, and as she gazed deeply into his brilliant turquoise eyes, it seemed as if they, too, were exchanging lasting promises once again. In her heart, and his, they silently renewed the vows they had entered into so hastily, and on Sam's part, reluctantly. This time Sam heard the words. This time she meant the promises she repeated silently to herself and to Travis. This time the pledge rang true.

Parson Aldrich pronounced Chas and Molly man and wife, his rich voice echoing through the church. Chas drew Molly into his arms for their first wedded kiss, and Alma, smiling from ear to ear, began thumping out Mendelssohn's *Wedding March* on the old organ, as if to rival the angel Gabriel on his horn. Then Sam was hugging Molly and kissing Chas on the cheek. Travis kissed the bride and shook his friend's hand. Parson Aldrich shook hands all around and wished everyone good fortune and a very merry Christmas. Various members of the church rose to congratulate the newlyweds, some of them coming forward to greet the new bride and wish the two of them well.

Amid all the confusion, Parson Aldrich caught at Travis's sleeve. Above the rising din of voices, he said, "Will you please remind Chas that he and Molly should both sign the marriage certificate before they leave? I felt so foolish when I realized that Samantha hadn't signed yours right away. Of course, how could she, when she'd fainted?"

The color drained from Travis's face. "Do you mean she—uh—isn't our—aren't we—"

Parson Aldrich stared at him curiously, then asked, "Do you mean to tell me that Sam didn't tell you? Why, I brought the matter to her attention months ago. In fact, as I recall, it was just a couple of weeks after your wedding, not too long before her brother escaped from jail. She signed it then."

Travis was stunned, his voice barely working. "She did?"

"Of course, she did," the parson said, shaking his head. "Why wouldn't she?"

Why, indeed? Travis knew all the reasons why Sam should have put up a fuss and refused to sign it. First he'd forced her to marry him, and then he'd regularly behaved like a jackass, especially after Billy's escape. He'd accused her of helping Billy escape, not believing her when Sam suggested that Nola Sandoval was the likely culprit.

The real question was, why had Sam gone ahead and willingly, without any force or argument at all, signed that marriage document that might have freed her from him legally if she had refused?

Instead, she had knowingly tied herself to him for a lifetime, and never said a single word to him about it. If not for Parson Aldrich, Travis might never have known how close he had come to losing her, if Sam had so wished.

She was standing a few feet away, smiling and talking with Molly, when Travis's searching gaze found her. Seconds later, she found herself swept into his arms, crushed tightly to him as his mouth hovered over hers. "I love you, Sam. As God is my witness, I love you with all my heart." Before she had a chance to reply, his lips were searing hers in a blistering kiss, and hers were answering with unmeasured passion.

They were still locked together, oblivious to everything else around them, when the church bells began to chime their midnight song, ringing in the Christmas morn, heralding the season of peace and love.

"Oh, Travis! It's beautiful! And it fits! It actually fits!" Hugging the pelisse about her, Sam almost danced for joy. It was a lovely full-length cloak with a fur-trimmed hood to keep the winter wind from whistling down her neck. Never had she possessed anything like it. Of course, she'd had little use for a dress cloak until now.

She bent to plant a kiss on his smiling lips and almost toppled over into his lap. With Hank and Elsie looking on with fond indulgence, Travis pulled her the rest of the way into his embrace, snuggling her against him. "I know you're disappointed not to be able to wear the riding skirt now," he said, nuzzling her neck. "But I wanted you to have something to look forward to. After you've recovered from having the baby, we'll go riding again, and you can wear it."

"It's a bribe, isn't it?" she asked, giggling.

"A bribe?"

She nodded. "So I won't wear boys' britches any more. That's why you got me a split ridin' skirt."

"Yeah, maybe it is a bribe. Do you like it?"

"I think it's a great idea."

She was also thrilled with the new quilted robe Travis had gifted her with and the slippers Elsie had knitted to match it. From Hank, she'd received winter gloves, but the best gift was having her brother here to share the holiday with them.

Sam, Travis, and Elsie had gotten Hank new clothes for Christmas. He'd brought so little with him when he'd come from Mexico, only one change of shirt and pants. Now that he was staying with them and working at the stables every day, Travis insisted that Hank take a bath at least every other day and change into clean clothing. Already, the reformation of Hank Downing from outlaw into a respectable citizen was beginning, and after all the struggles she had gone through, Sam didn't envy him in the least. She was simply glad she had most of that behind her now.

Elsie had not been forgotten by Saint Nicholas, either. Sam and Travis had gotten her a large bottle of her favorite lavender scent, and matching bath powder to go with it. As little as Hank had to spend, he'd managed to buy Elsie a small box of chocolate candies, his way of thanking her for all the little things she did for him each day, like making sure his clean socks found their way into his dresser drawer, and changing the linen on his bed.

For Travis, there had been a belt from Hank, a

bottle of his favorite whiskey from Lou Sprit, and a new shirt which Elsie had made for him. "I took pity on you," Elsie told him wryly. "Sam was considering sewing you a new one, but I talked her out of it."

His gifts from Sam truly surprised and delighted him, especially the hip-length leather coat with the fleece lining. "Sweetheart, I appreciate it more than I can tell you, and heaven knows, I sure can use it, but this must have cost you a pretty penny. Now, I know you didn't save by sewing this yourself and I also know you could never have saved enough out of your grocery money, 'cause we've all been eating too well. So, where did you get the money to buy this? Did you sell your mare and not tell me?"

Sam's temper had been rising until Travis tacked on that final question. She'd been afraid he was going to accuse her of stealing the coat, or of robbing someone in order to purchase it, and it had hurt to think that, after all this time, he still didn't trust her. But he did trust her after all, and her heart wanted to burst with joy.

She smiled up at him, watching as he stroked long fingers over the coat. "No, I didn't sell Bess. I told you I'd won a bundle during that week playin' poker at Lou's. If you'd have let me keep at it, we'd have been as rich as the Sandovals by now."

The grooming kit she'd given him for trimming his mustache brought a gruff laugh. "As many times as you've threatened to rip the thing off my lip, and now you give me this?" he chuckled in disbelief.

"Well," she said with a shrug, "at the risk of makin' you any more vain than you already are, I kinda like the blasted thing now. Guess I got used to it.''

It was when Sam went outdoors and came back in lugging a young armadillo in her arms, that Travis's heart overflowed. "Oh, Sam! Sam! Where did you get him? How?''

Gently, she transferred the trembling, armored creature into Travis's arms, where it promptly rolled over onto its back and pretended to faint.

"His name is Dilly, but you can change it if you want to. He's a little nervous right now so he's playin' possum, but he'll get used to you in no time. I just hope he learns to race as fast as Army. He's young yet, about nine months or so, as close as I can guess.''

"But where did you find him?''

"I figured old Army must have a lady friend around here somewhere, so I scouted around until I found her burrow. And what do you think I found, but a nest full of little ones! Of course, they've had to stay with their mama until just a few weeks ago. I've been hidin' Dilly under the porch for the past month now. I even made him a nice, leafy borrow all his own under there.''

"You crawled under the porch?" Travis asked in amazement. "In your condition? Lord, darlin'! It's a wonder you didn't get stuck under there!''

"I almost did once," she confessed. "Luckily, the ground is soft enough under there that I dug a trench for my belly and wriggled on out again!''

Travis didn't know what to say. She'd gone to so much trouble to make this day special for him. "Sam, I don't know how to thank you.''

"Oh, you'll think of somethin', I'm sure." She sent him a suggestive wink, and added for his ears only, "Why don't you trim your mustache? And I'll tell you if it still tickles the same after you do."

Christmas afternoon, friends came calling. Despite the fact that they were only wed a few hours, Chas and Molly stopped by to exchange gifts. They stayed to supper, and Molly helped Sam with the meal and the clean-up afterward since Elsie had gone to spend the rest of the day with her own family. Pastor and Alma Aldrich came by for a brief chat as did Doc Purdy. Though the Aldriches were expected elsewhere, Sam and Travis succeeded in talking the doctor into sharing the holiday meal with the rest of them.

Though Travis often received gifts from some of the townspeople, he was surprised when Purdy presented him with a present for him and Sam. Unwrapping it, he found a deck of cards and a complete set of checkers with the board. "What the devil?" he exclaimed softly, his brow wrinkling in confusion.

Then he turned red from the neck up, as Sam had only rarely seen him do. "Purdy, is this your subtle way of trying to tell me something?"

Doc nodded, not even trying to hide his smirk. "Sorry, Travis, but as Sam's doctor, I'm recommending a halt to more active games until the baby is born. Till then, it's cards and checkers for you, old man."

Purdy grinned; Travis frowned; Chas and Molly tried to pretend they hadn't heard a thing. Sam sat there with a devious, devilish glint growing in her eyes.

Later that night, Travis discovered what that look meant. He also learned that there were a few side benefits to be gained from Molly's bridal party. It seemed the "girls" had more interesting things to discuss than cooking and cleaning and trading cookie recipes. As Rose had so succinctly put it, "There's more than one way to skin a cat, and more than one way to make a rooster crow." Now, Sam was about to demonstrate exactly what was meant by that turn of phrase.

With her hands, mouth, and body, Sam set out to ignite his passions and then to satisfy them. Lightly, tauntingly, her nails scored his bare skin, not roughly to hurt or to mar his flesh, but enough to arouse every nerve in Travis's body to the height of perception. Where her nails scraped, her tongue then lapped, but the sensation was anything but soothing, particularly when her small white teeth nipped sharply here and there along the way.

For the longest time, she touched him everywhere except where he yearned for her the most, deftly skirting the proud proof of his arousal, while she stroked and nibbled her way over his tingling body. In a thousand ways, she teased him unmercifully until Travis thought he would lose his mind with the raging desire flooding through him.

Yet he lay willingly, if not still, beneath her avid investigation, letting her wield her feminine power over him. In some strange way, he felt stronger in giving Sam the freedom to explore him in all the ways she wished. It surprised him somewhat that she appeared to derive as much pleasure from touching him as she did when he caressed her, but he also understood it, for it was the same for him. The look on her face or the sounds she made as he stroked her silken body were enough to arouse him. That the same seemed true for her was a delightful discovery.

Still, he felt a little like a fly caught in the spider's web, waiting in anxious anticipation to be devoured by her, watching in helpless fascination as she spun her sensual, mystical magic intricately about him. As if to enforce the illusion, the long, silken strands of her hair trailed over his heated flesh like fragile fingers of lace, stroking and draping him in its sheer, shimmering veil. Her seeking hands roved his trembling body. Her lips covered his, her kiss hot and sweet, and he surrendered gladly to her wondrous ministrations.

Their tongues tangled, twining and writhing like fiery, dancing snakes, their breath mingling on a quivering sigh of intense longing as her body slithered tauntingly over his. Deliberately, slowly, Sam swayed over him, the hard, pebbled points of her breasts almost burning his chest as they funneled with delicious abrasion through the dense forest of hair that stood as no barrier at all against her wanton invasion.

Her mouth deserted his, peppering warm, wet kisses across his cheek. When her tongue darted into his ear, gooseflesh dotted his burning skin; the hot, feathery breath that followed sent a violent shudder trembling through him. "Sam, darlin', I can't stand much more of this."

A throaty, decidedly wicked laugh was her only reply as her tongue trailed a blazing path to his shoulder, nipping playfully along the sensitive curve. He was drowning in sweet, heady brandy, the fire of it licking through his veins and clouding his mind with smoldering desire. With trembling hands, he returned her silken caresses, clasping her to him as he drifted in a drugging mist of madly swirling need.

Her hair wafted over him like an elusive whisper as she slid slowly downward. Soft, warm lips closed over one flat nipple, and again her tongue flicked out to torment him, making him arch and groan in rising passion. Then her mouth closed over it tightly, suckling greedily, and rapture spiraled through him. The ache in his groin intensified until he was sure he would burst with wanting her. With a sigh of satisfaction, she turned her attention to his other nipple, and again he trembled at the touch of her mouth on his yearning flesh.

Her moist lips dragged across his ribs, her nails clawing sensuous patterns up his inner thighs as she eased her way inch by tantalizing inch closer to his throbbing arousal. "Sam! Sam!" He was torn between begging her to stop and pleading with her never, never to let this blissful torment end.

As her mouth closed over him, her hands stroking tentatively, he almost lurched from the bed. A low moan tore from him, his fingers tangling in the long, bright tendrils of her hair. A wavering curtain of red blurred his vision. A frantic pounding echoed the thunder of his racing heartbeat in his ears as his head thrashed back and forth in the throes of the sweetest, most searing agony he'd ever known. The pain-pleasure built within him, rising and billowing like a tumultuous storm until, suddenly, with the might of a ravaging tornado, it burst. With a wild cry, he exploded into ecstasy, a million suns bursting about him in blinding splendor.

Many minutes later, his hands still entangled in Sam's hair, her head cradled against his quivering stomach, Travis rasped, "I hope you know you almost killed me doing those things to me."

Laughing shakily, she smiled against his belly. "Yeah, but you'd have gone with a grin on your face."

"True, but you know that old saying, 'What's sauce for the goose, is sauce for the gander,' also goes the other way around," he warned, his deep chuckle reverberating through her.

"Then you'd better start heatin' the sauce, Mr. Gander," she countered brazenly, playfully nuzzling her nose into his navel, "'cause I'm one hungry goose, and I'm much too greedy to pass up an offer as sweet as that."

CHAPTER 28

It was the first Sunday of the new year, and 1878 was coming in with a blast of winter that shook northern Texas by its boot heels. The temperature had begun to plummet the night before, and the drizzling rain had fast turned to sleet. Now, in the cold light of morning, snow clouds hung heavy overhead, blown out of the mountains and across the plains on a bitter, gusting gale. Even now, the first fat flakes were streaking about, driven almost horizontally by the howling force of the wind, a wind that ripped through the streets of Tumble, whistled around corners, wailed mournfully at doors and windows, and crept into every nook and crevice it could find.

Church attendance was light this morning. Only the hardy had dared to brave the elements, and then only those who lived in town. With ice coating every bush, tree, and stray blade of grass for miles around, those in the outlying area were wise to stay safely at home. All the signs were right for a blizzard of immense proportions, and only a fool would stray far from the hearth today.

Seated next to Travis on the hard pew, Sam shivered and edged closer to his big body for warmth. Above the sound of the organ music, the windows rattled ominously, the board siding creaking as it took the weight of the wind battering it. Even inside the small building, it was as cold as a tomb. Through chattering teeth, Sam swore she saw her own breath, and for the hundredth time since she had inched out of bed this morning, Sam asked herself why they had bothered to attend the service. Surely even God understood the desire to stay home on a day like this! After all, He was the One responsible for such weather, wasn't He?

Parson Aldrich's pinched lips were almost blue as he began the sermon, and Sam thought surely the message would be short and sweet and to the point. The poor preacher looked too frozen to deliver a dissertation of any length. In fact, Sam had to wonder if the earlier, wavering tones of the ancient organ were caused by Alma's chilled fingers or a case of frozen pipes.

Tugging the hood of her pelisse up about her chin, Sam hunched down and attempted to apply her mind to the morning's lesson. Failing that, she tried to recall the blistering heat of last summer, a futile exercise at best. Her primary prayer was that she wouldn't get frostbite before they finally got home again.

Midway through the service, the doors of the church flew open, letting in a fresh blast of frigid air. That in itself drew everyone's attention, even before the ruddy-faced cowboy lurched stiffly down the aisle, yelling, "Marshal! Marshal Kincaid!"

Travis was on his feet, concern darkening his features, before the man could catch his breath. He recognized the cowhand as one of Sandoval's men, but could not readily recall his name.

"Marshal!" the man gasped, shivering violently. "You gotta come quick! Miss Nola sent me! Billy Downing's back, and Sandoval's fixin' to hang him!"

"What!" Travis's exclamation echoed the whirl of confusion that rocked through Sam. She tried to stand, but her legs had suddenly turned to butter, and she sank to the hard bench again, clutching the back of it with chilled fingers.

"Where are they? Is Nola all right?"

"Out at the ranch," the man puffed, still winded, "and Miss Nola is pitchin' a fit the likes of which I ain't never seen!"

"What about Billy?" Sam asked, her eyes wide and frightened.

"The boss has him tied up in the barn, and he ain't a pretty sight right now, but he's still breathin'. At least he was when I lit out for town."

Travis's long strides had already carried him to the coat rack at the rear of the church where he was strapping on his gunbelt. "Hank! Get over to the stable and get my horse saddled for me! And six others, the fastest ones there are! Now!" he barked when Hank just stared at him.

"Chas! Go to the office and break out the rifles and all the ammunition you can stuff into a couple of saddlebags. Ed! Frank! Joe! Bob! Will! Consider yourselves deputized! Let's get moving!"

"What about me?" Lou volunteered.

"You stay here and look after things in town. See that the women get home all right."

He was yanking the door open when Sam caught up to him, grabbing at his arm. "I'm goin' with you!"

Impatiently, he shook off her hand. Then, seeing how frightened she was, he hauled her back into his arms for a quick embrace. "No, Sam. I know you're worried, but there's nothing you can do. Let me take care of it, and I'll get word back to you as soon as I can."

"I can shoot!" she cried out. "Better than most of the men goin' along!"

He gave her one, short shake. "No! For once, think of the baby! Stop and take stock, Sam. Consider the danger!" His eyes cut to the building snowstorm. "This is turning into a full-fledged blizzard! I don't know if I can even get through to the ranch."

Her dark eyes searched his, and then she nodded in defeat. "All right, but at least take Lou with you. It'll give you another man, and he's got a lot of muscle, if it comes to that."

"Fine," he agreed, planting a quick kiss on her forehead. He wanted to stay and hold her, to comfort her, but there was no time. "Doc, Parson, will you two take over?" he called back.

Doc Purdy waved him on. "Go on. We'll see that everyone gets home safely."

As she watched him turn and lope down the street, Sam called after him, "Travis! Be careful!"

Through the swirling snow, she thought she saw him wave an arm in acknowledgement, but she couldn't be sure. "Oh, God, Travis!" she moaned to herself. "Please take care—and hurry!"

There seemed no sense in trying to reconvene the church service at this point, so Doc Purdy and Parson Aldrich divided the women who found themselves suddenly deserted by their husbands into two groups, and promptly escorted them home. By now, the threatening snowstorm was a reality, snow already blanketing the streets and beginning to drift.

Sam's fingers and toes were stiff and red by the time they reached her house, and she could only wonder how Travis and the others would manage to ride all that distance without freezing to death or becoming lost, let alone arrive in time to save Billy.

"Blast you, Billy Downing!" she raged, blinking back tears as she stood at the window and looked out at the storm. "You sure picked a fine time to need rescuin'!"

Battling the wind and snow, Travis was thinking much the same thing. As he hunched his neck deeper into the collar of his coat and settled deeper into his saddle, he wondered to himself why he couldn't have fallen in love with someone else—someone with a nice, ordinary law-abiding family that didn't always cause trouble at the most inopportune times!

No sooner had the thought crossed his mind, than he shrugged it away. He wouldn't trade Sam for anything in the world, and they both knew it. Besides, none of this was her fault. She couldn't help the way she was raised or who her family was or what they did. A grim smile etched his lips as Travis also admitted to himself that, whether Billy was her brother or not, Travis would most likely still have found himself braving this blizzard to save the boy's life. It was part and parcel of his job as marshal.

He was glad he'd been able to talk Sam out of coming with him as easily as he had. If it hadn't been for the baby, he knew she would have put up a better fight. As it was, he'd had a devil of a time convincing Hank that he couldn't come.

"You know the judge's orders, Hank," he'd reminded the boy sternly. "You're not to leave town, and since you can't carry a gun, you wouldn't be much help to us anyway. Stay here and look after Sam. If there is any way I can manage it, I'll bring Billy in safely."

"Sandoval better not have hung Billy, or Judge Andrews' orders won't mean spit!" Hank had warned. "I'll go after him and I'll kill him, if I have to do it with my bare hands!"

Not for the first time, it struck Travis that a large part of the blame for this latest fiasco belonged to that hot-headed father of Nola's. Granted, the man had every reason to want revenge against Billy for kidnapping Nola in the first place, but Rafe Sandoval had overstepped his bounds any number of times now. He had a bad habit of flying off the handle and charging into things without thinking them through.

He also had a nasty habit of taking the law into his own hands, which didn't set too well with Travis at all. Travis supposed that Sandoval had either conveniently forgotten or chosen to overlook the fact that Nola had been the one to set Billy free. With his land and his money, Sandoval seemed to think he could do as he damn well pleased, when and where it suited him to do so, and Travis had had a craw full of it. Travis looked forward to the day when someone more powerful and with more authority finally put Sandoval in his place, and he hoped he was around to see it happen.

The snow blew and shifted in a white blur that blinded the riders to all else. At best, they could see only three or four feet ahead of their horses. To keep from losing one another, as well as a vain attempt to form a slight barrier against the wind, they stayed bunched together. It didn't help much against the blustery gale. With visibility so limited, their progress was slow. A sudden misstep could send horse and rider tumbling off the edge of a steep gully, or snap a mount's leg in a snow-covered prairie dog hole.

If not for the extreme cold and the deepening drifts, Travis thought he could almost walk to the Sandoval ranch faster. As it was, they'd be lucky to make it by mid-afternoon sometime, if they didn't miss the entire spread by miles in this blizzard! Everything was one solid mass of white, with no sun and no identifiable landmarks to assure them that they were heading in the right direction. They had only their own sense of direction to guide them, and could only pray they were following them correctly.

Within an hour, Travis was wishing he'd at least taken the time to pull on an extra pair of socks. He couldn't even feel his toes anymore and he doubted any of the other riders were in better condition than he was. On the other hand, his fingers were stinging inside his gloves. His ears felt like frozen chunks of ice stuck to the sides of his head, and they hurt every time they brushed against the upturned collar of his coat. Though he'd tied a woolen scarf about his face and neck, his ears kept peeking out, and his cheeks felt numb and chapped. His nose felt as if it might snap off at the slightest touch. Snow encrusted his long eyelashes, making it harder to see.

"Dang!" Lou muttered next to him. "If I'd have stopped to think how cold it was gonna be out here, I'd have stayed with the women the way you wanted me to! I could be sittin' next to a roaring fire right now, drinkin' hot coffee and eatin' Sunday chicken."

"Aw, quit your bellyachin', Sprit," Frank grumbled. "As big as you are, you could live off your own fat for a month."

"Yeah," someone else added, "and right now I wish I had some o' that fat to keep me warm."

"It ain't fat, it's muscle, you lunkheads," Lou growled back.

"I wouldn't care what it was as long as it kept me warmer than I am right now," Chas put in. "If we don't get there soon, everything I've got is gonna freeze solid, and Molly never will get those kids she wants!"

By luck or sheer determination, they weren't sure which, the posse reached the Sandoval homestead about one o'clock. At first glance, the ranch yard looked deserted, but it was just an illusion created by the blowing snow. As they rode closer, they could see that the house was lit up like a cathedral, lamplight glowing from almost every room. It wasn't the house Travis was interested in, however, but the huge barn off to the side. From the amount of light gleaming through the dirty windows, he guessed there was a fair amount of activity going on in there, and he could only hope it wasn't a lynching.

With Chas and his other deputies right behind him, Travis strode into the brightly-lit barn, his rifle held in numb hands before him. The sight that met his eyes was not pretty. Billy, or a man Travis had to assume was Billy Downing, hung suspended by his wrists by a rope strung over a barn beam. His head drooped limply upon his bare chest, but from the little Travis could see of his face, he'd been beaten almost beyond recognition. His right eye was black and swollen, his lip was puffed out four times its normal size, blood drying all over his face. His nose appeared to be broken, and Travis guessed his jaw might be, too.

Sandoval was standing to one side, a bullwhip in his hands, he and his men so involved in their revenge that they took no notice of the new arrivals. There was an unholy gleam in Rafe's black eyes, his whole face twisted with hatred. Several of Sandoval's men were standing in a loose circle around Billy, witnesses, and perhaps participants, in the beating. If any of them had an ounce of sympathy for Downing, it did not show on their faces.

Before Travis could say anything, Sandoval raised the rawhide whip and sent it cracking against Billy's back. Despite his near-unconscious state and the way he hung there like a side of beef, Billy's body jerked, and he let out an agonized moan. The impetus of the lashing set his body spinning in a half-circle, and Travis counted at least a dozen bloody stripes across Billy's bare back.

"Sandoval!" Travis's roar echoed loudly from one end of the barn to the other. Heads spun about, hands reaching hastily for guns strapped at their sides.

Praying that his stiff fingers would not betray him now, Travis cocked his rifle, his blazing eyes daring anyone even to think of drawing on him. Behind him, every member of his posse did likewise. Sandoval's men backed down but not entirely. They stood warily waiting for further orders from their boss.

"What are you doing here, Kincaid?" Sandoval snarled. "No one invited you to come snooping around on my property!"

"You're mistaken," Travis drawled, stepping closer. "Seems at least one of your henchmen has developed a conscience and wants to see law and order done in the proper way."

With a nod of his head toward Billy's dangling form, Travis ordered, "Cut him down, Lou."

In the split instant that Travis's gaze had veered from him, Sandoval reached for a nearby rifle. Travis was faster. The loud report sounded at the same time that Sandoval's weapon skittered beyond the rancher's reach. "Try that again, Sandoval, and I'll probably have to kill you."

With several guns trained on them, the ranch hands did nothing more to try to stop him as Lou proceeded to cut Billy down. Catching the limp body as it fell, Lou slung Billy over his shoulder. "What now, Travis?" he asked.

"Now we borrow some decent clothes for Billy

from these fine gentlemen," Travis said with a smirk, "while Chas goes up to the house to fetch Nola."

Sandoval objected violently to this. "What do you need with my daughter, Kincaid? You've got what you came for. Now, just take that raping, robbing bastard and get the hell off my property!"

"Not yet, Sandoval. I want some kind of statement from Nola. In fact, I might have to arrest her and take her back with us, or had you forgotten that she's guilty of breaking Downing out of my jail last summer?"

While Sandoval blustered, cursed, and threatened, Lou wrapped Billy's back as best he could and dressed him in clothes begrudgingly given from the unwilling ranch hands. Though he groaned pitifully, Billy had passed out which Travis considered for the best right now. He'd be in a lot of pain once he awoke.

When she arrived, Nola dashed past Travis with a hasty, "Thank God you got here!" Then she fell on her knees next to Billy, tears streaming down her face as she tried to determine the extent of his injuries. "He's alive!" she cried, nearly wilting in relief.

"So far, and through no fault of your father's," Travis admitted dryly.

Before he could say anything else, or even attempt to question her, Nola rounded angrily on her father. "You brute! You hateful beast! How could you do this to him? My God! How far will your spite carry you?"

Sandoval's eyes narrowed. "As far as it takes to rid you of this vermin!"

Her face pale, Nola stood her ground. "He's my

husband!" she shouted, her announcement coming as a surprise to everyone but Rafe. "I love him!"

"You'll be his widow if I have anything to do with it!" Rafe countered bluntly.

"If you ever lay another hand on him, I'll never forgive you! Not as long as I draw breath! Furthermore," she stated, drawing herself up proudly, "if you had succeeded in killing him, that would not have been the end of it. I'm carrying his child!"

This shocked even Rafe into stunned silence. His black eyes scanned her figure. Finally, he found his tongue and stammered, "You—you're lying!"

"Am I? Time will tell, about five months from now!"

"Nola." Travis drew her attention, his brows drawn into a frown. "If you and Billy are married, why did you risk coming back? Last we heard, you were down in Mexico with Nan and Tom Downing."

"It's all my fault!" she wailed, tears brimming anew. "I got so awfully homesick, and then with the baby on the way, Billy didn't trust the doctors down there. He was afraid something might go wrong!"

"So he decided to bring you home where your father could look after you?" Travis deduced.

Nola nodded. "Yes. We talked about it and decided that he would drop me off at the south end of the ranch and ride on back down to Mexico. Then, after the baby was born and was old enough to travel with me, I was going to join him there." Her gaze turned toward Billy, regret and pain alive in her eyes. "But with the storm already starting, Billy had to come further than we'd planned. He was afraid I wouldn't make it safely on my own. That's when Daddy's men caught us."

"We're going to have to take Billy with us back to town, Nola," Travis told her.

"But the storm! He can't even ride in his condition!"

"We'll have to chance it. He's going to need medical care, and we sure can't leave him here, now can we?"

"No. No, you're right," she agreed. "We've got to get him to Doc Purdy. But I'm coming with you, Travis. I won't leave Billy, and after what my father has done, I won't spend one more night under his roof! I'll go get my things. Wait for me. Please."

As she started to leave, Sandoval stepped into her path, his face flushed with anger. "Nola! You can't do this! I forbid you to leave this ranch!"

Eyes every bit as dark and condemning as his flashed back at him. "You may rule this ranch, but you don't rule me! Not now, not ever! I'm a grown woman and I have a husband of my own! I don't know if I'll ever be able to forgive you for what you have done to Billy today, but if you ever want to see your grandchild or me again, you'd better do some serious soul-searching, Father. You have a lot to make up for before I want anything more to do with you! And you'd better pray real hard that Billy lives!"

Sam had almost worn a path in the rug by the time several riders rode up to the house. It was nearly dark, and she had to strain her eyes to make out Travis's tall form and Lou's bulk. Running to the door, she threw it open, ignoring the blast of icy air that nearly tore the breath from her body.

The breath the wind didn't steal, the sight of Billy's battered body did, and she had to cling to the door to remain standing as Lou carried Billy past her.

"My God! What have they done to him?" She stared after them, afraid to ask if her brother was still alive. She didn't even notice when Nola skirted past her.

"Hank!" Travis called to his brother-in-law who stood gaping in the hall. "We're putting Billy in your room. Show Lou the way, will you?"

He turned to Sam, his arms coming about her to steady her. "Doc Purdy is on the way, darlin'," he assured her, taking in her wide eyes and pale face.

"How . . . how bad is it?"

He pulled her away from the door and shut it. "Probably not as bad as it looks."

As much as Sam was trembling, she suddenly realized that Travis was shaking even more than she was. His face looked stiff with cold, moisture formed into icy crystals in his mustache. "Travis! You're frozen half to death!"

Suddenly Sam was all business, her mind clearing from its shock-induced fog. "You've got to get out of those clothes and into somethin' dry. I'll have Elsie heat some bath water for you, while I get you somethin' hot to drink. Are you hungry?"

As nice as it was to have her fussing over him, there were things to do first. "We're all chilled to the bone, Sam. Why don't you go make a hot pot of coffee, while I check on things upstairs? Oh, and see if Elsie can find that old army cot of mine. We'll put it in Hank's room for Nola."

"Nola?" Sam repeated stupidly. From some dim corner of her mind, she did recall having seen the woman come through the door. "What is she doin' here? Where is she?"

"She's probably upstairs, helping Lou tend to Billy." Travis's long, cold fingers tilted Sam's chin up so her eyes met his. "I know you don't care much for her, sweetheart, but try to be nice, okay? She and Billy are married now, and Nola says they're going to have a baby in a few months."

"Married?" she echoed again, her voice a squeak.

"Yeah," Travis drawled wryly, with that peculiarly lopsided grin of his. "Guess that makes us all one big, happy family now, doesn't it? Judge Andrews is just gonna love this!"

He loped up the stairs, leaving Sam staring after him, stunned speechless.

CHAPTER 29

Why Travis didn't put up a fuss and insist on putting Billy behind bars as he'd done when Billy had been shot, Sam didn't know. She was hesitant to ask. Maybe it had something to do with the fact that she and Travis were married now, whereas before Sam had only been living in Travis's house. Perhaps it was because both she and Hank were there, and he saw no real problem in having Billy there, too, at least until Billy recovered sufficiently. Besides, they were all family now.

Still, Sam could not help but think that Nola figured heavily in Travis's decision, and she could not help but writhe with jealousy that Nola would have more influence over Travis than she did as his wife, even while she was grateful to have Billy here instead of in jail. It seemed that she was forever battling that woman's charms! Seeing Nola again had brought back all of Sam's old insecurities and all the antagonism. Sam found herself gritting her teeth just to be moderately polite to Nola.

However, seeing the way Nola hovered continually at Billy's bedside, how she fretted over him and took over his care, went a long way toward lessening Sam's resentment. Nola honestly seemed to love Billy, and her tears and worry could not all be an act. Even while Sam continued to wonder what her brother saw in such a haughty, spoiled woman, beyond Nola's obvious beauty, Sam had to admit that Nola was presenting the picture of a truly devoted wife.

"I suppose I'll just have to give her the benefit of the doubt," she muttered disgruntledly to herself. "After all, she *is* family now, whether I approve or not."

When Sam finally worked up enough nerve to ask Travis why he'd housed Billy in the upstairs bedroom, she was surprised by his answer. It had nothing whatever to do with Nola or her baby. "Billy's back is in shreds from the lashing Sandoval gave him," he told her. "There is no way he can lie on his back right now, and it's almost impossible to lie comfortably on one of those jail cots. Under the circumstances, it seemed easier to move Billy in here for a while than to move a bed into one of the cells. Doc Purdy also warned that Billy's wounds require air and need to be kept clean, and the house is a lot warmer and cleaner than the jail. All in all, this seems the best arrangement until Billy is well."

Billy's back was, indeed, a mess. Thankfully, that was the worst of his injuries. Travis had been right when he'd said that Billy probably looked a lot worse than he was. His nose was broken. Luckily, his jaw was not, or Doc Purdy would have had to wire it shut, and Billy would have had to slurp liquids as best he could. Three cracked ribs added to the problem of finding a comfortable resting position, but once he regained consciousness, Billy considered himself lucky to be alive.

"That old man had murder in his eyes!" he confessed through bruised and swollen lips. Then, through the slits he had for eyes, his gaze sought Nola, the love radiating from his battered face. "It wasn't myself I was so bothered about, though. All the while they were hammerin' on me, all I could think of was Nola an' what that crazy father of hers might do to her an' the baby. It was pure hell to wonder an' not to be able to get free to help her if she needed me."

Nola went to her knees at his bedside, her hands clasping one of his and bringing it to her lips. "Oh, Billy! Billy! If I had it all to do over again, we would have stayed in Mexico. I'd give anything to have spared you this!"

"Now, honey, it's not your fault. I'm the one who wanted ya to have a proper doctor to look after ya an' the baby."

It was a poignant, private moment, and Sam felt her presence was an intrusion. Quietly, she tiptoed from the room, pulling Travis after her. "I guess she really does love him, as crazy as it seems. You know, Travis, at first, when Nola helped Billy escape, I thought it was all some kind of game with her or somethin', maybe just a way to defy her father for somethin' he'd done. From my dealings with her, she seemed nothin' more than a nasty, highfalutin rich girl who had to have her own way all the time and could care less about anyone but herself and what she wanted. I guess maybe I was wrong about her, at least a little bit."

"I suppose we're all a little guilty that way," Travis admitted, pulling Sam close to his side. "You're not the only one who has misjudged Nola."

"Did you?"

Travis laughed softly. "By a country mile! I liked her but I wasn't blind to her faults. I suppose I learned to accept Nola for what she was. I think loving Billy has had a lot to do with changing her. If not for that, she'd probably still be as self-centered as always. In ways, she probably still is, but this new Nola is a definite improvement, don't you think?"

Sam answered with an unladylike snort. "Hell, Travis! She couldn't have been much worse! Any change at all had to be for the better!"

It would have been too much to expect that being exposed to the blizzard would not have some ill effect, and two days after rescuing Billy, Travis came down with a terrible cold. It started in his head and swiftly settled into his chest, bringing with it a racking cough, a raging fever, fits of sneezing, and a sore throat. At first he tried to ignore it and go on about his work, but when he could barely drag himself out of bed in the morning, Sam put her foot down.

"You dad-blasted stubborn mule! Get your rear back into that bed, and don't even think about tryin' to get out again!" The determined glint in

Sam's eyes dared him to defy her. "Go on, Travis, before you fall flat on your face."

With his head thumping, his throat on fire, and the room starting to spin dizzily about him, he meekly obeyed. "Just for today, Sam," he croaked, sniffling back a sneeze. "I can't put all the work off on Chas for long."

On Travis's first day home, Sam found her hands full with a very grouchy patient. She thanked God for Elsie's presence and for Nola's. She brought Travis hot chicken soup, honey and lemon for his throat, and sponged him down when his fever rose. When Doc Purdy came by that morning to check on Billy, she asked him to look in on Travis, too. He left an enormous bottle of elixir and instructions to keep Travis in bed.

"Give him plenty of liquids, keep him warm, and try to keep his fever down as much as possible."

"What if it goes into pneumonia?" she worried.

"I'll be back around tomorrow to check on him and Billy, so don't worry, Sam. I'm sure it's only a cold. Travis is too ornery to get really sick."

Purdy hadn't seen ornery until Travis got sick! By the end of the day, Sam was ready to pull her hair out! She knew he felt miserable and she tried to be understanding, but he really was being a pain in the rear! It was like trying to deal with a two-year-old child, and Sam could only pray no child of hers would ever be this contrary.

He didn't want to use the chamber pot, he turned up his nose in disgust when she tried to dose him with the elixir, he complained about having to drink the tea she brought him, demanding that she bring him whiskey instead. When she refused, he glared at her sullenly. When he tried to get out of bed to fetch it himself, his legs gave out from under him, and she and Elsie had to drag him back into bed. He pouted through the early afternoon, until his fevered eyes closed wearily in sleep.

The first chance she got, Sam bundled up and dashed down to the jail, expecting to find Chas there, but the jailhouse was empty. Trudging through melting snow, she made her way to Chas's little house. Molly answered the door and invited her in.

"Is Chas here?" Sam asked, stomping the snow from her boots onto the little throw rug by the door.

"I was going to try and get a message to you," Molly told her. "Chas came home for lunch and almost passed out at the table. His face was all flushed, and he's chilling something awful. I sent him off to bed."

Sam sighed and nodded. "Sounds like he's caught the same cold as Travis."

Molly shook her head. "I guess we shouldn't be surprised with the day they spent last Sunday."

Sam refused Molly's offer of tea. "Some other time, Molly. Right now, I suppose I'd best get hold of Lou. With Travis and Chas both laid low, someone's got to take over as marshal, or deputy at least. Take good care of Chas, and let me know if you need anythin'."

Things were beginning to look difficult when Sam found Lou's barbershop locked up tight. When she knocked at the door of his living quarters over his shop, Lou answered her summons with a red nose and a tremendous sneeze. Sam didn't even bother to ask. She merely said, "I thought I'd check on you since your shop was closed. Do you want me to send Doc Purdy around to see you?"

"Doe, tanks," came the hacking reply.

Sam backed down the stairs. "I'll send Hank over later with some hot soup for you. Elsie swears by it."

Her next three stops brought the same results. Harry Jacobs's wife was managing the hotel by herself; Frank had the next thing to pneumonia; Ed Howard had a temperature so high it threatened to set the stable on fire, and he was cooped up in his little office, nursing his cold, while Hank ran the livery for him.

Sam was at her wits end! The only other halfway capable, intelligent men she could think of who were still healthy were Doc Purdy, Ike Harrison from the bank, and Parson Aldrich. Doc was likely run ragged by now; Ike Harrison couldn't shoot worth spit and was afraid of his own shadow; and, somehow, Sam couldn't quite picture Parson Aldrich being up to the job of deputy.

"All right, then," she muttered, drawing herself up and throwing her shoulders back. "I'll just have to do it myself!" Disregarding the fact that she was seven months pregnant and what Travis would say about all this, she waddled back to Chas and Molly's house.

"I've got to talk to Chas, Molly. It's important."

Molly led the way to the bedroom where Chas was huddled under the blankets, his teeth rattling with chills. "Hi, Samb!" he chattered.

She came straight to the point. "Chas, everyone in this whole blamed town is down sick, and there's no one left to handle things, so I want you to deputize me. I'd ask Travis, but he'd pitch a tizzy, and I know you have the authority, so do it."

"What!" He sat up in bed and stared at her through watery eyes, sure he was hallucinating from his fever. Molly gaped. "I can't do dat! I won't! Trabis would kill me, eben if I was willing, which I'b dot!"

Sam's face took on a cunning expression, her eyes glittering. "Then I guess I'll have to tell Molly what Travis told me about you and Nan Tucker."

Poor Chas frowned in confusion. "What are you talkin' aboud? Nuttin' eber habbened bedween be an' Dan."

Sam was torn between laughter and pity. The poor fellow was so sick, and he sounded so funny trying to talk through his stuffed nose. She didn't let him see any of this, however. She merely folded her arms over her chest and looked down her nose at him. "That's not what I heard, Chas."

"I'b tellin' you, it's dot true!" His eyes sought Molly's, begging her to believe him.

"True or not," Sam said in a pitiless voice, "it won't matter much, will it? Molly will still be mad, and the whole town will know what I know. I'm warnin' you, Chas. Now, lend me your badge and swear me in, or I blab to one and all."

Clutching his aching head, Chas groaned. As miserable as he felt, he couldn't even think straight, let alone hope to win an argument with Sam. He felt as weak as a kitten and all he wanted to do was lie down and sleep.

"Chas?" Sam prompted.

"Okay."

Two minutes later, Sam was walking toward their front door, a tin badge pinned to her coat and a wicked smile on her face. Before she could reach the door, Molly grabbed at her arm. "Sam? What's all this about Chas and Miss Tucker."

Smothering her laughter so Chas would not hear, Sam confessed, "Molly not one word of that was true. I made the whole thing up and I was lyin' through my teeth the entire time. I'm really sorry but I had to find a way to get Chas to deputize me, and that was the first thing I could come up with. Please don't tell Chas all this until he's back on his feet, but please don't give him any grief over it, either. The poor man is confused enough as it is."

Molly shook her head and laughed. "Someday, Sam, your devious ways are going to get you into a heap of trouble."

Pulling the door open, Sam threw back a wink. "What makes you think they haven't already?"

Sam judiciously withheld the news of Chas's illness from Travis. When Travis had a message to deliver to his deputy, Sam volunteered to see that he received it. When he wondered why Chas didn't come to visit or to share the news of what was happening in town, Sam explained that Chas had a cold, too, and he didn't want to exchange germs with Travis and possibly cause both of them to get worse. While Sam never lied to Travis outright, she became an expert at evading the truth.

Unwittingly, Travis also provided her with a handy excuse for not being available to him at all times. On the second day of his illness, Travis suddenly seemed to recall that Sam was pregnant. "I don't think you should be nursing me, Sam," he told her. "You might catch my cold, and in your condition, that wouldn't be good. Maybe you'd better stay away from me as much as you can until I'm over this. Elsie can bring me soup and tea as well as you can."

"Are you sure?" She fluffed his pillow.

He nodded, then sneezed and waved her away from him.

"Maybe you're right," she conceded, feeling just the teeniest bit guilty. "I'll look after things downstairs. Holler if you need me." With a quick kiss on his hot forehead, she scampered from the room. "Get well soon, sweetheart. I love you."

In the next few days, Sam hoped Travis would remember how much she loved him, especially once he got well and learned about her adventures as stand-in deputy. Fortunately, the bank didn't get robbed that week, no trigger-happy gunslingers rode into town, and the weekly stage arrived without problem. Everything was relatively quiet.

She did have to deal with a few minor incidents, however. Old Daniel Zimmerly got drunk in the middle of the week, as usual, and Sam had to arrest him for being disorderly. Actually, she only logged it into the records as being disorderly. In reality, he was caught peeping beneath the Widow Barker's window shade just as the lady was disrobing for the evening.

"You're lucky you could claim the excuse of being drunk, Dan," she told him as she clanked the cell door closed behind him. "You'd be in bigger trouble if you were sober and caught doin' such a thing." On second thought, imagining what Widow Barker who was seventy-five if she was a day must look like unclothed, Sam doubted Dan would have wanted to see the bony old woman like that if he'd been sober. Maybe he'd swear off liquor for a while, once he truly realized what he'd done!

Two days later, Stan Reed decided to beat up on his wife. Mary retaliated, giving Stan a wallop or two with her rolling pin in exchange for her own black eye. When the neighbors complained of the noise, Sam tried to put a stop to their marital dispute. The unhappy couple did not appreciate her interference, and Sam wasn't particularly thrilled either.

"Look, you two!" she finally told them angrily. "Personally, I could care less if the two of you beat one another senseless, but your neighbors would appreciate it if you'd do it quietly! If you disturb the peace again, I'll have to throw both of you in jail! Now, either learn to fight silently or find someplace out of town to scream at each other. There are people around town who are getting tired of hearin' you air your dirty linen all the time."

Then, on Saturday night, Sam was called to stop a fight at the Dance Palace, a local saloon. By the time Sam arrived the place was a free-for-all, fists flying in every direction, chairs sailing through the air, and girls in gaudy outfits hiding under tables. After screaming at the top of her lungs and still not being heard, Sam cocked her rifle and fired it into a heavy beam in the ceiling. There was an immediate pause in the fighting as everyone looked around to see who had fired off the shot and who had been hit by it.

By this time, Sam had crawled up onto the bar, with the help of the barkeeper, and was standing atop it. "Now that I've got your attention, maybe y'all can stop actin' like jackasses long enough to help clean this place up," she drawled. A mixture of grumbling and mocking laughter followed her statement.

"Who's gonna make me, little lady?" one rough-looking character guffawed, smirking up at her. "Just little ole you?"

Sam glared back, her rifle resting casually in the crook of her arm. "I don't need an army behind me to haul a little pissant like you off to jail, mister," she taunted.

When he growled and stepped toward her, she leveled the barrel of her rifle at him. "Keep comin', and you'll sing soprano in the church choir tomorrow."

Several of his drinking buddies laughed, but the burly man backed down. With outward calm, Sam heaved a secret sigh of relief. "Now, y'all have the choice of settlin' down or goin' to jail, and it would be a might crowded with all of you in there."

"You trying to say you can take all of us in, all by yourself?" another fellow hooted, deliberately eyeing her swollen stomach from where he now sat gathering a scattered deck of cards.

Without a word, Sam handed her rifle to the barkeeper. She knew she looked more than a little silly standing there with Travis's gunbelt strapped about her bulging belly, but she wasn't laughing, and within a heartbeat, neither was anyone else. In the blink of an eye, she had her pistol drawn and had fired a bullet straight through the center of the folded cards the man still held in his hands. A collective gasp rose from the crowd.

"Anyone else have any doubts about my abilities?" she asked softly, her dark gaze traveling the room, making them all aware of her waning patience. "Now, it's late, I'm tired, my feet hurt, and I'm in a real lousy mood, so make your choice fast and stick to it. 'Cause if I'm called back here again tonight, someone's gonna get hurt, and I can darn well guarantee it won't be me!"

Sam had her answer when the men started turning tables upright and putting chairs back where they belonged. She watched long enough to know that they had taken her warning seriously, and there would probably not be any more trouble out of them tonight. The grinning barkeeper helped her down from her perch, handed her back the rifle, and sent her home with a trusted escort, to make sure none of his patrons planned any revenge against her on the way.

"You make one hell of a fine deputy, Sam," he told her with a chuckle. "Maybe Travis ought to hire you full-time."

Sam's answering smile turned a little sick at the thought of how Travis was going to react when he heard about this.

Travis was more than upset. He was livid! "The minute my back is turned, you start your shenanigans! Damn it all, Sam, what did you think you were doing?"

"I was helpin' out," she told him with a weak smile that didn't soften his anger in the least. "Everyone else who was qualified was sick."

"So you took it upon yourself to play deputy!"

"I wasn't playin', Travis. I made sure it was all legal by havin' Chas deputize me first."

"I'll kill him! I'll skin him alive!"

"Travis, it's not Chas's fault. I caught him at a weak moment, when he was so sick he couldn't think straight."

This brought a reluctant smile. "Sounds like something you'd do."

She touched his arm, looking up at him with those big, dark eyes. "Don't be angry anymore, Travis. Please? Everythin' turned out all right, after all."

"You could have gotten hurt or killed," he groaned, pulling her into his arms and holding her close to his heart.

"Well, I didn't, and I did a real fine job, too." Then, before he could get angry all over again, she raised herself on tiptoe, pulled his face down to hers, and kissed him. The matter didn't arise again for sometime, and by then his temper had cooled a great deal more.

Billy didn't have a trial. He didn't even have a hearing before a judge, such as Sam had endured. To everyone's shock and Travis's indignation, Travis received a telegram direct from the governor, declaring that a pardon had been issued for one William Downing Jr., and the man was to be set free immediately.

"This is a travesty of the law! No trial? Nothing?" Travis railed, unable to share Sam's joy at such an unexpected turn of events. "I just don't understand it!"

Billy could not believe his good fortune. Travis could not believe his eyes. He read and reread the message, and even went so far as to verify its source. It was then that Travis began to understand what had happened. Rafe Sandoval, with his influence in high places and for some unknown reason, had contacted the governor and arranged for Billy's pardon. But, why? What was the man planning now?

They didn't have to wait long. The telegram arrived in the morning, and that evening Sandoval paid them all a visit at the Kincaid home. "Yes, I arranged for the pardon," he admitted freely. "I've decided I want my daughter back home to stay, and my future grandchild, and if that means having to take her husband in the bargain, so be it," he announced in his usual tyrannical manner. "But to accept a convicted bandit as part of our proud Sandoval family was unacceptable to me."

Sandoval stared hard at Billy for several seconds. "You can come to work for me at the ranch, and as long as you work hard and keep your nose clean, I'm willing to let bygones be bygones. We'll start over. But if you so much as stub your toe, boy, I'll be there to set you straight. Do we understand each other?"

Billy glared back. "Yeah, I understand ya all right, Sandoval. Ya want Nola back an' ya want me to be some kind o' slave in the bargain. Well, ya kin jest forget it. I'd rather go to jail than be your hired peon."

Sandoval sent Billy a nasty smirk. "That, too, could be arranged, Downing. I could always request that my friend, the governor, rescind your pardon."

"An' I could be back in Mexico with your daughter before your telegram even reached him," Billy countered with a hateful look of his own. "I owe ya for that beatin' ya gave me, an' I've been known to carry a grudge for a long time."

They were at a stalemate. Finally, with a disgusted sigh, Rafe said, "All right. What will it take to get my daughter back? What are your terms?"

"If we come to live at the ranch, you accept me as ya would any other man Nola might have chosen to marry—on equal terms. You may have your pride, Sandoval, but we Downings have our fair share, too. I won't be a hired hand around the place. I'll have a say in how things are run, an' there won't be any more of ya turning your men loose on me. You'll see that they give me proper respect, or Nola and I will find someplace else to settle down an' raise our family."

Silence reigned while Nola and Sam held their breath. At last, Rafe held out his hand toward Billy. "I agree but when I die, I won't leave the ranch to you. I'll will it to Nola and my grandchildren. Do we have a deal?"

Waiting long enough to make Sandoval sweat, Billy took his father-in-law's hand, giving it a brusque shake. "A deal," he agreed. "Jest don't forget, Rafe. I have witnesses."

CHAPTER 30

For Sam, January and February dragged by. Her stomach increased in size until she could no longer see her feet. She needed help just getting her shoes on in the morning, and many times her feet were so swollen that she wore her slippers most of the day instead. Inside her, the baby was so lively that Sam wondered if it intended to kick its way out rather than be born in the usual manner.

Toward the first of February, another ice storm hit, and Sam scared everyone when she slipped on a patch of ice and fell. She bruised her leg and sprained her wrist when she tried to break her fall. The worst of it was that her stomach started cramping almost immediately, and she had a burning sensation in her back.

Travis was frantic! He sent Elsie to fetch the

doctor, and hovered outside the bedroom door, pacing the hall while Purdy examined her. "It was a close call," Purdy admitted a short time later. "In fact, she still may go into early labor, and it's too soon yet. That's why I am insisting that Sam stay in bed until I'm assured the danger is past. She's not to get up for any reason."

Now, Sam knew what Travis had felt like when he'd been bedridden with his cold. All she could do was lie there all day and all night, with little to occupy her time. Billy and Nola were gone, living at the ranch now. Hank worked all day at the livery. Elsie tried to keep her company, but she was taking care of the household chores and doing all the cooking and could only spare a few minutes at a time to sit and talk. Travis took more time off than he should have during the day, but that still left hours and hours to be filled.

Never was Sam so grateful to Nan as now, for she was sure she would have gone stark-raving crazy if she hadn't learned to read. Travis raided the study shelves for anything and everything he thought might interest her. Alma and Parson Aldrich brought her more books from their house. Molly borrowed Chas's new copy of *The Adventures of Tom Sawyer*, and loaned it to Sam before Chas even had a chance to read it himself. It was a delightfully entertaining story, and Sam thoroughly enjoyed it.

It was Lou who really came to her rescue, however, when he showed up one afternoon with several dime novels. Some of them, the westerns, were his, but there were a couple of very risque women's novels included. Where he got these,

Sam didn't know. Lou didn't volunteer the information, and Sam didn't ask.

She was extremely grateful for such titillating reading, even if it did give her ideas she shouldn't be entertaining now. Certainly, there was nothing she could do about fulfilling the marvelous fantasies she accrued from reading such stories, but it was still a darn sight more interesting than most of the dull books she'd had to force herself to concentrate on to fill the time.

When he'd walk in and catch her reading one of them, thoroughly engrossed in the romantic theme, Travis would shake his head and grin. "How can you possibly enjoy reading that awful tripe?"

"It's not tripe, Travis. Truly, it's very romantic and intriguin'. B'sides, it's giving me a wealth of new ideas for after the baby is born."

"What sort of ideas?" he asked, arching a golden brow at her.

Her look was decidedly mischievous. "You'll have to wait and see. Far be it from me to get you all excited and not be able to do anythin' about it."

She was in bed for two solid weeks, and when Doc Purdy finally agreed that she could get up again, Sam was overjoyed. March finally arrived, and she looked forward to the birth of her baby at almost any time. Each morning, she awoke hoping that this would be the day. The cradle sat empty in the corner of their bedroom, all the tiny clothes and blankets waiting to be put to use. All was ready anytime the baby decided to come.

Even after she was up and about again, Travis

stayed close. He became agitated if he was called out of town for some reason, afraid that he would not be home when Sam's time came. He was hurrying home one evening before supper when he happened to notice something odd. He'd just waved at Mrs. Jenkins, who lived two doors down from Nan Tucker's little house, when he thought he saw something move across one of Nan's windows, from the inside. It was a fleeting impression, no more than a shadow, but it bothered him. The house had been closed up since Nan's abduction, and all her things were still inside, just as she'd left them. Was someone trying to steal something?

Cautiously, Travis approached the house, not wanting to alarm the intruder, if there was someone inside. From the corner of his eye, he saw Mrs. Jenkins watching him curiously, and he could only hope she wouldn't call out to him and ruin his chances of surprising the culprit. Stealthily mounting the steps of the small wooden porch, he reached for the doorknob. The door was locked, as it was supposed to be, but this didn't satisfy Travis or alleviate his suspicions any. Anyone not wanting to be seen would most likely have used the back door or crawled through a window to gain entry.

Travis knew Nan always kept a key to the front door hidden between the slats of the porch floor. Though it was growing dark now, he felt along the cracks until he found it. Once the door was unlocked, it swung open easily, without so much as a squeak, as he nudged it carefully with his boot.

All was dark and quiet within. Not a sound came to Travis's straining ears, and he began to think he'd been imagining things after all. Still, now that he was here, it wouldn't do any harm to go inside and check on things, to be certain that everything was still as it should be.

He walked inside, his eyes scanning the little parlor, wishing he could remember on which table Nan had kept her lamp. As his eyes adjusted a bit more to the interior, he spotted the lamp on a stand not far from the door. His hand was in his pocket, searching for a match, when the door suddenly slammed shut behind him. Whirling around, he faced the tall shadow of a man.

"Don't move, Marshal. I've got a gun aimed right at ya."

Travis didn't even breathe but he couldn't help being startled when the man said, "Nan, close the curtains over the windows before ya light the lamp."

"Downing?" Travis asked softly. "Tom Downing?"

"That's right." Before either of them could say more, Nan had the lamp lit, and Travis got his first really good look at his oldest brother-in-law. He was tall and dark, and Travis could see something of Sam around the eyes.

"Now," Tom said, "I want ya to keep your right hand in your pocket an' reach down slowly with your left an' unbuckle your gunbelt. Drop it on the floor. Do it real slow an' easy, now, because I'd hate to have to kill my baby sister's husband."

His jaw clenched at his own stupidity, Travis did as he was told. "You're taking quite a chance coming back to town like this," he muttered. "Mind telling me why?"

With his gun, Tom waved Travis toward a chair, indicating for Travis to sit. "Nan wanted to collect some of her things before we headed on, an' I was hoping to hear word of Sam and the boys. We haven't heard from Billy since he came back north with Nola. Did they make it awright?"

It was ridiculous, sitting here discussing Sam's family as if this were a friendly chat while Tom held him at gunpoint, but Travis was at a disadvantage. He could only pray for time and hope to come up with some way out of this. "They ran into some trouble with Nola's father, but everything has turned out all right. In fact, you should be pleased to know that Billy is a free man now."

"How? What happened?" Nan spoke up for the first time, drawing Travis's attention toward her.

Though he'd been aware of her standing in the background the entire time, now that he really took a good look at her, Travis was stunned. The change in her was dramatic! The little brown wren had turned into a lovely woman! Her hair hung in golden brown waves about her shoulders, no longer confined in a tight bun at her nape. Her face looked softer, fuller, her stance still straight, but more relaxed than rigid. Her eyes had a glow that lit up the rest of her features, making Travis wonder why he'd ever thought of her as plain. Gone were the prim little schoolmarm clothes, replaced by a flowing Mexican skirt and blouse.

"Nan!" he exclaimed softly, forgetting to answer her inquiry about Billy. "You look wonderful. Married life must agree with you."

She smiled shyly. "And you, Travis. How is Sam? Did she receive the letter and the locket we sent?"

"She got them. She's due to have our first child any day now. I was just on my way home to her when I thought I saw someone in the house. I was checking to make sure nobody was stealing anything."

"Ya should have gone on home," Tom put in. "We would have been here and gone by morning with no one the wiser, if ya had. Now we've got the problem of what to do with ya, while we get away safely."

"Have you thought about giving yourself up?"

Tom's answering laugh held little humor. "Yeah, I've thought about it, but hangin' or spendin' the rest of my life in jail doesn't hold much appeal, especially since I found Nan."

"There's always a chance you'd get a light sentence. Hank did. He's working at the livery stable now. We managed to satisfy the judge that Sam had mended her ways, and he seemed convinced enough to let her off."

"And Billy?" Nan asked. "You were going to tell us about Billy."

"Well, that's a horse of a different color." Travis's voice took on an edge. "It seems Sandoval had a sudden change of heart. He didn't want Nola married to a common criminal, so he bought Billy a pardon from the governor."

Nan's mouth dropped open in shock. "He what?"

"You heard me. He used his influence to arrange a pardon for his son-in-law. So, you see? There are ways of getting around the law, after all," he said with a bitter smile.

"Maybe," Tom conceded, "but that doesn't mean I would get off as easily. I can't chance it."

"Can't or won't? I thought you were the one who always wanted to be a preacher. How are you going to accomplish that or make a decent home for Nan if you're always on the run, always hiding behind a lie?"

"We'll manage somehow." Aside to Nan, Tom said, "See if ya can find some rope. We're gonna have to tie the marshal up an' leave him here while we ride out."

"But, Tom!"

"Don't worry, Nan. Someone will come lookin' for him an' find him b'fore too long."

"Someone already has," came a soft reply from the doorway. "Don't anybody move, especially you, dear brother."

"Sam!" Three startled voices echoed her name as Tom whirled about to face her. Sam stood watching with wide dark eyes, Travis's Colt in her hand.

"Put the gun down, Tom. Don't make me shoot you." Pain laced her voice.

Tom smiled confidently, keeping one eye, and the gun, on Travis while he talked to Sam. "Ya wouldn't kill your own brother. I know ya, Sam. Ya couldn't do that."

Sam's shoulder raised in a shrug. "I could always shoot your kneecaps off instead. Or maybe I'll just put a hole through your wrist. How would that be?" She seemed to wince a little at her own words, but stood firm.

Tom blanched, knowing she had the skill to do either with ease. "Now, Sam. Be reasonable. We jest need to buy enough time to get out o' town."

"Not this time, Tom. It's time to stop runnin' and face up to all the things you've done. Think about it, Tom. Pa's dead, Billy and Hank are here. We're family, and we'll help you all we can, but you've got to put the gun down and turn yourself in. It's the only way you stand any chance of bein' happy, of havin' things turn out all right."

A grimace crossed Sam's features, a frown drawing her brows together as she awaited his answer. When it didn't come, when Tom just stood there staring back at her, Sam lost her temper and yelled, "Damn it all! I'm gettin' sick and tired of all this! Every time Travis and I get our lives runnin' straight, one of my dear, darlin' brothers pops up like a bad penny! As much as I love you, all of you, there are times I wish I was an only child!

"Speakin' of which," she panted, suddenly breathless, "your time is runnin' real short, 'cause if I'm gonna have to shoot you, it's gonna have to be soon, before I have this baby right here where I stand!" Again, her face twisted in pain, but now they all realized the real reason why. Even as the contraction coursed through her, she held the gun steady, her eyes never veering from Tom's face.

At Sam's untimely announcement, Travis caught his breath in dismay. It was all he could do to remain still, to wait calmly and cautiously for an opportunity to act. His chance came almost immediately as Tom's mouth dropped open in amazement, his gaze wandering to Sam's enormous belly. In that one unguarded moment, Travis sprang from his chair. His elbow buried itself in Tom's stomach at the same time his hand chopped into Tom's wrist. The gun flew from Tom's hand, and before he could recover his breath, Travis had him face down on the floor, his hands behind his back.

"Nan, bring me my handcuffs from my gunbelt," Travis ordered gruffly.

Nan shook her head, tears streaming down her cheeks. "No. I can't stop you, but I won't help you, either."

Slowly, painfully, Sam eased herself to the floor beside the gunbelt. She called his name softly, just enough to get his attention, then tossed Travis the cuffs. "Do try to hurry, Travis," she groaned, biting her lip on a fresh wave of pain. "I wasn't lyin' about the baby comin'. B'sides," she added with shaky laugh, "supper's waitin', and you know how riled Elsie gets when the food goes cold."

Once more, Travis found himself pacing the floor, waiting for news of his wife and child. Elsie was unsuccessful in her efforts to get him to sit down and eat something, though she did distract him a little by getting him to tell her everything that had happened at Nan's.

As he'd carried Sam upstairs, after sending Hank running for Doc Purdy, Sam had told him how she'd come to find him at Nan's. It seemed that Mrs. Jenkins had become curious when she'd seen Travis go into the house and not come out. Thinking she had somehow missed seeing him, but still feeling uneasy, much too uneasy to investigate for herself, she had gone to the Kincaid home to find out if he had arrived home after all. When she discovered that Travis wasn't there, she related her tale to Sam and Elsie, feeling a little foolish, but still worried that something might have happened to him inside that dark house.

Sam had not felt quite herself since mid-morning. Her back had begun to ache again, horribly, and every once in a while, she'd gotten this twinge in her tummy. As the day progressed, so did the twinges, until Sam was certain she was going into labor. Because Doc Purdy had forewarned that it took hours, sometimes days, for a woman's first child to make its way into the world, Sam had said nothing to Elsie, lest the housekeeper alarm Travis too soon. The last thing Sam needed now was for Travis to hover over her and make her even more nervous than she already was.

Elsie was in the kitchen, and Sam upstairs dressing for dinner when Sam had felt a sudden, warm gush of water streaming down her legs. This, too, Doc Purdy had told her to expect, advising Sam that the pains would come harder and faster then. She hurried to clean herself up and dress, and was on her way downstairs to tell Elsie what had happened when Mrs. Jenkins had knocked on the door.

Upon hearing what Mrs. Jenkins had to say, the lady's unease quickly transferred itself to Sam, and she knew she would not rest until she'd gone to see for herself that Travis was all right. Disregarding the pains, which were fast becoming stronger and closer together, she'd set out for Nan's, telling Elsie she'd be back soon, and to watch for Travis in case they missed one another along the way.

When she reached the door, Sam had heard voices. Quietly letting herself in, she had instantly assessed the situation, and had enough presence of mind to arm herself before letting her presence be known. The rest Travis had seen for himself, and related to Elsie, as they waited together in the downstairs parlor. Tom was now safely behind bars with Chas guarding him, while Travis paced the house, going time and again to the bottom of the stairs and staring upward with agonized eyes.

At that moment, Sam would gladly have traded places with her husband. Never, in all her life, had she even imagined such pain. It came in waves that caught her up and tossed her down, never giving her time between to catch her breath. They clawed at her, like giant talons tearing through her until she had to bite her lip to stem the screams that rose to her throat.

"Go ahead and scream, Sam," Doc Purdy told her, wiping her drenched brow with a towel. "It's nothing I haven't heard before, and there's certainly no shame in it. God knows, if I were the one having this baby, I'd be screeching the roof off."

"T–Tr–Travis will hear!" she grunted between clenched teeth.

Purdy gave a chuckle. "Let him. It'll do him good to have to share some of the pain with you. Let's face it, Sam, he's had the easy part in all of this so far. You're the one who's had the nausea and the tender breasts and the big tummy and the swollen ankles—and now the labor." He held her hands through another contraction, urging her to try to relax and let herself go with the pain instead of fighting it so.

"How . . . much . . . long . . . er?"

"Not long now, honey. It's real close now."

What seemed like an eternity in hell, but was five minutes later according to Purdy's timing, Sam was straining and pushing her child into the doctor's waiting hands. "C'mon, Sam," he coaxed her gently. "I've got the head, let's see the rest of this little darling. One more good, hard push!"

The baby slipped from her body, and Sam collapsed against the sweat-dampened pillows. "It's a girl, Sam!" she heard him exclaim excitedly, even though he'd probably delivered hundreds of babies before hers. "You have a beautiful baby daughter!"

Through a haze, she watched as he cleared the baby's mouth and nose and gave it a light slap on the bottom. Her daughter gave a wavering wail then began to cry lustily. "Good!" Purdy praised. "Get those little lungs going!" Tenderly, he lay the squirming baby on Sam's tummy. "You two get better acquainted while I tend to the rest of this business. Then, as soon as we get you two cleaned up, we'll bring the new papa in to admire his fine work. I imagine he's getting pretty anxious about now."

By the time Purdy allowed Travis into the room, the baby was nursing, her tiny fingers curled upon her mother's breast. She suckled through rosebud lips, her chubby cheeks flexing, her eyes wide open in a fuzzy, newborn stare. "Oh, Sam!" he whispered in absolute awe. "She's the most delicate, beautiful thing I've seen, next to you, of course."

"Are you disappointed that she's not a boy?"

A tender smile curved his lips as he bent to kiss them both. "Never. She's perfect just the way she is! We'll have to get busy and choose a name for her now, though. We really can't have her going through life with a name like Little Who's It."

"I've already thought of a name I like, if it's all right with you," she told him. "I'd like to call her Harmony, Harmony Hope, because I'm hopin' her arrival will be the beginnin' of peace for all of us. I want you and my brothers, and their wives and all our children, to grow close and truly be a lovin' family. It's my hope for harmony between us, always."

It was September. It had been another hot, sticky summer, but not nearly as bad as the previous year. Harmony Hope Kincaid was now six months old, and learning to sit up by herself. Normally, she was a good baby, living up to her name, but now she was trying to cut her first tooth, and it was making her cranky. She had a mop of curling red-gold hair, and with every day her blue eyes took on more turquoise, like her daddy's.

Now, Harmony and her mother were sitting on the front porch swing, waiting for Travis to come home for lunch. Sam was humming a little tune and feeling very good about herself and life in general. In the past few months, things had turned out very well for all of them.

Nola had presented Billy with a new son two weeks before, and Rafe Sandoval was acting suspiciously like a proud grandfather. Hank was courting the daughter of one of the saloon keepers, and it looked like another wedding would be planned soon. Molly and Chas were expecting their first child around Christmas.

Though things were not quite as sunny for Tom and Nan right now, at least he'd not been hung. The judge had listened to Tom's side of things and then sentenced him to three years in a Kansas prison. He'd be paroled then, on the condition that he uphold his claim of wanting to become a preacher. While in prison, he was studying and training for his future vocation under the guidance of the prison chaplain.

Meanwhile, Nan had moved to Kansas and taken

a teaching position near the prison so that she could visit him regularly. She hadn't sold her little house, saying that one day they would move back to Tumble where they could be near all of Tom's family. Parson Aldrich had already told them that he'd be thrilled to have Tom as an assistant pastor in his church.

Sam was so deep in thought that she didn't notice Travis until he walked up onto the porch. Coming to them, he kissed Harmony on the top of her head then turned to catch Sam's lips with his own. The kiss deepened, sending waves of longing through them both, lasting until Harmony squealed for attention. Laughing, they drew apart, their eyes exchanging promises of delights to come when Harmony was put in her crib and sound asleep for the night.

"You have a letter, Sam," Travis told her, handing the envelope out to her and settling himself on the swing with Harmony in his lap.

She took it eagerly, thinking it was news from Nan, then frowned when she saw that it was from an attorney's office in Arkansas. "What on earth? I don't know anybody in Arkansas!"

"If you open it, we might found out what it's all about," Travis suggested wryly when she continued to stare at the address.

He waited patiently while she read it, watching her face light up with delight, then reflect sadness, and finally a combination of both. "Sam?" he prompted.

"Oh, Travis! I would have never guessed it! Sam Bass has left me his Hot Springs property!" Tears welled in her eyes as she recalled that day this past July when Travis had told her that Sam Bass had been killed in a shoot-out with the law. He'd died on his twenty-seventh birthday. In the weeks since, there had been a lot of rumors flying around that Bass had stashed a fortune in gold in some secret place, but no one knew where that might be.

Personally, Sam thought it was all a pack of lies. Bass could never have stolen that much gold if he'd lived another twenty years. The only thing of worth he'd owned had been his cabin on the mountain, and now he had bequeathed it all to Sam. "The letter says that he wanted me to have the property because I was the only one he knew who loved it as much as he did. Can you believe this?"

"You know, Sam. I think Bass must have been a little sweet on you at some time or other, even if he didn't say so."

"Maybe," she said with a self-conscious shrug. "Do you mind horribly?"

"No. You married me."

"And I love you, with all my heart." She leaned over to collect another tantalizing kiss. "I always will."

Harmony started to fuss again.

"You know, Sam," Travis chuckled, jiggling his daughter on his lap to quiet her, "I think it's about time you and I got off somewhere alone together for a while, don't you? Just the two of us."

Sam's smile was bright and sweet, and full of promise. She waggled the letter at him. "And I know just the place, sweetheart—our own private paradise for lovers."